LADY CHATTERLEY'S LOVER

◆

D. H. Lawrence

Introduction and Notes by
DAVID ELLIS
University of Kent at Canterbury

WORDSWORTH CLASSICS

In loving memory of
MICHAEL TRAYLER
the founder of Wordsworth Editions

9

Readers who are interested in other titles from
Wordsworth Editions are invited to visit our website at
www.wordsworth-editions.com

For our latest list and a full mail-order service, contact
Bibliophile Books, 5 Thomas Road, London E14 7BN
TEL: +44 (0)20 7515 9222 FAX: +44 (0)20 7538 4115
E-MAIL: orders@bibliophilebooks.com

First published 2005 by Wordsworth Editions Limited
8B East Street, Ware, Hertfordshire SG12 9HJ
Introduction and Notes added 2007

ISBN 978 1 84022 488 7

Typeset in Great Britain by Antony Gray
Printed and bound by Clays Ltd, St Ives plc

INTRODUCTION

Lady Chatterley's Lover made Lawrence a lot of money. It was first published in June 1928 and by the end of that year he was already a thousand pounds better off. This was a large sum for someone who had spent most of his previous life in modest circumstances and some of it (during the First World War) in extreme poverty. The money was useful because Lawrence was increasingly incapacitated by tuberculosis and therefore unable to rough it as he and his wife Frieda had so often done in the past. After a period in the seaside resort of Bandol in the South of France, he was moved to Vence, fifteen or so miles above Nice, and it was there that he died on 2 March 1930. Lawrence was fond of remembering that when at the end of 1910 his first novel (*The White Peacock*) had been published, a prominent London editor had written to his dying mother and predicted that her son would be riding in his own carriage by the time he was forty.[1] Had she lived long enough, Mrs Lawrence would not have been overjoyed to realise that although when the said son died at forty-four he had plenty of money in the bank, it was largely because of a book like *Lady Chatterley's Lover*. 'And you used to be such a dear good boy' is what he recalled her saying to him as he grew older.[2]

The reason Lawrence did so well out of *Lady Chatterley's Lover* is that he published it himself. In October 1926 he had finished a first version of the novel in which the sexual encounters between Connie Chatterley and the gamekeeper, who was then called Parkin, were not explicitly described. By that date Lawrence already had a reputation as someone who dealt with sexual matters in an uncomfortably direct fashion. His readers might well have remembered the meeting by the river of Paul Morel and Clara Dawes in *Sons and Lovers*, episodes between Ursula Brangwen and Rupert Birkin in *The Rainbow*, or the scene in *Women in Love* when

---

1   Roberts, Warren and Moore, Harry T. (eds), *Phoenix 2: Uncollected, Unpublished and Other Prose Works of D. H . Lawrence*, London, 1968, p. 260

2   Nehls, Edward (ed.), *D. H. Lawrence: A Composite Biography*, University of Wisconsin Press, 1958, Vol. 2, p. 44

Gerald Crich seeks consolation in the bed of Gudrun Brangwen. But in all these cases the most crucial moments of physical contact are left unstated, and there is heavy reliance on all that is implied in the use of such words as 'afterwards'. Feeling perhaps that sexual intercourse was more central to his new novel than it had been to the others, Lawrence wrote a second version of *Lady Chatterley's Lover* almost immediately after the first in which there was a minimum of elision and the descriptions were as explicit as he could make them. Real frankness, he must have decided, was impossible within the confines of 'polite' language and he therefore made use of cunt, fuck, shit, piss – words very rarely read in his time and usually only heard in hostile or aggressive contexts. One or two of these had made a fleeting appearance in the first version but they were now used without restraint.

The way in which the first version of *Lady Chatterley's Lover* was rewritten made it unpublishable by the usual channels but on 17 November 1927 Lawrence met in Florence a friend who published his own books and decided that he would to do the same. Rewriting the novel for a third and final time, he paid to have it printed in Florence and then sent out hundreds of leaflets offering it for sale in Britain and the United States. This was a risk but one which the net profit of a thousand pounds at the end of 1928 fully justified. The thousand or so copies he had printed quickly disappeared and the success of the novel led to a number of unauthorised, 'pirate' editions from the sale of which Lawrence himself received nothing. Enraged at the idea of people profiting from his labour in this way, he went to Paris in 1929 and arranged to have published there a cheap, second edition of his novel (the first had been sold at two and later four guineas). His chief intention was to make some money by underselling and therefore frustrating the pirates; but he was also anxious that ordinary people, of modest means, should read his work. It is altogether appropriate therefore that this present, Wordsworth edition of *Lady Chatterley's Lover* should be based on the text of the Paris edition.

It could well seem paradoxical that the novel which made Lawrence more money than he had ever had before was also the one in which modern society's preoccupation with money-making is most fiercely denounced. For many details of its setting he was reliant on both his memory and what proved to be his last visit to his native country and region in the late summer of 1926. This was at the time of the continuing miners' strike and observing its effects seems to have sharpened Lawrence's dislike of how British society had developed since the war. His novel is full of images and episodes which convey his bitter regret at the way the semi-rural Nottinghamshire of his youth was being destroyed by fresh industrial enterprises and raw new housing estates. The effect of increasing industrialisation on the rural environment is most memorably suggested by the description in Chapter 13 of Sir Clifford Chatterley's motorised bath chair crushing the flowers in the wood. Although Sir Clifford is presented as a relatively enlightened employer, Lawrence was inclined to blame the altered landscape of his native district on capitalist greed. But being critical of bosses did not mean that he was especially sympathetic to their workers since he clearly felt that, unlike his father, the miners of his own generation were only interested in wages. And yet Lawrence knew – and the diligence and efficiency with which he organised the distribution of *Lady Chatterley's Lover* showed he knew – that if man does not live by bread alone there has nevertheless to be a few loaves in the house for him to live at all. It is not everyone who is like Connie Chatterley in having a private income to fall back on. Talking about money one day, Lawrence defended a friend from the suggestion that she should give up her modest fifty-pound annuity because it was unearned, yet he went on to say that, 'Money, much money, has a really magical touch to make a man insensitive and so to make him wicked.'[3] In November 1927, just before he began to rewrite *Lady Chatterley's Lover* for the third time, he was visited by Michael Arlen, a friend from the war years whose recent best-seller, *The Green Hat*, had made him rich. Afterwards Lawrence reflected, 'We talked my poverty – it has got on my nerves lately. But next day had a horrible reaction, & felt a sort of pariah. People must feel like that who make their lives out of money. Definitely I hate the whole money-making world, Tom and Dick as well as en gros.' Yet then he added: 'But I won't be done by them either.'[4] If these remarks do not resolve the paradox of making money out of a book in which money-making is denounced, they at least throw light on it.

The visit of Arlen, and the feelings it excited, had a determining effect on the way Lawrence wrote his third version of *Lady Chatterley's Lover*. The attacks in the novel on greed, or what is called the Bitch Goddess of Success, are now extended to the literary field and Clifford becomes, in the first part, a writer whose essentially

3   Carswell, Catherine, *The Savage Pilgrimage: A Narrative of D. H. Lawrence*, Cambridge University Press, 1981, p. 245

4   See Ellis, David, *D. H. Lawrence: Dying Game*, Cambridge University Press, 1998, p. 388 (all the other details of Arlen's visit come from this source).

insignificant short stories bring him high financial returns. At the same time the wholly new character of Michaelis – clearly based on Arlen – is introduced. Arlen was a novelist rather than a playwright like Michaelis, but on his visit he had told Lawrence that the American stage adaptation of *The Green Hat* had brought him five thousand six hundred and fifty dollars in a single week. He is transposed into *Lady Chatterley's Lover* with only minor changes. To justify his sense of exclusion from the high society he depicts in his work, and has earned enough money to frequent, Lawrence makes Michaelis Irish whereas Arlen was in fact Armenian and wrongly thought by many to be Jewish. During the war years, when he still went by his real name of Dikran Kouyoumdjian, Lady Ottoline Morrell had referred to him disparagingly as a 'fat dark-blooded light-skinned Armenian Jew', and as he became successful Rebecca West mocked his pretensions to gentility by saying that he was 'every other inch a gentleman'.[5] Since the companies over which Lady Ottoline presided, and in which West moved, were not ones in which the working-class Lawrence ever felt entirely comfortable, there is a good deal of sympathy in the novel for Michaelis's outsider status.

Basing a character in his fiction as directly as Michaelis is based on Arlen is not uncommon in Lawrence's writing, but matters are usually more complicated. All novelists exploit their knowledge of others in the creation of their characters but the resulting figures are often amalgams and in any case narrative exigencies will frequently lead those figures to act and respond in ways quite alien to their supposed models. There is a good deal of Frieda in Connie Chatterley but also of other women Lawrence had known so that to think of Connie as a 'portrait' of his wife would be misleading. Less so is the common idea that Mellors is a portrait of the author, since he patently has many of Lawrence's own characteristics. Born into the industrial proletariat, he has become educated and can operate successfully in middle- or upper-class society, without ever feeling at home there. Tall but thin, his health is fragile and he suffers from a bad cough. The descriptions in Chapter 14 of the first two unnamed women who disappointed him are unmistakably portraits of two women friends from Lawrence's own early days, Jessie Chambers and Helen Cork. He is roughly the same age as his creator and holds

5   For Morrell's remark, see Gathorne-Hardy, Robert (ed.), *Ottoline at Garsington*, London, 1974; and for West's, Morgan, Ted, *Somerset Maugham*, London, 1980, p. 317.

identical opinions; yet in one crucial respect character and author are very different. In the 1950s Frieda wrote that, 'The terrible thing about Lady C. is that L. identified himself with both Clifford and Mellors; that took courage, that made me shiver, when I read it as he wrote it.'[6] What she was alluding to was that by 1927, whether or not Lawrence was technically impotent, he had certainly stopped having sexual relations with her. Lawrence may well have identified with Clifford in his impotence but his more obvious *spokesman* on this matter is Tommy Dukes who admits to being sexually inactive but continues to believe that the phallus is the only bridge to the future.

A friend of Arlen's reported him as having been flattered and pleased by the depiction of him in *Lady Chatterley's Lover*. Although Michaelis is often the recipient of the author's as well as Connie's sympathy, this is surprising given the inglorious sexual role he is chosen to play. The affair Connie has with him after her husband has been shipped back from the war, paralysed from the waist down, is represented as unsatisfactory largely because he is such an inadequate lover, someone who was 'always come and finished so quickly'. 'Like so many modern men,' Connie reflects, Michaelis 'was finished almost before he had begun,' and she refers at one point to his 'pathetic, two-second spasms'. All this is in contrast to Mellors who not only does not come too quickly, but can also come and come again within a relatively short period. For Arlen not to have been hurt and offended by this aspect of his characterisation would have taken a good deal of tolerance, or a subtle understanding of how most novelists work.

Connie's search for fulfilment outside marriage, with first Michaelis and then Mellors, inevitably raises the question of whether *Lady Chatterley's Lover* is in fact the 'good and proper' book Lawrence often insisted it was.[7] Conventional opinion of his time would have been offended by the novel because it dealt with adultery. So of course did many famous novels of the nineteenth century but in those the adulterous relationship was not across a class divide and in any case the results were eventually unhappy. At the end of *Anna Kerenina* the heroine commits suicide. Eighty years on, an objection of this kind hardly cuts much ice. Some modern readers may still be

---

6 Tedlock, E. W. (ed.), *Frieda Lawrence: Memoirs and Correspondence*, London, 1961, p. 352

7 For this particular phrase, see the Cambridge edition of Lawrence's *Letters*, Vol. 7, edited by Keith Sagar and James T. Boulton, Cambridge University Press, 1993, p. 34, but there are many similar ones elsewhere.

made uncomfortable by the moment in Chapter 13 when Connie kisses Mellors' hand as it lies on the back of the wheelchair just behind Clifford's head, but that partners in marriage are not always faithful to each other is hardly a shock now. Nor in fact could it have been so much of a shock in 1928 when the marriage tie was no longer regarded as it had been in the nineteenth century and there was a growing recognition that the inadequacy of one or other of the marriage partners might well make its continuance unreasonable. The more acute problem for the less hide-bound at that date was rather how and why Clifford had become inadequate. The chief reason offered is obviously his injury during the war and, only nine years after the conflict had ended, when people were still surrounded by visible indications of the human damage it had caused, this was a sensitive subject.

Lawrence later expressed some unease about his portrayal of Clifford. He had often been asked, he wrote, whether Clifford's injuries were meant to be symbolic. It had not been his conscious intention to make them so, he explained, but after he had read over the novel's first version,

> I recognised that the lameness of Clifford was symbolic of the paralysis, the deeper emotional or passional paralysis, of most men of his sort and class, today. I realised that it was perhaps taking an unfair advantage of Connie, to paralyse him technically. It made it so much more vulgar of her to leave him. Yet the story came as it did, by itself, so I left it alone. Whether we call it symbolism or not, it is, in the sense of its happening, inevitable.[8]

On one level Clifford may be a symbolic or, perhaps more accurately, a representative figure, but on another he is presented with so much particularity, and in such realistic detail, that it is difficult to avoid thinking of him as a poignant individual case, and one with which many readers of the time would have been familiar from their daily experience. To mitigate the impact of the character in this guise, and thereby protect Connie from the 'vulgarity' he mentions, Lawrence suggests that Clifford had been an indifferent lover before his injuries, and that he had never been very interested in sex. Apart therefore from the question of an heir to his estate and name, having to forgo a sexual life is not, it is suggested, the disaster it might have been for another kind of man.

Something of a disaster it nevertheless remains and in Lawrence's

8   'A Propos of *Lady Chatterley's Lover*', in *Phoenix 2*, p. 514

treatment of it there are traces of that stern Nietzschean morality which he had already displayed in such earlier writings as 'The Daughters of the Vicar' or 'The Fox'. This insists that no injuries on the scale Clifford suffers them are without corresponding psychological impairment and that therefore their victims necessarily become a threat to the healthy and undamaged. In Nietzsche's view, the weak are inclined to prey on the strong by exploiting the latter's feelings of sympathy and guilt, or their sense of duty. But this is immoral because, as he writes in *The Genealogy of Morals*, 'Our first rule on this earth should be that the sick must not contaminate the healthy . . . The right to exist of the full-toned bell is a thousand times greater than that of the cracked, miscast one: it alone heralds the future of mankind.'[9] Connie is tied to Clifford by pity but the consequence is that, denied both sexual and emotional fulfilment, she becomes ill. The novel insists on her moral right to that fulfilment rather than on her Christian duty to her crippled husband, although in doing so it softens the sharp, Nietzschean edges of the dilemma by showing that the special needs of that husband are in any case more than adequately met by Mrs Bolton, the nurse who willingly takes over from Connie her responsibilities of care. That it does this may indicate in Lawrence some recognition that Clifford cannot help being as he is any more than Michaelis can help being an inadequate lover. In one scheme of things, which combines easily enough with the Nietzschean, both these figures are predestined to failure while Mellors is a member of the elect. Calvinist as he sometimes is, this is partly Lawrence's feeling, yet in showing that both Clifford and Michaelis often make a bad situation worse, there is also a belief in individual moral responsibility which it is hard to imagine any great novelist being without.

There is more to *Lady Chatterley's Lover* than explicit accounts of sexual intercourse. The novel contains numerous fine descriptions of the natural and industrial landscape around Nottingham and there are many dramatic and sharply rendered human exchanges. Apart from the three principals and Michaelis, it could be thought short on characters since the 'cronies' who discuss sex and other matters of general interest with the Chatterleys are pasteboard figures belonging more to the novel of ideas than to the realist tradition within which *Lady Chatterley's Lover* is principally conceived. Yet

9 Nietzsche, Friedrich, *The Birth of Tragedy* and *The Genealogy of Morals*, translated by Francis Golffing, Doubleday, New York, 1956, p. 261

Mrs Bolton is a fully rounded figure who might easily have found a place in a novel by George Eliot or Thomas Hardy. In the words he gives to Mrs Bolton (her 'gossip'), Lawrence exhibits his remarkable ear for English colloquial speech with a regional inflection, and as Connie listens to them there occurs one of those memorable formulations which constitute another positive feature of the novel. 'Connie was fascinated, listening to her,' Lawrence writes,

> but afterwards always a little ashamed. She ought not to listen with this queer rabid curiosity. After all, one may hear the most private affairs of other people, but only in a spirit of respect for the struggling, battered thing which any human soul is . . .

For all its incidental strengths or attributes, *Lady Chatterley's Lover* is none the less a novel which is dominated by the sexual relations between Connie and Mellors. When the Director of Public Prosecutions attempted in 1960 to prevent Penguin Books from publishing an unexpurgated version, the chief prosecuting counsel may have been wrong to claim that it contained nothing except sex, but sexual relations are quite clearly and designedly its main topic. Just as clear is that Lawrence's intention in describing those relations in such detail was not to titillate, however often since that may have been the effect. No one more sternly disapproved of pornography than Lawrence. A writer in the nineteenth-century mould, he regarded himself as quite as much a teacher as an entertainer. Interviewed in 1925 by an American journalist, he was asked what it was that made him write. Egotism and the desire to let everyone know how clever he is, was the answer Frieda quickly gave on his behalf. But Lawrence himself protested that he wrote 'from a deep moral sense – for the race, as it were', and he added that,

> A writer writes because he can't help writing, and because he has something in him that he feels he can say better than it has been said before, and because it would be wrong, entirely wrong, to possess a talent and have thoughts without sharing them with the world.[10]

In his later novels especially, Lawrence used his fiction to share his thoughts with the world and to suggest remedies for the grave disorders with which he felt it was afflicted. The fervour with which he accepted the responsibilities of the novelist as teacher increased

10   The journalist's full account of the interview can be found in Nehls (ed.), *D. H. Lawrence: A Composite Biography*, Vol. 2, pp. 410–19.

as he grew older and serves both to acquit him of merely wanting to excite his readers in *Lady Chatterley's Lover* and explain why so many of those readers have found the earlier novels less satisfactory than the later.

In *Sons and Lovers* there is a certain glamour about the mine where the hero's father works and it was only in his later years that Lawrence blamed industry for the destruction of traditional ways of life and associated it with the obsession with money which he felt had corrupted every level of English society. This is the state of affairs he sets out to expose and denounce in *Lady Chatterley's Lover*, while at the same time showing that the only salvation lay in warm and tender human relationships, particularly those between men and women. But a warm relationship between a man and a woman, the novel insists, must be based on sex and not sex which is casual or frivolous but deeply serious. Because of modern society's ruthless exploitation of natural resources, most people have become fatally disconnected from their human and natural environment; but a satisfactory sexual relationship, in which the sex constituted a genuine sharing and was non-masturbatory, could be either a sign that, in the individuals concerned, the connection still existed, or a move towards its restoration. The importance of sex was that it made one part of a living, organic, natural world. In Lawrence's view, this truth could not be conveyed without the utmost frankness in his characters' discussions of sex and his own description of sexual encounters, a frankness only possible through avoidance of the usual polite euphemisms or medical terms and the rescue of words like 'cunt' and 'fuck' from the unpleasant contexts in which they generally appear. As he later explained in an essay he wrote on 'Pornography and Obscenity', it was also necessary to recognise that one reason why in the past sex had so often been regarded as a 'dirty little secret' was that the organs concerned had an excretory as well as a sexual function. Although in 'the really healthy human being the distinction between the two is instant', he felt that it was confusion on this issue which led many people to 'do dirt' on sex.[11] The solution was open recognition and clarity of the kind which Mellors exhibits when, as his fingertips touch 'the two secret openings of [Connie's] body, time after time, with a soft little brush of fire', he tells her: 'An' if tha shits and pisses, I'm glad. I don't want a woman as couldna shit nor piss.' A little later he links this statement with

11   The essay is reprinted in McDonald, Edward D. (ed.), *Phoenix: The Posthumous Papers of D. H. Lawrence*, 1936, pp. 170–87.

the general theme of the novel when he adds, 'An' if I only lived ten minutes, an' stroked thy arse an' got to know it, I should reckon I'd lived *one* life, see ter! Industrial system or not!'

It was in terms much like these I am using here that over thirty defence witnesses characterised *Lady Chatterley's Lover* in the 1960 trial and helped to secure a triumphant acquittal. Because very few of those who disliked the novel wanted to see it censored, it was only later that hard questions were raised about how the case had been presented, or some began to suggest that there were discrepancies between the experience of reading the book and the way Lawrence defended it in subsequent writings such as 'Pornography and Obscenity' but more particularly of course his 'A Propos of *Lady Chatterley's Lover*' ('Never trust the teller trust the tale' was one of his own rules for literary discussion). In a final address to the jury, the chief prosecuting counsel, who either had not wished or had not been able to call a single witness in support of his case, read out the passage from Chapter 16 which begins, 'It was a night of sensual passion . . .' (p. 218), hinting at what might be found objectionable in it but not explaining clearly what that was. It was only later that John Sparrow convincingly argued that the passage contained references to anal intercourse. He went on to observe that, although the defence witnesses had praised Lawrence's courageous frankness in talking about sex, these references were unusually obscure and only properly intelligible when read in conjunction with the discussions of Mellors' sexual preferences which occur in the letters sent to Connie while she is abroad.[12] What he might also have noted is that, while there had been much talk at the trial of the tenderness of the relation between Connie and Mellors, this final encounter before she leaves England involves 'piercing thrills of sensuality, different, sharper, more terrible than the thrills of tenderness'. Connie is at first an 'almost unwilling' partner, a 'little frightened', but the episode is presented as a burning out of shame, 'the deepest, oldest shames, in the most secret places': a question of penetrating to the 'last and deepest recess of organic shame' which, Lawrence insists, 'the phallus alone could explore'. Shame has to be defeated, the implication is, in order to avoid those fatal confusions which Lawrence describes in 'Pornography and Obscenity', but the process is not in its nature a loving one and it costs Connie an effort 'to let [Mellors] have his way and his will of her. She had to be a

12   See Sparrow, John, 'Regina versus Penguin Books Ltd: An Undisclosed Element in the Case', in *Encounter* (February 1962), pp. 35–43.

passive, consenting thing, like a slave, a physical slave'. Although this episode is not characteristic of the relationship between Connie and Mellors in general, it is surprising that it received so little attention from the prosecution in the 1960 trial and it was certainly in the interests of the defence counsel to ignore it.

In 'A Propos of *Lady Chatterley's Lover*', Lawrence writes warmly and appreciatively of marriage, citing it as the greatest contribution the Catholic Church ever made to Western culture. The kind of marriage he celebrates is indissoluble and yet Connie certainly dissolves hers. What might seem to save Lawrence from contradiction here is the insistence in 'A Propos' that 'marriage is no marriage which is not basically and permanently phallic' – a proviso which, as he puts it, 'crashes through our heart like a bullet'.[13] 'Phallic' could here be interpreted as meaning 'fully sexual', or even no more than warm and tender. Certainly when Lawrence talks of 'phallic consciousness' in his later writings he often means bodily awareness, or a way of living in close and intimate contact with both the human and the non-human environment. In this context sex becomes, as Mellors puts it on the last occasion he sees Connie, 'really only touch'. It is, however, he goes on to say, 'the closest of all touch' and it is hard not to think of his own warmth and connectedness as somehow dependent on a satisfactory sexual life, or at least on the memory of one. This would suggest that both the phallic consciousness he himself exhibits, and the phallic marriage to which Lawrence refers, cannot be easily separated from the phallus itself, the male organ; and it is with that organ – feminist writers increasingly complained after the 1960 trial – that there is in the novel an unhealthy preoccupation and one which indicated a masculine view of sexual experience both ignorant and unjust. Kate Millet, for example, in a highly influential book, first published in 1970, made Lawrence the centrepiece of her attack on male attitudes to women and began her section on his work by quoting the passage in which Connie observes with admiration and awe Mellors' erect penis. Since the light in this episode is provided by the sun shining through a low window, she is able to characterise it as 'a transfiguration scene with atmospheric clouds and lighting, and a pentacostal sunbeam . . . illuminating the ascension of the deity "thick and arching" before the reverent eyes of the faithful'.[14] This attitude to the phallus is for her symptomatic of the way in which

13   *Phoenix 2*, p. 505
14   Millet, Kate, *Sexual Politics*, London, 1977, p. 238

specifically female sexual experience is 'devalued in the novel. All Connie's meetings with Mellors may be seen from her point of view but the perspective is one which, for Millet, is too obviously inflected by the needs and priorities of the male author – in the episode involving anal intercourse, it seemed highly significant to her that the initially reluctant Connie is described as discovering that she had 'secretly wanted' this 'phallic hunting out' after all.

In Connie's encounters with Michaelis, she waits until he has ejaculated and then reaches her own climax while his erect penis is still inside her – bringing herself off, or 'grinding her own coffee' as Mellors terms it when denouncing the same practice in the wife from whom he is separated, Bertha Coutts. The first time Connie makes love with Mellors, the first half of this pattern repeats itself but Connie is disinclined to complete it, and in later meetings that need is in any case obviated by the satisfaction brought her by her new lover's powers of rapid recovery. The success of their physical relationship is attributed by Lawrence to the potency of Mellors but also, and perhaps even more importantly, to the way Connie allows him to take the initiative, becomes if not submissive then at least compliant. For Millet, the sexual relationship is a microcosm in which one can see reflected the power relations of society at large and Connie's submission to Mellors can therefore be regarded as yet one more illustration of the tyranny which for centuries men have exercised over women. But in Lawrence's traditionalist view there were innate differences between men and women which made the search for equality in the more private spheres of living a foolish enterprise, and he clearly believed that the feminists of his own day were on the wrong track. What he felt about them can partly be gauged by Mellors' harsh treatment of Connie's sister Hilda, and by the way the other 'independent' women who visit Wragby are presented.

Many of Millet's objections to *Lady Chatterley's Lover* were rearticulated twenty years after the publication of her *Sexual Politics* by Germaine Greer, who accused Lawrence of having enunciated 'all the great lies of phoney liberation'.[15] Of the features of the book she stigmatises which might fall into that category, the most important is perhaps vaginal orgasm, somehow separated by Lawrence from the clitoris. But Greer also refers to the damage she feels was done by his over-concern with lovers reaching their climax

15   Greer, Germaine, 'Sex, Lies and Old Pork Pies', in the *Independent on Sunday*, 3 June 1990, p. 9

simultaneously, and she objects as Millet had done, and as indeed anyone might, to the virulence with which Mellors denounces women who bring themselves off, and more particularly to his suggestion that they are nearly all lesbians. Her complaints are especially important in that she admits to having championed the novel in the sexual radicalism of her youth, only later discovering that its author had clay feet. She implicitly presents herself (that is) as a witness of the process whereby, from being a hero in the years leading up to the 1960 trial, Lawrence became a villain after it. In part because of the intensity of his relationship with his mother, Lawrence had developed a special insight into the feelings of women to which, during his lifetime, his many female admirers often testified; and he was unusual among male authors of his period in so often adopting female protagonists, the most notable of these being Ursula Brangwen in both *The Rainbow* and *Women in Love*. The risk he took in *Lady Chatterley's Lover* was to try to represent female experience at its most gender specific. For Mark Spilka, writing in 1980, 'the imaginative rendering of a woman's sexual experience' in *Lady Chatterley's Lover* was the novel's 'unassailable triumph'.[16] By that date many female critics were already taking a different view and their implied charge was that, just as the potency of Mellors was, for the Lawrence writing in 1928, an expression of wish-fulfilment, so the physical and psychological compliance of Connie was no more than an idealised, male view of what women ought to be, and how they ought to feel.

In the years after Lawrence's death in 1930, the growing reputation of his last novel was partly dependent on its being read according to the implied prescriptions in 'Pornography and Obscenity' or 'A Propos', and Mellors' address to Connie, 'Th'art good cunt, though, aren't ter? Best bit o' cunt left on earth,' could therefore serve as an illustration of the need for openness in any consideration of sexual matters. With the seismic shift of opinion which the new wave of feminism brought in the 1970s, these words inevitably began to sound as if Connie's cunt was for Mellors the only feature which defined her. Important changes of public feeling not only mean that identical aspects of a novel are differently interpreted but also that some which were previously neglected become salient while others

16 Spilka, Mark, 'Lawrence versus Peeperkorn on Abdication; or What Happens to the Pagan Vitalist When the Juice Runs Out', in *D. H, Lawrence: The Man Who Lived*, edited by Robert B. Partlow and Harry T, Moore, Southern Illinois Press, Carbondale, 1980, p. 116

sink into the background. Lawrence's complaints in *Lady Chatterley's Lover* about the way the search for profit has despoiled the countryside and brutalised the working classes may not have the force they once had because, comparing our time with his, we can reflect that he didn't know the half of it; but his description of Connie's drive through Tevershall in Chapter 11 still resonates powerfully. Critics of the novel will naturally concentrate on the bitterness of Mellors' denunciation of women, which seem less the dramatically appropriate consequence of his antecedents and more a result of his being used as a mouthpiece by the author; and their attention will be drawn to the 'night of sensual passion'. Yet in the main the book does tell a tender love story (as the witnesses at the 1960 trial said it did), and one in which there is not only an insistence on a woman's right to sexual satisfaction but also, unusually for Lawrence, to the satisfaction of her maternal instincts also. Connie desperately wants a baby but not on the terms Sir Clifford unimaginatively proposes. Although Germaine Greer characterises the disillusioned Mellors as 'a pretty boorish lay', the reader is made to feel that he will prove a reliable husband and father and that Connie will therefore be happy to go off with him to a remote farm, a contented wife and mother. This is not every woman's idea of fulfilment, and it is no doubt a weakness of the novel that Lawrence, whose temperament was naturally authoritarian, tends to imply it should be – that he ignores the huge *variety* of ways in which different people satisfy their sexual needs and manage to lead rich lives. Yet the case for Connie's solutions is powerfully and often movingly put. In 'A Propos' Lawrence talks of the need for marriage to be 'basically and *permanently* phallic' (my italics), but this is unlikely to mean that what will enrichen Connie's future life are sexual experiences of the same frequency and intensity as those described so graphically in the novel. What the final letter of Mellors suggests is rather that even the memory of such experiences would be enough to constitute a successful marriage, as it is shown to be for Mrs Bolton.

Lawrence accurately noted that *Lady Chatterley's Lover* had two chief enemies between which there was hardly any space to turn: puritanism and the advanced views of the young.[17] The first of these opponents was slow to rouse itself. By the time the British authorities finally confiscated copies of the novel coming into the country, the overwhelming majority had already been sold; but the Establishment had its revenge when the police raided an exhibition of Lawrence's paintings, which had opened in London in 1929, and seized all those in which there was any sign of pubic hair. He found this kind of response deeply irritating but must have known that those responsible for it were a dying breed, brought up in the repressive, late-Victorian moral atmosphere of his own youth. Far more formidable were the younger people who had learnt to dissipate the anxiety surrounding sex by making it more casual, depriving it of both centrality and what they considered its mystique, and reducing sexual intercourse to just one of the many things men and women could do together. The danger these attitudes represented to Lawrence's own point of view is evident from the fact that it is not so much puritanism which is stigmatised in his novel but the 'advanced' views of Clifford and his friends. Lawrence was after all a puritan himself although one who had struggled hard to rid himself of prudery. If he wanted to be frank about sex it was because nothing seemed to him more important, both for the individual and the community at large. The weakness he identified in advanced opinion was that it threatened to divorce function from feeling and in that context Clifford is its true representative when he suggests that Connie will be able to have herself impregnated by another man without that event having any significant effect on his own relationship with her. There are special reasons why he should adopt this view, yet it is one which we are made to feel would have been endorsed by all those visitors to Wragby derisively characterised by Lawrence as enlightened. Enlightened views on sex are a major target in *Lady Chatterley's Lover*, but with the advances in birth control which one of his characters predicts, and a further loosening of the moral standards once supported by Christianity, enlightenment has certainly had its revenge. It is impossible to respond to *Lady Chatterley's Lover* with the often naïve enthusiasm with which it was supported in the 1960 trial and any reading of the novel cannot now ignore what Millet and her successors had to say. Yet it still has much to recommend it, especially perhaps for those who are of an essentially conservative temperament but have nevertheless managed to rid themselves of their sexual inhibitions.

DAVID ELLIS
University of Kent

SUGGESTED READING

The biographical background to *Lady Chatterley's Lover* is fully explored in my own *D. H. Lawrence: Dying Game*, Cambridge University Press, 1998. On textual questions, and many other matters of interest, the reader should consult the Cambridge edition of the novel. This was published in 1993 and edited by Michael Squires. Squires is also the author of *The Creation of 'Lady Chatterley's Lover'*, Johns Hopkins University Press, 1983, and has edited – with Dennis Jackson – a useful collection of essays entitled *D. H. Lawrence's 'Lady': A New Look at 'Lady Chatterley's Lover'*, University of Georgia Press, 1985. There is an excellent account of how Lawrence's last visit to his native region in 1926 influenced his writing in Derek Brittan, *Lady Chatterley: The Making of the Novel*, Unwin Hyman, 1988.

A year after the *Lady Chatterley* trial, in 1961, Penguin Books published on invaluable transcript of the proceedings edited by C. H. Rolph. A nuanced development of Millett's attack on the book can be found in Hilary Simpson, *D. H. Lawrence and Feminism*, 1982. Very soon after Millett's book had first appeared, Norman Mailer attempted a rebuttal in *The Prisoner of Sex*, 1971, and it is to Mailer that Peter Balbert's spirited *D. H. Lawrence and the Phallic Imagination*, 1989, is much indebted. Most general books on Lawrence from the 1970s, 1980s and 1990s included a chapter on *Lady Chatterley's Lover*. The majority of them were also happy to recognise the important work done by F. R. Leavis in establishing Lawrence's reputation in the years after the Second World War. But Leavis did not like or, perhaps more accurately, did not approve of *Lady Chatterley's Lover*. For his strictures on the novel, see 'The Orthodoxy of Enlightenment', in *'Anna Kerenina' and Other Essays*, 1967, pp. 235–41.

A number of essays on *Lady Chatterley's Lover*, including the very important one by Mark Spilka cited in my Introduction (see footnote 16), can be found in Vol. 3 of *D. H. Lawrence: Critical Assessments*, edited by David Ellis and Ornella de Zordo, 1992; and readers might also find is useful to consult James C. Cowan, 'D. H. Lawrence's Sexual Fallacies', in *The Journal of the History of Sexuality*, Vol. 5, n. 1, July 1994. There is little very recent work on the novel because it has fallen so severely out of favour.

LADY CHATTERLEY'S LOVER

Chapter 1

OURS IS ESSENTIALLY a tragic age, so we refuse to take it tragically. The cataclysm has happened, we are among the ruins, we start to build up new little habitats, to have new little hopes. It is rather hard work: there is now no smooth road into the future: but we go round, or scramble over the obstacles. We've got to live, no matter how many skies have fallen.

This was more or less Constance Chatterley's position. The war had brought the roof down over her head. And she had realised that one must live and learn.

She married Clifford Chatterley in 1917, when he was home for a month on leave. They had a month's honeymoon. Then he went back to Flanders: to be shipped over to England again six months later, more or less in bits. Constance, his wife, was then twenty-three years old, and he was twenty-nine.

His hold on life was marvellous. He didn't die, and the bits seemed to grow together again. For two years he remained in the doctor's hands. Then he was pronounced a cure, and could return to life again, with the lower half of his body, from the hips down, paralysed for ever.

This was in 1920. They returned, Clifford and Constance, to his home, Wragby Hall, the family 'seat'. His father had died, Clifford was now a baronet, Sir Clifford, and Constance was Lady Chatterley. They came to start housekeeping and married life in the rather forlorn home of the Chatterleys on a rather inadequate income. Clifford had a sister, but she had departed. Otherwise there were no near relatives. The elder brother was dead in the war. Crippled for ever, knowing he could never have any children, Clifford came home to the smoky Midlands to keep the Chatterley name alive while he could.

He was not really downcast. He could wheel himself about in a wheeled chair, and he had a bath-chair with a small motor attachment, so he could drive himself slowly round the garden and into the fine melancholy park, of which he was really so proud, though he pretended to be flippant about it.

Having suffered so much, the capacity for suffering had to some extent left him. He remained strange and bright and cheerful, almost, one might say, chirpy, with his ruddy, healthy-looking face, and his pale-blue, challenging bright eyes. His shoulders were broad and strong, his hands were very strong. He was expensively dressed, and wore handsome neckties from Bond Street. Yet still in his face one saw the watchful look, the slight vacancy of a cripple.

He had so very nearly lost his life, that what remained was wonderfully precious to him. It was obvious in the anxious brightness of his eyes, how proud he was, after the great shock, of being alive, but he had been so much hurt that something inside him had perished, some of his feelings had gone. There was a blank of insentience.

Constance, his wife, was a ruddy, country-looking girl with soft brown hair and sturdy body, and slow movements, full of unusual energy. She had big, wondering eyes, and a soft mild voice, and seemed just to have come from her native village. It was not so at all. Her father was the once well-known R.A.,[1] old Sir Malcolm Reid. Her mother had been one of the cultivated Fabians[2] in the palmy, rather pre-Raphaelite days. Between artists and cultured socialists, Constance and her sister Hilda had had what might be called an aesthetically unconventional upbringing. They had been taken to Paris and Florence and Rome to breathe in art, and they had been taken also in the other direction, to the Hague and Berlin, to great Socialist conventions, where the speakers spoke in every civilised tongue, and no one was abashed.

The two girls, therefore, were from an early age not the least daunted by either art or ideal politics. It was their natural atmosphere. They were at once cosmopolitan and provincial, with the cosmopolitan provincialism of art that goes with pure social ideals.

They had been sent to Dresden at the age of fifteen, for music among other things. And they had had a good time there. They lived freely among the students, they argued with the men over philosophical, sociological and artistic matters, they were just as good as the men themselves: only better, since they were women. And they tramped off to the forests with sturdy youths bearing guitars, twang-twang! They sang the Wandervogel songs,[3] and they were free. Free! That was the great word. Out in the open world, out in the forests of the morning, with lusty and splendid-throated young fellows, free to do as they liked, and – above all – to say what they liked. It was the talk that mattered supremely: the impassioned interchange of talk. Love was only a minor accompaniment.

Both Hilda and Constance had had their tentative love affairs by the time they were eighteen. The young men with whom they talked so passionately and sang so lustily and camped under the trees in such freedom wanted, of course, the love connection. The girls were doubtful, but then the thing was so much talked about, it was supposed to be so important. And the men were so humble and craving. Why couldn't a girl be queenly, and give the gift of herself?

So they had given the gift of themselves, each to the youth with whom she had the most subtle and intimate arguments. The arguments, the discussions were the great thing: the love-making and connection were only a sort of primitive reversion and a bit of an anticlimax. One was less in love with the boy afterwards, and a little inclined to hate him, as if he had trespassed on one's privacy and inner freedom. For, of course, being a girl, one's whole dignity and meaning in life consisted in the achievement of an absolute, a perfect, a pure and noble freedom. What else did a girl's life mean? To shake off the old and sordid connections and subjections.

And however one might sentimentalise it, this sex business was one of the most ancient, sordid connections and subjections. Poets who glorified it were mostly men. Women had always known there was something better, something higher. And now they knew it more definitely than ever. The beautiful pure freedom of a woman was infinitely more wonderful than any sexual love. The only unfortunate thing was that men lagged so far behind women in the matter. They insisted on the sex thing like dogs.

And a woman had to yield. A man was like a child with his appetites. A woman had to yield him what he wanted, or like a child he would probably turn nasty and flounce away and spoil what was a very pleasant connection. But a woman could yield to a man without yielding her inner, free self. That the poets and talkers about sex did not seem to have taken sufficiently into account. A woman could take a man without really giving herself away. Certainly she could take him without giving herself into his power. Rather she could use this sex thing to have power over him. For she only had to hold herself back in sexual intercourse, and let him finish and expend himself without herself coming to the crisis: and then she could prolong the connection and achieve her orgasm and her crisis while he was merely her tool.

Both sisters had had their love experience by the time the war came, and they were hurried home. Neither was ever in love with a young man unless he and she were verbally very near: that is unless they were profoundly interested, TALKING to one another. The amazing, the profound, the unbelievable thrill there was in passionately talking to some really clever young man by the hour, resuming day after day for months . . . this they had never realised till it happened! The paradisal promise: Thou shalt have men to talk to! – had never been uttered. It was fulfilled before they knew what a promise it was.

And if after the roused intimacy of these vivid and soul-enlightened discussions the sex thing became more or less inevitable, then let it. It marked the end of a chapter. It had a thrill of its own too: a queer vibrating thrill inside the body, a final spasm of self-assertion, like the last word, exciting, and very like the row of asterisks that can be put to show the end of a paragraph, and a break in the theme.

When the girls came home for the summer holidays of 1913, when Hilda was twenty and Connie eighteen, their father could see plainly that they had had the love experience.

L'amour avait passé par là,[4] as somebody puts it. But he was a man of experience himself, and let life take its course. As for the mother, a nervous invalid in the last few months of her life, she only wanted her girls to be 'free', and to 'fulfil themselves'. She herself had never been able to be altogether herself: it had been denied her. Heaven knows why, for she was a woman who had her own income and her own way. She blamed her husband. But as a matter of fact, it was some old impression of authority on her own mind or soul that she could not get rid of. It had nothing to do with Sir Malcolm, who left his nervously hostile, high-spirited wife to rule her own roost, while he went his own way.

So the girls were 'free', and went back to Dresden, and their music, and the university and the young men. They loved their respective young men, and their respective young men loved them with all the passion of mental attraction. All the wonderful things the young men thought and expressed and wrote, they thought and expressed and wrote for the young women. Connie's young man was musical, Hilda's was technical. But they simply lived for their young women. In their minds and their mental excitements, that is. Somewhere else they were a little rebuffed, though they did not know it.

It was obvious in them too that love had gone through them: that is, the physical experience. It is curious what a subtle but unmistakable transmutation it makes, both in the body of men and women: the woman more blooming, more subtly rounded, her young angularities softened, and her expression either anxious or triumphant: the man much quieter, more inward, the very shapes of his shoulders and his buttocks less assertive, more hesitant.

In the actual sex-thrill within the body, the sisters nearly succumbed to the strange male power. But quickly they recovered themselves, took the sex-thrill as a sensation, and remained free. Whereas the men, in gratitude to the woman for the sex experience, let their souls go out to her. And afterwards looked rather as if they had lost a shilling and found sixpence. Connie's man could be a bit sulky, and Hilda's a bit jeering. But that is how men are! Ungrateful and never satisfied. When you don't have them they hate you because you won't; and when you do have them they hate you again, for some other reason. Or for no reason at all, except that they are discontented children, and can't be satisfied whatever they get, let a woman do what she may.

However, came the war. Hilda and Connie were rushed home again after having been home already in May, to their mother's funeral. Before Christmas of 1914 both their German young men were dead: whereupon the sisters wept, and loved the young men passionately, but underneath forgot them. They didn't exist any more.

Both sisters lived in their father's, really their mother's, Kensington house, and mixed with the young Cambridge group, the group that stood for 'freedom' and flannel trousers, and flannel shirts open at the neck, and a well-bred sort of emotional anarchy, and a whispering, murmuring sort of voice, and an ultra-sensitive sort of manner. Hilda, however, suddenly married a man ten years older than herself, an elder member of the same Cambridge group, a man with a fair amount of money, and a comfortable family job in the government: he also wrote philosophical essays. She lived with him in a smallish house in Westminster, and moved in that good sort of society of people in the government who are not tip-toppers, but who are, or would be, the real intelligent power in the nation: people who know what they're talking about, or talk as if they did.

Connie did a mild form of war-work, and consorted with the flannel-trousers Cambridge intransigents, who gently mocked at everything, so far. Her 'friend' was a Clifford Chatterley, a young man of twenty-two, who had hurried home from Bonn, where he was studying the technicalities of coal-mining. He had previously spent two years at Cambridge. Now he had become a first lieutenant in a smart regiment, so he could mock at everything more becomingly in uniform.

Clifford Chatterley was more upper-class than Connie. Connie was well-to-do intelligentsia, but he was aristocracy. Not the big sort, but still *it*. His father was a baronet, and his mother had been a viscount's daughter.

But Clifford, while he was better bred than Connie, and more 'society', was in his own way more provincial and more timid. He was at his ease in the narrow 'great world', that is, landed aristocracy society, but he was shy and nervous of all that other big world which consists of the vast hordes of the middle and lower classes, and foreigners. If the truth must be told, he was just a little bit frightened of middle- and lower-class humanity, and of foreigners not of his own class. He was, in some paralysing way, conscious of his own defencelessness, though he had all the defence of privilege. Which is curious, but a phenomenon of our day.

Therefore the peculiar soft assurance of a girl like Constance Reid fascinated him. She was so much more mistress of herself in that outer world of chaos than he was master of himself.

Nevertheless he too was a rebel: rebelling even against his class. Or perhaps rebel is too strong a word; far too strong. He was only caught in the general, popular recoil of the young against convention and against any sort of real authority. Fathers were ridiculous: his own obstinate one supremely so. And governments were ridiculous: our own wait-and-see sort especially so. And armies were ridiculous, and old buffers of generals altogether, the red-faced Kitchener[5] supremely. Even the war was ridiculous, though it did kill rather a lot of people.

In fact everything was a little ridiculous, or very ridiculous: certainly everything connected with authority, whether it were in the army or the government or the universities, was ridiculous to a degree. And as far as the governing class made any pretensions to govern, they were ridiculous too. Sir Geoffrey, Clifford's father, was intensely ridiculous, chopping down his trees, and weeding men out of his colliery to shove them into the war; and himself being so safe and patriotic; but, also, spending more money on his country than he'd got.

When Miss Chatterley – Emma – came down to London from the Midlands to do some nursing work, she was very witty in a quiet way about Sir Geoffrey and his determined patriotism. Herbert, the elder brother and heir, laughed outright, though it was his trees that were falling for trench props. But Clifford only smiled a little uneasily. Everything was ridiculous, quite true. But when it came too close and oneself became ridiculous too . . . ? At least people of a different class, like Connie, were earnest about something. They believed in something.

They were rather earnest about the Tommies,[6] and the threat of conscription, and the shortage of sugar and toffee for the children. In all these things, of course, the authorities were ridiculously at fault. But Clifford could not take it to heart. To him the authorities were ridiculous *ab ovo*, not because of toffee or Tommies.

And the authorities felt ridiculous, and behaved in a rather ridiculous fashion, and it was all a mad hatter's tea-party for a while. Till things developed over there, and Lloyd George[7] came to save the situation over here. And this surpassed even ridicule, the flippant young laughed no more.

In 1916 Herbert Chatterley was killed, so Clifford became heir. He was terrified even of this. His importance as son of Sir Geoffrey, and child of Wragby, was so ingrained in him, he could never escape it. And yet he knew that this too, in the eyes of the vast seething world, was ridiculous. Now he was heir and responsible for Wragby. Was that not terrible? and also splendid and at the same time, perhaps, purely absurd?

Sir Geoffrey would have none of the absurdity. He was pale and tense, withdrawn into himself, and obstinately determined to save his country and his own position, let it be Lloyd George or who it might. So cut off he was, so divorced from the England that was really England, so utterly incapable, that he even thought well of Horatio Bottomley.[8] Sir Geoffrey stood for England and Lloyd George as his forebears had stood for England and St George: and he never knew there was a difference. So Sir Geoffrey felled timber and stood for Lloyd George and England, England and Lloyd George.

And he wanted Clifford to marry and produce an heir. Clifford felt his father was a hopeless anachronism. But wherein was he himself any further ahead, except in a wincing sense of the ridiculousness of everything and the paramount ridiculousness of his own position? For willy-nilly he took his baronetcy and Wragby with the last seriousness.

The gay excitement had gone out of the war . . . dead. Too much death and horror. A man needed support and comfort. A man needed to have an anchor in the safe world. A man needed a wife.

The Chatterleys, two brothers and a sister, had lived curiously isolated, shut in with one another at Wragby, in spite of all their connections. A sense of isolation intensified the family tie, a sense of the weakness of their position, a sense of defencelessness, in spite of, or because of, the title and the land. They were cut off from those industrial Midlands in which they passed their lives. And they were cut off from their own class by the brooding, obstinate, shut-up nature of Sir Geoffrey, their father, whom they ridiculed, but whom they were so sensitive about.

The three had said they would all live together always. But now Herbert was dead, and Sir Geoffrey wanted Clifford to marry. Sir Geoffrey barely mentioned it: he spoke very little. But his silent, brooding insistence that it should be so was hard for Clifford to bear up against.

But Emma said No! She was ten years older than Clifford, and she felt his marrying would be a desertion and a betrayal of what the young ones of the family had stood for.

Clifford married Connie, nevertheless, and had his month's honeymoon with her. It was the terrible year 1917, and they were intimate as two people who stand together on a sinking ship. He had been virgin when he married: and the sex part did not mean much to him. They were so close, he and she, apart from that. And Connie exulted a little in this intimacy which was beyond sex, and beyond a man's 'satisfaction'. Clifford anyhow was not just keen on his 'satisfaction', as so many men seemed to be. No, the intimacy was deeper, more personal than that. And sex was merely an accident, or an adjunct: one of the curious obsolete, organic processes which persisted in its own clumsiness, but was not really necessary. Though Connie did want children: if only to fortify her against her sister-in-law Emma.

But early in 1918 Clifford was shipped home smashed, and there was no child. And Sir Geoffrey died of chagrin.

Chapter 2

CONNIE AND CLIFFORD came home to Wragby in the autumn of 1920. Miss Chatterley, still disgusted at her brother's defection, had departed and was living in a little flat in London.

Wragby was a long low old house in brown stone, begun about the middle of the eighteenth century, and added on to, till it was a warren of a place without much distinction. It stood on an eminence in a rather fine old park of oak trees, but alas, one could see in the near distance the chimney of Tebershall pit, with its clouds of steam and smoke, and on the damp, hazy distance of the hill the raw straggle of Teversall village, a village which began almost at the park gates, and trailed in utter hopeless ugliness for a long and gruesome mile: houses, rows of wretched, small, begrimed, brick houses, with black slate roofs for lids, sharp angles and wilful, blank dreariness.

Connie was accustomed to Kensington or the Scotch hills or the Sussex downs: that was her England. With the stoicism of the young she took in the utter, soulless ugliness of the coal-and-iron Midlands at a glance, and left it at what it was: unbelievable and not to be thought about. From the rather dismal rooms at Wragby she heard

the rattle-rattle of the screens at the pit, the puff of the w
engine, the clink-clink of shunting trucks, and the hoarse
whistle of the colliery locomotives. Tevershall pit-bank[9] was burn
had been burning for years, and it would cost thousands to put it out.
So it had to burn. And when the wind was that way, which was often,
the house was full of the stench of this sulphurous combustion of the
earth's excrement. But even on windless days the air always smelt of
something under-earth: sulphur, iron, coal, or acid. And even on the
Christmas roses the smuts settled persistently, incredible, like black
manna from skies of doom.

Well, there it was: fated like the rest of things! It was rather awful,
but why kick? You couldn't kick it away. It just went on. Life, like all
the rest! On the low dark ceiling of cloud at night red blotches
burned and quavered, dappling and swelling and contracting, like
burns that give pain. It was the furnaces. At first they fascinated
Connie with a sort of horror; she felt she was living underground.
Then she got used to them. And in the morning it rained.

Clifford professed to like Wragby better than London. This
country had a grim will of its own, and the people had guts. Connie
wondered what else they had: certainly neither eyes nor minds. The
people were as haggard, shapeless, and dreary as the countryside,
and as unfriendly. Only there was something in their deep-mouthed
slurring of the dialect, and the thresh-thresh of their hobnailed pit-
boots as they trailed home in gangs on the asphalt from work, that
was terrible and a bit mysterious.

There had been no welcome home for the young squire, no
festivities, no deputation, not even a single flower. Only a dank ride
in a motor car up a dark, damp drive, burrowing through gloomy
trees, out to the slope of the park where grey damp sheep were
feeding, to the knoll where the house spread its dark brown façade,
and the housekeeper and her husband were hovering, like unsure
tenants on the face of the earth, ready to stammer a welcome.

There was no communication between Wragby Hall and Tevershall
village, none. No caps were touched, no curtseys bobbed. The colliers
merely stared; the tradesmen lifted their caps to Connie as to an
acquaintance, and nodded awkwardly to Clifford; that was all. Gulf
impassable, and a quiet sort of resentment on either side. At first
Connie suffered from the steady drizzle of resentment that came from
the village. Then she hardened herself to it, and it became a sort of
tonic, something to live up to. It was not that she and Clifford were
unpopular, they merely belonged to another species altogether from
the colliers. Gulf impassable, breach indescribable, such as is perhaps

non-existent south of the Trent. But in the Midlands and the industrial North gulf impassable, across which no communication could take place. You stick to your side, I'll stick to mine! A strange denial of the common pulse of humanity.

Yet the village sympathised with Clifford and Connie in the abstract. In the flesh it was – You leave me alone! – on either side.

The rector was a nice man of about sixty, full of his duty, and reduced, personally, almost to a nonentity by the silent – You leave me alone! – of the village. The miners' wives were nearly all Methodists. The miners were nothing. But even so much official uniform as the clergyman wore was enough to obscure entirely the fact that he was a man like any other man. No, he was Mester Ashby, a sort of automatic preaching and praying concern.

This stubborn, instinctive – We think ourselves as good as you, if you *are* Lady Chatterley! – puzzled and baffled Connie at first extremely. The curious, suspicious, false amiability with which the miners' wives met her overtures; the curiously offensive tinge of – Oh dear me! I *am* somebody now, with Lady Chatterley talking to me! But she needn't think I'm not as good as her for all that! – which she always heard twanging in the women's half-fawning voices, was impossible. There was no getting past it. It was hopelessly and offensively nonconformist.

Clifford left them alone, and she learnt to do the same: she just went by without looking at them, and they stared as if she were a walking wax figure. When he had to deal with them, Clifford was rather haughty and contemptuous; one could no longer afford to be friendly. In fact he was altogether rather supercilious and contemptuous of anyone not in his own class. He stood his ground, without any attempt at conciliation. And he was neither liked nor disliked by the people: he was just part of things, like the pit-bank and Wragby itself.

But Clifford was really extremely shy and self-conscious now he was lamed. He hated seeing anyone except just the personal servants. For he had to sit in a wheeled chair or a sort of bath-chair. Nevertheless he was just as carefully dressed as ever, by his expensive tailors, and he wore the careful Bond Street neckties just as before, and from the top he looked just as smart and impressive as ever. He had never been one of the modern ladylike young men: rather bucolic even, with his ruddy face and broad shoulders. But his very quiet, hesitating voice, and his eyes, at the same time bold and frightened, assured and uncertain, revealed his nature. His manner was often offensively supercilious, and then again modest and self-effacing, almost tremulous.

Connie and he were attached to one another, in the aloof modern way. He was much too hurt in himself, the great shock of his maiming, to be easy and flippant. He was a hurt thing. And as such Connie stuck to him passionately.

But she could not help feeling how little connection he really had with people. The miners were, in a sense, his own men; but he saw them as objects rather than men, parts of the pit rather than parts of life, crude raw phenomena rather than human beings along with him. He was in some way afraid of them, he could not bear to have them look at him now he was lame. And their queer, crude life seemed as unnatural as that of hedgehogs.

He was remotely interested; but like a man looking down a microscope, or up a telescope. He was not in touch. He was not in actual touch with anybody, save, traditionally, with Wragby, and, through the close bond of family defence, with Emma. Beyond this nothing really touched him. Connie felt that she herself didn't really, not really touch him; perhaps there was nothing to get at ultimately; just a negation of human contact.

Yet he was absolutely dependent on her, he needed her every moment. Big and strong as he was, he was helpless. He could wheel himself about in a wheeled chair, and he had a sort of bath-chair with a motor attachment, in which he could puff slowly round the park. But alone he was like a lost thing. He needed Connie to be there, to assure him he existed at all.

Still he was ambitious. He had taken to writing stories; curious, very personal stories about people he had known. Clever, rather spiteful, and yet, in some mysterious way, meaningless. The observation was extraordinary and peculiar. But there was no touch, no actual contact. It was as if the whole thing took place in a vacuum. And since the field of life is largely an artificially-lighted stage today, the stories were curiously true to modern life, to the modern psychology, that is.

Clifford was almost morbidly sensitive about these stories. He wanted everyone to think them good, of the best, *ne plus ultra*.[10] They appeared in the most modern magazines, and were praised and blamed as usual. But to Clifford the blame was torture, like knives goading him. It was as if the whole of his being were in his stories.

Connie helped him as much as she could. At first she was thrilled. He talked everything over with her monotonously, insistently, persistently, and she had to respond with all her might. It was as if her whole soul and body and sex had to rouse up and pass into these stories of his. This thrilled her and absorbed her.

Of physical life they lived very little. She had to superintend the house. But the housekeeper had served Sir Geoffrey for many years, and the dried-up, elderly, superlatively correct female . . . you could hardly call her a parlourmaid, or even a woman . . . who waited at table, had been in the house for forty years. Even the very housemaids were no longer young. It was awful! What could you do with such a place, but leave it alone! All these endless rooms that nobody used, all the Midlands routine, the mechanical cleanliness and the mechanical order! Clifford had insisted on a new cook, an experienced woman who had served him in his rooms in London. For the rest the place seemed run by mechanical anarchy. Everything went on in pretty good order, strict cleanliness, and strict punctuality; even pretty strict honesty. And yet, to Connie, it was a methodical anarchy. No warmth of feeling united it organically. The house seemed as dreary as a disused street.

What could she do but leave it alone . . . ? So she left it alone. Miss Chatterley came sometimes, with her aristocratic thin face, and triumphed, finding nothing altered. She would never forgive Connie for ousting her from her union in consciousness with her brother. It was she, Emma, who should be bringing forth the stories, these books, with him; the Chatterley stories, something new in the world, that *they*, the Chatterleys, had put there. There was no other standard. There was no organic connection with the thought and expression that had gone before. Only something new in the world: the Chatterley books, entirely personal.

Connie's father, when he paid a flying visit to Wragby, said in private to his daughter: As for Clifford's writing, it's smart, but there's nothing in it. It won't last! . . . Connie looked at the burly Scottish knight who had done himself well all his life, and her eyes, her big, still-wondering blue eyes became vague. Nothing in it! What did he mean by *nothing in it*? If the critics praised it, and Clifford's name was almost famous, and it even brought in money . . . what did her father mean by saying there was nothing in Clifford's writing? What else could there be?

For Connie had adopted the standard of the young: what there was in the moment was everything. And moments followed one another without necessarily belonging to one another.

It was in her second winter at Wragby her father said to her: 'I hope, Connie, you won't let circumstances force you into being a demi-vierge.'

'A demi-vierge!' replied Connie vaguely. 'Why? Why not?'

'Unless you like it, of course!' said her father hastily. To Clifford he said the same, when the two men were alone: 'I'm afraid it doesn't quite suit Connie to be a demi-vierge.'

'A half-virgin!' replied Clifford, translating the phrase to be sure of it.

He thought for a moment, then flushed very red. He was angry and offended.

'In what way doesn't it suit her?' he asked stiffly.

'She's getting thin . . . angular. It's not her style. She's not the pilchard sort of little slip of a girl, she's a bonny Scotch trout.'

'Without the spots, of course!' said Clifford.

He wanted to say something later to Connie about the demi-vierge business . . . the half-virgin state of her affairs. But he could not bring himself to do it. He was at once too intimate with her and not intimate enough. He was so very much at one with her, in his mind and hers, but bodily they were non-existent to one another, and neither could bear to drag in the *corpus delicti*.[11] They were so intimate, and utterly out of touch.

Connie guessed, however, that her father had said something, and that something was in Clifford's mind. She knew that he didn't mind whether she were demi-vierge or *demi-monde*,[12] so long as he didn't absolutely know, and wasn't made to see. What the eye doesn't see and the mind doesn't know, doesn't exist.

Connie and Clifford had now been nearly two years at Wragby, living their vague life of absorption in Clifford and his work. Their interests had never ceased to flow together over his work. They talked and wrestled in the throes of composition, and felt as if something were happening, really happening, really in the void.

And thus far it was a life: in the void. For the rest it was non-existence. Wragby was there, the servants . . . but spectral, not really existing. Connie went for walks in the park, and in the woods that joined the park, and enjoyed the solitude and the mystery, kicking the brown leaves of autumn, and picking the primroses of spring. But it was all a dream; or rather it was like the simulacrum of reality. The oak-leaves were to her like oak-leaves seen ruffling in a mirror, she herself was a figure somebody had read about, picking primroses that were only shadows or memories, or words. No substance to her or anything . . . no touch, no contact! Only this life with Clifford, this endless spinning of webs of yarn, of the minutiae of consciousness, these stories Sir Malcolm said there was nothing in, and they wouldn't last. Why should there be anything in them, why should they last? Sufficient unto the day is the evil thereof. Sufficient unto the moment is the *appearance* of reality.

Clifford had quite a number of friends, acquaintances really, and he invited them to Wragby. He invited all sorts of people, critics and writers, people who would help to praise his books. And they were flattered at being asked to Wragby, and they praised. Connie understood it all perfectly. But why not? This was one of the fleeting patterns in the mirror. What was wrong with it?

She was hostess to these people . . . mostly men. She was hostess also to Clifford's occasional aristocratic relations. Being a soft, ruddy, country-looking girl, inclined to freckles, with big blue eyes, and curling, brown hair, and a soft voice, and rather strong, female loins she was considered a little old-fashioned and 'womanly'. She was not a 'little pilchard sort of fish', like a boy, with a boy's flat breast and little buttocks. She was too feminine to be quite smart.

So the men, especially those no longer young, were very nice to her indeed. But, knowing what torture poor Clifford would feel at the slightest sign of flirting on her part, she gave them no encouragement at all. She was quiet and vague, she had no contact with them and intended to have none. Clifford was extraordinarily proud of himself.

His relatives treated her quite kindly. She knew that the kindliness indicated a lack of fear, and that these people had no respect for you unless you could frighten them a little. But again she had no contact. She let them be kindly and disdainful, she let them feel they had no need to draw their steel in readiness. She had no real connection with them.

Time went on. Whatever happened, nothing happened, because she was so beautifully out of contact. She and Clifford lived in their ideas and his books. She entertained . . . there were always people in the house. Time went on as the clock does, half-past eight instead of half-past seven.

Chapter 3

CONNIE WAS AWARE, however, of a growing restlessness. Out of her disconnection, a restlessness was taking possession of her like madness. It twitched her limbs when she didn't want to twitch them, it jerked her spine when she didn't want to jerk upright but preferred to rest comfortably. It thrilled inside her body, in her womb, somewhere, till she felt she must jump into water and swim to get away from it; a mad restlessness. It made her heart beat violently for no reason. And she was getting thinner.

It was just restlessness. She would rush off across the park, and abandon Clifford, and lie prone in the bracken. To get away from the house . . . she must get away from the house and everybody. The wood was her one refuge, her sanctuary.

But it was not really a refuge, a sanctuary, because she had no connection with it. It was only a place where she could get away from the rest. She never really touched the spirit of the wood itself . . . if it had any such nonsensical thing.

Vaguely she knew herself that she was going to pieces in some way. Vaguely she knew she was out of connection: she had lost touch with the substantial and vital world. Only Clifford and his books, which did not exist . . . which had nothing in them! Void to void. Vaguely she knew. But it was like beating her head against a stone.

Her father warned her again: 'Why don't you get yourself a beau, Connie? Do you all the good in the world.'

That winter Michaelis came for a few days. He was a young Irishman who had already made a large fortune by his plays in America. He had been taken up quite enthusiastically for a time by smart society in London, for he wrote smart society plays. Then gradually smart society realised that it had been made ridiculous at the hands of a down-at-heel Dublin street-rat, and revulsion came. Michaelis was the last word in what was caddish and bounderish. He was discovered to be anti-English, and to the class that made this discovery this was worse than the dirtiest crime. He was cut dead, and his corpse thrown into the refuse-can.

Nevertheless Michaelis had his apartment in Mayfair, and walked down Bond Street the image of a gentleman, for you cannot get even the best tailors to cut their low-down customers, when the customers pay.

Clifford was inviting the young man of thirty at an inauspicious moment in the young man's career. Yet Clifford did not hesitate. Michaelis had the ear of a few million people, probably; and, being a hopeless outsider, he would no doubt be grateful to be asked down to Wragby at this juncture, when the rest of the smart world was cutting him. Being grateful, he would no doubt do Clifford 'good' over there in America. Kudos! A man gets a lot of kudos, whatever that may be, by being talked about in the right way, especially 'over there'. Clifford was a coming man; and it was remarkable what a sound publicity instinct he had. In the end Michaelis did him most nobly in a play, and Clifford was a sort of popular hero. Till the reaction, when he found he had been made ridiculous.

Connie wondered a little over Clifford's blind, imperious instinct to become known: known, that is, to the vast amorphous world he did not himself know, and of which he was uneasily afraid; known as a writer, as a first-class modern writer. Connie was aware from successful, old, hearty, bluffing Sir Malcolm, that artists did advertise themselves, and exert themselves to put their goods over. But her father used channels ready-made, used by all the other R.A.s who sold their pictures. Whereas Clifford discovered new channels of publicity, all kinds. He had all kinds of people at Wragby, without exactly lowering himself. But, determined to build himself a monument of a reputation quickly, he used any handy rubble in the making.

Michaelis arrived duly, in a very neat car, with a chauffeur and a manservant. He was absolutely Bond Street! But at sight of him something in Clifford's county soul recoiled. He wasn't exactly . . . not exactly . . . in fact, he wasn't at all, well, what his appearance intended to imply. To Clifford this was final and enough. Yet he was very polite to the man; to the amazing success in him. The bitch-goddess, as she is called, of Success, roamed, snarling and protective, round the half-humble, half-defiant Michaelis' heels, and intimidated Clifford completely: for he wanted to prostitute himself to the bitch-goddess, Success, also, if only she would have him.

Michaelis obviously wasn't an Englishman, in spite of all the tailors, hatters, barbers, booters of the very best quarter of London. No, no, he obviously wasn't an Englishman: the wrong sort of flattish, pale face and bearing; and the wrong sort of grievance. He had a grudge and a grievance: that was obvious to any true-born English gentleman, who would scorn to let such a thing appear blatant in his own demeanour. Poor Michaelis had been much kicked, so that he had a slightly tail-between-the-legs look even now. He had pushed his way by sheer instinct and sheerer effrontery on to the stage and to the front of it, with his plays. He had caught the public. And he had thought the kicking days were over. Alas, they weren't . . . They never would be. For he, in a sense, asked to be kicked. He pined to be where he didn't belong . . . among the English upper classes. And how they enjoyed the various kicks they got at him! And how he hated them!

Nevertheless he travelled with his manservant and his very neat car, this Dublin mongrel.

There was something about him that Connie liked. He didn't put on airs to himself; he had no illusions about himself. He talked to Clifford sensibly, briefly, practically about all the things Clifford wanted to know. He didn't expand or let himself go. He knew he had been asked down to Wragby to be made use of, and like an old, shrewd, almost indifferent business man, or big-business man, he let himself be asked questions, and he answered with as little waste of feeling as possible.

'Money!' he said. 'Money is a sort of instinct. It's a sort of property of nature in a man to make money. It's nothing you do. It's no trick you play. It's a sort of permanent accident of your own nature; once you start, you make money, and you go on; up to a point, I suppose.'

'But you've got to begin,' said Clifford.

'Oh quite! You've got to get *in*. You can do nothing if you are kept outside. You've got to beat your way in. Once you've done that, you can't help it.'

'But could you have made money except by plays?' asked Clifford.

'Oh probably not! I may be a good writer or I may be a bad one, but a writer and a writer of plays is what I am, and I've got to be. There's no question of that.'

'And you think it's a writer of popular plays that you've got to be?' asked Connie.

'There, exactly!' he said, turning to her in a sudden flash. 'There's nothing in it! There's nothing in popularity. There's nothing in the public, if it comes to that. There's nothing really in my plays to *make* them popular. It's not that. They just are, like the weather . . . the sort that will *have* to be . . . for the time being.'

He turned his slow, rather full eyes, that had been drowned in such fathomless disillusion, on Connie, and she trembled a little. He seemed so old . . . endlessly old, built up of layers of disillusion, going down in him generation after generation, like geological strata; and at the same time he was forlorn like a child. An outcast, in a certain sense; but with the desperate bravery of his rat-like existence.

'At least it's wonderful what you've done at your time of life,' said Clifford contemplatively.

'I'm thirty . . . yes, I'm thirty!' said Michaelis, sharply and suddenly, with a curious laugh; hollow, triumphant, and bitter.

'And are you alone?' asked Connie.

'How do you mean? Do I live alone? I've got my servant. He's a Greek, so he says, and quite incompetent. But I keep him. And I'm going to marry. Oh, yes, I must marry.'

'It sounds like going to have your tonsils cut,' laughed Connie. 'Will it be an effort?'

He looked at her admiringly. 'Well, Lady Chatterley, somehow it will! I find . . . excuse me . . . I find I can't marry an Englishwoman, not even an Irishwoman . . . '

'Try an American,' said Clifford.

'Oh, American!' He laughed a hollow laugh. 'No, I've asked my man if he will find me a Turk or something . . . something nearer to the Oriental.'

Connie really wondered at this queer, melancholy specimen of extraordinary success; it was said he had an income of fifty thousand dollars from America alone. Sometimes he was handsome: sometimes as he looked sideways, downwards, and the light fell on him, he had the silent, enduring beauty of a carved ivory Negro mask, with his rather full eyes, and the strong queerly-arched brows, the immobile, compressed mouth; that momentary but revealed immobility, an immobility, a timelessness which the Buddha aims at, and which Negroes express sometimes without ever aiming at it; something old, old, and acquiescent in the race! Aeons of acquiescence in race destiny, instead of our individual resistance. And then a swimming through, like rats in a dark river. Connie felt a sudden, strange leap of sympathy for him, a leap mingled with compassion, and tinged with repulsion, amounting almost to love. The outsider! The outsider! And they called him a bounder! How much more bounderish and assertive Clifford looked! How much stupider!

Michaelis knew at once he had made an impression on her. He turned his full, hazel, slightly prominent eyes on her in a look of pure detachment. He was estimating her, and the extent of the impression he had made. With the English nothing could save him from being the eternal outsider, not even love. Yet women sometimes fell for him . . . Englishwomen too.

He knew just where he was with Clifford. They were two alien dogs which would have liked to snarl at one another, but which smiled instead, perforce. But with the woman he was not quite so sure.

Breakfast was served in the bedrooms; Clifford never appeared before lunch, and the dining-room was a little dreary. After coffee Michaelis, restless and ill-sitting soul, wondered what he should do. It was a fine November day . . . fine for Wragby. He looked over the melancholy park. My God! What a place!

He sent a servant to ask, could he be of any service to Lady Chatterley: he thought of driving into Sheffield. The answer came, would he care to go up to Lady Chatterley's sitting-room.

Connie had a sitting-room on the third floor, the top floor of the central portion of the house. Clifford's rooms were on the ground floor, of course. Michaelis was flattered by being asked up to Lady Chatterley's own parlour. He followed blindly after the servant . . . he never noticed things, or had contact with his surroundings. In her room he did glance vaguely round at the fine German reproductions of Renoir and Cézanne.

'It's very pleasant up here,' he said, with his queer smile, as if it hurt him to smile, showing his teeth. 'You are wise to get up to the top.'

'Yes, I think so,' she said.

Her room was the only gay, modern one in the house, the only spot in Wragby where her personality was at all revealed. Clifford had never seen it, and she asked very few people up.

Now she and Michaelis sat on opposite sides of the fire and talked. She asked him about himself, his mother and father, his brothers . . . other people were always something of a wonder to her, and when her sympathy was awakened she was quite devoid of class feeling. Michaelis talked frankly about himself, quite frankly, without affectation, simply revealing his bitter, indifferent, stray-dog's soul, then showing a gleam of revengeful pride in his success.

'But why are you such a lonely bird?' Connie asked him; and again he looked at her, with his full, searching, hazel look.

'Some birds *are* that way,' he replied. Then, with a touch of familiar irony: 'but, look here, what about yourself? Aren't you by way of being a lonely bird yourself?' Connie, a little startled, thought about it for a few moments, and then she said: 'Only in a way! Not altogether, like you!'

'Am I altogether a lonely bird?' he asked, with his queer grin of a smile, as if he had toothache; it was so wry, and his eyes were so perfectly unchangingly melancholy, or stoical, or disillusioned, or afraid.

'Why?' she said, a little breathless, as she looked at him. 'You are, aren't you?'

She felt a terrible appeal coming to her from him, that made her almost lose her balance.

'Oh, you're quite right!' he said, turning his head away, and looking sideways, downwards, with that strange immobility of an old race that is hardly here in our present day. It was that that really made Connie lose her power to see him detached from herself.

He looked up at her with the full glance that saw everything, registered everything. At the same time, the infant crying in the night was crying out of his breast to her, in a way that affected her very womb.

'It's awfully nice of you to think of me,' he said laconically.

'Why shouldn't I think of you?' she exclaimed, with hardly breath to utter it.

He gave the wry, quick hiss of a laugh.

'Oh, in that way! . . . May I hold your hand for a minute?' he asked suddenly, fixing his eyes on her with almost hypnotic power, and sending out an appeal that affected her direct in the womb.

She stared at him, dazed and transfixed, and he went over and kneeled beside her, and took her two feet close in his two hands, and buried his face in her lap, remaining motionless. She was perfectly dim and dazed, looking down in a sort of amazement at the rather tender nape of his neck, feeling his face pressing her thighs. In all her burning dismay, she could not help putting her hand, with tenderness and compassion, on the defenceless nape of his neck, and he trembled, with a deep shudder.

Then he looked up at her with that awful appeal in his full, glowing eyes. She was utterly incapable of resisting it. From her breast flowed the answering, immense yearning over him; she must give him anything, anything.

He was a curious and very gentle lover, very gentle with the woman, trembling uncontrollably, and yet at the same time detached, aware, aware of every sound outside.

To her it meant nothing except that she gave herself to him. And at length he ceased to quiver any more, and lay quite still, quite still. Then, with dim, compassionate fingers, she stroked his head, that lay on her breast.

When he rose, he kissed both her hands, then both her feet, in their suede slippers, and in silence went away to the end of the room, where he stood with his back to her. There was silence for some minutes. Then he turned and came to her again as she sat in her old place by the fire.

'And now, I suppose you'll hate me!' he said in a quiet, inevitable way. She looked up at him quickly.

'Why should I?' she asked.

'They mostly do,' he said; then he caught himself up. 'I mean . . . a woman is supposed to.'

'This is the last moment when I ought to hate you,' she said resentfully.

'I know! I know! It should be so! You're *frightfully* good to me . . . ' he cried miserably.

She wondered why he should be miserable. 'Won't you sit down again?' she said. He glanced at the door.

'Sir Clifford!' he said, 'won't he . . . won't he be . . . ?' She paused a moment to consider. 'Perhaps!' she said. And she looked up at him. 'I don't want Clifford to know . . . not even to suspect. It would hurt him so much. But I don't think it's wrong, do you?'

'Wrong! Good God, no! You're only too infinitely good to me . . . I can hardly bear it.'

He turned aside, and she saw that in another moment he would be sobbing.

'But we needn't let Clifford know, need we?' she pleaded. 'It *would* hurt him so. And if he never knows, never suspects, it hurts nobody.'

'Me!' he said, almost fiercely; 'he'll know nothing from me! You see if he does. Me give myself away! Ha! Ha!' he laughed hollowly, cynically at such an idea. She watched him in wonder. He said to her: 'May I kiss your hand and go? I'll run into Sheffield I think, and lunch there, if I may, and be back to tea. May I do anything for you? May I be sure you don't hate me? – and that you won't?' – he ended with a desperate note of cynicism.

'No, I don't hate you,' she said. 'I think you're nice.'

'Ah!' he said to her fiercely, 'I'd rather you said that to me than said you love me! It means such a lot more . . . Till afternoon then. I've plenty to think about till then.' He kissed her hands humbly and was gone.

'I don't think I can stand that young man,' said Clifford at lunch.

'Why?' asked Connie.

'He's such a bounder underneath his veneer . . . just waiting to bounce us.'

'I think people have been so unkind to him,' said Connie.

'Do you wonder? And do you think he employs his shining hours doing deeds of kindness?'

'I think he has a certain sort of generosity.'

'Towards whom?'

'I don't quite know.'

'Naturally you don't. I'm afraid you mistake unscrupulousness for generosity.'

Connie paused. Did she? It was just possible. Yet the unscrupulousness of Michaelis had a certain fascination for her. He went whole lengths where Clifford only crept a few timid paces. In his way he had conquered the world, which was what Clifford wanted to do. Ways and means . . . ? Were those of Michaelis more despicable than those of Clifford? Was the way the poor outsider had shoved and bounced himself forward in person, and by the back doors, any worse than Clifford's way of advertising himself into prominence? The bitch-goddess, Success, was trailed by thousands of gasping dogs with lolling tongues. The one that got her first was the real dog among dogs, if you go by success! So Michaelis could keep his tail up.

The queer thing was, he didn't. He came back towards teatime with a large handful of violets and lilies, and the same hangdog expression. Connie wondered sometimes if it were a sort of mask to disarm opposition, because it was almost too fixed. Was he really such a sad dog?

His sad-dog sort of extinguished self persisted all the evening, though through it Clifford felt the inner effrontery. Connie didn't feel it, perhaps because it was not directed against women; only against men, and their presumptions and assumptions. That indestructible, inward effrontery in the meagre fellow was what made men so down on Michaelis. His very presence was an affront to a man of society, cloak it as he might in an assumed good manner.

Connie was in love with him, but she managed to sit with her embroidery and let the men talk, and not give herself away. As for Michaelis, he was perfect; exactly the same melancholic, attentive, aloof young fellow of the previous evening, millions of degrees remote from his hosts, but laconically playing up to them to the required amount, and never coming forth to them for a moment. Connie felt he must have forgotten the morning. He had not forgotten. But he knew where he was . . . in the same old place outside, where the born outsiders are. He didn't take the love-making altogether personally. He knew it would not change him from an ownerless dog, whom everybody begrudges its golden collar, into a comfortable society dog.

The final fact being that at the very bottom of his soul he *was* an outsider, and antisocial, and he accepted the fact inwardly, no matter how Bond-Streety he was on the outside. His isolation was a necessity to him; just as the appearance of conformity and mixing-in with the smart people was also a necessity.

But occasional love, as a comfort and soothing, was also a good thing, and he was not ungrateful. On the contrary, he was burningly, poignantly grateful for a piece of natural, spontaneous kindness: almost to tears. Beneath his pale, immobile, disillusioned face, his child's soul was sobbing with gratitude to the woman, and burning to come to her again; just as his outcast soul was knowing he would keep really clear of her.

He found an opportunity to say to her, as they were lighting the candles in the hall, 'May I come?'

'I'll come to you,' she said.

'Oh, good!'

He waited for her a long time . . . but she came.

He was the trembling excited sort of lover, whose crisis soon came, and was finished. There was something curiously childlike and defenceless about his naked body: as children are naked. His defences were all in his wits and cunning, his very instincts of cunning, and when these were in abeyance he seemed doubly naked and like a child, of unfinished, tender flesh, and somehow struggling helplessly.

He roused in the woman a wild sort of compassion and yearning, and a wild, craving physical desire. The physical desire he did not satisfy in her; he was always come and finished so quickly, then shrinking down on her breast, and recovering somewhat his effrontery while she lay dazed, disappointed, lost.

But then she soon learnt to hold him, to keep him there inside her when his crisis was over. And there he was generous and curiously potent; he stayed firm inside her, giving to her, while she was active . . . wildly, passionately active, coming to her own crisis. And as he felt the frenzy of her achieving her own orgasmic satisfaction from his hard, erect passivity, he had a curious sense of pride and satisfaction.

'Ah, how good!' she whispered tremulously, and she became quite still, clinging to him. And he lay there in his own isolation, but somehow proud.

He stayed that time only the three days, and to Clifford was exactly the same as on the first evening; to Connie also. There was no breaking down his external man.

He wrote to Connie with the same plaintive melancholy note as ever, sometimes witty, and touched with a queer, sexless affection. A kind of hopeless affection he seemed to feel for her, and the essential remoteness remained the same. He was hopeless at the very core of him, and he wanted to be hopeless. He rather hated hope. '*Une immense espérance a traversé la terre*,'[13] he read somewhere, and his comment was: 'and it's darned-well drowned everything worth having.'

Connie never really understood him, but, in her way, she loved him. And all the time she felt the reflection of his hopelessness in her. She couldn't quite, quite love in hopelessness. And he, being hopeless, couldn't ever quite love at all.

So they went on for quite a time, writing, and meeting occasionally in London. She still wanted the physical, sexual thrill she could get with him by her own activity, his little orgasm being over. And he still wanted to give it her. Which was enough to keep them connected.

And enough to give her a subtle sort of self-assurance, something blind and a little arrogant. It was an almost mechanical confidence in her own powers, and went with a great cheerfulness.

She was terrifically cheerful at Wragby. And she used all her aroused cheerfulness and satisfaction to stimulate Clifford, so that he wrote his best at this time, and was almost happy in his strange blind way. He really reaped the fruits of the sensual satisfaction she got out of Michaelis' male passivity erect inside her. But of course he never knew it, and if he had, he wouldn't have said thank-you!

Yet when those days of her grand joyful cheerfulness and stimulus were gone, quite gone, and she was depressed and irritable, how Clifford longed for them again! Perhaps if he'd known he might even have wished to get her and Michaelis together again.

Chapter 4

CONNIE ALWAYS HAD A FOREBODING of the hopelessness of her affair with Mick, as people called him. Yet other men seemed to mean nothing to her. She was attached to Clifford. He wanted a good deal of her life and she gave it to him. But she wanted a good deal from the life of a man, and this Clifford did not give her; could not. There were occasional spasms of Michaelis. But, as she knew by foreboding, that would come to an end. Mick *couldn't* keep anything up. It was part of his very being that he must break off any connection, and be loose, isolated, absolutely lone dog again. It was his major necessity, even though he always said: She turned me down!

The world is supposed to be full of possibilities, but they narrow down to pretty few in most personal experience. There's lots of good fish in the sea . . . maybe . . . but the vast masses seem to be mackerel or herring, and if you're not mackerel or herring yourself, you are likely to find very few good fish in the sea.

Clifford was making strides into fame, and even money. People came to see him. Connie nearly always had somebody at Wragby. But if they weren't mackerel they were herring, with an occasional catfish, or conger eel.

There were a few regular men, constants; men who had been at Cambridge with Clifford. There was Tommy Dukes, who had remained in the army, and was a Brigadier-General. 'The army leaves me time to think, and saves me from having to face the battle of life,' he said.

There was Charles May, an Irishman, who wrote scientifically about stars. There was Hammond, another writer. All were about the same age as Clifford; the young intellectuals of the day. They all believed in the life of the mind. What you did apart from that was your private affair, and didn't much matter. No one thinks of enquiring of another person at what hour he retires to the privy. It isn't interesting to anyone but the person concerned.

And so with most of the matters of ordinary life . . . how you make your money, or whether you love your wife, or if you have 'affairs'. All these matters concern only the person concerned, and, like going to the privy, have no interest for anyone else.

'The whole point about the sexual problem,' said Hammond, who was a tall thin fellow with a wife and two children, but much more closely connected with a typewriter, 'is that there is no point to it. Strictly there is no problem. We don't want to follow a man into the W.C., so why should we want to follow him into bed with a woman? And therein lies the problem. If we took no more notice of the one thing than the other, there'd be no problem. It's all utterly senseless and pointless; a matter of misplaced curiosity.'

'Quite, Hammond, quite! But if someone starts making love to Julia, you begin to simmer; and if he goes on, you are soon at boiling point.' . . . Julia was Hammond's wife.

'Why, exactly! So I should be if he began to urinate in a corner of my drawing-room. There's a place for all these things.'

'You mean you wouldn't mind if he made love to Julia in some discreet alcove?'

Charlie May was slightly satirical, for he had flirted a very little with Julia, and Hammond had cut up very roughly.

'Of course I should mind. Sex is a private thing between me and Julia; and of course I should mind anyone else trying to mix in.'

'As a matter of fact,' said the lean and freckled Tommy Dukes, who looked much more Irish than May, who was pale and rather fat: 'As a matter of fact, Hammond, you have a strong property instinct, and a strong will to self-assertion, and you want success. Since I've been in the army definitely, I've got out of the way of the world, and now I see how inordinately strong the craving for self-assertion and success is in men. It is enormously overdeveloped. All our individuality has run that way. And of course men like you think you'll get through better with a woman's backing. That's why you're so jealous. That's what sex is to you . . . a vital little dynamo between you and Julia, to bring success. If you began to be unsuccessful you'd begin to flirt, like Charlie, who isn't successful. Married people like you and Julia have labels on you, like travellers' trunks. Julia is labelled *Mrs Arnold B. Hammond* . . . just like a trunk on the railway that belongs to somebody. And you are labelled *Arnold B. Hammond, c/o Mrs Arnold B. Hammond*. Oh, you're quite right, you're quite right! The life of the mind needs a comfortable house and decent cooking. You're quite right. It even needs posterity. But it all hinges on the instinct for success. That is the pivot on which all things turn.'

Hammond looked rather piqued. He was rather proud of the integrity of his mind, and of his *not* being a time-server. None the less, he did want success.

'It's quite true, you can't live without cash,' said May. 'You've got to have a certain amount of it to be able to live and get along . . . even to be free to *think* you must have a certain amount of money, or your stomach stops you. But it seems to me you might leave the labels off sex. We're free to talk to anybody; so why shouldn't we be free to make love to any woman who inclines us that way?'

'There speaks the lascivious Celt,' said Clifford.

'Lascivious! well, why not – ? I can't see I do a woman any more harm by sleeping with her than by dancing with her . . . or even talking to her about the weather. It's just an interchange of sensations instead of ideas, so why not?'

'Be as promiscuous as the rabbits!' said Hammond.

'Why not? What's wrong with rabbits? Are they any worse than a neurotic, revolutionary humanity, full of nervous hate?'

'But we're not rabbits, even so,' said Hammond.

'Precisely! I have my mind: I have certain calculations to make in certain astronomical matters that concern me almost more than life or death. Sometimes indigestion interferes with me. Hunger would interfere with me disastrously. In the same way starved sex interferes with me. What then?'

'I should have thought sexual indigestion from surfeit would have interfered with you more seriously,' said Hammond satirically.

'Not it! I don't overeat myself, and I don't over-fuck myself. One has a choice about eating too much. But you would absolutely starve me.'

'Not at all! You can marry.'

'How do you know I can? It may not suit the process of my mind. Marriage might . . . and would . . . stultify my mental processes. I'm not properly pivoted that way . . . and so must I be chained in a kennel like a monk? All rot and funk, my boy. I must live and do my calculations. I need women sometimes. I refuse to make a mountain of it, and I refuse anybody's moral condemnation or prohibition. I'd be ashamed to see a woman walking round with my name-label on her, address and railway station, like a wardrobe trunk.'

These two men had not forgiven each other about the Julia flirtation.

'It's an amusing idea, Charlie,' said Dukes, 'that sex is just another form of talk, where you act the words instead of saying them. I suppose it's quite true. I suppose we might exchange as many sensations and emotions with women as we do ideas about the weather, and so on. Sex might be a sort of normal, physical conversation between a man and a woman. You don't talk to a woman unless you have ideas in common: that is you don't talk with any interest. And in the same way, unless you had some emotion or sympathy in common with a woman you wouldn't sleep with her. But if you had . . . '

'If you *have* the proper sort of emotion or sympathy with a woman, you *ought* to sleep with her,' said May. 'It's the only decent thing, to go to bed with her. Just as, when you are interested talking to someone, the only decent thing is to have the talk out. You don't prudishly put your tongue between your teeth and bite it. You just say out your say. And the same the other way.'

'No,' said Hammond. 'It's wrong. You, for example, May, you squander half your force with women. You'll never really do what you should do, with a fine mind such as yours. Too much of you goes the other way.'

'Maybe it does . . . and too little of you goes that way, Hammond, my boy, married or not. You can keep the purity and integrity of your mind, but it's going damned dry. Your pure mind is going as dry as fiddlesticks, from what I see of it. You're simply talking it down.'

Tommy Dukes burst into a laugh.

'Go it, you two minds!' he said. 'Look at me . . . I don't do any high and pure mental work, nothing but jot down a few ideas. And yet I neither marry nor run after women. I think Charlie's quite right; if he wants to run after the women, he's quite free not to run too often. But I wouldn't prohibit him from running. As for Hammond, he's got a property instinct, so naturally the straight road and the narrow gate are right for him. You'll see he'll be an English Man of Letters[14] before he's done. A.B.C. from top to toe. Then there's me. I'm nothing. Just a squib. And what about you, Clifford? Do you think sex is a dynamo to help a man on to success in the world?'

Clifford rarely talked much at these times. He never held forth; his ideas were really not vital enough for it, he was too confused and emotional. Now he blushed and looked uncomfortable.

'Well!' he said, 'being myself *hors de combat*,[15] I don't see I've anything to say on the matter.'

'Not at all,' said Dukes; 'the top of you's by no means *hors de combat*. You've got the life of the mind sound and intact. So let us hear your ideas.'

'Well,' stammered Clifford, 'even then I don't suppose I have much idea . . . I suppose marry-and-have-done-with-it would pretty well stand for what I think. Though of course between a man and woman who care for one another, it is a great thing.'

'What sort of great thing?' said Tommy.

'Oh . . . it perfects the intimacy,' said Clifford, uneasy as a woman in such talk.

'Well, Charlie and I believe that sex is a sort of communication like speech. Let any woman start a sex conversation with me, and it's natural for me to go to bed with her to finish it, all in due season. Unfortunately no woman makes any particular start with me, so I go to bed by myself; and am none the worse for it . . . I hope so, anyway, for how should I know? Anyhow I've no starry calculations to be interfered with, and no immortal works to write. I'm merely a fellow skulking in the army . . .'

Silence fell. The four men smoked. And Connie sat there and put another stitch in her sewing . . . Yes, she sat there! She had to sit mum. She had to be quiet as a mouse, not to interfere with the immensely important speculations of these highly-mental gentlemen. But she had to be there. They didn't get on so well without her; their ideas didn't flow so freely. Clifford was much more hedgy and nervous, he got cold feet much quicker in Connie's absence, and the talk didn't run. Tommy Dukes came off best; he was a little inspired by her presence. Hammond she didn't really like; he seemed so selfish in a mental way. And Charles May, though she liked something about him, seemed a little distasteful and messy, in spite of his stars.

How many evenings had Connie sat and listened to the manifestations of these four men! these, and one or two others. That they never seemed to get anywhere didn't trouble her deeply. She liked to hear what they had to say, especially when Tommy was there. It was fun. Instead of men kissing you, and touching you with their bodies, they revealed their minds to you. It was great fun! But what cold minds!

And also it was a little irritating. She had more respect for Michaelis, on whose name they all poured such withering contempt, as a little mongrel arriviste,[16] and uneducated bounder of the worst sort. Mongrel and bounder or not, he jumped to his own conclusions. He didn't merely walk round them with millions of words, in the parade of the life of the mind.

Connie quite liked the life of the mind, and got a great thrill out of it. But she did think it overdid itself a little. She loved being there, amidst the tobacco smoke of those famous evenings of the cronies, as she called them privately to herself. She was infinitely amused, and proud too, that even their talking they could not do, without her silent presence. She had an immense respect for thought . . . and these men, at least, tried to think honestly. But somehow there was a cat, and it wouldn't jump. They all alike talked at something, though what it was, for the life of her she couldn't say. It was something that Mick didn't clear, either.

But then Mick wasn't trying to do anything, but just get through his life, and put as much across other people as they tried to put across him. He was really antisocial, which was what Clifford and his cronies had against him. Clifford and his cronies were not antisocial; they were more or less bent on saving mankind, or on instructing it, to say the least.

There was a gorgeous talk on Sunday evening, when the conversation drifted again to love.

> 'Blest be the tie that binds
> Our hearts in kindred something-or-other' – [17]

said Tommy Dukes. 'I'd like to know what the tie is . . . The tie that binds *us* just now is mental friction on one another. And, apart from that, there's damned little tie between us. We bust apart, and say spiteful things about one another, like all the other damned intellectuals in the world. Damned everybodies, as far as that goes, for they all do it. Else we bust apart, and cover up the spiteful things we feel against one another by saying false sugaries. It's a curious thing that the mental life seems to flourish with its roots in spite, ineffable and fathomless spite. Always has been so! Look at Socrates, in Plato, and his bunch round him! The sheer spite of it all, just sheer joy in pulling somebody else to bits . . . Protagoras, or whoever it was! And Alcibiades,[18] and all the other little disciple dogs joining in the fray! I must say it makes one prefer Buddha, quietly sitting under a bo tree, or Jesus, telling his disciples little Sunday stories, peacefully, and without any mental fireworks. No, there's something wrong with the mental life, radically. It's rooted in spite and envy, envy and spite. Ye shall know the tree by its fruit.'

'I don't think we're altogether so spiteful,' protested Clifford.

'My dear Clifford, think of the way we talk each other over, all of us. I'm rather worse than anybody else, myself. Because I infinitely prefer the spontaneous spite to the concocted sugaries; now they *are* poison; when I begin saying what a fine fellow Clifford is, etc., etc., then poor Clifford is to be pitied. For God's sake, all of you, say spiteful things about me, then I shall know I mean something to you. Don't say sugaries, or I'm done.'

'Oh, but I do think we honestly like one another,' said Hammond.

'I tell you we must . . . we say such spiteful things to one another, about one another, behind our backs! I'm the worst.'

'And I do think you confuse the mental life with the critical activity. I agree with you, Socrates gave the critical activity a grand start, but he did more than that,' said Charlie May, rather magisterially. The cronies had such a curious pomposity under their assumed modesty. It was all so *ex cathedra*,[19] and it all pretended to be so humble.

Dukes refused to be drawn about Socrates.

'That's quite true, criticism and knowledge are not the same thing,' said Hammond.

'They aren't, of course,' chimed in Berry, a brown, shy young man, who had called to see Dukes, and was staying the night.

They all looked at him as if the ass had spoken.[20]

'I wasn't talking about knowledge . . . I was talking about the mental life,' laughed Dukes. 'Real knowledge comes out of the whole corpus of the consciousness; out of your belly and your penis as much as out of your brain and mind. The mind can only analyse and rationalise. Set the mind and the reason to cock it over the rest, and all they can do is to criticise, and make a deadness. I say *all* they can do. It is vastly important. My God, the world needs criticising today . . . criticising to death. Therefore let's live the mental life, and glory in our spite, and strip the rotten old show. But, mind you, it's like this: while you *live* your life, you are in some way an organic whole with all life. But once you start the mental life you pluck the apple. You've severed the connection between the apple and the tree: the organic connection. And if you've got nothing in your life *but* the mental life, then you yourself are a plucked apple . . . you've fallen off the tree. And then it is a logical necessity to be spiteful, just as it's a natural necessity for a plucked apple to go bad.'

Clifford made big eyes: it was all stuff to him. Connie secretly laughed to herself.

'Well then we're all plucked apples,' said Hammond, rather acidly and petulantly.

'So let's make cider of ourselves,' said Charlie.

'But what do you think of Bolshevism?' put in the brown Berry, as if everything had led up to it.

'Bravo!' roared Charlie. 'What do you think of Bolshevism?'

'Come on! Let's make hay of Bolshevism!' said Dukes.

'I'm afraid Bolshevism is a large question,' said Hammond, shaking his head seriously.

'Bolshevism, it seems to me,' said Charlie, 'is just a superlative hatred of the thing they call the bourgeois; and what the bourgeois is, isn't quite defined. It is Capitalism, among other things. Feelings and emotions are also so decidedly bourgeois that you have to invent a man without them.

'Then the individual, especially the *personal* man, is bourgeois: so he must be suppressed. You must submerge yourselves in the greater thing, the Soviet-social thing. Even an organism is bourgeois: so the ideal must be mechanical. The only thing that is a unit, non-organic, composed of many different, yet equally essential parts, is the machine. Each man a machine-part, and the driving power of the machine, hate . . . hate of the bourgeois. That, to me, is Bolshevism.'

'Absolutely!' said Tommy. 'But also, it seems to me a perfect description of the whole of the industrial ideal. It's the factory-owner's ideal in a nutshell; except that he would deny that the driving power was hate. Hate it is, all the same: hate of life itself. Just look at these Midlands, if it isn't plainly written up . . . but it's all part of the life of the mind, it's a logical development.'

'I deny that Bolshevism is logical, it rejects the major part of the premisses,' said Hammond.

'My dear man, it allows the material premiss; so does the pure mind . . . exclusively.'

'At least Bolshevism has got down to rock bottom,' said Charlie.

'Rock bottom! The bottom that has no bottom! The Bolshevists will have the finest army in the world in a very short time, with the finest mechanical equipment.'

'But this thing can't go on . . . this hate business. There must be a reaction . . . ' said Hammond.

'Well, we've been waiting for years . . . we wait longer. Hate's a growing thing like anything else. It's the inevitable outcome of forcing ideas on to life, of forcing one's deepest instincts; our deepest feelings we force according to certain ideas. We drive ourselves with a formula, like a machine. The logical mind pretends to rule the roost, and the roost turns into pure hate. We're all Bolshevists, only we are hypocrites. The Russians are Bolshevists without hypocrisy.'

'But there are many other ways,' said Hammond, 'than the Soviet way. The Bolshevists aren't really intelligent.'

'Of course not. But sometimes it's intelligent to be half-witted: if you want to make your end. Personally, I consider Bolshevism half-witted; but so do I consider our social life in the west half-witted. So I even consider our far-famed mental life half-witted. We're all as cold as cretins, we're all as passionless as idiots. We're all of us Bolshevists, only we give it another name. We think we're gods . . . men like gods! It's just the same as Bolshevism. One has to be human, and have a heart and a penis if one is going to escape being either a god or a Bolshevist . . . for they are the same thing: they're both too good to be true.'

Out of the disapproving silence came Berry's anxious question: 'You do believe in love then, Tommy, don't you?'

'You lovely lad!' said Tommy. 'No, my cherub, nine times out of ten, no! Love's another of those half-witted performances today. Fellows with swaying waists fucking little jazz girls with small boy buttocks, like two collar studs! Do you mean that sort of love? Or the joint-property, make-a-success-of-it, My-husband-my-wife sort of love? No, my fine fellow, I don't believe in it at all!'

'But you do believe in something?'

'Me? Oh, intellectually I believe in having a good heart, a chirpy penis, a lively intelligence, and the courage to say "shit!" in front of a lady.'

'Well, you've got them all,' said Berry.

Tommy Dukes roared with laughter. 'You angel boy! If only I had! If only I had! No; my heart's as numb as a potato, my penis droops and never lifts its head up, I dare rather cut him clean off than say "shit!" in front of my mother or my aunt . . . they are real ladies, mind you; and I'm not really intelligent, I'm only a "mental-lifer". It would be wonderful to be intelligent: then one would be alive in all the parts mentioned and unmentionable. The penis rouses his head and says: How do you do? – to any really intelligent person. Renoir said he painted his pictures with his penis . . . he did too, lovely pictures! I wish I did something with mine. God! when one can only talk! Another torture added to Hades! And Socrates started it.'

'There are nice women in the world,' said Connie, lifting her head up and speaking at last.

The men resented it . . . she should have pretended to hear nothing. They hated her admitting she had attended so closely to such talk.

'My God!

> *If they be not nice to me*
> *What care I how nice they be?*[21]

'No, it's hopeless! I just simply can't vibrate in unison with a woman. There's no woman I can really want when I'm faced with her, and I'm not going to start forcing myself to it . . . My God, no! I'll remain as I am, and lead the mental life. It's the only honest thing I can do. I can be quite happy *talking* to women; but it's all pure, hopelessly pure. Hopelessly pure! What do you say, Hildebrand,[22] my chicken?'

'It's much less complicated if one stays pure,' said Berry.

'Yes, life is all too simple!'

Chapter 5

ON A FROSTY MORNING with a little February sun, Clifford and Connie went for a walk across the park to the wood. That is, Clifford chuffed in his motor-chair, and Connie walked beside him.

The hard air was still sulphurous, but they were both used to it. Round the near horizon went the haze, opalescent with frost and smoke, and on the top lay the small blue sky; so that it was like being inside an enclosure, always inside. Life always a dream or a frenzy, inside an enclosure.

The sheep coughed in the rough, sere grass of the park, where frost lay bluish in the sockets of the tufts. Across the park ran a path to the wood-gate, a fine ribbon of pink. Clifford had had it newly gravelled with sifted gravel from the pit-bank. When the rock and refuse of the underworld had burned and given off its sulphur, it turned bright pink, shrimp-coloured on dry days, darker, crab-coloured on wet. Now it was pale shrimp-colour, with a bluish-white hoar of frost. It always pleased Connie, this underfoot of sifted, bright pink. It's an ill wind that brings nobody good.

Clifford steered cautiously down the slope of the knoll from the hall, and Connie kept her hand on the chair. In front lay the wood, the hazel thicket nearest, the purplish density of oaks beyond. From the wood's edge rabbits bobbed and nibbled. Rooks suddenly rose in a black train, and went trailing off over the little sky.

Connie opened the wood-gate, and Clifford puffed slowly through into the broad riding[23] that ran up an incline between the clean-whipped thickets of the hazel. The wood was a remnant of the great forest where Robin Hood hunted, and this riding was an old, old thoroughfare coming across country. But now, of course, it was only a riding through the private wood. The road from Mansfield swerved round to the north.

In the wood everything was motionless, the old leaves on the ground keeping the frost on their underside. A jay called harshly, many little birds fluttered. But there was no game; no pheasants. They had been killed off during the war, and the wood had been left unprotected, till now Clifford had got his gamekeeper again.

Clifford loved the wood; he loved the old oak trees. He felt they were his own through generations. He wanted to protect them. He wanted this place inviolate, shut off from the world.

The chair chuffed slowly up the incline, rocking and jolting on the frozen clods. And suddenly, on the left, came a clearing where there was nothing but a ravel of dead bracken, a thin and spindly sapling leaning here and there, big sawn stumps, showing their tops and their grasping roots, lifeless. And patches of blackness where the woodmen had burned the brushwood and rubbish.

This was one of the places that Sir Geoffrey had cut during the war for trench timber. The whole knoll, which rose softly on the right of the riding, was denuded and strangely forlorn. On the crown of the knoll where the oaks had stood, now was bareness; and from there you could look out over the trees to the colliery railway, and the new works at Stacks Gate. Connie had stood and looked, it was a breach in the pure seclusion of the wood. It let in the world. But she didn't tell Clifford.

This denuded place always made Clifford curiously angry. He had been through the war, had seen what it meant. But he didn't get really angry till he saw this bare hill. He was having it replanted. But it made him hate Sir Geoffrey.

Clifford sat with a fixed face as the chair slowly mounted. When they came to the top of the rise he stopped; he would not risk the long and very jolty down-slope. He sat looking at the greenish sweep of the riding downwards, a clear way through the bracken and oaks. It swerved at the bottom of the hill and disappeared; but it had such a lovely easy curve, of knights riding and ladies on palfreys.

'I consider this is really the heart of England,' said Clifford to Connie, as he sat there in the dim February sunshine.

'Do you?' she said, seating herself, in her blue knitted dress, on a stump by the path.

'I do! this is the old England, the heart of it; and I intend to keep it intact.'

'Oh yes!' said Connie. But, as she said it she heard the eleven-o'clock hooters at Stacks Gate colliery. Clifford was too used to the sound to notice.

'I want this wood perfect . . . untouched. I want nobody to trespass in it,' said Clifford.

There was a certain pathos. The wood still had some of the mystery of wild, old England; but Sir Geoffrey's cuttings during the war had given it a blow. How still the trees were, with their crinkly, innumerable twigs against the sky, and their grey, obstinate trunks rising from the brown bracken! How safely the birds flitted among them! And once there had been deer, and archers, and monks padding along on asses. The place remembered, still remembered.

Clifford sat in the pale sun, with the light on his smooth, rather blond hair, his reddish full face inscrutable.

'I mind more, not having a son, when I come here, than any other time,' he said.

'But the wood is older than your family,' said Connie gently.

'Quite!' said Clifford. 'But we've preserved it. Except for us it would go . . . it would be gone already, like the rest of the forest. One must preserve some of the old England!'

'Must one?' said Connie. 'If it has to be preserved, and preserved against the new England? It's sad, I know.'

'If some of the old England isn't preserved, there'll be no England at all,' said Clifford. 'And we who have this kind of property, and the feeling for it, *must* preserve it.'

There was a sad pause.

'Yes, for a little while,' said Connie.

'For a little while! It's all we can do. We can only do our bit. I feel every man of my family has done his bit here, since we've had the place. One may go against convention, but one must keep up tradition.' Again there was a pause.

'What tradition?' asked Connie.

'The tradition of England! of this!'

'Yes,' she said slowly.

'That's why having a son helps; one is only a link in a chain,' he said.

Connie was not keen on chains, but she said nothing. She was thinking of the curious impersonality of his desire for a son.

'I'm sorry we can't have a son,' she said.

He looked at her steadily, with his full, pale-blue eyes.

'It would almost be a good thing if you had a child by another man,' he said. 'If we brought it up at Wragby, it would belong to us and to the place. I don't believe very intensely in fatherhood. If we had the child to rear, it would be our own, and it would carry on. Don't you think it's worth considering?'

Connie looked up at him at last. The child, her child, was just an 'it' to him. It . . . it . . . it!

'But what about the other man?' she asked.

'Does it matter very much? Do these things really affect us very deeply? . . . You had that lover in Germany . . . what is it now? Nothing almost. It seems to me that it isn't these little acts and little connections we make in our lives that matter so very much. They pass away, and where are they? Where . . . Where are the snows of yesteryear?[24] . . . It's what endures through one's life that matters; my own life matters to me, in its long continuance and development. But what do the occasional connections matter? And the occasional sexual connections especially! If people don't exaggerate them ridiculously, they pass like the mating of birds. And so they should. What does it matter? It's the lifelong companionship that matters. It's the living together from day to day, not the sleeping together once or twice. You and I are married, no matter what happens to us. We have the habit of each other. And habit, to my thinking, is more vital than any occasional excitement. The long, slow, enduring thing . . . that's what we live by . . . not the occasional spasm of any sort. Little by little, living together, two people fall into a sort of unison, they vibrate so intricately to one another. That's the real secret of marriage, not sex; at least not the simple function of sex. You and I are interwoven in a marriage. If we stick to that we ought to be able to arrange this sex thing, as we arrange going to the dentist; since fate has given us a checkmate physically there.'

Connie sat and listened in a sort of wonder, and a sort of fear. She did not know if he was right or not. There was Michaelis, whom she loved; so she said to herself. But her love was somehow only an excursion from her marriage with Clifford; the long, slow habit of intimacy, formed through years of suffering and patience. Perhaps the human soul needs excursions, and must not be denied them. But the point of an excursion is that you come home again.

'And wouldn't you mind *what* man's child I had?' she asked.

'Why, Connie, I should trust your natural instinct of decency and selection. You just wouldn't let the wrong sort of fellow touch you.'

She thought of Michaelis! He was absolutely Clifford's idea of the wrong sort of fellow.

'But men and women may have different feelings about the wrong sort of fellow,' she said.

'No,' he replied. 'You care for me. I don't believe you would ever care for a man who was purely antipathetic to me. Your rhythm wouldn't let you.'

She was silent. Logic might be unanswerable because it was so absolutely wrong.

'And should you expect me to tell you?' she asked, glancing up at him almost furtively.

'Not at all. I'd better not know . . . But you do agree with me, don't you, that the casual sex thing is nothing, compared to the long life lived together? Don't you think one can just subordinate the sex thing to the necessities of a long life? Just use it, since that's what we're driven to? After all, *do* these temporary excitements matter? Isn't the whole problem of life the slow building up of an integral personality, through the years? living an integrated life? There's no point in a disintegrated life. If lack of sex is going to disintegrate you, then go out and have a love affair. If lack of a child is going to disintegrate you, then have a child if you possibly can. But only do these things so that you have an integrated life, that makes a long harmonious thing. And you and I can do that together . . . don't you think? . . . if we adapt ourselves to the necessities, and at the same time weave the adaptation together into a piece with our steadily-lived life. Don't you agree?'

Connie was a little overwhelmed by his words. She knew he was right theoretically. But when she actually touched her steadily-lived life with him she . . . hesitated. Was it actually her destiny to go on weaving herself into his life all the rest of her life? Nothing else?

Was it just that? She was to be content to weave a steady life with him, all one fabric, but perhaps brocaded with the occasional flower of an adventure. But how could she know what she would feel next year? How could one ever know? How could one say Yes? for years and years? The little yes, gone on a breath! Why should one be pinned down by that butterfly word? Of course it had to flutter away and be gone, to be followed by other yes's and no's! Like the straying of butterflies.

'I think you're right, Clifford. And as far as I can see I agree with you. Only life may turn quite a new face on it all.'

'But until life turns a new face on it all, you do agree?'

'Oh yes! I think I do, really.'

She was watching a brown spaniel that had run out of a side-path, and was looking towards them with lifted nose, making a soft, fluffy bark. A man with a gun strode swiftly, softly out after the dog, facing their way as if about to attack them; then stopped instead, saluted, and was turning downhill. It was only the new gamekeeper, but he had frightened Connie, he seemed to emerge with such a swift menace. That was how she had seen him, like the sudden rush of a threat out of nowhere.

He was a man in dark green velveteens and gaiters . . . the old style, with a red face and red moustache and distant eyes. He was going quickly downhill.

'Mellors!' called Clifford.

The man faced lightly round, and saluted with a quick little gesture, a soldier!

'Will you turn the chair round and get it started? That makes it easier,' said Clifford.

The man at once slung his gun over his shoulder, and came forward with the same curious swift, yet soft movements, as if keeping invisible. He was moderately tall and lean, and was silent. He did not look at Connie at all, only at the chair.

'Connie, this is the new gamekeeper, Mellors. You haven't spoken to her ladyship yet, Mellors?'

'No, Sir!' came the ready, neutral words.

The man lifted his hat as he stood, showing his thick, almost fair hair. He stared straight into Connie's eyes, with a perfect, fearless, impersonal look, as if he wanted to see what she was like. He made her feel shy. She bent her head to him shyly, and he changed his hat to his left hand and made her a slight bow, like a gentleman; but he said nothing at all. He remained for a moment still, with his hat in his hand.

'But you've been here some time, haven't you?' Connie said to him.

'Eight months, Madam . . . your Ladyship!' he corrected himself calmly.

'And do you like it?'

She looked him in the eyes. His eyes narrowed a little, with irony, perhaps with impudence.

'Why, yes, thank you, your Ladyship! I was reared here . . .' He gave another slight bow, turned, put his hat on, and strode to take hold of the chair. His voice on the last words had fallen into the heavy broad drag of the dialect . . . perhaps also in mockery, because there had been no trace of dialect before. He might almost be a gentleman. Anyhow, he was a curious, quick, separate fellow, alone, but sure of himself.

Clifford started the little engine, the man carefully turned the chair, and set it nose-forwards to the incline that curved gently to the dark hazel thicket.

'Is that all then, Sir Clifford?' asked the man.

'No, you'd better come along in case she sticks. The engine isn't really strong enough for the uphill work.' The man glanced round for his dog . . . a thoughtful glance. The spaniel looked at him and faintly moved its tail. A little smile, mocking or teasing her, yet gentle, came into his eyes for a moment, then faded away, and his face was expressionless. They went fairly quickly down the slope, the man with his hand on the rail of the chair, steadying it. He looked like a free soldier rather than a servant. And something about him reminded Connie of Tommy Dukes.

When they came to the hazel grove, Connie suddenly ran forward, and opened the gate into the park. As she stood holding it, the two men looked at her in passing, Clifford critically, the other man with a curious, cool wonder; impersonally wanting to see what she looked like. And she saw in his blue, impersonal eyes a look of suffering and detachment, yet a certain warmth. But why was he so aloof, apart?

Clifford stopped the chair, once through the gate, and the man came quickly, courteously, to close it.

'Why did you run to open?' asked Clifford in his quiet, calm voice, that showed he was displeased. 'Mellors would have done it.'

'I thought you would go straight ahead,' said Connie.

'And leave you to run after us?' said Clifford.

'Oh, well, I like to run sometimes!'

Mellors took the chair again, looking perfectly unheeding, yet Connie felt he noted everything. As he pushed the chair up the steepish rise of the knoll in the park, he breathed rather quickly, through parted lips. He was rather frail really. Curiously full of vitality, but a little frail and quenched. Her woman's instinct sensed it.

Connie fell back, let the chair go on. The day had greyed over: the small blue sky that had poised low on its circular rims of haze was closed in again, the lid was down, there was a raw coldness. It was going to snow. All grey, all grey! the world looked worn out.

The chair waited at the top of the pink path. Clifford looked round for Connie.

'Not tired, are you?' he asked.

'Oh, no!' she said.

But she was. A strange, weary yearning, a dissatisfaction had started in her. Clifford did not notice: those were not things he was aware of. But the stranger knew. To Connie, everything in her world and life seemed worn out, and her dissatisfaction was older than the hills.

They came to the house, and round to the back, where there were no steps. Clifford managed to swing himself over on to the low, wheeled house-chair; he was very strong and agile with his arms. Then Connie lifted the burden of his dead legs after him.

The keeper, waiting at attention to be dismissed, watched

everything narrowly, missing nothing. He went pale, with a sort of fear, when he saw Connie lifting the inert legs of the man in her arms, into the other chair, Clifford pivoting round as she did so. He was frightened.

'Thanks, then, for the help, Mellors,' said Clifford casually, as he began to wheel down the passage to the servants' quarters.

'Nothing else, Sir?' came the neutral voice, like one in a dream.

'Nothing, good morning!'

'Good-morning, Sir.'

'Good-morning! it was kind of you to push the chair up that hill . . . I hope it wasn't heavy for you,' said Connie, looking back at the keeper outside the door.

His eyes came to hers in an instant, as if wakened up. He was aware of her.

'Oh no, not heavy!' he said quickly. Then his voice dropped again into the broad sound of the vernacular: 'Good mornin' to your Ladyship!'

'Who is your gamekeeper?' Connie asked at lunch.

'Mellors! You saw him,' said Clifford.

'Yes, but where did he come from?'

'Nowhere! He was a Tevershall boy . . . son of a collier, I believe.'

'And was he a collier himself?'

'Blacksmith on the pit-bank, I believe: overhead smith. But he was keeper here for two years before the war . . . before he joined up. My father always had a good opinion of him, so when he came back, and went to the pit for a blacksmith's job, I just took him back here as keeper. I was really very glad to get him . . . it's almost impossible to find a good man round here, for a gamekeeper . . . and it needs a man who knows the people.'

'And isn't he married?'

'He was. But his wife went off with . . . with various men . . . but finally with a collier at Stacks Gate, and I believe she's living there still.'

'So this man is alone?'

'More or less! He has a mother in the village . . . and a child, I believe.'

Clifford looked at Connie, with his pale, slightly prominent blue eyes, in which a certain vagueness was coming. He seemed alert in the foreground, but the background was like the Midlands atmosphere, haze, smoky mist. And the haze seemed to be creeping forward. So when he stared at Connie in his peculiar way, giving her his peculiar, precise information, she felt all the background of his mind filling up with mist, with nothingness. And it frightened her. It made him seem impersonal, almost to idiocy.

And dimly she realised one of the great laws of the human soul: that when the emotional soul receives a wounding shock, which does not kill the body, the soul seems to recover as the body recovers. But this is only appearance. It is really only the mechanism of the reassumed habit. Slowly, slowly the wound to the soul begins to make itself felt, like a bruise, which only slowly deepens its terrible ache, till it fills all the psyche. And when we think we have recovered and forgotten, it is then that the terrible after-effects have to be encountered at their worst.

So it was with Clifford. Once he was 'well', once he was back at Wragby, and writing his stories, and feeling sure of life, in spite of all, he seemed to forget, and to have recovered all his equanimity. But now, as the years went by, slowly, slowly, Connie felt the bruise of fear and horror coming up, and spreading in him. For a time it had been so deep as to be numb, as it were non-existent. Now slowly it began to assert itself in a spread of fear, almost paralysis. Mentally he still was alert. But the paralysis, the bruise of the too-great shock, was gradually spreading in his affective self.

And as it spread in him, Connie felt it spread in her. An inward dread, an emptiness, an indifference to everything gradually spread in her soul. When Clifford was roused, he could still talk brilliantly, and, as it were, command the future: as when, in the wood, he talked about her having a child, and giving an heir to Wragby. But the day after, all the brilliant words seemed like dead leaves, crumpling up and turning to powder, meaning really nothing, blown away on any gust of wind. They were not the leafy words of an effective life, young with energy and belonging to the tree. They were the hosts of fallen leaves of a life that is ineffectual.

So it seemed to her everywhere. The colliers at Tevershall were talking again of a strike, and it seemed to Connie there again it was not a manifestation of energy, it was the bruise of the war that had been in abeyance, slowly rising to the surface and creating the great ache of unrest, and stupor of discontent. The bruise was deep, deep, deep . . . the bruise of the false inhuman war. It would take many years for the living blood of the generations to dissolve the vast black clot of bruised blood, deep inside their souls and bodies. And it would need a new hope.

Poor Connie! As the years drew on it was the fear of nothingness in her life that affected her. Clifford's mental life and hers gradually began to feel like nothingness. Their marriage, their integrated life based on a habit of intimacy, that he talked about: there were days when it all became utterly blank and nothing. It was words, just so many words. The only reality was nothingness, and over it a hypocrisy of words.

There was Clifford's success: the bitch-goddess! It was true he was almost famous, and his books brought him in a thousand pounds. His photograph appeared everywhere. There was a bust of him in one of the galleries, and a portrait of him in two galleries. He seemed the most modern of modern voices. With his uncanny lame instinct for publicity, he had become in four or five years one of the best known of the young 'intellectuals'. Where the intellect came in, Connie did not quite see. Clifford was really clever at that slightly humorous analysis of people and motives which leaves everything in bits at the end. But it was rather like puppies tearing the sofa cushions to bits; except that it was not young and playful, but curiously old, and rather obstinately conceited. It was weird and it was nothing. This was the feeling that echoed and re-echoed at the bottom of Connie's soul: it was all nothing, a wonderful display of nothingness. At the same time a display. A display! a display! a display!

Michaelis had seized upon Clifford as the central figure for a play; already he had sketched in the plot, and written the first act. For Michaelis was even better than Clifford at making a display of nothingness. It was the last bit of passion left in these men: the passion for making a display. Sexually they were passionless, even dead. And now it was not money that Michaelis was after. Clifford had never been primarily out for money, though he made it where he could, for money is the seal and stamp of success. And success was what they wanted. They wanted, both of them, to make a real display . . . a man's own very display of himself, that should capture for a time the vast populace.

It was strange . . . the prostitution to the bitch-goddess. To Connie, since she was really outside of it, and since she had grown numb to the thrill of it, it was again nothingness. Even the prostitution to the bitch-goddess was nothingness, though the men prostituted themselves innumerable times. Nothingness even that.

Michaelis wrote to Clifford about the play. Of course she knew about it long ago. And Clifford was again thrilled. He was going to be displayed again this time, somebody was going to display him, and to advantage. He invited Michaelis down to Wragby with Act I.

Michaelis came: in summer, in a pale-coloured suit and white suede gloves, with mauve orchids for Connie, very lovely, and Act I was a great success. Even Connie was thrilled . . . thrilled to what bit of marrow she had left. And Michaelis, thrilled by his power to thrill, was really wonderful . . . and quite beautiful, in Connie's eyes. She saw in him that ancient motionlessness of a race that can't be disillusioned any more, an extreme, perhaps, of impurity that is pure. On the far side of his supreme prostitution to the bitch-goddess he seemed pure, pure as an African ivory mask that dreams impurity into purity, in its ivory curves and planes.

His moment of sheer thrill with the two Chatterleys, when he simply carried Connie and Clifford away, was one of the supreme moments of Michaelis' life. He had succeeded: he had carried them away. Even Clifford was temporarily in love with him . . . if that is the way one can put it.

So next morning Mick was more uneasy than ever: restless, devoured, with his hands restless in his trousers pockets. Connie had not visited him in the night . . . and he had not known where to find her. Coquetry! . . . at his moment of triumph.

He went up to her sitting-room in the morning. She knew he would come. And his restlessness was evident. He asked her about his play . . . did she think it good? He *had* to hear it praised: that affected him with the last thin thrill of passion beyond any sexual orgasm. And she praised it rapturously. Yet all the while, at the bottom of her soul, she knew it was nothing.

'Look here!' he said suddenly at last. 'Why don't you and I make a clean thing of it? Why don't we marry?'

'But I am married,' she said, amazed, and yet feeling nothing.

'Oh that! . . . he'll divorce you all right . . . Why don't you and I marry? I want to marry. I know it would be the best thing for me . . . marry and lead a regular life. I lead the deuce of a life, simply tearing myself to pieces. Look here, you and I, we're made for one another . . . hand and glove. Why don't we marry? Do you see any reason why we shouldn't?'

Connie looked at him amazed: and yet she felt nothing. These men, they were all alike, they left everything out. They just went off from the top of their heads as if they were squibs, and expected you to be carried heavenwards along with their own thin sticks.

'But I am married already,' she said. 'I can't leave Clifford, you know.'

'Why not? but why not?' he cried. 'He'll hardly know you've gone, after six months. He doesn't know that anybody exists, except himself. Why the man has no use for you at all, as far as I can see; he's entirely wrapped up in himself.'

Connie felt there was truth in this. But she also felt that Mick was hardly making a display of selflessness.

'Aren't all men wrapped up in themselves?' she asked.

'Oh, more or less, I allow. A man's got to be, to get through. But that's not the point. The point is, what sort of a time can a man give a woman? Can he give her a damn good time, or can't he? If he can't he's no right to the woman . . . ' He paused and gazed at her with his full, hazel eyes, almost hypnotic. 'Now I consider,' he added, 'I can give a woman the darndest good time she can ask for. I think I can guarantee myself.'

'And what sort of a good time?' asked Connie, gazing on him still with a sort of amazement, that looked like thrill; and underneath feeling nothing at all.

'Every sort of a good time, damn it, every sort! Dress, jewels up to a point, any nightclub you like, know anybody you want to know, live the pace . . . travel and be somebody wherever you go . . . Darn it, every sort of good time.'

He spoke it almost in a brilliancy of triumph, and Connie looked at him as if dazzled, and really feeling nothing at all. Hardly even the surface of her mind was tickled at the glowing prospects he offered her. Hardly even her most outside self responded, that at any other time would have been thrilled. She just got no feeling from it all, she couldn't 'go off'. She just sat and stared and looked dazzled, and felt nothing, only somewhere she smelt the extraordinarily unpleasant smell of the bitch-goddess.

Mick sat on tenterhooks, leaning forward in his chair, glaring at her almost hysterically: and whether he was more anxious out of vanity for her to say Yes! or whether he was more panic-stricken for fear she *should* say Yes! – who can tell?

'I should have to think about it,' she said. 'I couldn't say now. It may seem to you Clifford doesn't count, but he does. When you think how disabled he is . . . '

'Oh damn it all! if a fellow's going to trade on his disabilities, I might begin to say how lonely I am, and always have been, and all the rest of the my-eye-Betty-Martin[25] sob-stuff! Damn it all, if a fellow's got nothing but disabilities to recommend him . . . '

He turned aside, working his hands furiously in his trouser pockets. That evening he said to her, 'You're coming round to my room tonight, aren't you? I don't darned know where your room is.'

'All right!' she said.

He was a more excited lover that night, with his strange, small boy's frail nakedness. Connie found it impossible to come to her crisis before he had really finished his. And he roused a certain craving passion in her, with his little boy's nakedness and softness; she had to go on after he had finished, in the wild tumult and heaving of her loins, while he heroically kept himself up, and present in her, with all his will and self-offering, till she brought about her own crisis, with weird little cries.

When at last he drew away from her, he said, in a bitter, almost sneering little voice, 'You couldn't go off at the same time as a man, could you? You'd have to bring yourself off! You'd have to run the show!'

This little speech, at the moment, was one of the shocks of her life. Because that passive sort of giving himself was so obviously his only real mode of intercourse.

'What do you mean?' she said.

'You know what I mean. You keep on for hours after I've gone off . . . and I have to hang on with my teeth till you bring yourself off by your own exertions.'

She was stunned by this unexpected piece of brutality, at the moment when she was glowing with a sort of pleasure beyond words, and a sort of love for him. Because, after all, like so many modern men, he was finished almost before he had begun. And that forced the woman to be active.

'But you want me to go on, to get my own satisfaction?' she said.

He laughed grimly: 'I want it!' he said. 'That's good! I want to hang on with my teeth clenched, while you go for me!'

'But don't you?' she insisted.

He avoided the question. 'All the darned women are like that,' he said. 'Either they don't go off at all, as if they were dead in there . . . or else they wait till a chap's really done, and then they start in to bring themselves off, and a chap's got to hang on. I never had a woman yet who went off just at the same moment as I did.'

Connie only half heard this piece of novel, masculine information. She was only stunned by his feeling against her . . . his incomprehensible brutality. She felt so innocent.

'But you want me to have my satisfaction too, don't you?' she repeated.

'Oh, all right! I'm quite willing. But I'm darned if hanging on waiting for a woman to go off is much of a game for a man . . .'

This speech was one of the crucial blows of Connie's life. It killed something in her. She had not been so very keen on Michaelis; till he started it, she did not want him. It was as if she never positively wanted him. But once he had started her, it seemed only natural for her to come to her own crisis with him. Almost she had loved him for it . . . almost that night she loved him, and wanted to marry him.

Perhaps instinctively he knew it, and that was why he had to bring down the whole show with a smash; the house of cards. Her whole sexual feeling for him, or for any man, collapsed that night. Her life fell apart from his as completely as if he had never existed.

And she went through the days drearily. There was nothing now but this empty treadmill of what Clifford called the integrated life, the long living together of two people, who are in the habit of being in the same house with one another.

Nothingness! To accept the great nothingness of life seemed to be the one end of living. All the many busy and important little things that make up the grand sum-total of nothingness!

Chapter 6

'WHY DON'T MEN AND WOMEN really like one another nowadays?' Connie asked Tommy Dukes, who was more or less her oracle.

'Oh, but they do! I don't think since the human species was invented, there has ever been a time when men and women have liked one another as much as they do today. Genuine liking! Take myself . . . I really *like* women better than men; they are braver, one can be more frank with them.'

Connie pondered this.

'Ah, yes, but you never have anything to do with them!' she said.

'I? What am I doing but talking perfectly sincerely to a woman at this moment?'

'Yes, talking . . . '

'And what more could I do if you were a man, than talk perfectly sincerely to you?'

'Nothing perhaps. But a woman . . . '

'A woman wants you to like her and talk to her, and at the same time love her and desire her; and it seems to me the two things are mutually exclusive.'

'But they shouldn't be!'

'No doubt water ought not to be so wet as it is; it overdoes it in wetness. But there it is! I like women and talk to them, and therefore I don't love them and desire them. The two things don't happen at the same time in me.'

'I think they ought to.'

'All right. The fact that things ought to be something else than what they are, is not my department.'

Connie considered this. 'It isn't true,' she said. 'Men can love women and talk to them. I don't see how they can love them *without* talking, and being friendly and intimate. How can they?'

'Well,' he said, 'I don't know. What's the use of my generalising? I only know my own case. I like women, but I don't desire them. I like talking to them; but talking to them, though it makes me intimate in one direction, sets me poles apart from them as far as kissing is concerned. So there you are! But don't take me as a general example, probably I'm just a special case: one of the men who like women, but don't love women, and even hate them if they force me into a pretence of love, or an entangled appearance.'

'But doesn't it make you sad?'

'Why should it? Not a bit! I look at Charlie May, and the rest of the men who have affairs . . . No, I don't envy them a bit! If fate sent me a woman I wanted, well and good. Since I don't know any woman I want, and never see one . . . why, I presume I'm cold, and really *like* some women very much.'

'Do you like me?'

'Very much! And you see there's no question of kissing between us, is there?'

'None at all!' said Connie. 'But oughtn't there to be?'

'*Why*, in God's name? I like Clifford, but what would you say if I went and kissed him?'

'But isn't there a difference?'

'Where does it lie, as far as we're concerned? We're all intelligent human beings, and the male and female business is in abeyance. Just in abeyance. How would you like me to start acting up like a continental male at this moment, and parading the sex thing?'

'I should hate it.'

'Well then! I tell you, if I'm really a male thing at all, I never run across the female of my species. And I don't miss her, I just *like* women. Who's going to force me into loving, or pretending to love them, working up the sex game?'

'No, I'm not. But isn't something wrong?'

'You may feel it, I don't.'

'Yes, I feel something is wrong between men and women. A woman has no glamour for a man any more.'

'Has a man for a woman?'

She pondered the other side of the question.

'Not much,' she said truthfully.

'Then let's leave it all alone, and just be decent and simple, like proper human beings with one another. Be damned to the artificial sex-compulsion! I refuse it!'

Connie knew he was right, really. Yet it left her feeling so forlorn, so forlorn and stray. Like a chip on a dreary pond, she felt. What was the point, of her or anything?

It was her youth which rebelled. These men seemed so old and cold. Everything seemed old and cold. And Michaelis let one down so; he was no good. The men didn't want one; they just didn't really want a woman, even Michaelis didn't.

And the bounders who pretended they did, and started working the sex game, they were worse than ever.

It was just dismal, and one had to put up with it. It was quite true, men had no real glamour for a woman: if you could fool yourself into thinking they had, even as she had fooled herself over Michaelis, that was the best you could do. Meanwhile you just lived on and there was nothing to it. She understood perfectly well why people had cocktail parties, and jazzed, and Charlestoned[26] till they were ready to drop. You had to take it out some way or other, your youth, or it ate you up. But what a ghastly thing, this youth! You felt as old as Methuselah,[27] and yet the thing fizzed somehow, and didn't let you be comfortable. A mean sort of life! And no prospect! She almost wished she had gone off with Mick, and made her life one long cocktail party, and jazz evening. Anyhow that was better than just mooning yourself into the grave.

On one of her bad days she went out alone to walk in the wood, ponderously, heeding nothing, not even noticing where she was. The report of a gun not far off startled and angered her.

Then, as she went, she heard voices, and recoiled. People! She didn't want people. But her quick ear caught another sound, and she roused; it was a child sobbing. At once she attended – someone was ill-treating a child. She strode swinging down the wet drive, her sullen resentment uppermost. She felt just prepared to make a scene.

Turning the corner, she saw two figures in the drive beyond her: the keeper, and a little girl in a purple coat and moleskin cap, crying.

'Ah, shut it up, tha false little bitch!' came the man's angry voice, and the child sobbed louder.

Constance strode nearer, with blazing eyes. The man turned and looked at her, saluting coolly, but he was pale with anger.

'What's the matter? Why is she crying?' demanded Constance, peremptory but a little breathless.

A faint smile like a sneer came on the man's face. 'Nay, yo' mun ax 'er,' he replied callously, in broad vernacular.

Connie felt as if he had hit her in the face, and she changed colour. Then she gathered her defiance, and looked at him, her dark blue eyes blazing rather vaguely.

'I asked *you*,' she panted.

He gave a queer little bow, lifting his hat. 'You did, your Ladyship,' he said; then, with a return to the vernacular – 'but I canna tell yer.' And he became a soldier, inscrutable, only pale with annoyance.

Connie turned to the child, a ruddy, black-haired thing of nine or ten. 'What is it, dear? Tell me why you're crying!' she said, with the conventionalised sweetness suitable. More violent sobs, self-conscious. Still more sweetness on Connie's part.

'There, there, don't you cry! Tell me what they've done to you!' . . . an intense tenderness of tone. At the same time she felt in the pocket of her knitted jacket, and luckily found a sixpence.

'Don't you cry then!' she said, bending in front of the child. 'See what I've got for you!'

Sobs, snuffles, a fist taken from a blubbered face, and a black shrewd eye cast for a second on the sixpence. Then more sobs, but subduing. 'There, tell me what's the matter, tell me!' said Connie, putting the coin into the child's chubby hand, which closed over it.

'It's the . . . it's the . . . pussy!'

Shudders of subsiding sobs.

'What pussy, dear?'

After a silence the shy fist, clenching on sixpence, pointed into the bramble brake.

'There!'

Connie looked, and there, sure enough, was a big black cat, stretched out grimly, with a bit of blood on it.

'Oh!' she said in repulsion.

'A poacher, your Ladyship,' said the man satirically.

She glanced at him angrily. 'No wonder the child cried,' she said, 'if you shot it when she was there. No wonder she cried!'

He looked into Connie's eyes, laconic, contemptuous, not hiding his feelings. And again Connie flushed; she felt she had been making a scene, the man did not respect her.

'What is your name?' she said playfully to the child. 'Won't you tell me your name?'

Sniffs; then very affectedly in a piping voice: 'Connie Mellors!'

'Connie Mellors! Well, that's a nice name! And did you come out with your Daddy, and he shot a pussy? But it was a bad pussy!'

The child looked at her, with bold, dark eyes of scrutiny, sizing her up, and her condolence.

'I wanted to stop with my Gran,' said the little girl.

'Did you? But where is your Gran?'

The child lifted an arm, pointing down the drive. 'At th' cottidge.'

'At the cottage! And would you like to go back to her?'

Sudden, shuddering quivers of reminiscent sobs. 'Yes!'

'Come then, shall I take you? Shall I take you to your Gran? Then your Daddy can do what he has to do.' She turned to the man. 'It is your little girl, isn't it?'

He saluted, and made a slight movement of the head in affirmation.

'I suppose I can take her to the cottage?' asked Connie.

'If your Ladyship wishes.'

Again he looked into her eyes, with that calm, searching detached glance. A man very much alone, and on his own.

'Would you like to come with me to the cottage, to your Gran, dear?'

The child peeped up again. 'Yes!' she simpered.

Connie disliked her, the spoilt, false little female. Nevertheless she wiped her face, and took her hand. The keeper saluted in silence.

'Good-morning!' said Connie.

It was nearly a mile to the cottage, and Connie senior was well bored by Connie junior by the time the gamekeeper's picturesque little home was in sight. The child was already as full to the brim with tricks as a little monkey, and so self-assured.

At the cottage the door stood open, and there was a rattling heard inside. Connie lingered, the child slipped her hand, and ran indoors.

'Gran! Gran!'

'Why, are yer back a'ready!'

The grandmother had been blackleading[28] the stove, it was Saturday morning. She came to the door in her sacking apron, a blacklead-brush in her hand, and a black smudge on her nose. She was a little, rather dry woman.

'Why, whatever?' she said, hastily wiping her arm across her face as she saw Connie standing outside.

'Good-morning!' said Connie. 'She was crying, so I just brought her home.'

The grandmother looked round swiftly at the child: 'Why, wheer was yer Dad?'

The little girl clung to her grandmother's skirts and simpered.

'He was there,' said Connie, 'but he'd shot a poaching cat, and the child was upset.'

'Oh, you'd no right t'ave bothered, Lady Chatterley, I'm sure! I'm sure it was very good of you, but you shouldn't 'ave bothered. Why, did ever you see!' – and the old woman turned to the child: 'Fancy Lady Chatterley takin' all that trouble over yer! Why, she shouldn't 'ave bothered!'

'It was no bother, just a walk,' said Connie smiling.

'Why, I'm sure 'twas very kind of you, I must say! So she was crying! I knew there'd be something afore they got far. She's frightened of 'im, that's wheer it is. Seems 'e's almost a stranger to 'er, fair a stranger, and I don't think they're two as'd hit it off very easy. He's got funny ways.'

Connie didn't know what to say.

'Look, Gran!' simpered the child.

The old woman looked down at the sixpence in the little girl's hand.

'An' sixpence an' all! Oh, your Ladyship, you shouldn't, you shouldn't. Why, isn't Lady Chatterley good to yer! My word, you're a lucky girl this morning!'

She pronounced the name, as all the people did: Chat'ley. 'Isn't Lady Chat'ley *good* to you!' Connie couldn't help looking at the old woman's nose, and the latter again vaguely wiped her face with the back of her wrist, but missed the smudge.

Connie was moving away . . . 'Well, thank you ever so much, Lady Chat'ley, I'm sure. Say thank you to Lady Chat'ley!' – this last to the child.

'Thank you,' piped the child.

'There's a dear!' laughed Connie, and she moved away, saying 'Good-morning', heartily relieved to get away from the contact. Curious, she thought, that that thin, proud man should have that little, sharp woman for a mother!

And the old woman, as soon as Connie had gone, rushed to the bit of mirror in the scullery, and looked at her face. Seeing it, she stamped her foot with impatience. 'Of *course* she had to catch me in my coarse apron, and a dirty face! Nice idea she'd get of me!'

Connie went slowly home to Wragby. 'Home!' . . . it was a warm word to use for that great, weary warren. But then it was a word that had had its day. It was somehow cancelled. All the great words, it seemed to Connie, were cancelled for her generation: love, joy, happiness, home, mother, father, husband, all these great, dynamic words were half dead now, and dying from day to day. Home was a place you lived in, love was a thing you didn't fool yourself about, joy was a word you applied to a good Charleston, happiness was a term of hypocrisy used to bluff other people, a father was an individual who enjoyed his own existence, a husband was a man you lived with and kept going in spirits. As for sex, the last of the great words, it was just a cocktail term for an excitement that bucked you up for a while, then left you more raggy than ever. Frayed! It was as if the very material you were made of was cheap stuff, and was fraying out to nothing.

All that really remained was a stubborn stoicism: and in that there was a certain pleasure. In the very experience of the nothingness of life, phase after phase, *étape* after *étape*,[29] there was a certain grisly satisfaction. So that's *that*! Always this was the last utterance: home, love, marriage, Michaelis: So that's *that*! And when one died, the last words to life would be: So that's *that*!

Money? Perhaps one couldn't say the same there. Money one always wanted. Money, success, the bitch-goddess, as Tommy Dukes persisted in calling it, after Henry James,[30] that was a permanent necessity. You couldn't spend your last sou, and say finally: So that's *that*! No, if you lived even another ten minutes, you wanted a few more sous for something or other. Just to keep the business mechanically going, you needed money. You had to have it. Money you *have* to have. You needn't really have anything else. So that's that!

Since, of course, it's not your own fault you are alive. Once you are alive, money is a necessity, and the only absolute necessity. All the rest you can get along without, at a pinch. But not money. Emphatically, that's *that*!

She thought of Michaelis, and the money she might have had with him; and even that she didn't want. She preferred the lesser amount which she helped Clifford to make by his writing. That she actually helped to make. 'Clifford and I together, we make twelve hundred a year out of writing'; so she put it to herself. Make money! Make it! Out of nowhere. Wring it out of the thin air! The last feat to be humanly proud of! The rest all-my-eye-Betty-Martin.

So she plodded home to Clifford, to join forces with him again, to make another story out of nothingness: and a story meant money. Clifford seemed to care very much whether his stories were considered first-class literature or not. Strictly, she didn't care. Nothing in it! said her father. Twelve hundred pounds last year! was the retort simple and final.

If you were young, you just set your teeth, and bit on and held on, till the money began to flow from the invisible; it was a question of power. It was a question of will; a subtle, subtle, powerful emanation of will out of yourself brought back to you the mysterious nothingness of money: a word on a bit of paper. It was a sort of magic, certainly it was triumph. The bitch-goddess! Well, if one had to prostitute oneself, let it be to a bitch-goddess! One could always despise her even while one prostituted oneself to her, which was good.

Clifford, of course, had still many childish taboos and fetishes. He wanted to be thought 'really good', which was all cock-a-hoopy[31] nonsense. What was really good was what actually caught on. It was no good being really good and getting left with it. It seemed as if most of the 'really good' men just missed the bus. After all you only lived one life, and if you missed the bus, you were just left on the pavement, along with the rest of the failures.

Connie was contemplating a winter in London with Clifford, next winter. He and she had caught the bus all right, so they might as well ride on top for a bit, and show it.

The worst of it was, Clifford tended to become vague, absent, and to fall into fits of vacant depression. It was the wound to his psyche coming out. But it made Connie want to scream. Oh God, if the mechanism of the consciousness itself was going to go wrong, then what was one to do? Hang it all, one did one's bit! Was one to be let down *absolutely*?

Sometimes she wept bitterly, but even as she wept she was saying to herself: Silly fool, wetting hankies! As if that would get you anywhere!

Since Michaelis, she had made up her mind she wanted nothing. That seemed the simplest solution of the otherwise insoluble. She wanted nothing more than what she'd got; only she wanted to get ahead with what she'd got: Clifford, the stories, Wragby, the Lady-Chatterley business, money, and fame, such as it was . . . she wanted to go ahead with it all. Love, sex, all that sort of stuff, just water-ices! Lick it up and forget it. If you don't hang on to it in your mind, it's nothing. Sex especially . . . nothing! Make up your mind to it, and you've solved the problem. Sex and a cocktail: they both lasted about as long, had the same effect, and amounted to about the same thing.

But a child, a baby! that was still one of the sensations. She would venture very gingerly on that experiment. There was the man to consider, and it was curious, there wasn't a man in the world whose children you wanted. Mick's children! Repulsive thought! As lief have a child to a rabbit! Tommy Dukes? . . . he was very nice, but somehow you couldn't associate him with a baby, another generation. He ended in himself. And out of all the rest of Clifford's pretty wide acquaintance, there was not a man who did not rouse her contempt, when she thought of having a child by him. There were several who would have been quite possible as lovers, even Mick. But to let them breed a child on you! Ugh! Humiliation and abomination.

So that was that!

Nevertheless, Connie had the child at the back of her mind. Wait! wait! She would sift the generations of men through her sieve, and see if she couldn't find one who would do. 'Go ye into the streets[32] and byways of Jerusalem, and see if ye can find a *man*.' It had been impossible to find a man in the Jerusalem of the prophet, though there were thousands of male humans. But a *man*! *C'est une autre chose!*[33]

She had an idea that he would have to be a foreigner: not an Englishman, still less an Irishman. A real foreigner.

But wait! wait! Next winter she would get Clifford to London; the following winter she would get him abroad to the South of France, Italy. Wait! She was in no hurry about the child. That was her own private affair, and the one point on which, in her own queer, female way, she was serious to the bottom of her soul. She was not going to risk any chance comer, not she! One might take a lover almost at any moment, but a man who should beget a child on one . . . wait! wait! it's a very different matter. 'Go ye into the streets and byways of Jerusalem . . . ' It was not a question of love; it was a question of a *man*. Why, one might even rather hate him, personally. Yet if he was the man, what would one's personal hate matter? This business concerned another part of oneself.

It had rained as usual, and the paths were too sodden for Clifford's chair, but Connie would go out. She went out alone every day now, mostly in the wood, where she was really alone. She saw nobody there.

This day, however, Clifford wanted to send a message to the keeper, and as the boy was laid up with influenza – somebody always seemed to have influenza at Wragby – Connie said she would call at the cottage.

The air was soft and dead, as if all the world were slowly dying. Grey and clammy and silent, even from the shuffling of the collieries, for the pits were working short time, and today they were stopped altogether. The end of all things!

In the wood all was utterly inert and motionless, only great drops fell from the bare boughs, with a hollow little crash. For the rest, among the old trees was depth within depth of grey, hopeless inertia, silence, nothingness.

Connie walked dimly on. From the old wood came an ancient melancholy, somehow soothing to her, better than the harsh insentience of the outer world. She liked the *inwardness* of the remnant of forest, the unspeaking reticence of the old trees. They seemed a very power of silence, and yet a vital presence. They, too, were waiting: obstinately, stoically waiting, and giving off a potency of silence. Perhaps they were only waiting for the end; to be cut down, cleared away, the end of the forest, for them the end of all things. But perhaps their strong and aristocratic silence, the silence of strong trees, meant something else.

As she came out of the wood on the north side, the keeper's cottage, a rather dark, brown stone cottage, with gables and a handsome chimney, looked uninhabited, it was so silent and alone. But a thread of smoke rose from the chimney, and the little railed-in garden in the front of the house was dug and kept very tidy. The door was shut.

Now she was here she felt a little shy of the man, with his curious far-seeing eyes. She did not like bringing him orders, and felt like going away again. She knocked softly, no one came. She knocked again, but still not loudly. There was no answer. She peeped through the window, and saw the dark little room, with its almost sinister privacy, not wanting to be invaded.

She stood and listened, and it seemed to her she heard sounds from the back of the cottage. Having failed to make herself heard, her mettle was roused, she would not be defeated.

So she went round the side of the house. At the back of the cottage the land rose steeply, so the back yard was sunken, and enclosed by a low stone wall. She turned the corner of the house and stopped. In the little yard two paces beyond her, the man was washing himself, utterly unaware. He was naked to the hips, his velveteen breeches slipping down over his slender loins. And his white slim back was curved over a big bowl of soapy water, in which he ducked his head, shaking his head with a queer, quick little motion, lifting his slender white arms, and pressing the soapy water from his ears, quick, subtle as a weasel playing with water, and utterly alone. Connie backed away round the corner of the house, and hurried away to the wood. In spite of herself, she had had a shock. After all, merely a man washing himself; commonplace enough, Heaven knows!

Yet in some curious way it was a visionary experience: it had hit her in the middle of the body. She saw the clumsy breeches slipping down over the pure, delicate, white loins, the bones showing a little, and the sense of aloneness, of a creature purely alone, overwhelmed her. Perfect, white, solitary nudity of a creature that lives alone, and inwardly alone. And beyond that, a certain beauty of a pure creature. Not the stuff of beauty, not even the body of beauty, but a lambency, the warm, white flame of a single life, revealing itself in contours that one might touch: a body!

Connie had received the shock of vision in her womb, and she knew it; it lay inside her. But with her mind she was inclined to ridicule. A man washing himself in a back yard! No doubt with evil-smelling yellow soap! She was rather annoyed; why should she be made to stumble on these vulgar privacies?

So she walked away from herself, but after a while she sat down on a stump. She was too confused to think. But in the coil of her confusion, she was determined to deliver her message to the fellow. She would not be balked. She must give him time to dress himself, but not time to go out. He was probably preparing to go out somewhere.

So she sauntered slowly back, listening. As she came near, the cottage looked just the same. A dog barked, and she knocked at the door, her heart beating in spite of herself.

She heard the man coming lightly downstairs. He opened the door quickly, and startled her. He looked uneasy himself, but instantly a laugh came on his face.

'Lady Chatterley!' he said. 'Will you come in?'

His manner was so perfectly easy and good, she stepped over the threshold into the rather dreary little room.

'I only called with a message from Sir Clifford,' she said in her soft, rather breathless voice.

The man was looking at her with those blue, all-seeing eyes of his, which made her turn her face aside a little. He thought her comely, almost beautiful, in her shyness, and he took command of the situation himself at once.

'Would you care to sit down?' he asked, presuming she would not. The door stood open.

'No thanks! Sir Clifford wondered if you would . . . ' and she delivered her message, looking unconsciously into his eyes again. And now his eyes looked warm and kind, particularly to a woman, wonderfully warm, and kind, and at ease.

'Very good, your Ladyship. I will see to it at once.'

Taking an order, his whole self had changed, glazed over with a sort of hardness and distance. Connie hesitated, she ought to go. But she looked round the clean, tidy, rather dreary little sitting-room with something like dismay.

'Do you live here quite alone?' she asked.

'Quite alone, your Ladyship.'

'But your mother . . . ?'

'She lives in her own cottage in the village.'

'With the child?' asked Connie.

'With the child!'

And his plain, rather worn face took on an indefinable look of derision. It was a face that changed all the time, baffling.

'No,' he said, seeing Connie stand at a loss, 'my mother comes and cleans up for me on Saturdays; I do the rest myself.'

Again Connie looked at him. His eyes were smiling again, a little mockingly, but warm and blue, and somehow kind. She wondered at him. He was in trousers and flannel shirt and a grey tie, his hair soft and damp, his face rather pale and worn-looking. When the eyes ceased to laugh they looked as if they had suffered a great deal, still without losing their warmth. But a pallor of isolation came over him, she was not really there for him.

She wanted to say so many things, and she said nothing. Only she looked up at him again, and remarked: 'I hope I didn't disturb you?'

The faint smile of mockery narrowed his eyes.

'Only combing my hair, if you don't mind. I'm sorry I hadn't a coat on, but then I had no idea who was knocking. Nobody knocks here, and the unexpected sounds ominous.'

He went in front of her down the garden path to hold the gate. In his shirt, without the clumsy velveteen coat, she saw again how slender he was, thin, stooping a little. Yet, as she passed him, there was something young and bright in his fair hair, and his quick eyes. He would be a man about thirty-seven or -eight.

She plodded on into the wood, knowing he was looking after her; he upset her so much, in spite of herself.

And he, as he went indoors, was thinking: 'She's nice, she's real! She's nicer than she knows.'

She wondered very much about him; he seemed so unlike a gamekeeper, so unlike a working-man anyhow; although he had something in common with the local people. But also something very uncommon.

'The gamekeeper, Mellors, is a curious kind of person,' she said to Clifford; 'he might almost be a gentleman.'

'Might he?' said Clifford. 'I hadn't noticed.'

'But isn't there something special about him?' Connie insisted.

'I think he's quite a nice fellow, but I know very little about him. He only came out of the army last year, less than a year ago. From India, I rather think. He may have picked up certain tricks out there, perhaps he was an officer's servant, and improved on his position. Some of the men were like that. But it does them no good, they have to fall back into their old place when they get home again.'

Connie gazed at Clifford contemplatively. She saw in him the peculiar tight rebuff against anyone of the lower classes who might be really climbing up, which she knew was characteristic of his breed.

'But don't you think there is something special about him?' she asked.

'Frankly, no! Nothing I had noticed.'

He looked at her curiously, uneasily, half-suspiciously. And she felt he wasn't telling her the real truth; he wasn't telling himself the real truth, that was it. He disliked any suggestion of a really exceptional human being. People must be more or less at his level, or below it.

Connie felt again the tightness, niggardliness of the men of her generation. They were so tight, so scared of life!

Chapter 7

WHEN CONNIE WENT UP to her bedroom she did what she had not done for a long time: took off all her clothes, and looked at herself naked in the huge mirror. She did not know what she was looking for, or at, very definitely, yet she moved the lamp till it shone full on her.

And she thought, as she had thought so often . . . what a frail, easily hurt, rather pathetic thing a human body is, naked; somehow a little unfinished, incomplete!

She had been supposed to have rather a good figure, but now she was out of fashion: a little too female, not enough like an adolescent boy. She was not very tall, a bit Scottish and short; but she had a certain fluent, down-slipping grace that might have been beauty. Her skin was faintly tawny, her limbs had a certain stillness, her body should have had a full, down-slipping richness; but it lacked something.

Instead of ripening its firm, down-running curves, her body was flattening and going a little harsh. It was as if it had not had enough sun and warmth; it was a little greyish and sapless.

Disappointed of its real womanhood, it had not succeeded in becoming boyish, and unsubstantial, and transparent; instead it had gone opaque.

Her breasts were rather small, and dropping pear-shaped. But they were unripe, a little bitter, without meaning hanging there. And her belly had lost the fresh, round gleam it had had when she was young, in the days of her German boy, who really loved her physically. Then it was young and expectant, with a real look of its own. Now it was going slack, and a little flat, thinner, but with a slack thinness. Her thighs, too, that used to look so quick and glimpsy in their female roundness, somehow they too were going flat, slack, meaningless.

Her body was going meaningless, going dull and opaque, so much insignificant substance. It made her feel immensely depressed and hopeless. What hope was there? She was old, old at twenty-seven, with no gleam and sparkle in the flesh. Old through neglect and denial, yes, denial. Fashionable women kept their bodies bright like delicate porcelain, by external attention. There was nothing inside the porcelain; but she was not even as bright as that. The mental life! Suddenly she hated it with a rushing fury, the swindle!

She looked in the other mirror's reflection at her back, her waist, her loins. She was getting thinner, but to her it was not becoming. The crumple of her waist at the back, as she bent back to look, was a little weary; and it used to be so gay-looking. And the longish slope of her haunches and her buttocks had lost its gleam and its sense of richness. Gone! Only the German boy had loved it, and he was ten years dead, very nearly. How time went by! Ten years dead, and she was only twenty-seven. The healthy boy with his fresh, clumsy sensuality that she had then been so scornful of! Where would she find it now? It was gone out of men. They had their pathetic, two-seconds spasms like Michaelis; but no healthy human sensuality, that warms the blood and freshens the whole being.

Still she thought the most beautiful part of her was the long-sloping fall of the haunches from the socket of the back, and the slumberous, round stillness of the buttocks. Like hillocks of sand the Arabs say, soft and downward-slipping with a long slope. Here the life still lingered hoping. But here too she was thinner, and going unripe, astringent.

But the front of her body made her miserable. It was already beginning to slacken, with a slack sort of thinness, almost withered, going old before it had ever really lived. She thought of the child she might somehow bear. Was she fit, anyhow?

She slipped into her nightdress, and went to bed, where she sobbed bitterly. And in her bitterness burned a cold indignation against Clifford, and his writings and his talk: against all the men of his sort who defrauded a woman even of her own body.

Unjust! Unjust! The sense of deep physical injustice burned to her very soul.

But in the morning, all the same, she was up at seven, and going downstairs to Clifford. She had to help him in all the intimate things, for he had no man, and refused a woman-servant. The housekeeper's husband, who had known him as a boy, helped him, and did any heavy lifting; but Connie did the personal things, and she did them willingly. It was a demand on her, but she had wanted to do what she could.

So she hardly ever went away from Wragby, and never for more than a day or two; when Mrs Betts, the housekeeper, attended to Clifford. He, as was inevitable in the course of time, took all the service for granted. It was natural he should.

And yet, deep inside herself, a sense of injustice, of being defrauded, began to burn in Connie. The physical sense of injustice is a dangerous feeling, once it is awakened. It must have outlet, or it eats away the one in whom it is aroused. Poor Clifford, he was not to blame. His was the greater misfortune. It was all part of the general catastrophe.

And yet was he not in a way to blame? This lack of warmth, this lack of the simple, warm, physical contact, was he not to blame for that? He was never really warm, nor even kind, only thoughtful, considerate, in a well-bred, cold sort of way! But never warm as a man can be warm to a woman, as even Connie's father could be warm to her, with the warmth of a man who did himself well, and intended to, but who still could comfort a woman with a bit of his masculine glow.

But Clifford was not like that. His whole race was not like that. They were all inwardly hard and separate, and warmth to them was just bad taste. You had to get on without it, and hold your own; which was all very well if you were of the same class and race. Then you could keep yourself cold and be very estimable, and hold your own, and enjoy the satisfaction of holding it. But if you were of another class and another race it wouldn't do; there was no fun merely holding your own, and feeling you belonged to the ruling class. What was the point, when even the smartest aristocrats had really nothing positive of their own to hold, and their rule was really a farce, not rule at all? What was the point? It was all cold nonsense.

A sense of rebellion smouldered in Connie. What was the good of it all? What was the good of her sacrifice, her devoting her life to Clifford? What was she serving, after all? A cold spirit of vanity, that had no warm human contacts, and that was as corrupt as any low-born Jew, in craving for prostitution to the bitch-goddess, Success. Even Clifford's cool and contactless assurance that he belonged to the ruling class didn't prevent his tongue lolling out of his mouth, as he panted after the bitch-goddess. After all, Michaelis was really more dignified in the matter, and far, far more successful. Really, if you looked closely at Clifford, he was a buffoon, and a buffoon is more humiliating than a bounder.

As between the two men, Michaelis really had far more use for her than Clifford had. He had even more need of her. Any good nurse can attend to crippled legs! And as for the heroic effort, Michaelis was a heroic rat, and Clifford was very much of a poodle showing off.

There were people staying in the house, among them Clifford's Aunt Eva, Lady Bennerley. She was a thin woman of sixty, with a red nose, a widow, and still something of a *grande dame*. She belonged to one of the best families, and had the character to carry it off. Connie liked her, she was so perfectly simple and frank, as far as she intended to be frank, and superficially kind. Inside herself she was a past-mistress in holding her own, and holding other people a little lower. She was not at all a snob: far too sure of herself. She was perfect at the social sport of coolly holding her own, and making other people defer to her.

She was kind to Connie, and tried to worm into her woman's soul with the sharp gimlet of her well-born observations.

'You're quite wonderful, in my opinion,' she said to Connie. 'You've done wonders for Clifford. I never saw any budding genius myself, and there he is all the rage.' Aunt Eva was quite complacently proud of Clifford's success. Another feather in the family cap! She didn't care a straw about his books, but why should she?

'Oh, I don't think it's my doing,' said Connie.

'It must be! Can't be anybody else's. And it seems to me you don't get enough out of it.'

'How?'

'Look at the way you are shut up here. I said to Clifford: If that child rebels one day you'll have yourself to thank!'

'But Clifford never denies me anything,' said Connie.

'Look here, my dear child' – and Lady Bennerley laid her thin hand on Connie's arm. 'A woman has to live her life, or live to repent not having lived it. Believe me!' And she took another sip of brandy, which maybe was her form of repentance.

'But I do live my life, don't I?'

'Not in my idea! Clifford should bring you to London, and let you go about. His sort of friends are all right for him, but what are they for you? If I were you I should think it wasn't good enough. You'll let your youth slip by, and you'll spend your old age, and your middle age too, repenting it.'

Her ladyship lapsed into contemplative silence, soothed by the brandy.

But Connie was not keen on going to London, and being steered into the smart world by Lady Bennerley. She didn't feel really smart, it wasn't interesting. And she did feel the peculiar, withering coldness under it all; like the soil of Labrador, which has gay little flowers on its surface, and a foot down is frozen.

Tommy Dukes was at Wragby, and another man, Harry Winterslow, and Jack Strangeways with his wife Olive. The talk was much more desultory than when only the cronies were there, and everybody was a bit bored, for the weather was bad, and there was only billiards, and the pianola to dance to.

Olive was reading a book about the future, when babies would be bred in bottles, and women would be 'immunised'.

'Jolly good thing too!' she said. 'Then a woman can live her own life.' Strangeways wanted children, and she didn't.

'How'd you like to be immunised?' Winterslow asked her, with an ugly smile.

'I hope I am; naturally,' she said. 'Anyhow the future's going to have more sense, and a woman needn't be dragged down by her *functions*.'

'Perhaps she'll float off into space altogether,' said Dukes.

'I do think sufficient civilisation ought to eliminate a lot of the physical disabilities,' said Clifford. 'All the love-business for example, it might just as well go. I suppose it would if we could breed babies in bottles.'

'No!' cried Olive. 'That might leave all the more room for fun.'

'I suppose,' said Lady Bennerley, contemplatively, 'if the love-business went, something else would take its place. Morphia, perhaps. A little morphine in all the air. It would be wonderfully refreshing for everybody.'

'The government releasing ether into the air on Saturdays, for a cheerful weekend!' said Jack. 'Sounds all right, but where should we be by Wednesday?'

'So long as you can forget your body you are happy,' said Lady Bennerley. 'And the moment you begin to be aware of your body, you are wretched. So, if civilisation is any good, it has to help us to forget our bodies, and then time passes happily without our knowing it.'

'Help us to get rid of our bodies altogether,' said Winterslow. 'It's quite time man began to improve on his own nature, especially the physical side of it.'

'Imagine if we floated like tobacco smoke,' said Connie.

'It won't happen,' said Dukes. 'Our old show will come flop; our civilisation is going to fall. It's going down the bottomless pit, down the chasm. And believe me, the only bridge across the chasm will be the phallus!'

'Oh do! *do* be impossible, General!' cried Olive.

'I believe our civilisation is going to collapse,' said Aunt Eva.

'And what will come after it?' asked Clifford.

'I haven't the faintest idea, but something, I suppose,' said the elderly lady.

'Connie says people like wisps of smoke, and Olive says immunised women, and babies in bottles, and Dukes says the phallus is the bridge to what comes next. I wonder what it will really be?' said Clifford.

'Oh, don't bother! let's get on with today,' said Olive. 'Only hurry up with the breeding bottle, and let us poor women off.'

'There might even be real men, in the next phase,' said Tommy. 'Real, intelligent, wholesome men, and wholesome nice women! Wouldn't that be a change, an enormous change from us? *We're* not men, and the women aren't women. We're only celebrating make-shifts, mechanical and intellectual experiments. There may even come a civilisation of genuine men and women, instead of our little lot of clever-jacks, all at the intelligence-age of seven. It would be even more amazing than men of smoke or babies in bottles.'

'Oh, when people begin to talk about real women, I give up,' said Olive.

'Certainly nothing but the spirit in us is worth having,' said Winterslow.

'Spirits!' said Jack, drinking his whisky and soda.

'Think so? Give me the resurrection of the body!' said Dukes. 'But it'll come, in time, when we've shoved the cerebral stone away a bit, the money and the rest. Then we'll get a democracy of touch, instead of a democracy of pocket.'

Something echoed inside Connie: 'Give me the democracy of touch, the resurrection of the body!' She didn't at all know what it meant, but it comforted her, as meaningless things may do.

Anyhow everything was terribly silly, and she was exasperatedly bored by it all, by Clifford, by Aunt Eva, by Olive and Jack, and Winterslow, and even by Dukes. Talk, talk, talk! What hell it was, the continual rattle of it!

Then, when all the people went, it was no better. She continued plodding on, but exasperation and irritation had got hold of her lower body, she couldn't escape. The days seemed to grind by, with curious painfulness, yet nothing happened. Only she was getting thinner; even the housekeeper noticed it, and asked her about herself. Even Tommy Dukes insisted she was not well, though she said she was all right. Only she began to be afraid of the ghastly white tombstones, that peculiar loathsome whiteness of Carrara marble, detestable as false teeth, which stuck up on the hillside, under Tevershall church, and which she saw with such grim painfulness from the park. The bristling of the hideous false teeth of tombstones on the hill affected her with a grisly kind of horror. She felt the time not far off when she would be buried there, added to the ghastly host under the tombstones and the monuments, in these filthy Midlands.

She needed help, and she knew it; so she wrote a little *cri de coeur* [34] to her sister, Hilda. 'I'm not well lately, and I don't know what's the matter with me.'

Down posted Hilda from Scotland, where she had taken up her abode. She came in March, alone, driving herself in a nimble two-seater. Up the drive she came, tooting up the incline, then sweeping round the oval of grass, where the two great wild beech trees stood, on the flat in front of the house.

Connie had run out to the steps. Hilda pulled up her car, got out, and kissed her sister.

'But Connie!' she said. 'Whatever is the matter?'

'Nothing!' said Connie, rather shamefacedly; but she knew how she had suffered in contrast to Hilda. Both sisters had the same rather golden, glowing skin, and soft brown hair, and naturally strong, warm physique. But now Connie was thin and earthy-looking, with a scraggy, yellowish neck, that stuck out of her jumper.

'But you're ill, child!' said Hilda, in the soft, rather breathless voice, that both sisters had alike. Hilda was nearly, but not quite, two years older than Connie.

'No, not ill. Perhaps I'm bored,' said Connie a little pathetically.

The light of battle glowed in Hilda's face: she was a woman, soft and still as she seemed, of the old amazon sort, not made to fit with men.

'This wretched place!' she said softly, looking at poor, old, lumbering Wragby with real hate. She looked soft and warm herself, as a ripe pear, and she was an amazon of the real old breed.

She went quietly in to Clifford. He thought how handsome she looked, but also he shrank from her. His wife's family did not have his sort of manners, or his sort of etiquette. He considered them rather outsiders, but once they got inside they made him jump through the hoop.

He sat square and well-groomed in his chair, his hair sleek and blond, and his face fresh, his blue eyes pale, and a little prominent, his expression inscrutable, but well-bred. Hilda thought it sulky and stupid, and he waited. He had an air of aplomb, but Hilda didn't care what he had an air of; she was up in arms, and if he'd been Pope or Emperor it would have been just the same.

'Connie's looking awfully unwell,' she said in her soft voice, fixing him with her beautiful, glowering grey eyes. She looked so maidenly, so did Connie; but he well knew the stone of Scottish obstinacy underneath.

'She's a little thinner,' he said.

'Haven't you done anything about it?'

'Do you think it necessary?' he asked, with his suavest English stiffness, for the two things often go together.

Hilda only glowered at him without replying; repartee was not her forte, nor Connie's; so she glowered, and he was much more uncomfortable than if she had said things.

'I'll take her to a doctor,' said Hilda at length. 'Can you suggest a good one round here?'

'I'm afraid I can't.'

'Then I'll take her to London, where we have a doctor we trust.'

Though boiling with rage, Clifford said nothing.

'I suppose I may as well stay the night,' said Hilda, pulling off her gloves, 'and I'll drive her to town tomorrow.'

Clifford was yellow at the gills with anger, and at evening the whites of his eyes were a little yellow too. He ran to liver. But Hilda was consistently modest and maidenly.

'You must have a nurse or somebody, to look after you personally. You should really have a manservant,' said Hilda as they sat, with apparent calmness, at coffee after dinner. She spoke in her soft, seemingly gentle way, but Clifford felt she was hitting him on the head with a bludgeon.

'You think so?' he said coldly.

'I'm sure! It's necessary. Either that, or Father and I must take Connie away for some months. This can't go on.'

'What can't go on?'

'Haven't you looked at the child?' asked Hilda, gazing at him full stare. He looked rather like a huge, boiled crayfish, at the moment; or so she thought.

'Connie and I will discuss it,' he said.

'I've already discussed it with her,' said Hilda.

Clifford had been long enough in the hands of nurses; he hated them, because they left him no real privacy. And a manservant! . . . he couldn't stand a man hanging round him. Almost better any woman. But why not Connie?

The two sisters drove off in the morning, Connie looking rather like an Easter lamb, rather small beside Hilda, who held the wheel. Sir Malcolm was away, but the Kensington house was open.

The doctor examined Connie carefully, and asked her all about her life. 'I see your photograph, and Sir Clifford's, in the illustrated papers sometimes. Almost notorieties, aren't you? That's how the quiet little girls grow up, though you're only a quiet little girl even now, in spite of the illustrated papers. No, no! There's nothing organically wrong, but it won't do! it won't do! Tell Sir Clifford he's got to bring you to town, or take you abroad, and amuse you. You've got to be amused, got to! Your vitality is much too low; no reserves, no reserves. The nerves of the heart a bit queer already: oh, yes! Nothing but nerves; I'd put you right in a month at Cannes or Biarritz. But it mustn't go on, *mustn't*, I tell you, or I won't be answerable for consequences. You're spending your life without renewing it. You've got to be amused, properly, healthily amused. You're spending your vitality without making any. Can't go on, you know. Depression! avoid depression!'

Hilda set her jaw, and that meant something.

Michaelis heard they were in town, and came running with roses. 'Why, whatever's wrong?' he cried. 'You're a shadow of yourself. Why, I never saw such a change! Why ever didn't you let me know? Come to Nice with me! Come down to Sicily! Go on, come to Sicily with me, it's lovely there just now. You want sun! You want life! Why, you're wasting away! Come away with me! Come to Africa! Oh, hang Sir Clifford! Chuck him, and come along with me. I'll marry you the minute he divorces you. Come along and try a life! God's love! That place Wragby would kill anybody. Beastly place! Foul place! Kill anybody! Come away with me into the sun! It's the sun you want, of course, and a bit of normal life.'

But Connie's heart simply stood still at the thought of abandoning Clifford there and then. She couldn't do it. No . . . no! She just couldn't. She had to go back to Wragby.

Michaelis was disgusted. Hilda didn't like Michaelis, but she *almost* preferred him to Clifford. Back went the sisters to the Midlands.

Hilda talked to Clifford, who still had yellow eyeballs when they got back. He, too, in his way, was overwrought; but he had to listen to all Hilda said, to all the doctor had said, not what Michaelis had said, of course, and he sat mum through the ultimatum.

'Here is the address of a good manservant, who was with an invalid patient of the doctor's till he died last month. He is really a good man, and fairly sure to come.'

'But I'm *not* an invalid, and I will *not* have a manservant,' said Clifford, poor devil.

'And here are the addresses of two women; I saw one of them, she would do very well; a woman of about fifty, quiet, strong, kind, and in her way cultured . . .'

Clifford only sulked, and would not answer.

'Very well, Clifford. If we don't settle something by tomorrow, I shall telegraph to Father, and we shall take Connie away.'

'Will Connie go?' asked Clifford.

'She doesn't want to, but she knows she must. Mother died of cancer, brought on by fretting. We're not running any risks.'

So next day Clifford suggested Mrs Bolton, Teyershall parish nurse. Apparently Mrs Betts had thought of her. Mrs Bolton was just retiring from her parish duties to take up private nursing jobs. Clifford had a queer dread of delivering himself into the hands of a stranger, but this Mrs Bolton had once nursed him through scarlet fever, and he knew her.

The two sisters at once called on Mrs Bolton, in a newish house in a row, quite select for Teyershall. They found a rather good-looking woman of forty-odd, in a nurse's uniform, with a white collar and apron, just making herself tea, in a small, crowded sitting-room.

Mrs Bolton was most attentive and polite, seemed quite nice, spoke with a bit of a broad slur, but in heavily correct English, and from having bossed the sick colliers for a good many years, had a very good opinion of herself, and a fair amount of assurance. In short, in her tiny way, one of the governing class in the village, very much respected.

'Yes, Lady Chatterley's not looking at all well! Why, she used to be that bonny, didn't she now? But she's been failing all winter! Oh, it's hard, it is. Poor Sir Clifford! Eh, that war, it's a lot to answer for.'

And Mrs Bolton would come to Wragby at once, if Dr Shardlow would let her off. She had another fortnight's parish nursing to do, by rights, but they might get a substitute, you know.

Hilda posted off to Dr Shardlow, and on the following Sunday Mrs Bolton drove up in Leiver's cab to Wragby, with two trunks. Hilda had talks with her; Mrs Bolton was ready at any moment to talk. And she seemed so young! the way the passion would flush in her rather pale cheek. She was forty-seven.

Her husband, Ted Bolton, had been killed in the pit, twenty-two years ago, twenty-two years last Christmas, just at Christmas time, leaving her with two children, one a baby in arms. Oh the baby was married now, Edith, to a young man in Boots Cash Chemists in Sheffield. The other one was a schoolteacher in Chesterfield; she came home weekends, when she wasn't asked out somewhere. Young folks enjoyed themselves nowadays, not like when she, Ivy Bolton, was young.

Ted Bolton was twenty-eight when he was killed in an explosion down th' pit. The butty[35] in front shouted to them all to lie down quick, there were four of them. And they all lay down in time, only Ted, and it killed him. Then at the inquiry, on the masters' side they said Ted had been frightened, and trying to run away, and not obeying orders, so it was like his fault really. So the compensation was only three hundred pounds, and they made out as if it was more of a gift than legal compensation, because it was really the man's own fault. And they wouldn't let her have the money down; she wanted to have a little shop. But they said she'd no doubt squander it, perhaps in drink! So she had to draw it thirty shillings a week. Yes, she had to go every Monday morning down to the offices, and stand there a couple of hours waiting her turn; yes, for almost four years she went every Monday. And what could she do with two little children on her hands? But Ted's mother was very good to her. When the baby could toddle she'd keep both the children for the day, while she, Ivy Bolton, went to Sheffield, and attended classes in ambulance, and then the fourth year she even took a nursing course and got qualified. She was determined to be independent and keep her children. So she was assistant at Uthwaite hospital, just a little place, for a while. But when the Company, the Tevershall Colliery Company, really Sir Geoffrey, saw that she could get on by herself, they were very good to her, gave her the parish nursing, and stood by her, she would say that for them. And she'd done it ever since, till now it was getting a bit much for her, she needed something a bit lighter, there was such a lot of traipsing round if you were a district nurse.

'Yes, the Company's been very good to *me*, I always say it. But I should never forget what they said about Ted, for he was as steady and fearless a chap as ever set foot on the cage, and it was as good as branding him a coward. But there, he was dead, and could say nothing to none of 'em.'

It was a queer mixture of feelings the woman showed as she talked. She liked the colliers, whom she had nursed for so long; but she felt very superior to them. She felt almost upper class; and at the same time a resentment against the ruling class smouldered in her. The masters! In a dispute between masters and men, she was always for the men. But when there was no question of contest, she was pining to be superior, to be one of the upper classes. The upper classes fascinated her, appealing to her peculiar English passion for superiority. She was thrilled to come to Wragby; thrilled to talk to Lady Chatterley, my word, different from the common colliers' wives! She said so in so many words. Yet one could see a grudge against the Chatterleys peep out in her; the grudge against the masters.

'Why, yes, of course, it would wear Lady Chatterley out! It's a mercy she had a sister to come and help her. Men don't think, high and low alike, they take what a woman does for them for granted. Oh, I've told the colliers off about it many a time. But it's very hard for Sir Clifford, you know, crippled like that. They were always a haughty family, standoffish in a way, as they've a right to be. But then to be brought down like that! And it's very hard on Lady Chatterley, perhaps harder on her. What she misses! I only had Ted three years, but my word, while I had him I had a husband I could never forget. He was one in a thousand, and jolly as the day. Who'd ever have thought he'd get killed? I don't believe it to this day somehow, I've never believed it, though I washed him with my own hands. But he was never dead for me, he never was. I never took it in.'

This was a new voice in Wragby, very new for Connie to hear; it roused a new ear in her.

For the first week or so, Mrs Bolton, however, was very quiet at Wragby; her assured, bossy manner left her, and she was nervous. With Clifford she was shy, almost frightened, and silent. He liked that, and soon recovered his self-possession, letting her do things for him without even noticing her.

'She's a useful nonentity!' he said. Connie opened her eyes in wonder, but did not contradict him. So different are impressions on two different people!

And he soon became rather superb, somewhat lordly with the nurse. She had rather expected it, and he played up without knowing. So susceptible we are to what is expected of us! The colliers had been so like children, talking to her, and telling her what hurt them, while she bandaged them, or nursed them. They had always made her feel so grand, almost superhuman in her administrations. Now Clifford made her feel small, and like a servant, and she accepted it without a word, adjusting herself to the upper classes.

She came very mute, with her long, handsome face, and downcast eyes, to administer to him. And she said very humbly: 'Shall I do this now, Sir Clifford? Shall I do that?'

'No, leave it for a time. I'll have it done later.'

'Very well, Sir Clifford.'

'Come in again in half an hour.'

'Very well, Sir Clifford.'

'And just take those old papers out, will you?'

'Very well, Sir Clifford.'

She went softly, and in half an hour she came softly again. She was bullied, but she didn't mind. She was experiencing the upper classes. She neither resented nor disliked Clifford; he was just part of a phenomenon, the phenomenon of the high-class folks, so far unknown to her, but now to be known. She felt more at home with Lady Chatterley, and after all it's the mistress of the house matters most.

Mrs Bolton helped Clifford to bed at night, and slept across the passage from his room, and came if he rang for her in the night. She also helped him in the morning, and soon valeted him completely, even shaving him, in her soft, tentative woman's way. She was very good and competent, and she soon knew how to have him in her power. He wasn't so very different from the colliers after all, when you lathered his chin, and softly rubbed the bristles. The stand-offishness and the lack of frankness didn't bother her; she was having a new experience.

Clifford, however, inside himself, never quite forgave Connie for giving up her personal care of him to a strange hired woman. It killed, he said to himself, the real flower of the intimacy between him and her. But Connie didn't mind that. The fine flower of their intimacy was to her rather like an orchid, a bulb stuck parasitic on her tree of life, and producing, to her eyes, a rather shabby flower.

Now she had more time to herself she could softly play the piano, up in her room, and sing: 'Touch not the nettle . . . for the bonds of love are ill to loose.'[36] She had not realised till lately how ill to loose they were, these bonds of love. But thank Heaven she had loosened them! She was so glad to be alone, not always to have to talk to him. When he was alone he tapped-tapped-tapped on a typewriter, to infinity. But when he was not 'working', and she was there, he talked, always talked; infinite small analysis of people and motives, and results, characters and personalities, till now she had had enough. For years she had loved it, until she had enough, and then suddenly it was too much. She was thankful to be alone.

It was as if thousands and thousands of little roots and threads of consciousness in him and her had grown together into a tangled mass, till they could crowd no more, and the plant was dying. Now quietly, subtly she was unravelling the tangle of his consciousness and hers, breaking the threads gently, one by one, with patience and impatience to get clear. But the bonds of such love are more ill to loose even than most bonds; though Mrs Bolton's coming had been a great help.

But he still wanted the old intimate evenings of talk with Connie: talk or reading aloud. But now she could arrange that Mrs Bolton should come at ten to disturb them. At ten o'clock Connie could go upstairs and be alone. Clifford was in good hands with Mrs Bolton.

Mrs Bolton ate with Mrs Betts in the housekeeper's room, since they were all agreeable. And it was curious how much closer the servants' quarters seemed to have come; right up to the doors of Clifford's study, when before they were so remote. For Mrs Betts would sometimes sit in Mrs Bolton's room, and Connie heard their lowered voices, and felt somehow the strong, other vibration of the working people almost invading the sitting-rooms, when she and Clifford were alone. So changed was Wragby merely by Mrs Bolton's coming.

And Connie felt herself released, in another world, she felt she breathed differently. But still she was afraid of how many of her roots, perhaps mortal ones, were tangled with Clifford's. Yet still, she breathed freer, a new phase was going to begin in her life.

Chapter 8

MRS BOLTON ALSO KEPT a cherishing eye on Connie, feeling she must extend to her her female and professional protection. She was always urging her ladyship to walk out, to drive to Uthwaite, to be in the air. For Connie had got into the habit of sitting still by the fire, pretending to read, or to sew feebly, and hardly going out at all.

It was a blowy day soon after Hilda had gone, that Mrs Bolton said: 'Now why don't you go for a walk through the wood, and look at the daffs behind the keeper's cottage? They're the prettiest sight you'd see in a day's march. And you could put some in your room; wild daffs are always so cheerful-looking, aren't they?'

Connie took it in good part, even daffs for daffodils. Wild daffodils! After all, one should not stew in one's own juice. The spring came back . . . 'Seasons return, but not to me returns Day, or the sweet approach of Ev'n or Morn.'[37]

And the keeper, his thin, white body, like a lonely pistil of an invisible flower! She had forgotten him in her unspeakable depression. But now something roused . . . 'Pale beyond porch and portal'[38] . . . the thing to do was to pass the porches and the portals.

She was stronger, she could walk better, and in the wood the wind would not be so tiring as it was across the park, flattening against her. She wanted to forget, to forget the world, and all the dreadful, carrion-bodied people. 'Ye must be born again! I believe in the resurrection of the body![39] Except a grain of wheat fall into the earth and die, it shall by no means bring forth.[40] When the crocus cometh forth I too will emerge and see the sun!' In the wind of March endless phrases swept through her consciousness.

Little gusts of sunshine blew, strangely bright, and lit up the celandines at the wood's edge, under the hazel-rods, they spangled out bright and yellow. And the wood was still, stiller, but yet gusty with crossing sun. The first windflowers were out, and all the wood seemed pale with the pallor of endless little anemones, sprinkling the shaken floor. 'The world has grown pale with thy breath.'[41] But it was the breath of Persephone, this time; she was out of hell on a cold morning. Cold breaths of wind came, and overhead there was an anger of entangled wind caught among the twigs. It, too, was caught and trying to tear itself free, the wind, like Absalom.[42] How cold the anemones looked, bobbing their naked white shoulders over crinoline skirts of green. But they stood it. A few first bleached little primroses too, by the path, and yellow buds unfolding themselves.

The roaring and swaying was overhead, only cold currents came down below. Connie was strangely excited in the wood, and the colour flew in her cheeks, and burned blue in her eyes. She walked ploddingly, picking a few primroses and the first violets, that smelled sweet and cold, sweet and cold. And she drifted on without knowing where she was.

Till she came to the clearing, at the far end of the wood, and saw the green-stained stone cottage, looking almost rosy, like the flesh underneath a mushroom, its stone warmed in a burst of sun. And there was a sparkle of yellow jasmine by the door; the closed door. But no sound; no smoke from the chimney; no dog barking.

She went quietly round to the back, where the bank rose up; she had an excuse, to see the daffodils.

And they were there, the short-stemmed flowers, rustling and fluttering and shivering, so bright and alive, but with nowhere to hide their faces, as they turned them away from the wind.

They shook their bright, sunny little rags in bouts of distress. But perhaps they liked it really; perhaps they really liked the tossing.

Constance sat down with her back to a young pine tree, that swayed against her with curious life, elastic, and powerful, rising up. The erect, alive thing, with its top in the sun! And she watched the daffodils turn golden, in a burst of sun that was warm on her hands and lap. Even she caught the faint, tarry scent of the flowers. And then, being so still and alone, she seemed to get into the current of her own proper destiny. She had been fastened by a rope, and jagging and snarring like a boat at its moorings; now she was loose and adrift.

The sunshine gave way to chill; the daffodils were in shadow, dipping silently. So they would dip through the day and the long cold night. So strong in their frailty!

She rose, a little stiff, took a few daffodils, and went down. She hated breaking the flowers, but she wanted just one or two to go with her. She would have to go back to Wragby and its walls, and now she hated it, especially its thick walls. Walls! Always walls! Yet one needed them in this wind.

When she got home Clifford asked her, 'Where did you go?'

'Right across the wood! Look, aren't the little daffodils adorable? To think they should come out of the earth!'

'Just as much out of the air and sunshine,' he said.

'But modelled in the earth,' she retorted, with a prompt contradiction, that surprised her a little.

The next afternoon she went to the wood again. She followed the broad riding that swerved round and up through the larches to a spring called John's Well. It was cold on this hillside, and not a flower in the darkness of larches. But the icy little spring softly pressed upwards from its tiny well-bed of pure, reddish-white pebbles. How icy and clear it was! Brilliant! The new keeper had no doubt put in fresh pebbles. She heard the faint tinkle of water, as the tiny overflow trickled over and downhill. Even above the hissing boom of the larchwood, that spread its bristling, leafless, wolfish darkness on the down-slope, she heard the tinkle as of tiny water-bells.

This place was a little sinister, cold, damp. Yet the well must have been a drinking-place for hundreds of years. Now no more. Its tiny cleared space was lush and cold and dismal.

She rose and went slowly towards home. As she went she heard a faint tapping away on the right, and stood still to listen. Was it hammering, or a woodpecker? It was surely hammering.

She walked on, listening. And then she noticed a narrow track between young fir trees, a track that seemed to lead nowhere. But she felt it had been used. She turned down it adventurously, between the thick young firs, which gave way soon to the old oak wood. She followed the track, and the hammering grew nearer, in the silence of the windy wood, for trees make a silence even in their noise of wind.

She saw a secret little clearing, and a secret little hut made of rustic poles. And she had never been here before! She realised it was the quiet place where the growing pheasants were reared; the keeper in his shirt-sleeves was kneeling, hammering. The dog trotted forward with a short, sharp bark, and the keeper lifted his face suddenly and saw her. He had a startled look in his eyes.

He straightened himself and saluted, watching her in silence, as she came forward with weakening limbs. He resented the intrusion, he cherished his solitude as his only and last freedom in life.

'I wondered what the hammering was,' she said, feeling weak and breathless, and a little afraid of him, as he looked so straight at her.

'Ah'm gettin' th' coops ready for th' young bods,' he said, in broad vernacular.

She did not know what to say, and she felt weak.

'I should like to sit down a bit,' she said.

'Come and sit 'ere i' th' 'ut,' he said, going in front of her to the hut, pushing aside some timber and stuff, and drawing out a rustic chair, made of hazel sticks.

'Am Ah t' light yer a little fire?' he asked, with the curious naïveté of the dialect.

'Oh, don't bother,' she replied.

But he looked at her hands: they were rather blue. So he quickly took some larch twigs to the little brick fireplace in the corner, and in a moment the yellow flame was running up the chimney. He made a place by the brick hearth.

'Sit 'ere then a bit, and warm yer,' he said.

She obeyed him. He had that curious kind of protective authority she obeyed at once. So she sat and warmed her hands at the blaze, and dropped logs on the fire, whilst outside he was hammering again. She did not really want to sit, poked in a corner by the fire; she would rather have watched from the door, but she was being looked after, so she had to submit.

The hut was quite cosy, panelled with unvarnished deal, having a little rustic table and stool beside her chair, and a carpenter's bench, then a big box, tools, new boards, nails; and many things hung from pegs: axe, hatchet, traps, things in sacks, his coat. It had no window, the light came in through the open door. It was a jumble, but also it was a sort of little sanctuary.

She listened to the tapping of the man's hammer; it was not so happy. He was oppressed. Here was a trespass on his privacy, and a dangerous one! A woman! He had reached the point where all he wanted on earth was to be alone. And yet he was powerless to preserve his privacy; he was a hired man, and these people were his masters.

Especially he did not want to come into contact with a woman again. He feared it; for he had a big wound from old contacts. He felt if he could not be alone, and if he could not be left alone, he would die. His recoil away from the outer world was complete; his last refuge was this wood; to hide himself there!

Connie grew warm by the fire, which she had made too big: then she grew hot. She went and sat on the stool in the doorway, watching the man at work. He seemed not to notice her, but he knew. Yet he worked on, as if absorbedly, and his brown dog sat on her tail near him, and surveyed the untrustworthy world.

Slender, quiet and quick, the man finished the coop he was making, turned it over, tried the sliding door, then set it aside. Then he rose, went for an old coop, and took it to the chopping-log where he was working. Crouching, he tried the bars; some broke in his hands; he began to draw the nails. Then he turned the coop over and deliberated, and he gave absolutely no sign of awareness of the woman's presence.

So Connie watched him fixedly. And the same solitary aloneness she had seen in him naked, she now saw in him clothed: solitary, and intent, like an animal that works alone, but also brooding, like a soul that recoils away, away from all human contact. Silently, patiently, he was recoiling away from her even now. It was the stillness, and the timeless sort of patience, in a man impatient and passionate, that touched Connie's womb. She saw it in his bent head, the quick, quiet hands, the crouching of his slender, sensitive loins; something patient and withdrawn. She felt his experience had been deeper and wider than her own; much deeper and wider, and perhaps more deadly. And this relieved her of herself; she felt almost irresponsible.

So she sat in the doorway of the hut in a dream, utterly unaware of time and of particular circumstances. She was so drifted away that he glanced up at her quickly, and saw the utterly still, waiting look on her face. To him it was a look of waiting. And a little thin tongue of fire suddenly flickered in his loins, at the root of his back, and he groaned in spirit. He dreaded with a repulsion almost of death, any further close human contact. He wished above all things she would go away, and leave him to his own privacy. He dreaded her will, her female will, and her modern female insistency. And above all he dreaded her cool, upper-class impudence of having her own way. For after all he was only a hired man. He hated her presence there.

Connie came to herself with sudden uneasiness. She rose. The afternoon was turning to evening, yet she could not go away. She went over to the man, who stood up at attention, his worn face stiff and blank, his eyes watching her.

'It is so nice here, so restful,' she said. 'I have never been here before.'

'No?'

'I think I shall come and sit here sometimes.'

'Yes?'

'Do you lock the hut when you're not here?'

'Yes, your Ladyship.'

'Do you think I could have a key too, so that I could sit here sometimes? Are there two keys?'

'Not as Ah know on, ther' isna.'

He had lapsed into the vernacular. Connie hesitated; he was putting up an opposition. Was it his hut, after all?

'Couldn't we get another key?' she asked in her soft voice, that underneath had the ring of a woman determined to get her way.

'Another!' he said, glancing at her with a flash of anger, touched with derision.

'Yes, a duplicate,' she said, flushing.

''Appen Sir Clifford 'ud know,' he said, putting her off.

'Yes!' she said, 'he might have another. Otherwise we could have one made from the one you have. It would only take a day or so, I suppose. You could spare your key for so long.'

'Ah canna tell yer, m' Lady! Ah know nob'dy as ma'es keys round 'ere.'

Connie suddenly flushed with anger.

'Very well!' she said. 'I'll see to it.'

'All right, your Ladyship.'

Their eyes met. His had a cold, ugly look of dislike and contempt, and indifference to what would happen. Hers were hot with rebuff.

But her heart sank, she saw how utterly he disliked her, when she went against him. And she saw him in a sort of desperation.

'Good-afternoon!'

'Afternoon, my Lady!' He saluted and turned abruptly away. She had wakened the sleeping dogs of old voracious anger in him, anger against the self-willed female. And he was powerless, powerless. He knew it!

And she was angry against the self-willed male. A servant too! She walked sullenly home.

She found Mrs Bolton under the great beech tree on the knoll, looking for her.

'I just wondered if you'd be coming, my Lady,' the woman said brightly.

'Am I late?' asked Connie.

'Oh . . . only Sir Clifford was waiting for his tea.'

'Why didn't *you* make it then?'

'Oh, I don't think it's hardly my place. I don't think Sir Clifford would like it at all, my Lady.'

'I don't see why not,' said Connie.

She went indoors to Clifford's study, where the old brass kettle was simmering on the tray.

'Am I late, Clifford?' she said, putting down the few flowers and taking up the tea-caddy, as she stood before the tray in her hat and scarf. 'I'm sorry! Why didn't you let Mrs Bolton make the tea?'

'I didn't think of it,' he said ironically. 'I don't quite see her presiding at the tea-table.'

'Oh, there's nothing sacrosanct about a silver teapot,' said Connie.

He glanced up at her curiously.

'What did you do all afternoon?' he said.

'Walked and sat in a sheltered place. Do you know there are still berries on the big holly tree?'

She took off her scarf, but not her hat, and sat down to make tea. The toast would certainly be leathery. She put the tea-cosy over the teapot, and rose to get a little glass for her violets. The poor flowers hung over, limp on their stalks.

'They'll revive again!' she said, putting them before him in their glass for him to smell.

'Sweeter than the lids of Juno's eyes,'[43] he quoted.

'I don't see a bit of connection with the actual violets,' she said. 'The Elizabethans are rather upholstered.'

She poured him his tea.

'Do you think there is a second key to that little hut not far from John's Well, where the pheasants are reared?' she said.

'There may be. Why?'

'I happened to find it today – and I'd never seen it before. I think it's a darling place. I could sit there sometimes, couldn't I?'

'Was Mellors there?'

'Yes! That's how I found it: his hammering. He didn't seem to like my intruding at all. In fact he was almost rude when I asked about a second key.'

'What did he say?'

'Oh nothing: just his manner; and he said he knew nothing about keys.'

'There may be one in Father's study. Betts knows them all; they're all there. I'll get him to look.'

'Oh do!' she said.

'So Mellors was almost rude?'

'Oh, nothing, really! But I don't think he wanted me to have the freedom of the castle, quite.'

'I don't suppose he did.'

'Still, I don't see why he should mind. It's not his home, after all! It's not his private abode. I don't see why I shouldn't sit there if I want to.'

'Quite!' said Clifford. 'He thinks too much of himself, that man.'

'Do you think he does?'

'Oh decidedly! He thinks he's something exceptional. You know he had a wife he didn't get on with, so he joined up in 1915 and was sent out to India, I believe. Anyhow he was blacksmith to the cavalry in Egypt for a time; always was connected with horses, a clever fellow that way. Then some Indian colonel took a fancy to him, and he was made a lieutenant. Yes, they gave him a commission. I believe he went back to India with his colonel, and up to the north-west frontier. He was ill; he has a pension. He didn't come out of the army till last year, I believe, and then, naturally, it isn't easy for a man like that to get back to his own level. He's bound to flounder. But he does his duty all right, as far as I'm concerned. Only I'm not having any of the Lieutenant Mellors touch.'

'How could they make him an officer when he speaks broad Derbyshire?'

'He doesn't . . . except by fits and starts. He can speak perfectly well, for him. I suppose he has an idea if he's come down to the ranks again, he'd better speak as the ranks speak.'

'Why didn't you tell me about him before?'

'Oh, I've no patience with these romances. They're the ruin of all order. It's a thousand pities they ever happened.'

Connie was inclined to agree. What was the good of discontented people who fitted in nowhere?

In the spell of fine weather Clifford, too, decided to go to the wood. The wind was cold, but not so tiresome, and the sunshine was like life itself, warm and full.

'It's amazing,' said Connie, 'how different one feels when there's a really fresh fine day. Usually one feels the very air is half dead. People are killing the very air.'

'Do you think people are doing it?' he asked.

'I do. The steam of so much boredom, and discontent and anger out of all the people, just kills the vitality in the air. I'm sure of it.'

'Perhaps some condition of the atmosphere lowers the vitality of the people?' he said.

'No, it's man that poisons the universe,' she asserted.

'Fouls his own nest,' remarked Clifford.

The chair puffed on. In the hazel copse catkins were hanging pale gold, and in sunny places the wood-anemones were wide open, as if exclaiming with the joy of life, just as good as in past days, when people could exclaim along with them. They had a faint scent of apple-blossom. Connie gathered a few for Clifford.

He took them and looked at them curiously.

'Thou still unravished bride of quietness,'[44] he quoted. 'It seems to fit flowers so much better than Greek vases.'

'Ravished is such a horrid word!' she said. 'It's only people who ravish things.'

'Oh, I don't know . . . snails and things,' he said.

'Even snails only eat them, and bees don't ravish.'

She was angry with him, turning everything into words. Violets were Juno's eyelids, and windflowers were unravished brides. How she hated words, always coming between her and life: they did the ravishing, if anything did: ready-made words and phrases, sucking all the life-sap out of living things.

The walk with Clifford was not quite a success. Between him and Connie there was a tension that each pretended not to notice, but there it was. Suddenly, with all the force of her female instinct, she was shoving him off. She wanted to be clear of him, and especially of his consciousness, his words, his obsession with himself, his endless treadmill obsession with himself, and his own words.

The weather came rainy again. But after a day or two she went out in the rain, and she went to the wood. And once there, she went towards the hut. It was raining, but not so cold, and the wood felt so silent and remote, inaccessible in the dusk of rain.

She came to the clearing. No one there! The hut was locked. But she sat on the log doorstep, under the rustic porch, and snuggled into her own warmth. So she sat, looking at the rain, listening to the many noiseless noises of it, and to the strange soughings of wind in upper branches, when there seemed to be no wind. Old oak trees stood around, grey, powerful trunks, rain-blackened, round and vital, throwing off reckless limbs. The ground was fairly free of undergrowth, the anemones sprinkled, there was a bush or two, elder, or guelder-rose, and a purplish tangle of bramble; the old russet of bracken almost vanished under green anemone ruffs.

Perhaps this was one of the unravished places. Unravished! The whole world was ravished.

Some things can't be ravished. You can't ravish a tin of sardines. And so many women are like that; and men. But the earth . . . !

The rain was abating. It was hardly making darkness among the oaks any more. Connie wanted to go; yet she sat on. But she was getting cold; yet the overwhelming inertia of her inner resentment kept her there as if paralysed.

Ravished! How ravished one could be without ever being touched. Ravished by dead words become obscene, and dead ideas become obsessions.

A wet brown dog came running and did not bark, lifting a wet feather of a tail. The man followed in a wet black oilskin jacket, like a chauffeur, and face flushed a little. She felt him recoil in his quick walk, when he saw her. She stood up in the handbreadth of dryness under the rustic porch. He saluted without speaking, coming slowly near. She began to withdraw.

'I'm just going,' she said.

'Was yer waitin' to get in?' he asked, looking at the hut, not at her.

'No, I only sat a few minutes in the shelter,' she said, with quiet dignity.

He looked at her. She looked cold.

'Sir Clifford 'adnt got no other key, then?' he asked.

'No, but it doesn't matter. I can sit perfectly dry under this porch. Good-afternoon!' She hated the excess of vernacular in his speech.

He watched her closely, as she was moving away. Then he hitched up his jacket, and put his hand in his breeches pocket, taking out the key of the hut.

''Appen yer'd better 'ave this key, an' Ah mun fend for t' bods some other road.'

She looked at him.

'What do you mean?' she asked.

'I mean as 'appen Ah can find anuther pleece as'll du for rearin' th' pheasants. If yer want ter be 'ere, yo'll non want me messin' abaht a' th' time.'

She looked at him, getting his meaning through the fog of the dialect.

'Why don't you speak ordinary English?' she said coldly.

'Me! Ah thowt it *wor* ordinary.'

She was silent for a few moments in anger.

'So if yer want t' key, yer'd better ta'e it. Or 'appen Ah'd better gi'e 't yer termorrer, an' clear all t' stuff aht fust. Would that du for yer?'

She became more angry.

'I didn't want your key,' she said. 'I don't want you to clear anything out at all. I don't in the least want to turn you out of your hut, thank you! I only wanted to be able to sit here sometimes, like today. But I can sit perfectly well under the porch, so please say no more about it.'

He looked at her again, with his wicked blue eyes.

'Why,' he began, in the broad slow dialect. 'Your Ladyship's as welcome as Christmas ter th' hut an' th' key an' iverythink as is. On'y this time o' th' year ther's bods ter set, an' Ah've got ter be potterin' abaht a good bit, seein' after 'em, an' a'. Winter time Ah ned 'ardly come nigh th' pleece. But what wi' spring, an' Sir Clifford wantin' ter start th' pheasants . . . An' your Ladyship'd non want me tinkerin' around an' about when she was 'ere, all th' time.'

She listened with a dim kind of amazement.

'Why should I mind your being here?' she asked.

He looked at her curiously.

'T'nuisance on me!' he said briefly, but significantly. She flushed. 'Very well!' she said finally. 'I won't trouble you. But I don't think I should have minded at all sitting and seeing you look after the birds. I should have liked it. But since you think it interferes with you, I won't disturb you, don't be afraid. You are Sir Clifford's keeper, not mine.'

The phrase sounded queer, she didn't know why. But she let it pass.

'Nay, your Ladyship. It's your Ladyship's own 'ut. It's as your Ladyship likes an' pleases, every time. Yer can turn me off at a wik's notice. It wor only . . . '

'Only what?' she asked, baffled.

He pushed back his hat in an odd comic way.

'On'y as 'appen yo'd like the place ter yersen, when yer did come, an' not me messin' abaht.'

'But why?' she said, angry. 'Aren't you a civilised human being? Do you think I ought to be afraid of you? Why should I take any notice of you and your being here or not? Why is it important?'

He looked at her, all his face glimmering with wicked laughter.

'It's not, your Ladyship. Not in the very least,' he said.

'Well why then?' she asked.

'Shall I get your Ladyship another key then?'

'No thank you! I don't want it.'

'Ah'll get it anyhow. We'd best 'ave two keys ter th' place.'

'And I consider you are insolent,' said Connie, with her colour up, panting a little.

'Nay, nay!' he said quickly. 'Dunna yer say that! Nay, nay! I niver meant nuthink. Ah on'y thought as if yo' come 'ere, Ah s'd 'ave ter clear out, an' it'd mean a lot o' work, settin' up somewheres else. But if your Ladyship isn't going ter take no notice o' me, then . . . it's Sir Clifford's 'ut, an' everythink is as your Ladyship likes, everythink is as your Ladyship likes an' pleases, barrin' yer take no notice o' me, doin' th' bits of jobs as Ah've got ter do.'

Connie went away completely bewildered. She was not sure whether she had been insulted and mortally offended, or not. Perhaps the man really only meant what he said; that he thought she would expect him to keep away. As if she would dream of it! And as if he could possibly be so important, he and his stupid presence.

She went home in confusion, not knowing what she thought or felt.

Chapter 9

CONNIE WAS SURPRISED at her own feeling of aversion from Clifford. What is more, she felt she had always really disliked him. Not hate: there was no passion in it. But a profound physical dislike. Almost it seemed to her, she had married him because she disliked him, in a secret, physical sort of way. But of course, she had married him really because in a mental way he attracted her and excited her. He had seemed, in some way, her master, beyond her.

Now the mental excitement had worn itself out and collapsed, and she was aware only of the physical aversion. It rose up in her from her depths: and she realised how it had been eating her life away.

She felt weak and utterly forlorn. She wished some help would come from outside. But in the whole world there was no help. Society was terrible because it was insane. Civilised society is insane. Money and so-called love are its two great manias; money a long way first. The individual asserts himself in his disconnected insanity in these two modes: money and love. Look at Michaelis! His life and activity were just insanity. His love was a sort of insanity.

And Clifford the same. All that talk! All that writing! All that wild struggling to push himself forwards! It was just insanity. And it was getting worse, really maniacal.

Connie felt washed-out with fear. But at least, Clifford was shifting his grip from her on to Mrs Bolton. He did not know it. Like many insane people, his insanity might be measured by the things he was *not* aware of; the great desert tracts in his consciousness.

Mrs Bolton was admirable in many ways. But she had that queer sort of bossiness, endless assertion of her own will, which is one of the signs of insanity in modern woman. She *thought* she was utterly subservient and living for others. Clifford fascinated her because he always, or so often, frustrated her will, as if by a finer instinct. He had a finer, subtler will of self-assertion than herself. This was his charm for her.

Perhaps that had been his charm, too, for Connie.

'It's a lovely day, today!' Mrs Bolton would say in her caressive, persuasive voice. 'I should think you'd enjoy a little run in your chair today, the sun's just lovely.'

'Yes? Will you give me that book – there, that yellow one. And I think I'll have those hyacinths taken out.'

'Why they're so beautiful!' She pronounced it with the 'y' sound: be-yutiful! 'And the scent is simply gorgeous.'

'The scent is what I object to,' he said. 'It's a little funereal.'

'Do you think so!' she exclaimed in surprise, just a little offended, but impressed. And she carried the hyacinths out of the room, impressed by his higher fastidiousness.

'Shall I shave you this morning, or would you rather do it yourself?' Always the same soft, caressive, subservient, yet managing voice.

'I don't know. Do you mind waiting a while. I'll ring when I'm ready.'

'Very good, Sir Clifford!' she replied, so soft and submissive, withdrawing quietly. But every rebuff stored up new energy of will in her.

When he rang, after a time, she would appear at once. And then he would say, 'I think I'd rather you shaved me this morning.'

Her heart gave a little thrill, and she replied with extra softness: 'Very good, Sir Clifford!'

She was very deft, with a soft, lingering touch, a little slow. At first he had resented the infinitely soft touch of her fingers on his face. But now he liked it, with a growing voluptuousness. He let her shave him nearly every day: her face near his, her eyes so very concentrated, watching that she did it right. And gradually her fingertips knew his cheeks and lips, his jaw and chin and throat perfectly. He was well-fed and well-liking, his face and throat were handsome enough, and he was a gentleman.

She was handsome too, pale, her face rather long and absolutely still, her eyes bright, but revealing nothing. Gradually, with infinite softness, almost with love, she was getting him by the throat, and he was yielding to her.

She now did almost everything for him, and he felt more at home with her, less ashamed of accepting her menial offices, than with Connie. She liked handling him. She loved having his body in her charge, absolutely, to the last menial offices. She said to Connie one day: 'All men are babies, when you come to the bottom of them. Why, I've handled some of the toughest customers as ever went down Tevershall pit. But let anything ail them so that you have to do for them, and they're babies, just big babies. Oh, there's not much difference in men!'

At first Mrs Bolton had thought there really was something different in a gentleman, a *real* gentleman, like Sir Clifford. So Clifford had got a good start of her. But gradually, as she came to the bottom of him, to use her own term, she found he was like the rest, a baby grown to man's proportions: but a baby with a queer temper and a fine manner and power in its control, and all sorts of odd knowledge that she had never dreamed of, with which he could still bully her.

Connie was sometimes tempted to say to him, 'For God's sake, don't sink so horribly into the hands of that woman!' But she found she didn't care for him enough to say it, in the long run.

It was still their habit to spend the evening together, till ten o'clock. Then they would talk, or read together, or go over his manuscript. But the thrill had gone out of it. She was bored by his manuscripts. But she still dutifully typed them out for him. But in time Mrs Bolton would do even that.

For Connie had suggested to Mrs Bolton that she should learn to use a typewriter. And Mrs Bolton, always ready, had begun at once, and practised assiduously. So now Clifford would sometimes dictate a letter to her, and she would take it down rather slowly, but correctly. And he was very patient, spelling for her the difficult words, or the occasional phrases in French. She was so thrilled, it was almost a pleasure to instruct her.

Now Connie would sometimes plead a headache as an excuse for going up to her room after dinner.

'Perhaps Mrs Bolton will play piquet with you,' she said to Clifford.

'Oh, I shall be perfectly all right. You go to your own room and rest, darling.'

But no sooner had she gone, than he rang for Mrs Bolton, and asked her to take a hand at piquet or bezique,[45] or even chess. He had taught her all these games. And Connie found it curiously objectionable to see Mrs Bolton, flushed and tremulous like a little girl, touching her queen or her knight with uncertain fingers, then drawing away again. And Clifford, faintly smiling with a half-teasing superiority, saying to her: 'You must say j'adoube!'[46]

She looked up at him with bright, startled eyes, then murmured shyly, obediently, 'J'adoube!'

Yes, he was educating her. And he enjoyed it, it gave him a sense of power. And she was thrilled. She was coming bit by bit into possession of all that the gentry knew, all that made them upper class: apart from the money. That thrilled her. And at the same time, she was making him want to have her there with him. It was a subtle deep flattery to him, her genuine thrill.

To Connie, Clifford seemed to be coming out in his true colours: a little vulgar, a little common, and uninspired; rather fat. Ivy Bolton's tricks and humble bossiness were also only too transparent. But Connie did wonder at the genuine thrill which the woman got out of Clifford. To say she was in love with him would be putting it wrongly. She was thrilled by her contact with a man of the upper class, this titled gentleman, this author who could write books and poems, and whose photograph appeared in the illustrated newspapers. She was thrilled to a weird passion. And his 'educating' her roused in her a passion of excitement and response much deeper than any love affair could have done. In truth, the very fact that there could *be* no love affair left her free to thrill to her very marrow with this other passion, the peculiar passion of *knowing*, knowing as he knew.

There was no mistake that the woman was in some way in love with him: whatever force we give to the word love. She looked so handsome and so young, and her grey eyes were sometimes marvellous. At the same time, there was a lurking soft satisfaction about her, even of triumph, and private satisfaction. Ugh, that private satisfaction! How Connie loathed it!

But no wonder Clifford was caught by the woman! She absolutely adored him, in her persistent fashion, and put herself absolutely at his service, for him to use as he liked. No wonder he was flattered!

Connie heard long conversations going on between the two. Or rather, it was mostly Mrs Bolton talking. She had unloosed to him the stream of gossip about Tevershall village. It was more than gossip. It was Mrs Gaskell and George Eliot and Miss Mitford[47] all rolled in one, with a great deal more, that these women left out. Once started, Mrs Bolton was better than any book, about the lives of the people. She knew them all so intimately, and had such a peculiar, flamey zest in all their affairs, it was wonderful, if just a *trifle* humiliating to listen to her. At first she had not ventured to 'talk Tevershall', as she called it, to Clifford. But once started, it went on. Clifford was listening for 'material', and he found it in plenty. Connie realised that his so-called genius was just this: a perspicuous talent for personal gossip, clever and apparently detached. Mrs Bolton, of course, was very warm when she 'talked Tevershall'. Carried away, in fact. And it was marvellous, the things that happened and that she knew about. She would have run to dozens of volumes.

Connie was fascinated, listening to her. But afterwards always a little ashamed. She ought not to listen with this queer rabid curiosity. After all, one may hear the most private affairs of other people, but only in a spirit of respect for the struggling, battered thing which any human soul is, and in a spirit of fine, discriminative sympathy. For even satire is a form of sympathy. It is the way our sympathy flows and recoils that really determines our lives. And here lies the vast importance of the novel, properly handled. It can inform and lead into new places the flow of our sympathetic consciousness, and it can lead our sympathy away in recoil from things gone dead. Therefore, the novel, properly handled, can reveal the most secret places of life: for it is in the *passional* secret places of life, above all, that the tide of sensitive awareness needs to ebb and flow, cleansing and freshening.

But the novel, like gossip, can also excite spurious sympathies and recoils, mechanical and deadening to the psyche. The novel can glorify the most corrupt feelings, so long as they are *conventionally* 'pure'. Then the novel, like gossip, becomes at last vicious, and, like gossip, all the more vicious because it is always ostensibly on the side of the angels. Mrs Bolton's gossip was always on the side of the angels. 'And he was such a *bad* fellow, and she was such a *nice* woman.' Whereas, as Connie could see even from Mrs Bolton's gossip, the woman had been merely a mealy-mouthed sort, and the man angrily honest. But angry honesty made a 'bad man' of him, and mealy-mouthedness made a 'nice woman' of her, in the vicious, conventional channelling of sympathy by Mrs Bolton.

For this reason, the gossip was humiliating. And for the same reason, most novels, especially popular ones, are humiliating too. The public responds now only to an appeal to its vices.

Nevertheless, one got a new vision of Tevershall village from Mrs Bolton's talk. A terrible, seething welter of ugly life it seemed: not at all the flat drabness it looked from outside. Clifford of course knew by sight most of the people mentioned, Connie knew only one or two. But it sounded really more like a Central African jungle than an English village.

'I suppose you heard as Miss Allsopp was married last week! Would you ever! Miss Allsopp, old James's daughter, the boot-and-shoe Allsopp. You know they built a house up at Pye Croft. The old man died last year from a fall; eighty-three, he was, an' nimble as a lad. An' then he slipped on Bestwood Hill, on a slide as the lads 'ad made last winter, an' broke his thigh, and that finished him, poor old man, it did seem a shame. Well he left all his money to Tattie: didn't leave the boys a penny. And Tattie, I know, is five years – yes, she's fifty-three last autumn. And you know they were such Chapel people, my word! She taught Sunday school for thirty years, till her father died. And then she started carrying on with a fellow from Kinbrook, I don't know if you know him, an oldish fellow with a red nose, rather dandified, Willcock, 'as works in Harrison's woodyard. Well he's sixty-five if he's a day, yet you'd have thought they were a pair of young turtle-doves, to see them, arm in arm, and kissing at the gate: yes, an' she sitting on his knee right in the bay window on Pye Croft Road, for anybody to see. And he's got sons over forty: only lost his wife two years ago. If old James Allsopp hasn't risen from his grave, it's because there is no rising: for he kept her that strict! Now they're married and gone to live down at Kinbrook, and they say she goes round in a dressing-gown from morning to night, a veritable sight. I'm sure it's awful, the way the old ones go on! Why they're a lot worse than the young, and a sight more disgusting. I lay it down to the pictures, myself. But you can't keep them away. I was always saying: go to a good instructive film, but do for goodness' sake keep away from these melodramas and love films. Anyhow keep the children away! But there you are, the grown-ups are worse than the children: and the old ones beat the band. Talk about morality! nobody cares a thing. Folks does as they like, and much better off they are for it, I must say. But they're having to draw their horns in nowadays, now th' pits are working so bad, and they haven't got the money. And the grumbling they do, it's awful, especially the women. The men are so good and patient! What can they do, poor chaps! But the women, oh, they do carry on! They go and show off, giving contributions for a wedding present for Princess Mary,[48] and then when they see all the grand things that's been given, they simply rave: who's she, any better than anybody else! Why doesn't Swan & Edgar[49] give me *one* fur coat, instead of giving her six. I wish I'd kept my ten shillings! What's she going to give *me*, I should like to know? Here I can't get a new spring coat, my dad's working that bad, and she gets van-loads. It's time as poor folks had some money to spend, rich ones 'as 'ad it long enough. I want a new spring coat, I do, an' wheer am I going to get it? – I say to them, be thankful you're well fed and well clothed, without all the new finery you want! – And they fly back at me: "Why isn't Princess Mary thankful to go about in her old rags, then, an' have nothing! Folks like *her* get van-loads, an' I can't have a new spring coat. It's a damned shame. Princess! bloomin' rot about Princess! It's munney as matters, an' cos she's got lots, they give her more! Nobody's givin' me any, an' I've as much right as anybody else. Don't talk to me about education. It's munney as matters. I want a new spring coat, I do, an' I shan't get it, cos there's no munney . . . ' That's all they care about, clothes. They think nothing of giving seven and eight guineas for a winter coat – colliers' daughters, mind you – and two guineas for a child's summer hat. And then they go to the Primitive Chapel in their two-guinea hat, girls as would have been proud of a three-and-sixpenny one in my day. I heard that at the Primitive Methodist[50] anniversary this year, when they have a built-up platform for the Sunday School children, like a grandstand going almost up to th' ceiling, I heard Miss Thompson, who has the first class of girls in the Sunday School, say there'd be over a thousand pounds in new Sunday clothes sitting on that platform! And times are what they are! But you can't stop them. They're mad for clothes. And boys the same. The lads spend every penny on themselves, clothes, smoking, drinking in the Miners' Welfare, jaunting off to Sheffield two or three times a week. Why, it's another world. And they fear nothing, and they respect nothing, the young don't. The older men are that patient and good, really, they let the women take everything. And this is what it leads to. The women are positive demons. But the lads aren't like their dads. They're sacrificing nothing, they aren't: they're all for self. If you tell them they ought to be putting a bit by, for a home, they say: That'll keep, that will, I'm goin' t' enjoy myself while I can. Owt else'll keep! – Oh, they're rough an' selfish, if you like. Everything falls on the older men, an' it's a bad lookout all round.'

Clifford began to get a new idea of his own village. The place had always frightened him, but he had thought it more or less stable. Now – ?

'Is there much Socialism, Bolshevism, among the people?' he asked.

'Oh!' said Mrs Bolton, 'you hear a few loud-mouthed ones. But they're mostly women who've got into debt. The men take no notice. I don't believe you'll ever turn our Te
vershall men into reds. They're too decent for that. But the young ones blether sometimes. Not that they care for it really. They only want a bit of money in their pocket, to spend at the Welfare, or go gadding to Sheffield. That's all they care. When they've got no money, they'll listen to the reds spouting. But nobody believes in it, really.'

'So you think there's no danger?'

'Oh no! Not if trade was good, there wouldn't be. But if things were bad for a long spell, the young ones might go funny. I tell you, they're a selfish, spoilt lot. But I don't see how they'd ever do anything. They aren't ever serious about anything, except showing off on motorbikes and dancing at the Palais-de-danse[51] in Sheffield. You can't *make* them serious. The serious ones dress up in evening clothes and go off to the Pally to show off before a lot of girls and dance these new Charlestons and what not. I'm sure sometimes the bus'll be full of young fellows in evening suits, collier lads, off to the Pally: let alone those that have gone with their girls in motors or on motorbikes. They don't give a serious thought to a thing – save Doncaster races, and the Derby: for they all of them bet on every race. And football! But even football's not what it was, not by a long chalk. It's too much like hard work, they say. No, they'd rather be off on motorbikes to Sheffield or Nottingham, Saturday afternoons.'

'But what do they do when they get there?'

'Oh, hang around – and have tea in some fine tea-place like the Mikado – and go to the Pally or the pictures or the Empire, with some girl. The girls are as free as the lads. They do just what they like.'

'And what do they do when they haven't the money for these things?'

'They seem to get it, somehow. And they begin talking nasty then. But I don't see how you're going to get Bolshevism, when all the lads want is just money to enjoy themselves, and the girls the same, with fine clothes: and they don't care about another thing. They haven't the brains to be Socialists. They haven't enough seriousness to take anything really serious, and they never will have.'

Connie thought, how extremely like all the rest of the classes the lower classes sounded. Just the same thing over again, Tevershall or Mayfair or Kensington. There was only one class nowadays: moneyboys. The moneyboy and the moneygirl, the only difference was how much you'd got, and how much you wanted.

Under Mrs Bolton's influence, Clifford began to take a new interest in the mines. He began to feel he belonged. A new sort of self-assertion came into him. After all, he was the real boss in Tevershall, he was really the pits. It was a new sense of power, something he had till now shrunk from with dread.

Tevershall pits were running thin. There were only two collieries: Tevershall itself, and New London. Tevershall had once been a famous mine, and had made famous money. But its best days were over. New London was never very rich, and in ordinary times just got along decently. But now times were bad, and it was pits like New London that got left.

'There's a lot of Tevershall men left and gone to Stacks Gate and Whiteover,' said Mrs Bolton. 'You've not seen the new works at Stacks Gate, opened after the war, have you, Sir Clifford? Oh, you must go one day, they're something quite new: great big chemical works at the pit-head, doesn't look a bit like a colliery. They say they get more money out of the chemical by-products than out of the coal – I forget what it is. And the grand new houses for the men, fair mansions! Of course it's brought a lot of riff-raff from all over the country. But a lot of Tevershall men got on there, and doin' well, a lot better than our own men. They say Tevershall's done, finished: only a question of a few more years, and it'll have to shut down. And New London'll go first. My word, won't it be funny, when there's no Tevershall pit working. It's bad enough during a strike, but my word, if it closes for good, it'll be like the end of the world. Even when I was a girl it was the best pit in the country, and a man counted himself lucky if he could get on here. Oh, there's been some money made in Tevershall. And now the men say it's a sinking ship, and it's time they all got out. Doesn't it sound awful! But of course there's a lot as'll never go till they have to. They don't like these newfangled mines, such a depth, and all machinery to work them. Some of them simply dreads those iron men, as they call them, those machines for hewing the coal, where men always did it before. And they say it's wasteful as well. But what goes in waste is saved in wages, and a lot more. It seems soon there'll be no use for men on the face of the earth, it'll be all machines. But they say that's what folks said when they had to give up the old stocking frames.[52] I can remember one or two. But my word, the more machines, the more people, that's what it looks like! They say you can't get the same chemicals out of Tevershall coal as you can out of Stacks Gate, and that's funny, they're not three miles apart. But they say so. But everybody says it's a shame something can't be started, to keep the men going a bit better, and employ the girls. All the girls traipsing off to Sheffield every day! My word, it would be something to talk about if Tevershall Collieries took a new lease of life, after everybody saying they're finished, and a sinking ship, and the men ought to leave them like rats leave a sinking ship. But folks talk so much. Of course there was a boom during the war. When Sir Geoffrey made a trust of himself and got the money safe for ever, somehow. So they say! But they say even the masters and the owners don't get much out of it now. You can hardly believe it, can you! Why I always thought the pits would go on for ever and ever. Who'd have thought, when I was a girl! But New England's shut down, so is

Colwick Wood: yes, it's fair haunting to go through that coppy[53] and see Colwick Wood standing there deserted among the trees, and bushes growing up all over the pit-head, and the lines red rusty. It's like death itself, a dead colliery. Why whatever we should do if Tevershall shut down – ? it doesn't bear thinking of. Always that throng it's been, except at strikes, and even then the fan-wheels didn't stand, except when they fetched the ponies up. I'm sure it's a funny world, you don't know where you are from year to year, you really don't.'

It was Mrs Bolton's talk that really put a new fight into Clifford. His income, as she pointed out to him, was secure, from his father's trust, even though it was not large. The pits did not really concern him. It was the other world he wanted to capture, the world of literature and fame: the popular world, not the working world.

Now he realised the distinction between popular success and working success: the populace of pleasure and the populace of work. He, as a private individual, had been catering with his stories for the populace of pleasure. And he had caught on. But beneath the populace of pleasure lay the populace of work, grim, grimy, and rather terrible. They too had to have their providers. And it was a much grimmer business, providing for the populace of work, than for the populace of pleasure. While he was doing his stories, and 'getting on' in the world, Tevershall was going to the wall.

He realised now that the bitch-goddess of Success had two main appetites: one for flattery, adulation, stroking and tickling such as writers and artists gave her; but the other a grimmer appetite for meat and bones. And the meat and bones for the bitch-goddess were provided by the men who made money in industry.

Yes, there were two great groups of dogs wrangling for the bitch-goddess: the group of the flatterers, those who offered her amusement, stories, films, plays: and the other, much less showy, much more savage breed, those who gave her meat, the real substance of money. The well-groomed showy dogs of amusement wrangled and snarled among themselves for the favours of the bitch-goddess. But it was nothing to the silent fight-to-the-death that went on among the indispensables, the bone-bringers.

But under Mrs Bolton's influence, Clifford was tempted to enter this other fight, to capture the bitch-goddess by brute means of industrial production. Somehow, he got his pecker up. In one way, Mrs Bolton made a man of him, as Connie never did. Connie kept him apart, and made him sensitive and conscious of himself and his own states. Mrs Bolton made him aware only of outside things.

Inwardly he began to go soft as pulp. But outwardly he began to be effective.

He even roused himself to go to the mines once more: and when he was there, he went down in a tub, and in a tub he was hauled out into the workings. Things he had learned before the war, and seemed utterly to have forgotten, now came back to him. He sat there, crippled, in a tub, with the underground manager showing him the seam with a powerful torch. And he said little. But his mind began to work.

He began to read again his technical works on the coal-mining industry, he studied the government reports, and he read with care the latest things on mining and the chemistry of coal and of shale which were written in German. Of course the most valuable discoveries were kept secret as far as possible. But once you started a sort of research in the field of coal-mining, a study of methods and means, a study of by-products and the chemical possibilities of coal, it was astounding, the ingenuity and the almost uncanny cleverness of the modern technical mind, as if really the devil himself had lent fiend's wits to the technical scientists of industry. It was far more interesting than art, than literature, poor emotional half-witted stuff, was this technical science of industry. In this field, men were like gods, or demons, inspired to discoveries, and fighting to carry them out. In this activity, men were beyond any mental age calculable. But Clifford knew that when it did come to the emotional and human life, these self-made men were of a mental age of about thirteen, feeble boys. The discrepancy was enormous and appalling.

But let that be. Let man slide down to general idiocy in the emotional and 'human' mind, Clifford did not care. Let all that go hang. He was interested in the technicalities of modern coal-mining, and in pulling Tevershall out of the hole.

He went down to the pit day after day, he studied, he put the general manager, and the overhead manager, and the underground manager, and the engineers through a mill they had never dreamed of. Power! He felt a new sense of power flowing through him: power over all these men, over the hundreds and hundreds of colliers. He was finding out: and he was getting things into his grip.

And he seemed verily to be reborn. *Now* life came into him! He had been gradually dying, with Connie, in the isolated private life of the artist and the conscious being. Now let all that go. Let it sleep. He simply felt life rush into him out of the coal, out of the pit. The very stale air of the colliery was better than oxygen to him. It gave him a sense of power, power. He was doing something: and he was

going to do something. He was going to win, to win: not as he had
won with his stories, mere publicity, amid a whole sapping of energy
and malice. But a man's victory.

At first he thought the solution lay in electricity: convert the coal
into electric power. Then a new idea came. The Germans invented
a new locomotive engine with a self-feeder, that did not need a
fireman. And it was to be fed with a new fuel, that burnt in small
quantities at a great heat, under peculiar conditions.

The idea of a new concentrated fuel that burnt with a hard
slowness at a fierce heat was what first attracted Clifford. There
must be some sort of external stimulus to the burning of such fuel,
not merely air supply. He began to experiment, and got a clever
young fellow, who had proved brilliant in chemistry, to help him.

And he felt triumphant. He had at last got out of himself. He had
fulfilled his lifelong secret yearning to get out of himself. Art had not
done it for him. Art had only made it worse. But now, now he had
done it.

He was not aware how much Mrs Bolton was behind him. He did
not know how much he depended on her. But for all that, it was
evident that when he was with her his voice dropped to an easy
rhythm of intimacy, almost a trifle vulgar.

With Connie, he was a little stiff. He felt he owed her everything,
everything, and he showed her the utmost respect and consideration,
so long as she gave him mere outward respect. But it was obvious
he had a secret dread of her. The new Achilles[54] in him had a heel,
and in this heel the woman, the woman like Connie his wife, could
lame him fatally. He went in a certain half-subservient dread of
her, and was extremely nice to her. But his voice was a little tense
when he spoke to her, and he began to be silent whenever she was
present.

Only when he was alone with Mrs Bolton did he really feel a lord
and a master, and his voice ran on with her almost as easily and
garrulously as her own could run. And he let her shave him or
sponge all his body as if he were a child, really as if he were a child.

Chapter 10

CONNIE WAS A GOOD DEAL ALONE now, fewer people came to
Wragby. Clifford no longer wanted them. He had turned against
even the cronies. He was queer. He preferred the radio, which he
had installed at some expense, with a good deal of success at last. He

could sometimes get Madrid or Frankfurt, even there in the uneasy Midlands.

And he would sit alone for hours listening to the loudspeaker bellowing forth. It amazed and stunned Connie. But there he would sit, with a blank entranced expression on his face, like a person losing his mind, and listen, or seem to listen, to the unspeakable thing.

Was he really listening? Or was it a sort of soporific he took, whilst something else worked on underneath in him? Connie did not know. She fled up to her room, or out of doors to the wood. A kind of terror filled her sometimes, a terror of the incipient insanity of the whole civilised species.

But now that Clifford was drifting off to this other weirdness of industrial activity, becoming almost a *creature*, with a hard, efficient shell of an exterior and a pulpy interior, one of the amazing crabs and lobsters of the modern, industrial and financial world, invertebrates of the crustacean order, with shells of steel, like machines, and inner bodies of soft pulp, Connie herself was really completely stranded.

She was not even free, for Clifford must have her there. He seemed to have a nervous terror that she should leave him. The curious pulpy part of him, the emotional and humanly-individual part, depended on her with terror, like a child, almost like an idiot. She must be there, there at Wragby, a Lady Chatterley, his wife. Otherwise he would be lost like an idiot on a moor.

This amazing dependence Connie realised with a sort of horror. She heard him with his pit managers, with the members of his Board, with young scientists, and she was amazed at his shrewd insight into things, his power, his uncanny material power over what is called practical men. He had become a practical man himself, and an amazingly astute and powerful one, a master. Connie attributed it to Mrs Bolton's influence upon him, just at the crisis in his life.

But this astute and practical man was almost an idiot when left alone to his own emotional life. He worshipped Connie, she was his wife, a higher being, and he worshipped her with a queer, craven idolatry, like a savage, a worship based on enormous fear, and even hate of the power of the idol, the dread idol. All he wanted was for Connie to swear, to swear not to leave him, not to give him away.

'Clifford,' she said to him – but this was after she had the key to the hut – 'would you really like me to have a child one day?'

He looked at her with a furtive apprehension in his rather prominent pale eyes.

'I shouldn't mind, if it made no difference between us,' he said.

'No difference to what?' she asked.

'To you and me; to our love for one another. If it's going to affect that, then I'm all against it. Why, I might even one day have a child of my own!'

She looked at him in amazement.

'I mean, it might come back to me one of these days.'

She still stared in amazement, and he was uncomfortable.

'So you would not like it if I had a child?' she said.

'I tell you,' he replied quickly, like a cornered dog, 'I am quite willing, provided it doesn't touch your love for me. If it would touch that, I am dead against it.'

Connie could only be silent in cold fear and contempt. Such talk was really the gabbling of an idiot. He no longer knew what he was talking about.

'Oh, it wouldn't make any difference to my feeling for you,' she said, with a certain sarcasm.

'There!' he said. 'That is the point! In that case I don't mind in the least. I mean it would be awfully nice to have a child running about the house, and feel one was building up a future for it. I should have something to strive for then, and I should know it was your child, shouldn't I, dear? And it would seem just the same as my own. Because it is you who count in these matters. You know that, don't you, dear? I don't enter, I am a cypher. You are the great I-am! as far as life goes. You know that, don't you? I mean, as far as I am concerned. I mean, but for you I am absolutely nothing. I live for your sake and your future. I am nothing to myself.'

Connie heard it all with deepening dismay and repulsion. It was one of the ghastly half-truths that poison human existence. What man in his senses would say such things to a woman! But men aren't in their senses. What man with a spark of honour would put this ghastly burden of life-responsibility upon a woman, and leave her there, in the void?

Moreover, in half an hour's time, Connie heard Clifford talking to Mrs Bolton, in a hot, impulsive voice, revealing himself in a sort of passionless passion to the woman, as if she were half mistress, half foster-mother to him. And Mrs Bolton was carefully dressing him in evening clothes, for there were important business guests in the house.

Connie really sometimes felt she would die at this time. She felt she was being crushed to death by weird lies, and by the amazing cruelty of idiocy. Clifford's strange business efficiency in a way overawed her, and his declaration of private worship put her into a panic. There was nothing between them. She never even touched

him nowadays, and he never touched her. He never even took her
hand and held it kindly. No, and because they were so utterly out of
touch, he tortured her with his declaration of idolatry. It was the
cruelty of utter impotence. And she felt her reason would give way,
or she would die.

She fled as much as possible to the wood. One afternoon, as she sat
brooding, watching the water bubbling coldly in John's Well, the
keeper had strode up to her.

'I got you a key made, my Lady!' he said, saluting, and he offered
her the key.

'Thank you so much!' she said, startled.

'The hut's not very tidy, if you don't mind,' he said. 'I cleared it
what I could.'

'But I didn't want you to trouble!' she said.

'Oh, it wasn't any trouble. I am setting the hens in about a week.
But they won't be scared of you. I s'll have to see to them morning
and night, but I shan't bother you any more than I can help.'

'But you wouldn't bother me,' she pleaded. 'I'd rather not go to
the hut at all, if I am going to be in the way.'

He looked at her with his keen blue eyes. He seemed kindly, but
distant. But at least he was sane, and wholesome, if even he looked
thin and ill. A cough troubled him.

'You have a cough,' she said.

'Nothing – a cold! The last pneumonia left me with a cough, but
it's nothing.'

He kept distant from her, and would not come any nearer.

She went fairly often to the hut, in the morning or in the afternoon,
but he was never there. No doubt he avoided her on purpose. He
wanted to keep his own privacy.

He had made the hut tidy, put the little table and chair near the
fireplace, left a little pile of kindling and small logs, and put the tools
and traps away as far as possible, effacing himself. Outside, by the
clearing, he had built a low little roof of boughs and straw, a shelter
for the birds, and under it stood the five coops. And, one day when
she came, she found two brown hens sitting alert and fierce in the
coops, sitting on pheasants' eggs, and fluffed out so proud and deep
in all the heat of the pondering female blood. This almost broke
Connie's heart. She, herself, was so forlorn and unused, not a female
at all, just a mere thing of terrors.

Then all the five coops were occupied by hens, three brown and a
grey and a black. All alike, they clustered themselves down on the
eggs in the soft nestling ponderosity of the female urge, the female

nature, fluffing out their feathers. And with brilliant eyes they watched Connie, as she crouched before them, and they gave short sharp clucks of anger and alarm, but chiefly of female anger at being approached.

Connie found corn in the corn-bin in the hut. She offered it to the hens in her hand. They would not eat it. Only one hen pecked at her hand with a fierce little jab, so Connie was frightened. But she was pining to give them something, the brooding mothers who neither fed themselves nor drank. She brought water in a little tin, and was delighted when one of the hens drank.

Now she came every day to the hens, they were the only things in the world that warmed her heart. Clifford's protestations made her go cold from head to foot. Mrs Bolton's voice made her go cold, and the sound of the business men who came. An occasional letter from Michaelis affected her with the same sense of chill. She felt she would surely die if it lasted much longer.

Yet it was spring, and the bluebells were coming in the wood, and the leaf-buds on the hazels were opening like the spatter of green rain. How terrible it was that it should be spring, and everything cold-hearted, cold-hearted. Only the hens, fluffed so wonderfully on the eggs, were warm with their hot, brooding female bodies! Connie felt herself living on the brink of fainting all the time.

Then, one day, a lovely sunny day with great tufts of primroses under the hazels, and many violets dotting the paths, she came in the afternoon to the coops and there was one tiny, tiny perky chicken tinily prancing round in front of a coop, and the mother hen clucking in terror. The slim little chick was greyish-brown with dark markings, and it was the most alive little spark of a creature in seven kingdoms at that moment. Connie crouched to watch in a sort of ecstasy. Life, life! Pure, sparky, fearless new life! New life! So tiny and so utterly without fear! Even when it scampered a little scramblingly into the coop again, and disappeared under the hen's feathers in answer to the mother hen's wild alarm-cries, it was not really frightened, it took it as a game, the game of living. For in a moment a tiny sharp head was poking through the gold-brown feathers of the hen, and eyeing the Cosmos.

Connie was fascinated. And at the same time, never had she felt so acutely the agony of her own female forlornness. It was becoming unbearable.

She had only one desire now, to go to the clearing in the wood. The rest was a kind of painful dream. But sometimes she was kept all day at Wragby, by her duties as hostess. And then she felt as if she too were going blank, just blank and insane.

One evening, guests or no guests, she escaped after tea. It was late, and she fled across the park like one who fears to be called back. The sun was setting rosy as she entered the wood, but she pressed on among the flowers. The light would last long overhead.

She arrived at the clearing flushed and semi-conscious. The keeper was there, in his shirt-sleeves, just closing up the coops for the night, so the little occupants would be safe. But still one little trio was pattering about on tiny feet, alert drab mites, under the straw shelter, refusing to be called in by the anxious mother.

'I had to come and see the chickens!' she said, panting, glancing shyly at the keeper, almost unaware of him. 'Are there any more?'

'Thurty-six so far!' he said. 'Not bad!'

He too took a curious pleasure in watching the young things come out.

Connie crouched in front of the last coop. The three chicks had run in. But still their cheeky heads came poking sharply through the yellow feathers, then withdrawing, then only one beady little head eyeing forth from the vast mother-body.

'I'd love to touch them,' she said, putting her fingers gingerly through the bars of the coop. But the mother-hen pecked at her hand fiercely, and Connie drew back startled and frightened.

'How she pecks at me! She hates me!' she said in a wondering voice. 'But I wouldn't hurt them!'

The man standing above her laughed, and crouched down beside her, knees apart, and put his hand with quiet confidence slowly into the coop. The old hen pecked at him, but not so savagely. And slowly, softly, with sure gentle fingers, he felt among the old bird's feathers and drew out a faintly-peeping chick in his closed hand.

'There!' he said, holding out his hand to her. She took the little drab thing between her hands, and there it stood, on its impossible little stalks of legs, its atom of balancing life trembling through its almost weightless feet into Connie's hands. But it lifted its handsome, clean-shaped little head boldly, and looked sharply round, and gave a little 'peep'. 'So adorable! So cheeky!' she said softly.

The keeper, squatting beside her, was also watching with an amused face the bold little bird in her hands. Suddenly he saw a tear fall on to her wrist.

And he stood up, and stood away, moving to the other coop. For suddenly he was aware of the old flame shooting and leaping up in his loins, that he had hoped was quiescent for ever. He fought against it, turning his back to her. But it leapt, and leapt downwards, circling in his knees.

He turned again to look at her. She was kneeling and holding her two hands slowly forward, blindly, so that the chicken should run in to the mother-hen again. And there was something so mute and forlorn in her, compassion flamed in his bowels for her.

Without knowing, he came quickly towards her and crouched beside her again, taking the chick from her hands, because she was afraid of the hen, and putting it back in the coop. At the back of his loins the fire suddenly darted stronger.

He glanced apprehensively at her. Her face was averted, and she was crying blindly, in all the anguish of her generation's forlornness. His heart melted suddenly, like a drop of fire, and he put out his hand and laid his fingers on her knee.

'You shouldn't cry,' he said softly.

But then she put her hands over her face and felt that really her heart was broken and nothing mattered any more.

He laid his hand on her shoulder, and softly, gently, it began to travel down the curve of her back, blindly, with a blind stroking motion, to the curve of her crouching loins. And there his hand softly, softly, stroked the curve of her flank, in the blind instinctive caress.

She had found her scrap of handkerchief and was blindly trying to dry her face.

'Shall you come to the hut?' he said, in a quiet, neutral voice.

And closing his hand softly on her upper arm, he drew her up and led her slowly to the hut, not letting go of her till she was inside. Then he cleared aside the chair and table, and took a brown soldier's blanket from the tool chest, spreading it slowly. She glanced at his face, as she stood motionless.

His face was pale and without expression, like that of a man submitting to fate.

'You lie there,' he said softly, and he shut the door, so that it was dark, quite dark.

With a queer obedience, she lay down on the blanket. Then she felt the soft, groping, helplessly desirous hand touching her body, feeling for her face. The hand stroked her face softly, softly, with infinite soothing and assurance, and at last there was the soft touch of a kiss on her cheek.

She lay quite still, in a sort of sleep, in a sort of dream. Then she quivered as she felt his hand groping softly, yet with queer thwarted clumsiness, among her clothing. Yet the hand knew, too, how to unclothe her where it wanted. He drew down the thin silk sheath, slowly, carefully, right down and over her feet. Then with a quiver of exquisite pleasure he touched the warm soft body, and touched her navel for a moment in a kiss. And he had to come in to her at once, to enter the peace on earth of her soft, quiescent body. It was the moment of pure peace for him, the entry into the body of the woman.

She lay still, in a kind of sleep, always in a kind of sleep. The activity, the orgasm was his, all his; she could strive for herself no more. Even the tightness of his arms round her, even the intense movement of his body, and the springing of his seed in her, was a kind of sleep, from which she did not begin to rouse till he had finished and lay softly panting against her breast.

Then she wondered, just dimly wondered, why? Why was this necessary? Why had it lifted a great cloud from her and given her peace? Was it real? Was it real?

Her tormented modern-woman's brain still had no rest. Was it real? And she knew, if she gave herself to the man, it was real. But if she kept herself for herself, it was nothing. She was old; millions of years old, she felt. And at last, she could bear the burden of herself no more. She was to be had for the taking. To be had for the taking.

The man lay in a mysterious stillness. What was he feeling? What was he thinking? She did not know. He was a strange man to her, she did not know him. She must only wait, for she did not dare to break his mysterious stillness. He lay there with his arms round her, his body on hers, his wet body touching hers, so close. And completely unknown. Yet not unpeaceful. His very stillness was peaceful.

She knew that, when at last he roused and drew away from her. It was like an abandonment. He drew her dress in the darkness down over her knees and stood a few moments, apparently adjusting his own clothing. Then he quietly opened the door and went out.

She saw a very brilliant little moon shining above the afterglow over the oaks. Quickly she got up and arranged herself; she was tidy. Then she went to the door of the hut.

All the lower wood was in shadow, almost darkness. Yet the sky overhead was crystal. But it shed hardly any light. He came through the lower shadow towards her, his face lifted like a pale blotch.

'Shall we go, then?' he said.

'Where?'

'I'll go with you to the gate.'

He arranged things his own way. He locked the door of the hut and came after her.

'You aren't sorry, are you?' he asked, as he went at her side.

'No! No! Are you?' she said.

'For that! No!' he said. Then after a while he added: 'But there's the rest of things.'

'What rest of things?' she said.

'Sir Clifford. Other folks. All the complications.'

'Why complications?' she said, disappointed.

'It's always so. For you as well as for me. There's always complications.' He walked on steadily in the dark.

'And are you sorry?' she said.

'In a way!' he replied, looking up at the sky. 'I thought I'd done with it all. Now I've begun again.'

'Begun what?'

'Life.'

'Life!' she re-echoed, with a queer thrill.

'It's life,' he said. 'There's no keeping clear. And if you do keep clear you might almost as well die. So if I've got to be broken open again, I have.'

She did not quite see it that way, but still . . .

'It's just love,' she said cheerfully.

'Whatever that may be,' he replied.

They went on through the darkening wood in silence, till they were almost at the gate.

'But you don't hate me, do you?' she said wistfully.

'Nay, nay,' he replied. And suddenly he held her fast against his breast again, with the old connecting passion. 'Nay, for me it was good, it was good. Was it for you?'

'Yes, for me too,' she answered, a little untruthfully, for she had not been conscious of much.

He kissed her softly, softly, with the kisses of warmth.

'If only there weren't so many other people in the world,' he said lugubriously.

She laughed. They were at the gate to the park. He opened for her.

'I won't come any further,' he said.

'No!' And she held out her hand, as if to shake hands. But he took it in both his.

'Shall I come again?' she asked wistfully.

'Yes! Yes!'

She left him and went across the park.

He stood back and watched her going into the dark, against the pallor of the horizon. Almost with bitterness he watched her go. She had connected him up again, when he had wanted to be alone. She had cost him that bitter privacy of a man who at last wants only to be alone.

He turned into the dark of the wood. All was still, the moon had set. But he was aware of the noises of the night, the engines at Stacks Gate, the traffic on the main road. Slowly he climbed the denuded knoll. And from the top he could see the country, bright rows of lights at Stacks Gate, smaller lights at Tevershall pit, the yellow lights of Tevershall and lights everywhere, here and there, on the dark country, with the distant blush of furnaces, faint and rosy, since the night was clear, the rosiness of the outpouring of white-hot metal. Sharp, wicked electric lights at Stacks Gate! An undefinable quick of evil in them! And all the unease, the ever-shifting dread of the industrial night in the Midlands. He could hear the winding-engines at Stacks Gate turning down the seven-o'clock miners. The pit worked three shifts.

He went down again into the darkness and seclusion of the wood. But he knew that the seclusion of the wood was illusory. The industrial noises broke the solitude, the sharp lights, though unseen, mocked it. A man could no longer be private and withdrawn. The world allows no hermits. And now he had taken the woman, and brought on himself a new cycle of pain and doom. For he knew by experience what it meant.

It was not woman's fault, nor even love's fault, nor the fault of sex. The fault lay there, out there, in those evil electric lights and diabolical rattlings of engines. There, in the world of the mechanical greedy, greedy mechanism and mechanised greed, sparkling with lights and gushing hot metal and roaring with traffic, there lay the vast evil thing, ready to destroy whatever did not conform. Soon it would destroy the wood, and the bluebells would spring no more. All vulnerable things must perish under the rolling and running of iron.

He thought with infinite tenderness of the woman. Poor forlorn thing, she was nicer than she knew, and oh! so much too nice for the tough lot she was in contact with. Poor thing, she too had some of the vulnerability of the wild hyacinths, she wasn't all tough rubber-goods and platinum, like the modern girl. And they would do her in! As sure as life, they would do her in, as they do in all naturally tender life. Tender! Somewhere she was tender, tender with a tenderness of the growing hyacinths, something that has gone out of the celluloid women of today. But he would protect her with his heart for a little while. For a little while, before the insentient iron world and the Mammon of mechanised greed did them both in, her as well as him.

He went home with his gun and his dog, to the dark cottage, lit the lamp, started the fire, and ate his supper of bread and cheese, young onions and beer. He was alone, in a silence he loved. His room was clean and tidy, but rather stark. Yet the fire was bright, the hearth white, the petroleum lamp hung bright over the table, with its white oilcloth. He tried to read a book about India, but tonight he could not read. He sat by the fire in his shirt-sleeves, not smoking, but with a mug of beer in reach. And he thought about Connie.

To tell the truth, he was sorry for what had happened, perhaps most for her sake. He had a sense of foreboding. No sense of wrong or sin; he was troubled by no conscience in that respect. He knew that conscience was chiefly fear of society, or fear of oneself. He was not afraid of himself. But he was quite consciously afraid of society, which he knew by instinct to be a malevolent, partly-insane beast.

The woman! If she could be there with him, and there were nobody else in the world! The desire rose again, his penis began to stir like a live bird. At the same time an oppression, a dread of exposing himself and her to that outside Thing that sparkled viciously in the electric lights, weighed down his shoulders. She, poor young thing, was just a young female creature to him; but a young female creature whom he had gone into and whom he desired again.

Stretching with the curious yawn of desire, for he had been alone and apart from man or woman for four years, he rose and took his coat again, and his gun, lowered the lamp and went out into the starry night, with the dog. Driven by desire and by dread of the malevolent Thing outside, he made his round in the wood, slowly, softly. He loved the darkness and folded himself into it. It fitted the turgidity of his desire which, in spite of all, was like a riches; the stirring restlessness of his penis, the stirring fire in his loins! Oh, if only there were other men to be with, to fight that sparkling electric Thing outside there, to preserve the tenderness of life, the tenderness of women, and the natural riches of desire. If only there were men to fight side by side with! But the men were all outside there, glorying in the Thing, triumphing or being trodden down in the rush of mechanised greed or of greedy mechanism.

Constance, for her part, had hurried across the park, home, almost without thinking. As yet she had no afterthought. She would be in time for dinner.

She was annoyed to find the doors fastened, however, so that she had to ring. Mrs Bolton opened.

'Why there you are, your Ladyship! I was beginning to wonder if you'd gone lost!' she said a little roguishly. 'Sir Clifford hasn't asked for you, though; he's got Mr Linley in with him, talking over something. It looks as if he'd stay to dinner, doesn't it, my Lady?'

'It does rather,' said Connie.

'Shall I put dinner back a quarter of an hour? That would give you time to dress in comfort.'

'Perhaps you'd better.'

Mr Linley was the general manager of the collieries, an elderly man from the north, with not quite enough punch to suit Clifford; not up to post-war conditions, nor post-war colliers either, with their 'ca' canny'[55] creed. But Connie liked Mr Linley, though she was glad to be spared the toadying of his wife.

Linley stayed to dinner, and Connie was the hostess men liked so much, so modest, yet so attentive and aware, with big, wide blue eyes and a soft repose that sufficiently hid what she was really thinking. Connie had played this woman so much, it was almost second nature to her; but still, decidedly second. Yet it was curious how everything disappeared from her consciousness while she played it.

She waited patiently till she could go upstairs and think her own thoughts. She was always waiting, it seemed to be her *forte*.

Once in her room, however, she felt still vague and confused. She didn't know what to think. What sort of a man was he, really? Did he really like her? Not much, she felt. Yet he was kind. There was something, a sort of warm naïve kindness, curious and sudden, that almost opened her womb to him. But she felt he might be kind like that to any woman. Though even so, it was curiously soothing, comforting. And he was a passionate man, wholesome and passionate. But perhaps he wasn't quite individual enough; he might be the same with any woman as he had been with her. It really wasn't personal. She was only really a female to him.

But perhaps that was better. And after all, he was kind to the female in her, which no man had ever been. Men were very kind to the *person* she was, but rather cruel to the female, despising her or ignoring her altogether. Men were awfully kind to Constance Reid or to Lady Chatterley; but not to her womb they weren't kind. And he took no notice of Constance or of Lady Chatterley; he just softly stroked her loins or her breasts.

She went to the wood next day. It was a grey, still afternoon, with the dark-green dogs'-mercury spreading under the hazel copse, and all the trees making a silent effort to open their buds. Today she could almost feel it in her own body, the huge heave of the sap in the massive trees, upwards, up, up to the bud-tips, there to push into little flamey oak-leaves, bronze as blood. It was like a tide running turgid upward, and spreading on the sky.

She came to the clearing, but he was not there. She had only half expected him. The pheasant chicks were running lightly abroad, light as insects, from the coops where the yellow hens clucked anxiously. Connie sat and watched them, and waited. She only waited. Even the chicks she hardly saw. She waited.

The time passed with dream-like slowness, and he did not come. She had only half expected him. He never came in the afternoon. She must go home to tea. But she had to force herself to leave.

As she went home, a fine drizzle of rain fell.

'Is it raining again?' said Clifford, seeing her shake her hat.

'Just drizzle.'

She poured tea in silence, absorbed in a sort of obstinacy. She did want to see the keeper today, to see if it were really real. If it were really real.

'Shall I read a little to you afterwards?' said Clifford.

She looked at him. Had he sensed something?

'The spring makes me feel queer – I thought I might rest a little,' she said.

'Just as you like. Not feeling really unwell, are you?'

'No! Only rather tired – with the spring. Will you have Mrs Bolton to play something with you?'

'No! I think I'll listen in.'

She heard the curious satisfaction in his voice. She went upstairs to her bedroom. There she heard the loudspeaker begin to bellow, in an idiotically velveteen-genteel sort of voice, something about a series of street-cries, the very cream of genteel affectation imitating old criers. She pulled on her old violet-coloured mackintosh, and slipped out of the house at the side door.

The drizzle of rain was like a veil over the world, mysterious, hushed, not cold. She got very warm as she hurried across the park. She had to open her light waterproof.

The wood was silent, still and secret in the evening drizzle of rain, full of the mystery of eggs and half-open buds, half-unsheathed flowers. In the dimness of it all trees glistened naked and dark as if they had unclothed themselves, and the green things on earth seemed to hum with greenness.

There was still no one at the clearing. The chicks had nearly all gone under the mother-hens, only one or two lost adventurous ones still dibbed about[56] in the dryness under the straw roof-shelter. And they were doubtful of themselves.

So! He still had not been. He was staying away on purpose. Or perhaps something was wrong. Perhaps she should go to the cottage and see.

But she was born to wait. She opened the hut with her key. It was all tidy, the corn put in the bin, the blankets folded on the shelf, the straw neat in a corner; a new bundle of straw. The hurricane lamp hung on a nail. The table and chair had been put back where she had lain.

She sat down on a stool in the doorway. How still everything was! The fine rain blew very softly, filmily, but the wind made no noise. Nothing made any sound. The trees stood like powerful beings, dim, twilit, silent and alive. How alive everything was!

Night was drawing near again; she would have to go. He was avoiding her.

But suddenly he came striding into the clearing, in his black oilskin jacket like a chauffeur, shining with wet. He glanced quickly at the hut, half-saluted, then veered aside and went on to the coops. There he crouched in silence, looking carefully at everything, then carefully shutting the hens and chicks up safe against the night.

At last he came slowly towards her. She still sat on her stool. He stood before her under the porch.

'You come then,' he said, using the intonation of the dialect.

'Yes,' she said, looking up at him. 'You're late!'

'Ay!' he replied, looking away into the wood.

She rose slowly, drawing aside her stool.

'Did you want to come in?' she asked.

He looked down at her shrewdly.

'Won't folks be thinkin' somethink, you comin' here every night?' he said.

'Why?' She looked up at him, at a loss. 'I said I'd come. Nobody knows.'

'They soon will, though,' he replied. 'An' what then?'

She was at a loss for an answer.

'Why should they know?' she said.

'Folks always does,' he said fatally.

Her lip quivered a little.

'Well I can't help it,' she faltered.

'Nay,' he said. 'You can help it by not comin' – if yer want to,' he added, in a lower tone.

'But I don't want to,' she murmured.

He looked away into the wood, and was silent.

'But what when folks finds out?' he asked at last. 'Think about it! Think how lowered you'll feel, one of your husband's servants.'

She looked up at his averted face.

'Is it,' she stammered, 'is it that you don't want me?'

'Think!' he said. 'Think what if folks find out – Sir Clifford an' a' – an' everybody talkin' – '

'Well, I can go away.'

'Where to?'

'Anywhere! I've got money of my own. My mother left me twenty thousand pounds in trust, and I know Clifford can't touch it. I can go away.'

'But 'appen you don't want to go away.'

'Yes, yes! I don't care what happens to me.'

'Ay, you think that! But you'll care! You'll have to care, everybody has. You've got to remember your Ladyship is carrying on with a gamekeeper. It's not as if I was a gentleman. Yes, you'd care. You'd care.'

'I shouldn't. What do I care about my ladyship! I hate it really. I feel people are jeering every time they say it. And they are, they are! Even you jeer when you say it.'

'Me!'

For the first time he looked straight at her, and into her eyes.

'I don't jeer at you,' he said.

As he looked into her eyes she saw his own eyes go dark, quite dark, the pupils dilating.

'Don't you care about a' the risk?' he asked in a husky voice. 'You should care. Don't care when it's too late!'

There was a curious warning pleading in his voice.

'But I've nothing to lose,' she said fretfully. 'If you knew what it is, you'd think I'd be glad to lose it. But are you afraid for yourself?'

'Ay!' he said briefly. 'I am. I'm afraid. I'm afraid. I'm afraid o' things.'

'What things?' she asked.

He gave a curious backward jerk of his head, indicating the outer world.

'Things! Everybody! The lot of 'em.'

Then he bent down and suddenly kissed her unhappy face.

'Nay, I don't care,' he said. 'Let's have it, an' damn the rest. But if you was to feel sorry you'd ever done it – !'

'Don't put me off,' she pleaded.

He put his fingers to her cheek and kissed her again suddenly.

'Let me come in then,' he said softly. 'An' take off your mackintosh.'

He hung up his gun, slipped out of his wet leather jacket, and reached for the blankets.

'I brought another blanket,' he said, 'so we can put one over us if you like.'

'I can't stay long,' she said. 'Dinner is half-past seven.'

He looked at her swiftly, then at his watch.

'All right,' he said.

He shut the door, and lit a tiny light in the hanging hurricane lamp.

'One time we'll have a long time,' he said.

He put the blankets down carefully, one folded for her head. Then he sat down a moment on the stool, and drew her to him, holding her close with one arm, feeling for her body with his free hand. She heard the catch of his intaken breath as he found her. Under her frail petticoat she was naked.

'Eh! what it is to touch thee!' he said, as his finger caressed the delicate, warm, secret skin of her waist and hips. He put his face down and rubbed his cheek against her belly and against her thighs again and again. And again she wondered a little over the sort of rapture it was to him. She did not understand the beauty he found in her, through touch upon her living secret body, almost the ecstasy of beauty. For passion alone is awake to it. And when passion is dead, or absent, then the magnificent throb of beauty is incomprehensible and even a little despicable; warm, live beauty of contact, so much deeper than the beauty of vision. She felt the glide of his cheek on her thighs and belly and buttocks, and the close brushing of his moustache and his soft thick hair, and her knees began to quiver. Far down in her she felt a new stirring, a new nakedness emerging. And she was half afraid. Half she wished he would not caress her so. He was encompassing her somehow. Yet she was waiting, waiting.

And when he came into her, with an intensification of relief and consummation that was pure peace to him, still she was waiting. She felt herself a little left out. And she knew, partly it was her own fault. She willed herself into this separateness. Now perhaps she was condemned to it. She lay still, feeling his motion within her, his deep-sunk intentness, the sudden quiver of him at the springing of his seed, then the slow-subsiding thrust. That thrust of the buttocks, surely it was a little ridiculous. If you were a woman, and apart in all the business, surely that thrusting of the man's buttocks was supremely ridiculous. Surely the man was intensely ridiculous in this posture and this act!

But she lay still, without recoil. Even when he had finished, she did not rouse herself to get a grip on her own satisfaction, as she had done with Michaelis; she lay still, and the tears slowly filled and ran from her eyes.

He lay still, too. But he held her close and tried to cover her poor naked legs with his legs, to keep them warm. He lay on her with a close, undoubting warmth.

'Are yer cold?' he asked, in a soft, small voice, as if she were close, so close. Whereas she was left out, distant.

'No! But I must go,' she said gently.

He sighed, held her closer, then relaxed to rest again.

He had not guessed her tears. He thought she was there with him.

'I must go,' she repeated.

He lifted himself, kneeled beside her a moment, kissed the inner side of her thighs, then drew down her skirts, buttoning his own clothes unthinking, not even turning aside, in the faint, faint light from the lantern.

'Tha mun come ter th' cottage one time,' he said, looking down at her with a warm, sure, easy face.

But she lay there inert, and was gazing up at him thinking: Stranger! Stranger! She even resented him a little.

He put on his coat and looked for his hat, which had fallen, then he slung on his gun.

'Come then!' he said, looking down at her with those warm, peaceful sort of eyes.

She rose slowly. She didn't want to go. She also rather resented staying. He helped her with her thin waterproof, and saw she was tidy.

Then he opened the door. The outside was quite dark. The faithful dog under the porch stood up with pleasure seeing him. The drizzle of rain drifted greyly past upon the darkness. It was quite dark.

'Ah mun ta'e th' lantern,' he said. 'The'll be nob'dy.'

He walked just before her in the narrow path, swinging the hurricane lamp low, revealing the wet grass, the black shiny tree-roots like snakes, wan flowers. For the rest, all was grey rain-mist and complete darkness.

'Tha mun come to the cottage one time,' he said, 'shall ta? We might as well be hung for a sheep as for a lamb.'

It puzzled her, his queer, persistent wanting her, when there was nothing between them, when he never really spoke to her, and in spite of herself she resented the dialect. His 'tha mun come' seemed not addressed to her, but some common woman. She recognised the foxglove leaves of the riding and knew, more or less, where they were.

'It's quarter past seven,' he said, 'you'll do it.' He had changed his voice, seemed to feel her distance. As they turned the last bend in the riding towards the hazel wall and the gate, he blew out the light. 'We'll see from here,' he said, taking her gently by the arm.

But it was difficult, the earth under their feet was a mystery, but he felt his way by tread: he was used to it. At the gate he gave her his electric torch. 'It's a bit lighter in the park,' he said; 'but take it for fear you get off th' path.'

It was true, there seemed a ghost-glimmer of greyness in the open space of the park. He suddenly drew her to him and whipped his hand under her dress again, feeling her warm body with his wet, chill hand.

'I could die for the touch of a woman like thee,' he said in his throat. 'If tha' would stop another minute.' She felt the sudden force of his wanting her again.

'No, I must run,' she said, a little wildly.

'Ay,' he replied, suddenly changed, letting her go.

She turned away, and on the instant she turned back to him saying: 'Kiss me.'

He bent over her indistinguishable and kissed her on the left eye. She held her mouth and he softly kissed it, but at once drew away. He hated mouth kisses.

'I'll come tomorrow,' she said, drawing away; 'if I can,' she added.

'Ay! not so late,' he replied out of the darkness. Already she could not see him at all.

'Good-night,' she said.

'Good-night, your Ladyship,' his voice.

She stopped and looked back into the wet dark. She could just see the bulk of him. 'Why did you say that?' she said.

'Nay,' he replied. 'Good-night then, run!'

She plunged on in the dark-grey tangible night. She found the side door open, and slipped into her room unseen. As she closed the door the gong sounded, but she would take her bath all the same – she must take her bath. 'But I won't be late any more,' she said to herself; 'it's too annoying.'

The next day she did not go to the wood. She went instead with Clifford to Uthwaite. He could occasionally go out now in the car, and had got a strong young man as chauffeur, who could help him out of the car if need be. He particularly wanted to see his godfather, Leslie Winter, who lived at Shipley Hall, not far from Uthwaite. Winter was an elderly gentleman now, wealthy, one of the wealthy coal-owners who had had their heyday in King Edward's time.[57] King Edward had stayed more than once at Shipley, for the shooting.

It was a handsome old stucco hall, very elegantly appointed, for Winter was a bachelor and prided himself on his style; but the place was beset by collieries. Leslie Winter was attached to Clifford, but personally did not entertain a great respect for him, because of the photographs in illustrated papers and the literature. The old man was a buck of the King Edward school, who thought life was life and the scribbling fellows were something else. Towards Connie the Squire was always rather gallant; he thought her an attractive demure maiden and rather wasted on Clifford, and it was a thousand pities she stood no chance of bringing forth an heir to Wragby. He himself had no heir.

Connie wondered what he would say if he knew that Clifford's gamekeeper had been having intercourse with her, and saying to her, 'Tha mun come to th' cottage one time.' He would detest and despise her, for he had come almost to hate the shoving forward of the working classes. A man of her own class he would not mind, for Connie was gifted from nature with this appearance of demure, submissive maidenliness, and perhaps it was part of her nature. Winter called her 'dear child' and gave her a rather lovely miniature of an eighteenth-century lady, rather against her will.

But Connie was preoccupied with her affair with the keeper. After all, Mr Winter, who was really a gentleman and a man of the world, treated her as a person and a discriminating individual; he did not lump her together with all the rest of his female womanhood in his 'thee' and 'tha'.

She did not go to the wood that day nor the next, nor the day following. She did not go so long as she felt, or imagined she felt, the man waiting for her, wanting her. But the fourth day she was terribly unsettled and uneasy. She still refused to go to the wood and open her thighs once more to the man. She thought of all the things she might do – drive to Sheffield, pay visits, and the thought of all these things was repellent. At last she decided to take a walk, not towards the wood, but in the opposite direction; she would go to Marehay, through the little iron gate in the other side of the park fence. It was a quiet grey day of spring, almost warm. She walked on unheeding, absorbed in thoughts she was not even conscious of. She was not really aware of anything outside her, till she was startled by the loud barking of the dog at Marehay Farm. Marehay Farm! Its pastures ran up to Wragby park fence, so they were neighbours, but it was some time since Connie had called.

'Bell!' she said to the big white bull-terrier. 'Bell! have you forgotten me? Don't you know me?' She was afraid of dogs, and Bell stood back and bellowed, and she wanted to pass through the farmyard on to the warren[58] path.

Mrs Flint appeared. She was a woman of Constance's own age, had been a schoolteacher, but Connie suspected her of being rather a false little thing.

'Why, it's Lady Chatterley! Why!' And Mrs Flint's eyes glowed again, and she flushed like a young girl. 'Bell, Bell. Why! barking at Lady Chatterley! Bell! Be quiet!' She darted forward and slashed at the dog with a white cloth she held in her hand, then came forward to Connie.

'She used to know me,' said Connie, shaking hands. The Flints were Chatterley tenants.

'Of course she knows your Ladyship! She's just showing off,' said Mrs Flint, glowing and looking up with a sort of flushed confusion, 'but it's so long since she's seen you. I do hope you are better.'

'Yes thanks, I'm all right.'

'We've hardly seen you all winter. Will you come in and look at the baby?'

'Well!' Connie hesitated. 'Just for a minute.'

Mrs Flint flew wildly in to tidy up, and Connie came slowly after her, hesitating in the rather dark kitchen where the kettle was boiling by the fire. Back came Mrs Flint.

'I do hope you'll excuse me,' she said. 'Will you come in here?'

They went into the living-room, where a baby was sitting on the rag hearthrug, and the table was roughly set for tea. A young servant-girl backed down the passage, shy and awkward.

The baby was a perky little thing of about a year, with red hair like its father, and cheeky pale-blue eyes. It was a girl, and not to be daunted. It sat among cushions and was surrounded with rag dolls and other toys in modern excess.

'Why, what a dear she is!' said Connie, 'and how she's grown! A big girl! A big girl!'

She had given it a shawl when it was born, and celluloid ducks for Christmas.

'There, Josephine! Who's that come to see you? Who's this, Josephine? Lady Chatterley – you know Lady Chatterley, don't you?'

The queer pert little mite gazed cheekily at Connie. Ladyships were still all the same to her.

'Come! Will you come to me?' said Connie to the baby.

The baby didn't care one way or another, so Connie picked her up and held her in her lap. How warm and lovely it was to hold a child in one's lap, and the soft little arms, the unconscious cheeky little legs.

'I was just having a rough cup of tea all by myself. Luke's gone to market, so I can have it when I like. Would you care for a cup, Lady Chatterley? I don't suppose it's what you're used to, but if you would . . . '

Connie would, though she didn't want to be reminded of what she was used to. There was a great re-laying of the table, and the best cups brought and the best teapot.

'If only you wouldn't take any trouble,' said Connie.

But if Mrs Flint took no trouble, where was the fun! So Connie played with the child and was amused by its little female dauntlessness, and got a deep voluptuous pleasure out of its soft young warmth. Young life! And so fearless! So fearless, because so defenceless. All the other people, so narrow with fear!

She had a cup of tea, which was rather strong, and very good bread and butter, and bottled damsons. Mrs Flint flushed and glowed and bridled with excitement, as if Connie were some gallant knight. And they had a real female chat, and both of them enjoyed it.

'It's a poor little tea, though,' said Mrs Flint.

'It's much nicer than at home,' said Connie truthfully.

'Oh-h!' said Mrs Flint, not believing, of course.

But at last Connie rose.

'I must go,' she said. 'My husband has no idea where I am. He'll be wondering all kinds of things.'

'He'll never think you're here,' laughed Mrs Flint excitedly. 'He'll be sending the crier round.'

'Goodbye, Josephine,' said Connie, kissing the baby and ruffling its red, wispy hair.

Mrs Flint insisted on opening the locked and barred front door. Connie emerged in the farm's little front garden, shut in by a privet hedge. There were two rows of auriculas by the path, very velvety and rich.

'Lovely auriculas,' said Connie.

'Recklesses, as Luke calls them,' laughed Mrs Flint. 'Have some.'

And eagerly she picked the velvet and primrose flowers.

'Enough! Enough!' said Connie.

They came to the little garden gate.

'Which way were you going?' asked Mrs Flint.

'By the warren.'

'Let me see! Oh yes, the cows are in the gin close.[59] But they're not up yet. But the gate's locked, you'll have to climb.'

'I can climb,' said Connie.

'Perhaps I can just go down the close with you.'

They went down the poor, rabbit-bitten pasture. Birds were whistling in wild evening triumph in the wood. A man was calling up the last cows, which trailed slowly over the path-worn pasture.

'They're late, milking, tonight,' said Mrs Flint severely. 'They know Luke won't be back till after dark.'

They came to the fence, beyond which the young fir-wood bristled dense. There was a little gate, but it was locked. In the grass on the inside stood a bottle, empty.

. 'There's the keeper's empty bottle for his milk,' explained Mrs Flint. 'We bring it as far as here for him, and then he fetches it himself.'

'When?' said Connie.

'Oh, any time he's around. Often in the morning. Well, goodbye Lady Chatterley! And do come again. It was so lovely having you.'

Connie climbed the fence into the narrow path between the dense, bristling young firs. Mrs Flint went running back across the pasture, in a sun-bonnet, because she was really a schoolteacher. Constance didn't like this dense new part of the wood; it seemed gruesome and choking. She hurried on with her head down, thinking of the Flints' baby. It was a dear little thing, but it would be a bit bow-legged like its father. It showed already, but perhaps it would grow out of it. How warm and fulfilling somehow to have a baby, and how Mrs Flint had showed it off! She had something anyhow that Connie hadn't got, and apparently couldn't have. Yes, Mrs Flint had flaunted her motherhood. And Connie had been just a bit, just a little bit jealous. She couldn't help it.

She started out of her muse, and gave a little cry of fear. A man was there.

It was the keeper. He stood in the path like Balaam's ass,[60] barring her way.

'How's this?' he said in surprise.

'How did you come?' she panted.

'How did you? Have you been to the hut?'

'No! No! I went to Marehay.'

He looked at her curiously, searchingly, and she hung her head a little guiltily.

'And were you going to the hut now?' he asked rather sternly.

'No! I mustn't. I stayed at Marehay. No one knows where I am. I'm late. I've got to run.'

'Giving me the slip, like?' he said, with a faint ironic smile.

'No! No. Not that. Only – '

'Why, what else?' he said. And he stepped up to her, and put his arms around her. She felt the front of his body terribly near to her, and alive.

'Oh, not now, not now,' she cried, trying to push him away.

'Why not? It's only six o'clock. You've got half an hour. Nay! Nay! I want you.'

He held her fast and she felt his urgency. Her old instinct was to fight for her freedom. But something else in her was strange and inert and heavy. His body was urgent against her, and she hadn't the heart any more to fight.

He looked around.

'Come – come here! Through here,' he said, looking penetratingly into the dense fir trees, that were young and not more than half-grown.

He looked back at her. She saw his eyes, tense and brilliant, fierce, not loving. But her will had left her. A strange weight was on her limbs. She was giving way. She was giving up.

He led her through the wall of prickly trees, that were difficult to come through, to a place where was a little space and a pile of dead boughs. He threw one or two dry ones down, put his coat and waistcoat over them, and she had to lie down there under the boughs of the tree, like an animal, while he waited, standing there in his shirt and breeches, watching her with haunted eyes. But still he was provident – he made her lie properly, properly. Yet he broke the band of her underclothes, for she did not help him, only lay inert.

He too had bared the front part of his body and she felt his naked flesh against her as he came into her. For a moment he was still inside her, turgid there and quivering. Then as he began to move, in the sudden helpless orgasm, there awoke in her new strange thrills rippling inside her. Rippling, rippling, rippling, like a flapping overlapping of soft flames, soft as feathers, running to points of brilliance, exquisite, exquisite and melting her all molten inside. It was like bells rippling up and up to a culmination. She lay unconscious of the wild little cries she uttered at the last. But it was over too soon, too soon, and she could no longer force her own conclusion with her own activity. This was different, different. She could do nothing. She could no longer harden and grip for her own satisfaction upon him. She could only wait, wait and moan in spirit as she felt him withdrawing, withdrawing and contracting, coming to the terrible moment when he would slip out of her and be gone. Whilst all her womb was open and soft, and softly clamouring, like a sea-anemone under the tide, clamouring for him to come in again and make a fulfilment for her. She clung to him unconscious in passion, and he never quite slipped from her, and she felt the soft bud of him within her stirring, and strange rhythms flushing up into her with a strange rhythmic growing motion, swelling and swelling till it filled all her cleaving consciousness, and then began again the unspeakable motion that was not really motion, but pure deepening whirlpools of sensation swirling deeper and deeper through all her tissue and consciousness, till she was one perfect concentric fluid of feeling, and she lay there crying in unconscious inarticulate cries. The voice out of the uttermost night, the life! The man heard it beneath him with a kind of awe, as his life sprang out into her. And as it subsided, he subsided too and lay utterly still, unknowing, while her grip on him slowly relaxed, and she lay inert. And they lay and knew nothing, not even of each other, both lost. Till at last he began to rouse and become aware of his defenceless nakedness, and she was aware that his body was loosening its clasp on her. He was coming apart; but in her breast she felt she could not bear him to leave her uncovered. He must cover her now for ever.

But he drew away at last, and kissed her and covered her over, and began to cover himself. She lay looking up to the boughs of the tree, unable as yet to move. He stood and fastened up his breeches, looking round. All was dense and silent, save for the awed dog that lay with its paws against its nose. He sat down again on the brushwood and took Connie's hand in silence.

She turned and looked at him. 'We came off together that time,' he said.

She did not answer.

'It's good when it's like that. Most folks live their lives through and they never know it,' he said, speaking rather dreamily.

She looked into his brooding face.

'Do they?' she said. 'Are you glad?'

He looked back into her eyes. 'Glad,' he said. 'Ay, but never mind.' He did not want her to talk. And he bent over her and kissed her, and she felt, so he must kiss her for ever.

At last she sat up.

'Don't people often come off together?' she asked with naïve curiosity.

'A good many of them never. You can see by the raw look of them.' He spoke unwittingly, regretting he had begun.

'Have you come off like that with other women?'

He looked at her amused.

'I don't know,' he said, 'I don't know.'

And she knew he would never tell her anything he didn't want to tell her. She watched his face, and the passion for him moved in her bowels. She resisted it as far as she could, for it was the loss of herself to herself.

He put on his waistcoat and his coat, and pushed a way through to the path again.

The last level rays of the sun touched the wood. 'I won't come with you,' he said; 'better not.'

She looked at him wistfully before she turned. His dog was waiting so anxiously for him to go, and he seemed to have nothing whatever to say. Nothing left.

Connie went slowly home, realising the depth of the other thing in her. Another self was alive in her, burning molten and soft in her womb and bowels, and with this self she adored him. She adored him till her knees were weak as she walked. In her womb and bowels she was flowing and alive now and vulnerable, and helpless in adoration of him as the most naïve woman. It feels like a child, she said to herself; it feels like a child in me. And so it did, as if her womb, that had always been shut, had opened and filled with new life, almost a burden, yet lovely.

'If I had a child!' she thought to herself; 'if I had him inside me as a child!' – and her limbs turned molten at the thought, and she realised the immense difference between having a child to oneself, and having a child to a man whom one's bowels yearned towards. The former seemed in a sense ordinary: but to have a child to a man whom one adored in one's bowels and one's womb, it made her feel she was very different from her old self, and as if she was sinking deep, deep to the centre of all womanhood and the sleep of creation.

It was not the passion that was new to her, it was the yearning adoration. She knew she had always feared it, for it left her helpless; she feared it still, lest if she adored him too much, then she would lose herself, become effaced, and she did not want to be effaced, a slave, like a savage woman. She must not become a slave. She feared her adoration, yet she would not at once fight against it. She knew she could fight it. She had a devil of self-will in her breast that could have fought the full soft heaving adoration of her womb and crushed it. She could even now do it, or she thought so, and she could then take up her passion with her own will.

Ah yes, to be passionate like a Bacchante, like a Bacchanal fleeing through the woods, to call on Iacchos,[61] the bright phallos that had no independent personality behind it, but was pure god-servant to the woman! The man, the individual, let him not dare intrude. He was but a temple-servant, the bearer and keeper of the bright phallos, her own.

So, in the flux of new awakening, the old hard passion flamed in her for a time, and the man dwindled to a contemptible object, the mere phallos-bearer, to be torn to pieces when his service was performed. She felt the force of the Bacchae in her limbs and her body, the woman gleaming and rapid, beating down the male; but while she felt this, her heart was heavy. She did not want it, it was known and barren, birthless; the adoration was her treasure. It was so fathomless, so soft, so deep and so unknown. No, no, she would give up her hard bright female power; she was weary of it, stiffened with it; she would sink in the new bath of life, in the depths of her womb and her bowels that sang the voiceless song of adoration. It was early yet to begin to fear the man.

'I walked over by Marehay, and I had tea with Mrs Flint,' she said to Clifford. 'I wanted to see the baby. It's so adorable, with hair like red cobwebs. Such a dear! Mr Flint had gone to market, so she and I and the baby had tea together. Did you wonder where I was?'

'Well, I wondered, but I guessed you had dropped in somewhere to tea,' said Clifford jealously. With a sort of second sight he sensed something new in her, something to him quite incomprehensible, but he ascribed it to the baby. He thought that all that ailed Connie was that she did not have a baby, automatically bring one forth, so to speak.

'I saw you go across the park to the iron gate, my Lady,' said Mrs Bolton; 'so I thought perhaps you'd called at the Rectory.'

'I nearly did, then I turned towards Marehay instead.'

The eyes of the two women met: Mrs Bolton's grey and bright and searching; Connie's blue and veiled and strangely beautiful. Mrs Bolton was almost sure she had a lover, yet how could it be, and who could it be? Where was there a man?

'Oh, it's so good for you, if you go out and see a bit of company sometimes,' said Mrs Bolton. 'I was saying to Sir Clifford, it would do her Ladyship a world of good if she'd go out among people more.'

'Yes, I'm glad I went, and such a quaint dear cheeky baby, Clifford,' said Connie. 'It's got hair just like spider-webs, and bright orange, and the oddest, cheekiest, pale-blue china eyes. Of course it's a girl, or it wouldn't be so bold, bolder than any little Sir Francis Drake.'

'You're right, my Lady – a regular little Flint. They were always a forward sandy-headed family,' said Mrs Bolton.

'Wouldn't you like to see it, Clifford? I've asked them to tea for you to see it.'

'Who?' he asked, looking at Connie in great uneasiness.

'Mrs Flint and the baby, next Monday.'

'You can have them to tea up in your room,' he said.

'Why, don't you want to see the baby?' she cried.

'Oh, I'll see it, but I don't want to sit through a tea-time with them.'

'Oh,' said Connie, looking at him with wide veiled eyes.

She did not really see him, he was somebody else.

'You can have a nice cosy tea up in your room, my Lady, and Mrs Flint will be more comfortable than if Sir Clifford was there,' said Mrs Bolton.

She was sure Connie had a lover, and something in her soul exulted. But who was he? Who was he? Perhaps Mrs Flint would provide a clue.

Connie would not take her bath this evening. The sense of his flesh touching her, his very stickiness upon her, was dear to her, and in a sense holy.

Clifford was very uneasy. He would not let her go after dinner, and she had wanted so much to be alone. She looked at him, but was curiously submissive.

'Shall we play a game, or shall I read to you, or what shall it be?' he asked uneasily.

'You read to me,' said Connie.

'What shall I read – verse or prose? Or drama?'

'Read Racine,' she said.

It had been one of his stunts in the past, to read Racine in the real French grand manner, but he was rusty now, and a little self-conscious; he really preferred the loudspeaker. But Connie was sewing, sewing a little silk frock of primrose silk, cut out of one of her dresses, for Mrs Flint's baby. Between coming home and dinner she had cut it out, and she sat in the soft quiescent rapture of herself, sewing, while the noise of the reading went on.

Inside herself she could feel the humming of passion, like the after-humming of deep bells.

Clifford said something to her about the Racine. She caught the sense after the words had gone.

'Yes! Yes!' she said, looking up at him. 'It *is* splendid.'

Again he was frightened at the deep blue blaze of her eyes, and of her soft stillness, sitting there. She had never been so utterly soft and still. She fascinated him helplessly, as if some perfume about her intoxicated him. So he went on helplessly with his reading, and the throaty sound of the French was like the wind in the chimneys to her. Of the Racine she heard not one syllable.

She was gone in her own soft rapture, like a forest soughing with the dim, glad moan of spring, moving into bud. She could feel in the same world with her the man, the nameless man, moving on beautiful feet, beautiful in the phallic mystery. And in herself, in all her veins, she felt him and his child. His child was in all her veins, like a twilight.

'For hands she hath none, nor eyes, nor feet, nor golden Treasure of hair . . .'[62]

She was like a forest, like the dark interlacing of the oak-wood, humming inaudibly with myriad unfolding buds. Meanwhile the birds of desire were asleep in the vast interlaced intricacy of her body.

But Clifford's voice went on, clapping and gurgling with unusual sounds. How extraordinary it was! How extraordinary he was, bent there over the book, queer and rapacious and civilised, with broad shoulders and no real legs! What a strange creature, with the sharp, cold inflexible will of some bird, and no warmth, no warmth at all! One of those creatures of the afterwards, that have no soul, but an extra-alert will, cold will. She shuddered a little, afraid of him. But then, the soft warm flame of life was stronger than he, and the real things were hidden from him.

The reading finished. She was startled. She looked up, and was more startled still to see Clifford watching her with pale, uncanny eyes, like hate.

'Thank you *so* much! You do read Racine beautifully!' she said softly.

'Almost as beautifully as you listen to him,' he said cruelly.

'What are you making?' he asked.

'I'm making a child's dress, for Mrs Flint's baby.'

He turned away. A child! A child! That was all her obsession.

'After all,' he said, in a declamatory voice, 'one gets all one wants out of Racine. Emotions that are ordered and given shape are more important than disorderly emotions.'

She watched him with wide, vague, veiled eyes.

'Yes, I'm sure they are,' she said.

'The modern world has only vulgarised emotion by letting it loose. What we need is classic control.'

'Yes,' she said slowly, thinking of him listening with vacant face to the emotional idiocy of the radio. 'People pretend to have emotions, and they really feel nothing. I suppose that is being romantic.'

'Exactly!' he said.

As a matter of fact, he was tired. This evening had tired him. He would rather have been with his technical books, or his pit-manager, or listening-in to the radio.

Mrs Bolton came in with two glasses of malted milk: for Clifford, to make him sleep, and for Connie, to fatten her again. It was a regular nightcap she had introduced.

Connie was glad to go, when she had drunk her glass, and thankful she needn't help Clifford to bed. She took his glass and put it on the tray, then took the tray, to leave it outside.

'Good-night Clifford! *Do* sleep well! The Racine gets into one like a dream. Good-night!'

She had drifted to the door. She was going without kissing him good-night. He watched her with sharp, cold eyes. So! She did not even kiss him good-night, after he had spent an evening reading to her. Such depths of callousness in her! Even if the kiss was but a formality, it was on such formalities that life depends. She was a Bolshevik, really. Her instincts were Bolshevistic! He gazed coldly and angrily at the door whence she had gone. Anger!

And again the dread of the night came on him. He was a network of nerves, and when he was not braced up to work, and so full of energy: or when he was not listening-in, and so utterly neuter: then he was haunted by anxiety and a sense of dangerous impending void. He was afraid. And Connie could keep the fear off him, if she would. But it was obvious she wouldn't, she wouldn't. She was callous, cold and callous to all that he did for her. He gave up his life for her, and she was callous to him. She only wanted her own way. 'The lady loves her will.'

Now it was a baby she was obsessed by. Just so that it should be her own, all her own, and not his!

Clifford was so healthy, considering. He looked so well and ruddy in the face, his shoulders were broad and strong, his chest deep, he had put on flesh. And yet, at the same time, he was afraid of death. A terrible hollow seemed to menace him somewhere, somehow, a void, and into this void his energy would collapse. Energyless, he felt at times he was dead, really dead.

So his rather prominent pale eyes had a queer look, furtive, and yet a little cruel, so cold: and at the same time, almost impudent. It was a very odd look, this look of impudence: as if he were triumphing over life in spite of life. 'Who knoweth the mysteries of the will – for it can triumph even against the angels – ' [63]

But his dread was the nights when he could not sleep. Then it was awful indeed, when annihilation pressed in on him on every side. Then it was ghastly, to exist without having any life: lifeless, in the night, to exist.

But now he could ring for Mrs Bolton. And she would always come.

That was a great comfort. She would come in her dressing-gown, with her hair in a plait down her back, curiously girlish and dim, though the brown plait was streaked with grey. And she would make him coffee or camomile tea, and she would play chess or piquet with him. She had a woman's queer faculty of playing even chess well enough, when she was three parts asleep, well enough to make her worth beating. So, in the silent intimacy of the night, they sat, or she sat and he lay on the bed, with the reading-lamp shedding its solitary light on them, she almost gone in sleep, he almost gone in a sort of fear, and they played, played together – then they had a cup of coffee and a biscuit together, hardly speaking, in the silence of night, but being a reassurance to one another.

And this night she was wondering who Lady Chatterley's lover was. And she was thinking of her own Ted, so long dead, yet for her never quite dead. And when she thought of him, the old, old grudge against the world rose up, but especially against the masters, that they had killed him. They had not really killed him. Yet, to her, emotionally, they had. And somewhere deep in herself, because of it, she was a nihilist, and really anarchic.

In her half-sleep, thoughts of her Ted and thoughts of Lady Chatterley's unknown lover commingled, and then she felt she shared with the other woman a great grudge against Sir Clifford and all he stood for. At the same time she was playing piquet with him, and they were gambling sixpences. And it was a source of satisfaction to be playing piquet with a baronet, and even losing sixpences to him.

When they played cards, they always gambled. It made him forget himself. And he usually won. Tonight too he was winning. So he would not go to sleep till the first dawn appeared. Luckily it began to appear at half-past four or thereabouts.

Connie was in bed, and fast asleep all this time. But the keeper, too, could not rest. He had closed the coops and made his round of the wood, then gone home and eaten supper. But he did not go to bed. Instead he sat by the fire and thought.

He thought of his boyhood in Tevershall, and of his five or six years of married life. He thought of his wife, and always bitterly. She had seemed so brutal. But he had not seen her now since 1915, in the spring when he joined up. Yet there she was, not three miles away, and more brutal than ever. He hoped never to see her again while he lived.

He thought of his life abroad, as a soldier. India, Egypt, then India again: the blind, thoughtless life with the horses: the colonel who had loved him and whom he had loved: the several years that he had been an officer, a lieutenant with a very fair chance of being a captain. Then the death of the colonel from pneumonia, and his own narrow escape from death: his damaged health: his deep restlessness: his leaving the army and coming back to England to be a working man again.

He was temporising with life. He had thought he would be safe, at least for a time, in this wood. There was no shooting as yet: he had to rear the pheasants. He would have no guns to serve. He would be alone, and apart from life, which was all he wanted. He had to have some sort of a background. And this was his native place. There was even his mother, though she had never meant very much to him. And he could go on in life, existing from day to day, without connection and without hope. For he did not know what to do with himself.

He did not know what to do with himself. Since he had been an officer for some years, and had mixed among the other officers and civil servants, with their wives and families, he had lost all ambition to 'get on'. There was a toughness, a curious rubber-necked toughness and unlivingness about the middle and upper classes, as he had known them, which just left him feeling cold and different from them.

So, he had come back to his own class. To find there, what he had forgotten during his absence of years, a pettiness and a vulgarity of manner extremely distasteful. He admitted now at last, how important manner was. He admitted, also, how important it was even *to pretend* not to care about the halfpence and the small things of life. But among the common people there was no pretence. A penny more or less on the bacon was worse than a change in the Gospel. He could not stand it.

And again, there was the wage-squabble. Having lived among the owning classes, he knew the utter futility of expecting any solution of the wage-squabble. There was no solution, short of death. The only thing was not to care, not to care about the wages.

Yet, if you were poor and wretched you *had* to care. Anyhow, it was becoming the only thing they did care about. The *care* about money was like a great cancer, eating away the individuals of all classes. He refused to *care* about money.

And what then? What did life offer apart from the care of money? Nothing.

Yet he could live alone, in the wan satisfaction of being alone, and raise pheasants to be shot ultimately by fat men after breakfast. It was futility, futility to the nth power.

But why care, why bother? And he had not cared nor bothered till now, when this woman had come into his life. He was nearly ten years older than she. And he was a thousand years older in experience, starting from the bottom. The connection between them was growing closer. He could see the day when it would clinch up and they would have to make a life together. 'For the bonds of love are ill to loose!'

And what then? What then? Must he start again, with nothing to start on? Must he entangle this woman? Must he have the horrible broil with her lame husband? And also some sort of horrible broil with his own brutal wife, who hated him? Misery! lots of misery! And he was no longer young and merely buoyant. Neither was he the insouciant sort. Every bitterness and every ugliness would hurt him: and the woman!

But even if they got clear of Sir Clifford and of his own wife, even if they got clear, what were they going to do? What was he, himself, going to do? What was he going to do with his life? For he must do something. He couldn't be a mere hanger-on, on her money and his own very small pension.

It was the insoluble. He could only think of going to America, to try a new air. He disbelieved in the dollar utterly. But perhaps, perhaps there was something else.

He could not rest nor even go to bed. After sitting in a stupor of bitter thoughts until midnight, he got suddenly from his chair and reached for his coat and gun.

'Come on, lass,' he said to the dog. 'We're best outside.'

It was a starry night, but moonless. He went on a slow, scrupulous, soft-stepping and stealthy round. The only thing he had to contend with was the colliers setting snares for rabbits, particularly the Stacks Gate colliers, on the Marehay side. But it was breeding season, and even colliers respected it a little. Nevertheless the stealthy beating of the round in search of poachers soothed his nerves and took his mind off his thoughts.

But when he had done his slow, cautious beating of his bounds – it was nearly a five-mile walk – he was tired. He went to the top of the knoll and looked out. There was no sound save the noise, the faint shuffling noise from Stacks Gate colliery, that never ceased working: and there were hardly any lights, save the brilliant electric rows at the works. The world lay darkly and fumily sleeping. It was half-past two. But even in its sleep it was an uneasy, cruel world, stirring with the noise of a train or some great lorry on the road, and flashing with some rosy lightning-flash from the furnaces. It was a world of iron and coal, the cruelty of iron and the smoke of coal, and the endless, endless greed that drove it all. Only greed, greed stirring in its sleep.

It was cold, and he was coughing. A fine cold draught blew over the knoll. He thought of the woman. Now he would have given all he had or ever might have to hold her warm in his arms, both of them wrapped in one blanket, and sleep. All hopes of eternity and all gain from the past he would have given to have her there, to be wrapped warm with him in one blanket, and sleep, only sleep. It seemed the sleep with the woman in his arms was the only necessity.

He went to the hut, and wrapped himself in the blanket and lay on the floor to sleep. But he could not, he was cold. And besides, he felt cruelly his own unfinished nature. He felt his own unfinished condition of aloneness cruelly. He wanted her, to touch her, to hold her fast against him in one moment of completeness and sleep.

He got up again and went out, towards the park gates this time: then slowly along the path towards the house. It was nearly four o'clock, still clear and cold, but no sign of dawn. He was used to the dark, he could see well.

Slowly, slowly the great house drew him, as a magnet. He wanted to be near her. It was not desire, not that. It was the cruel sense of unfinished aloneness, that needed a silent woman folded in his arms. Perhaps he could find her. Perhaps he could even call her out to him: or find some way in to her. For the need was imperious.

He slowly, silently climbed the incline to the hall. Then he came round the great trees at the top of the knoll, on to the drive, which made a grand sweep round a lozenge of grass in front of the entrance. He could already see the two magnificent beeches which stood in this big level lozenge in front of the house, detaching themselves darkly in the dark air.

There was the house, low and long and obscure, with one light burning downstairs, in Sir Clifford's room. But which room she was in, the woman who held the other end of the frail thread which drew him so mercilessly, that he did not know.

He went a little nearer, gun in hand, and stood motionless on the drive, watching the house. Perhaps even now he could find her, come at her in some way. The house was not impregnable: he was as clever as burglars are. Why not come to her?

He stood motionless, waiting, while the dawn faintly and imperceptibly paled behind him. He saw the light in the house go out. But he did not see Mrs Bolton come to the window and draw back the old curtain of dark-blue silk, and stand herself in the dark room, looking out on the half-dark of the approaching day, looking for the longed-for dawn, waiting, waiting for Clifford to be really reassured that it was daybreak. For when he was sure of daybreak, he would sleep almost at once.

She stood blind with sleep at the window, waiting. And as she stood, she started, and almost cried out. For there was a man out there on the drive, a black figure in the twilight. She woke up greyly, and watched, but without making a sound to disturb Sir Clifford.

The daylight began to rustle into the world, and the dark figure seemed to go smaller and more defined. She made out the gun and gaiters and baggy jacket – it would be Oliver Mellors, the keeper. Yes, for there was the dog nosing around like a shadow, and waiting for him!

And what did the man want? Did he want to rouse the house? What was he standing there for, transfixed, looking up at the house like a love-sick male dog outside the house where the bitch is?

Goodness! The knowledge went through Mrs Bolton like a shot. He was Lady Chatterley's lover! He! He!

To think of it! Why, she, Ivy Bolton, had once been a tiny bit in love with him herself! When he was a lad of sixteen and she a woman of twenty-six. It was when she was studying, and he had helped her a lot with the anatomy and things she had had to learn. He'd been a clever boy, had a scholarship for Sheffield Grammar School, and learned French and things: and then after all had become an over-head blacksmith shoeing horses, because he was fond of horses, he said: but really because he was frightened to go out and face the world, only he'd never admit it.

But he'd been a nice lad, a nice lad, had helped her a lot, so clever at making things clear to you. He was quite as clever as Sir Clifford, and always one for the women. More with women than men, they said.

Till he'd gone and married that Bertha Coutts, as if to spite himself. Some people do marry to spite themselves, because they're disappointed of something. And no wonder it had been a failure. For years he was gone, all the time of the war: and a lieutenant and all: quite the gentleman, really quite the gentleman! Then to come back to Tevershall and go as a gamekeeper! Really, some people can't take their chances when they've got them! And talking broad Derbyshire again like the worst, when she, Ivy Bolton, knew he spoke like any gentleman, *really*.

Well, well! So her Ladyship had fallen for him! Well – her Ladyship wasn't the first: there was something about him. But fancy! A Tevershall lad born and bred, and she her Ladyship in

Wragby Hall! My word, that was a slap back at the high-and-mighty Chatterleys!

But he, the keeper, as the day grew, had realised: it's no good! It's no good trying to get rid of your own aloneness. You've got to stick to it all your life. Only at times, at times, the gap will be filled in. At times! But you have to wait for the times. Accept your own aloneness and stick to it, all your life. And then accept the times when the gap is filled in, when they come. But they've got to come. You can't force them.

With a sudden snap the bleeding desire that had drawn him after her broke. He had broken it, because it must be so. There must be a coming together on both sides. And if she wasn't coming to him, he wouldn't track her down. He mustn't. He must go away, till she came.

He turned slowly, ponderingly, accepting again the isolation. He knew it was better so. She must come to him: it was no use his trailing after her. No use!

Mrs Bolton saw him disappear, saw his dog run after him.

'Well, well!' she said. 'He's the one man I never thought of; and the one man I might have thought of. He was nice to me when he was a lad, after I lost Ted. Well, well! Whatever would *he* say if he knew!'

And she glanced triumphantly at the already sleeping Clifford, as she stepped softly from the room.

Chapter 11

CONNIE WAS SORTING OUT one of the Wragby lumber rooms. There were several: the house was a warren, and the family never sold anything. Sir Geoffrey's father had liked pictures and Sir Geoffrey's mother had liked *cinquecento*[65] furniture. Sir Geoffrey himself had liked old carved oak chests, vestry chests. So it went on through the generations. Clifford collected very modern pictures, at very moderate prices.

So in the lumber room there were bad Sir Edwin Landseers and pathetic William Henry Hunt[66] birds' nests: and other Academy stuff, enough to frighten the daughter of an R.A. She determined to look through it one day, and clear it all. And the grotesque furniture interested her.

Wrapped up carefully to preserve it from damage and dry-rot was the old family cradle, of rosewood. She had to unwrap it, to look at it. It had a certain charm: she looked at it a long time.

'It's a thousand pities it won't be called for,' sighed Mrs Bolton, who was helping. 'Though cradles like that are out of date nowadays.'

'It might be called for. I might have a child,' said Connie casually, as if saying she might have a new hat.

'You mean if anything happened to Sir Clifford!' stammered Mrs Bolton.

'No! I mean as things are. It's only muscular paralysis with Sir Clifford – it doesn't affect *him*,' said Connie, lying as naturally as breathing.

Clifford had put the idea into her head. He had said: 'Of course *I* may have a child yet. I'm not really mutilated at all. The potency may easily come back, even if the muscles of the hips and legs are paralysed. And then the seed may be transferred.'

He really felt, when he had his periods of energy and worked so hard at the question of the mines, as if his sexual potency were returning. Connie had looked at him in terror. But she was quite quick-witted enough to use his suggestion for her own preservation. For she would have a child if she could: but not his.

Mrs Bolton was for a moment breathless, flabbergasted. Then she didn't believe it: she saw in it a ruse. Yet doctors could do such things nowadays. They might sort of graft seed.

'Well, my Lady, I only hope and pray you may. It would be lovely for you: and for everybody. My word, a child in Wragby, what a difference it would make!'

'Wouldn't it!' said Connie.

And she chose three R.A. pictures of sixty years ago, to send to the Duchess of Shortlands for that lady's next charitable bazaar. She was called 'the bazaar duchess', and she always asked all the county to send things for her to sell. She would be delighted with three framed R.A.s. She might even call, on the strength of them. How furious Clifford was when she called!

But oh my dear! Mrs Bolton was thinking to herself. Is it Oliver Mellors' child you're preparing us for? Oh my dear, that *would* be a Tevershall baby in the Wragby cradle, my word! Wouldn't shame it, neither!

Among other monstrosities in this lumber room was a largeish black japanned box, excellently and ingeniously made some sixty or seventy years ago, and fitted with every imaginable object. On top was a concentrated toilet set: brushes, bottles, mirrors, combs, boxes, even three beautiful little razors in safety sheaths, shaving-bowl and all. Underneath came a sort of escritoire outfit: blotters, pens, ink-bottles, paper, envelopes, memorandum books: and then a perfect sewing-outfit, with three different-sized scissors, thimbles, needles, silks and cottons, darning egg, all of the very best quality and perfectly finished. Then there was a little medicine store, with bottles labelled Laudanum, Tincture of Myrrh, Ess. Cloves and so on: but empty. Everything was perfectly new, and the whole thing, when shut up, was as big as a small, but fat weekend bag. And inside, it fitted together like a puzzle. The bottles could not possibly have spilled: there wasn't room.

The thing was wonderfully made and contrived, excellent craftsmanship of the Victorian order. But somehow it was monstrous. Some Chatterley must even have felt it, for the thing had never been used. It had a peculiar soullessness.

Yet Mrs Bolton was thrilled.

'Look what beautiful brushes, so expensive, even the shaving brushes, three perfect ones! No! and those scissors! They're the best that money could buy. Oh, I call it lovely!'

'Do you?' said Connie. 'Then you have it.'

'Oh no, my Lady!'

'Of course! It will only lie here till Doomsday. If you won't have it, I'll send it to the Duchess as well as the pictures, and she doesn't deserve so much. Do have it!'

'Oh your Ladyship! Why, I shall never be able to thank you.'

'You needn't try,' laughed Connie.

And Mrs Bolton sailed down with the huge and very black box in her arms, flushing bright pink in her excitement.

Mr Betts drove her in the trap to her house in the village, with the box. And she *had* to have a few friends in, to show it: the schoolmistress, the chemist's wife, Mrs Weedon the under-cashier's wife. They thought it marvellous. And then started the whisper of Lady Chatterley's child.

'Wonders'll never cease!' said Mrs Weedon.

But Mrs Bolton was *convinced*, if it did come, it would be Sir Clifford's child. So there!

Not long after, the rector said gently to Clifford, 'And may we really hope for an heir to Wragby? Ah, that would be the hand of God in mercy, indeed!'

'Well! We may *hope*,' said Clifford, with a faint irony, and at the same time, a certain conviction. He had begun to believe it really possible it might even be *his* child.

Then one afternoon came Leslie Winter, Squire Winter, as everybody called him: lean, immaculate, and seventy: and every inch a gentleman, as Mrs Bolton said to Mrs Betts. Every millimetre indeed!

And with his old-fashioned, rather haw-haw! manner of speaking, he seemed more out of date than bag wigs.[67] Time, in her flight, drops these fine old feathers.

They discussed the collieries. Clifford's idea was, that his coal, even the poor sort, could be made into hard concentrated fuel that would burn at great heat if fed with certain damp, acidulated air at a fairly strong pressure. It had long been observed that in a particularly strong, wet wind the pit-bank burned very vivid, gave off hardly any fumes, and left a fine powder of ash, instead of the slow pink gravel.

'But where will you find the proper engines for burning your fuel?' asked Winter.

'I'll make them myself. And I'll use my fuel myself. And I'll sell electric power. I'm certain I could do it.'

'If you can do it, then splendid, splendid, my dear boy. Haw! Splendid! If I can be of any help, I shall be delighted. I'm afraid I am a little out of date, and my collieries are like me. But who knows, when I'm gone, there may be men like you. Splendid! It will employ all the men again, and you won't have to sell your coal, or fail to sell it. A splendid idea, and I hope it will be a success. If I had sons of my own, no doubt they would have up-to-date ideas for Shipley: no doubt! By the way, dear boy, is there any foundation to the rumour that we may entertain hopes of an heir to Wragby?'

'Is there a rumour?' asked Clifford.

'Well, my dear boy, Marshall from Fillingwood asked *me*, that's all I can say about a rumour. Of course I wouldn't repeat it for the world, if there were no foundation.'

'Well, Sir,' said Clifford uneasily, but with strange bright eyes. 'There is a hope. There is a hope.'

Winter came across the room and wrung Clifford's hand.

'My dear boy, my dear lad, can you believe what it means to me, to hear that! And to hear you are working in the hopes of a son: and that you may again employ every man at Tevershall. Ah, my boy! to keep up the level of the race, and to have work waiting for any man who cares to work! – '

The old man was really moved.

Next day Connie was arranging tall yellow tulips in a glass vase.

'Connie,' said Clifford, 'did you know there was a rumour that you are going to supply Wragby with a son and heir?'

Connie felt dim with terror, yet she stood quite still, touching the flowers.

'No!' she said. 'Is it a joke? Or malice?'

He paused before he answered: 'Neither, I hope. I hope it may be a prophecy.'

Connie went on with her flowers.

'I had a letter from Father this morning,' she said. 'He wants to know if I am aware he has accepted Sir Alexander Cooper's invitation for me for July and August, to the Villa Esmeralda in Venice.'

'July *and* August?' said Clifford.

'Oh, I wouldn't stay all that time. Are you sure you wouldn't come?'

'I won't travel abroad,' said Clifford promptly.

She took her flowers to the window.

'Do you mind if I go?' she said. You know it was promised, for this summer.'

'For how long would you go?'

'Perhaps three weeks.'

There was silence for a time.

'Well,' said Clifford slowly, and a little gloomily, 'I suppose I could stand it for three weeks: if I were absolutely sure you'd want to come back.'

'I should want to come back,' she said, with quiet simplicity, heavy with conviction. She was thinking of the other man.

Clifford felt her conviction, and somehow he believed her, he believed it was for him. He felt immensely relieved, joyful at once.

'In that case,' he said, 'I think it would be all right, don't you?'

'I think so,' she said.

'You'd enjoy the change?'

She looked up at him with strange blue eyes.

'I should like to see Venice again,' she said, 'and to bathe from one of the shingle islands across the lagoon. But you know I loathe the Lido! And I don't fancy I shall like Sir Alexander Cooper and Lady Cooper. But if Hilda is there, and we have a gondola of our own: yes, it will be rather lovely. I *do* wish you'd come.'

She said it sincerely. She would so love to make him happy, in these ways.

'Ah, but think of me, though, at the Gare du Nord:[68] at Calais quay!'

'But why not? I see other men carried in litter-chairs, who have been wounded in the war. Besides, we'd motor all the way.'

'We should need to take two men.'

'Oh no! We'd manage with Field. There would always be another man there.'

But Clifford shook his head.

'Not this year, dear! Not this year! Next year probably I'll try.'

She went away gloomily. Next year! What would next year bring? She herself did not really want to go to Venice: not now, now there was the other man. But she was going as a sort of discipline: and also because, if she had a child, Clifford could think she had a lover in Venice.

It was already May, and in June they were supposed to start. Always these arrangements! Always one's life arranged for one! Wheels that worked one and drove one, and over which one had no real control!

It was May, but cold and wet again. A cold wet May, good for corn and hay! Much the corn and hay matter nowadays! Connie had to go into Uthwaite, which was their little town, where the Chatterleys were still *the* Chatterleys. She went alone, Field driving her.

In spite of May and a new greenness, the country was dismal. It was rather chilly, and there was smoke on the rain, and a certain sense of exhaust vapour in the air. One just had to live from one's resistance. No wonder these people were ugly and tough.

The car ploughed uphill through the long squalid straggle of Tevershall, the blackened brick dwellings, the black slate roofs glistening their sharp edges, the mud black with coal-dust, the pavements wet and black. It was as if dismalness had soaked through and through everything. The utter negation of natural beauty, the utter negation of the gladness of life, the utter absence of the instinct for shapely beauty which every bird and beast has, the utter death of the human intuitive faculty was appalling. The stacks of soap in the grocers' shops, the rhubarb and lemons in the green-grocers! the awful hats in the milliners! all went by ugly, ugly, ugly, followed by the plaster-and-gilt horror of the cinema with its wet picture announcements, 'A Woman's Love!', and the new big Primitive chapel, primitive enough in its stark brick and big panes of greenish and raspberry glass in the windows. The Wesleyan chapel, higher up, was of blackened brick and stood behind iron railings and blackened shrubs. The Congregational chapel, which thought itself superior, was built of rusticated sandstone and had a steeple, but not a very high one. Just beyond were the new school buildings, expensive pink brick, and gravelled playground inside iron railings, all very imposing, and mixing the suggestion of a chapel and a prison. Standard Five girls were having a singing lesson, just finishing the la-me-doh-la exercises and beginning a 'sweet children's song'. Anything more unlike song, spontaneous song, would be impossible to imagine: a strange bawling yell that followed the outlines of a tune. It was not like savages: savages have subtle rhythms. It was not like animals: animals *mean* something when they yell. It was like nothing on earth, and it was called singing. Connie sat and listened with her heart in her boots, as Field was filling petrol. What could possibly become of such a people, a people in whom the living intuitive faculty was dead as nails, and only queer mechanical yells and uncanny will-power remained?

A coal-cart was coming downhill, clanking in the rain. Field started upwards, past the big but weary-looking drapers and clothing shops, the post-office, into the little market-place of forlorn space, where Sam Black was peering out of the door of the Sun, that called itself an inn, not a pub, and where the commercial travellers stayed, and was bowing to Lady Chatterley's car.

The church was away to the left among black trees. The car slid on downhill, past the Miners' Arms. It had already passed the Wellington, the Nelson, the Three Tunns and the Sun, now it passed the Miners' Arms, then the Mechanics' Hall, then the new and almost gaudy Miners' Welfare and so, past a few new 'villas', out into the blackened road between dark hedges and dark green fields, towards Stacks Gate.

Teamshall! That was Tevershall! Merrie England! Shakespeare's England! No, but the England of today, as Connie had realised since she had come to live in it. It was producing a new race of mankind, over-conscious in the money and social and political side, on the spontaneous, intuitive side dead, but dead. Half-corpses, all of them: but with a terrible insistent consciousness in the other half. There was something uncanny and underground about it all. It was an underworld. And quite incalculable. How shall we understand the reactions in half-corpses? When Connie saw the great lorries full of steel-workers from Sheffield, weird, distorted smallish beings like men, off for an excursion to Matlock, her bowels fainted and she thought: Ah God, what has man done to man? What have the leaders of men been doing to their fellow men? They have reduced them to less than humanness; and now there can be no fellowship any more! It is just a nightmare.

She felt again in a wave of terror the grey, gritty hopelessness of it all. With such creatures for the industrial masses, and the upper classes as she knew them, there was no hope, no hope any more. Yet she was wanting a baby, and an heir to Wragby! An heir to Wragby! She shuddered with dread.

Yet Mellors had come out of all this! Yes, but he was as apart from it all as she was. Even in him there was no fellowship left. It was dead. The fellowship was dead. There was only apartness and hopelessness, as far as all this was concerned. And this was England, the vast bulk of England: as Connie knew, since she had motored from the centre of it.

The car was rising towards Stacks Gate. The rain was holding off, and in the air came a queer pellucid gleam of May. The country rolled away in long undulations, south towards the Peak, east towards Mansfield and Nottingham. Connie was travelling South.

As she rose on to the high country, she could see on her left, on a height above the rolling land, the shadowy, powerful bulk of Warsop Castle, dark grey, with below it the reddish plastering of miners' dwellings, newish, and below those the plumes of dark smoke and white steam from the great colliery which put so many thousand pounds per annum into the pockets of the Duke and the other shareholders. The powerful old castle was a ruin, yet still it hung its bulk on the low skyline, over the black plumes and the white that waved on the damp air below.

A turn, and they ran on the high level to Stacks Gate. Stacks Gate, as seen from the high road, was just a huge and gorgeous new hotel, the Coningsby Arms, standing red and white and gilt in barbarous isolation off the road. But if you looked, you saw on the left rows of handsome 'modern' dwellings, set down like a game of dominoes, with spaces and gardens, a queer game of dominoes that some weird 'masters' were playing on the surprised earth. And beyond these blocks of dwellings, at the back, rose all the astonishing and frightening overhead erections of a really modern mine, chemical works and long galleries, enormous, and of shapes not before known to man. The head-stocks and pit-bank of the mine itself were insignificant among the huge new installations. And in front of this, the game of dominoes stood forever in a sort of surprise, waiting to be played.

This was Stacks Gate, new on the face of the earth, since the war. But as a matter of fact, though even Connie did not know it, down-hill half a mile below the 'hotel' was old Stacks Gate, with a little old colliery and blackish old brick dwellings, and a chapel or two and a shop or two and a little pub or two.

But that didn't count any more. The vast plumes of smoke and vapour rose from the new works up above, and this was now Stacks Gate: no chapels, no pubs, even no shops. Only the great 'works', which are the modern Olympia with temples to all the gods; then the model dwellings: then the hotel. The hotel in actuality was nothing but a miners' pub, though it looked first-classy.

Even since Connie's arrival at Wragby this new place had arisen on the face of the earth, and the model dwellings had filled with riff-raff drifting in from anywhere, to poach Clifford's rabbits among other occupations.

The car ran on along the uplands, seeing the rolling county spread out. The county! It had once been a proud and lordly county. In front, looming again and hanging on the brow of the skyline, was the huge and splendid bulk of Chadwick Hall,[69] more window than wall, one of the most famous Elizabethan houses. Noble it stood alone above a great park, but out of date, passed over. It was still kept up, but as a show place. 'Look how our ancestors lorded it!'

That was the past. The present lay below. God alone knows where the future lies. The car was already turning, between little old blackened miners' cottages, to descend to Uthwaite. And Uthwaite, on a damp day, was sending up a whole array of smoke plumes and steam, to whatever gods there be. Uthwaite down in the valley, with all the steel threads of the railways to Sheffield drawn through it, and the coal-mines and the steel-works sending up smoke and glare from long tubes, and the pathetic little corkscrew spire of the church, that is going to tumble down, still pricking the fumes, always affected Connie strangely. It was an old market-town, centre of the dales. One of the chief inns was the Chatterley Arms. There, in Uthwaite, Wragby was known as Wragby, as if it were a whole place, not just a house, as it was to outsiders: Wragby Hall, near Tevershall: Wragby, a 'seat'.

The miners' cottages, blackened, stood flush on the pavement, with that intimacy and smallness of colliers' dwellings over a hundred years old. They lined all the way. The road had become a street, and as you sank, you forgot instantly the open, rolling country where the castles and big houses still dominated, but like ghosts. Now you were just above the tangle of naked railway-lines, and foundries and other 'works' rose about you, so big you were only aware of walls. And iron clanked with a huge reverberating clank, and huge lorries shook the earth, and whistles screamed.

Yet again, once you had got right down and into the twisted and crooked heart of the town, behind the church, you were in the world of two centuries ago, in the crooked streets where the Chatterley Arms stood, and the old pharmacy, streets which used to lead out to the wild open world of the castles and stately couchant houses.

But at the corner a policeman held up his hand as three lorries loaded with iron rolled past, shaking the poor old church. And not till the lorries were past could he salute her Ladyship.

So it was. Upon the old crooked burgess streets hordes of oldish, blackened miners' dwellings crowded, lining the roads out. And immediately after these came the newer, pinker rows of rather larger houses, plastering the valley: the homes of more modern workmen. And beyond that again, in the wide rolling regions of the castles, smoke waved against steam, and patch after patch of raw reddish brick showed the newer mining settlements, sometimes in the hollows, sometimes gruesomely ugly along the skyline of the slopes. And between, in between, were the tattered remnants of the old coaching and cottage England, even the England of Robin Hood, where the miners prowled with the dismalness of suppressed sporting instincts, when they were not at work.

England my England! But which is *my* England? The stately homes of England make good photographs, and create the illusion of a connection with the Elizabethans. The handsome old halls are there, from the days of Good Queen Anne and Tom Jones.[70] But smuts fall and blacken on the drab stucco, that has long ceased to be golden. And one by one, like the stately homes, they were abandoned. Now they are being pulled down. As for the cottages of England – there they are – great plasterings of brick dwellings on the hopeless countryside.

Now they are pulling down the stately homes, the Georgian halls are going. Fritchley, a perfect old Georgian mansion, was even now, as Connie passed in the car, being demolished. It was in perfect repair: till the war the Weatherleys had lived in style there. But now it was too big, too expensive, and the country had become too uncongenial. The gentry were departing to pleasanter places, where they could spend their money without having to see how it was made.

This is history. One England blots out another. The mines had made the halls wealthy. Now they were blotting them out, as they had already blotted out the cottages. The industrial England blots out the agricultural England. One meaning blots out another. The new England blots out the old England. And the continuity is not organic, but mechanical.

Connie, belonging to the leisured classes, had clung to the remnants of the old England. It had taken her years to realise that it was really blotted out by this terrifying new and gruesome England, and that the blotting out would go on till it was complete. Fritchley was gone, Eastwood was gone, Shipley was going: Squire Winter's beloved Shipley.

Connie called for a moment at Shipley. The park gates, at the back, opened just near the level crossing of the colliery railway; the Shipley colliery itself stood just beyond the trees. The gates stood open, because through the park was a right-of-way that the colliers used. They hung around the park.

The car passed the ornamental ponds, in which the colliers threw their newspapers, and took the private drive to the house. It stood above, aside, a very pleasant stucco building from the middle of the eighteenth century. It had a beautiful alley of yew trees, that had approached an older house, and the hall stood serenely spread out, winking its Georgian panes as if cheerfully. Behind, there were really beautiful gardens.

Connie liked the interior much better than Wragby. It was much lighter, more alive, shapen and elegant. The rooms were panelled with creamy-painted panelling, the ceilings were touched with gilt, and everything was kept in exquisite order, all the appointments were perfect, regardless of expense. Even the corridors managed to be ample and lovely, softly curved and full of life.

But Leslie Winter was alone. He had adored his house. But his park was bordered by three of his own collieries. He had been a generous man in his ideas. He had almost welcomed the colliers in his park. Had the miners not made him rich! So, when he saw the gangs of unshapely men lounging by his ornamental waters – not on the *private* part of the park, no, he drew the line there – he would say: 'The miners are perhaps not so ornamental as deer, but they are far more profitable.'

But that was in the golden – monetarily – latter half of Queen Victoria's reign. Miners were then 'good working men'.

Winter had made this speech, half apologetic, to his guest, the then Prince of Wales. And the Prince had replied, in his rather guttural English, 'You are quite right. If there were coal under Sandringham,[71] I would open a mine on the lawns, and think it first-rate landscape gardening. Oh, I am quite willing to exchange roe-deer for colliers, at the price. Your men are good men too, I hear.'

But then, the Prince had perhaps an exaggerated idea of the beauty of money, and the blessings of industrialism.

However, the Prince had been a King, and the King had died, and now there was another King, whose chief function seemed to be to open soup-kitchens.

And the good working men were somehow hemming Shipley in. New mining villages crowded on the park, and the squire felt somehow that the population was alien. He used to feel, in a good-natured but quite grand way, lord of his own domain and of his own colliers. Now, by a subtle pervasion of the new spirit, he had somehow been pushed out. It was he who did not belong any more.

There was no mistaking it. The mines, the industry, had a will of its own, and this will was against the gentleman-owner. All the colliers took part in the will, and it was hard to live up against it. It either shoved you out of the place, or out of life altogether.

Squire Winter, a soldier, had stood it out. But he no longer cared to walk in the park after dinner. He almost hid, indoors. Once he had walked, bareheaded, and in his patent-leather shoes and purple silk socks, with Connie down to the gate, talking to her in his well-bred rather haw-haw fashion. But when it came to passing the little gangs of colliers who stood and stared without either salute or anything else, Connie felt how the lean, well-bred old man winced, winced as an elegant antelope stag in a cage winces from the vulgar stare. The colliers were not *personally* hostile: not at all. But their spirit was cold, and shoving him out. And deep down, there was a profound grudge. They 'worked for him'. And in their ugliness, they resented his elegant, well-groomed, well-bred existence. 'Who's he!' It was the *difference* they resented.

And somewhere, in his secret English heart, being a good deal of a soldier, he believed they were right to resent the difference. He felt himself a little in the wrong, for having all the advantages. Nevertheless he represented a system, and he would not be shoved out.

Except by death. Which came on him soon after Connie's call, suddenly. And he remembered Clifford handsomely in his will.

The heirs at once gave out the order for the demolishing of Shipley. It cost too much to keep up. No one would live there. So it was broken up. The avenue of yews was cut down. The park was denuded of its timber, and divided into lots. It was near enough to Uthwaite. In the strange, bald desert of this still-one-more no-man's-land, new little streets of semi-detacheds were run up, very desirable! The Shipley Hall Estate!

Within a year of Connie's last call, it had happened. There stood Shipley Hall Estate, an array of red-brick semi-detached 'villas' in new streets. No one would have dreamed that the stucco hall had stood there twelve months before.

But this is a later stage of King Edward's landscape gardening, the sort that has an ornamental coal-mine on the lawn.

One England blots out another. The England of the Squire Winters and the Wragby Halls was gone, dead. The blotting out was only not yet complete.

What would come after? Connie could not imagine. She could only see the new brick streets spreading into the fields, the new erections rising at the collieries, the new girls in their silk stockings, the new collier lads lounging into the Pally or the Welfare. The younger generation were utterly unconscious of the old England. There was a gap in the continuity of consciousness, almost American: but industrial really. What next?

Connie always felt there was no next. She wanted to hide her head in the sand: or at least, in the bosom of a living man.

The world was so complicated and weird and gruesome! The common people were so many, and really so terrible. So she thought as she was going home, and saw the colliers trailing from the pits, grey-black, distorted, one shoulder higher than the other, slurring their heavy ironshod boots. Underground grey faces, whites of eyes rolling, necks cringing from the pit roof, shoulders out of shape. Men! Men! Alas, in some ways patient and good men. In other ways, non-existent. Something that men *should* have was bred and killed out of them. Yet they were men. They begot children. One might bear a child to them. Terrible, terrible thought! They were good and kindly. But they were only half, only the grey half of a human being. As yet, they were 'good'. But even that was the goodness of their halfness. Supposing the dead in them ever rose up! But no, it was too terrible to think of. Connie was absolutely afraid of the industrial masses. They seemed so *weird* to her. A life with utterly no beauty in it, no intuition, always 'in the pit'.

Children from such men! Oh God, oh God!

Yet Mellors had come from such a father. Not quite. Forty years had made a difference, an appalling difference in manhood. The iron and the coal had eaten deep into the bodies and souls of the men.

Incarnate ugliness, and yet alive! What would become of them all? Perhaps with the passing of the coal they would disappear again, off the face of the earth. They had appeared out of nowhere in their thousands, when the coal had called for them. Perhaps they were only weird fauna of the coal-seams. Creatures of another reality, they were elementals, serving the elements of coal, as the metal-workers were elementals, serving the element of iron. Men not men, but animas of coal and iron and clay. Fauna of the elements, carbon, iron, silicon: elementals. They had perhaps some of the weird, inhuman beauty of minerals, the lustre of coal, the weight and blueness and resistance of iron, the transparency of glass. Elemental creatures, weird and distorted, of the mineral world! They belonged to the coal, the iron, the clay, as fish belong to the sea and worms to dead wood. The anima of mineral disintegration!

Connie was glad to be home, to bury her head in the sand. She was glad even to babble to Clifford. For her fear of the mining and iron Midlands affected her with a queer feeling that went all over her, like influenza.

'Of course I had to have tea in Miss Bentley's shop,' she said.

'Really! Winter would have given you tea.'

'Oh yes, but I daren't disappoint Miss Bentley.'

Miss Bentley was a sallow old maid with a rather large nose and romantic disposition, who served tea with a careful intensity worthy of a sacrament.

'Did she ask after me?' said Clifford.

'Of course! *May* I ask your Ladyship how Sir Clifford is! I believe she ranks you even higher than Nurse Cavell!'[72]

'And I suppose you said I was blooming.'

'Yes! And she looked as rapt as if I had said the heavens had opened to you. I said if she ever came to Tevershall she was to come to see you.'

'Me! Whatever for! See me!'

'Why yes, Clifford. You can't be so adored without making some slight return. Saint George of Cappadocia[73] was nothing to you, in her eyes.'

'And do you think she'll come?'

'Oh, she blushed! and looked quite beautiful for a moment, poor thing! Why don't men marry the women who would really adore them?'

'The women start adoring too late. But did she say she'd come?'

'Oh!' Connie imitated the breathless Miss Bentley, 'your Ladyship, if ever I should dare to presume!'

'Dare to presume! how absurd! But I hope to God she won't turn up. And how was her tea?'

'Oh, Lipton's and *very* strong! But Clifford, do you realise you are the *Roman de la rose*[74] of Miss Bentley and lots like her?'

'I'm not flattered, even then.'

'They treasure up every one of your pictures in the illustrated papers, and probably pray for you every night. It's rather wonderful.'

She went upstairs to change.

That evening he said to her, 'You do think, don't you, that there is something eternal in marriage?'

She looked at him.

'But Clifford, you make eternity sound like a lid or a long, long chain that trailed after one, no matter how far one went.'

He looked at her, annoyed.

'What I mean,' he said, 'is that if you go to Venice, you won't go in the hopes of some love affair that you can take *au grand sérieux*, will you?'

'A love affair in Venice *au grand sérieux*? No, I assure you! No, I'd never take a love affair in Venice more than *au très petit sérieux*.'[75]

She spoke with a queer kind of contempt. He knitted his brows, looking at her.

Coming downstairs in the morning, she found the keeper's dog Flossie sitting in the corridor outside Clifford's room, and whimpering very faintly.

'Why Flossie!' she said softly. 'What are you doing here?'

And she quietly opened Clifford's door. Clifford was sitting up in bed, with the bed-table and typewriter pushed aside, and the keeper was standing at attention at the foot of the bed. Flossie ran in. With a faint gesture of head and eyes, Mellors ordered her to the door again, and she slunk out.

'Oh good-morning, Clifford!' Connie said. 'I didn't know you were busy.' Then she looked at the keeper, saying good-morning to him. He murmured his reply, looking at her as if vaguely. But she felt a whiff of passion touch her, from his mere presence.

'Did I interrupt you, Clifford? I'm sorry.'

'No, it's nothing of any importance.'

She slipped out of the room again, and up to the blue boudoir on the first floor. She sat in the window, and saw him go down the drive, with his curious, silent motion, effaced. He had a natural sort of quiet distinction, an aloof pride, and also a certain look of frailty. A hireling! One of Clifford's hirelings! 'The fault, dear Brutus, is not in our stars, but in ourselves, that we are underlings.'[76]

Was he an underling? Was he? What did he think of *her*?

It was a sunny day, and Connie was working in the garden, and Mrs Bolton was helping her. For some reason, the two women had drawn together, in one of the unaccountable flows and ebbs of sympathy that exist between people. They were pegging down carnations, and putting in small plants for the summer. It was work they both liked. Connie especially felt a delight in putting the soft roots of young plants into a soft black puddle, and cradling them down. On this spring morning she felt a quiver in her womb too, as if the sunshine had touched it and made it happy.

'It is many years since you lost your husband?' she said to Mrs Bolton, as she took up another little plant and laid it in its hole.

'Twenty-three!' said Mrs Bolton, as she carefully separated the young columbines into single plants. 'Twenty-three years since they brought him home.'

Connie's heart gave a lurch, at the terrible finality of it. 'Brought him home!'

'Why did he get killed, do you think?' she asked. 'He was happy with you?'

It was a woman's question to a woman. Mrs Bolton put aside a strand of hair from her face, with the back of her hand.

'I don't know, my Lady! He sort of wouldn't give in to things: he wouldn't really go with the rest. And then he hated ducking his head for anything on earth. A sort of obstinacy, that *gets* itself killed. You see he didn't really care. I lay it down to the pit. He ought never to have been down pit. But his dad made him go down, as a lad; and then, when you're over twenty, it's not very easy to come out.'

'Did he say he hated it?'

'Oh no! Never! He never said he hated anything. He just made a funny face. He was one of those who wouldn't take care: like some of the first lads as went off so blithe to the war and got killed right away. He wasn't really wezzle-brained.[77] But he wouldn't care. I used to say to him: "You care for nought nor nobody!" But he did! The way he sat when my first baby was born, motionless, and the sort of fatal eyes he looked at me with, when it was over! I had a bad time, but I had to comfort *him*. "It's all right, lad, it's all right!" I said to him. And he gave me a look, and that funny sort of smile. He never said anything. But I don't believe he had any right pleasure with me at nights after; he'd never really let himself go. I used to say to him: Oh, let thysen go, lad! I'd talk broad to him sometimes. And he said nothing. But he wouldn't let himself go, or he couldn't. He didn't want me to have any more children. I always blamed his mother, for letting him in th' room. He'd no right t'ave been there. Men makes so much more of things than they should, once they start brooding.'

'Did he mind so much?' said Connie in wonder.

'Yes, he sort of couldn't take it for natural, all that pain. And it spoilt his pleasure in his bit of married love. I said to him: "If I don't care, why should you? It's my look-out!" But all he'd ever say was: "It's not right!" '

'Perhaps he was too sensitive,' said Connie.

'That's it! When you come to know men, that's how they are: too sensitive in the wrong place. And I believe, unbeknown to himself, he hated the pit, just hated it. He looked so quiet when he was dead, as if he'd got free. He was such a nice-looking lad. It just broke my heart to see him, so still and pure looking, as if he'd *wanted* to die. Oh, it broke my heart, that did. But it was the pit.'

She wept a few bitter tears, and Connie wept more. It was a warm spring day, with a perfume of earth and of yellow flowers, many things rising to bud, and the garden still with the very sap of sunshine.

'It must have been terrible for you!' said Connie.

'Oh, my Lady! I never realised at first. I could only say: Oh my lad, what did you want to leave me for! That was all my cry. But somehow I felt he'd come back.'

'But he *didn't* want to leave you,' said Connie.

'Oh no, my Lady! That was only my silly cry. And I kept expecting him back. Especially at nights. I kept waking up thinking: Why he's not in bed with me! It was as if my *feelings* wouldn't believe he'd gone. I just felt he'd *have* to come back and lie against me, so I could feel him with me. That was all I wanted, to feel him there with me, warm. And it took me a thousand shocks before I knew he wouldn't come back, it took me years.'

'The touch of him,' said Connie.

'That's it, my Lady, the touch of him! I've never got over it to this day, and never shall. And if there's a heaven above, he'll be there, and will lie up against me so I can sleep.'

Connie glanced at the handsome, brooding face in fear. Another passionate one out of Tevershall! The touch of him! For the bonds of love are ill to loose!

'It's terrible, once you've got a man into your blood!' she said.

'Oh, my Lady! And that's what makes you feel so bitter. You feel folks *wanted* him killed. You feel the pit fair *wanted* to kill him. Oh, I felt, if it hadn't been for the pit, an' them as runs the pit, there'd have been no leaving me. But they all *want* to separate a woman and a man, if they're together.'

'If they're physically together,' said Connie.

'That's right, my Lady! There's a lot of hard-hearted folks in the world. And every morning when he got up and went to th' pit, I felt it was wrong, wrong. But what else could he do? What can a man do?'

A queer hate flared in the woman.

'But can a touch last so long?' Connie asked suddenly. 'That you could feel him so long?'

'Oh my Lady, what else is there to last? Children grows away from you. But the man, well – ! But even *that* they'd like to kill in you, the very thought of the touch of him. Even your own children! Ah well! We might have drifted apart, who knows. But the feeling's something different. It's 'appen better never to care. But there, when I look at women who's never really been warmed through by a man, well, they seem to me poor dool-owls[78] after all, no matter how they may dress up and gad. No, I'll abide by my own. I've not much respect for people.'

Chapter 12

CONNIE WENT TO THE WOOD directly after lunch. It was really a lovely day, the first dandelions making suns, the first daisies so white. The hazel thicket was a lace-work of half-open leaves, and the last dusty perpendicular of the catkins. Yellow celandines now were in crowds, flat open, pressed back in urgency, and the yellow glitter of themselves. It was the yellow, the powerful yellow of early summer. And primroses were broad, and full of pale abandon, thick-clustered primroses no longer shy. The lush, dark green of hyacinths was a sea, with buds rising like pale corn, while in the riding the forget-me-nots were fluffing up, and columbines were unfolding their ink-purple ruches, and there were bits of blue bird's-eggshell under a bush. Everywhere the bud-knots and the leap of life!

The keeper was not at the hut. Everything was serene, brown chickens running lustily. Connie walked on towards the cottage, because she wanted to find him.

The cottage stood in the sun, off the wood's edge. In the little garden the double daffodils rose in tufts, near the wide-open door, and red double daisies made a border to the path. There was the bark of a dog, and Flossie came running.

The wide-open door! so he was at home. And the sunlight falling on the red-brick floor! As she went up the path, she saw him through the window, sitting at the table in his shirt-sleeves, eating. The dog wuffed softly, slowly wagging her tail.

He rose, and came to the door, wiping his mouth with a red handkerchief, still chewing.

'May I come in?' she said.

'Come in!'

The sun shone into the bare room, which still smelled of a mutton chop, done in a dutch oven[79] before the fire, because the dutch oven still stood on the fender, with the black potato-saucepan on a piece of paper, beside it on the white hearth. The fire was red, rather low, the bar dropped, the kettle singing.

On the table was his plate, with potatoes and the remains of the chop; also bread in a basket, salt, and a blue mug with beer. The tablecloth was white oilcloth, he stood in the shade.

'You are very late,' she said. 'Do go on eating!'

She sat down on a wooden chair, in the sunlight by the door.

'I had to go to Uthwaite,' he said, sitting down at table but not eating.

'Do eat,' she said.

But he did not touch the food.

'Shall y'ave something?' he asked her. 'Shall y'ave a cup of tea? t' kettle's on t' boil.' He half rose again from his chair.

'If you'll let me make it myself,' she said, rising. He seemed sad, and she felt she was bothering him.

'Well, teapot's in there' – he pointed to a little, drab corner cupboard; 'an' cups. An' tea's on t' mantel ower yer 'ead.'

She got the black teapot, and the tin of tea from the mantelshelf. She rinsed the teapot with hot water, and stood a moment wondering where to empty it.

'Throw it out,' he said, aware of her. 'It's clean.'

She went to the door and threw the drop of water down the path. How lovely it was here, so still, so really woodland. The oaks were putting out ochre yellow leaves; in the garden the red daisies were like red plush buttons. She glanced at the big, hollow sandstone slab of the threshold, now crossed by so few feet.

'But it's lovely here,' she said. 'Such a beautiful stillness, everything alive and still.'

He was eating again, rather slowly and unwillingly, and she could feel he was discouraged. She made the tea in silence, and set the teapot on the hob, as she knew the people did. He pushed his plate aside and went to the back place; she heard a latch click, then he came back with cheese on a plate, and butter.

She set the two cups on the table; there were only two.

'Will you have a cup of tea?' she said.

'If you like. Sugar's in th' cupboard, an' there's a little cream-jug. Milk's in a jug in th' pantry.'

'Shall I take your plate away?' she asked him. He looked up at her with a faint ironical smile.

'Why . . . if you like,' he said, slowly eating bread and cheese. She went to the back, into the penthouse scullery, where the pump was. On the left was a door, no doubt the pantry door. She unlatched it, and almost smiled at the place he called a pantry, a long narrow whitewashed slip of a cupboard. But it managed to contain a little barrel of beer, as well as a few dishes and bits of food. She took a little milk from the yellow jug.

'How do you get your milk?' she asked him, when she came back to the table.

'Flints! They leave me a bottle at the warren end. You know, where I met you!'

But he was discouraged.

She poured out the tea, poising the cream-jug.

'No milk,' he said; then he seemed to hear a noise, and looked keenly through the doorway.

''Appen we'd better shut,' he said.

'It seems a pity,' she replied. 'Nobody will come, will they?'

'Not unless it's one time in a thousand, but you never know.'

'And even then it's no matter,' she said. 'It's only a cup of tea. Where are the spoons?'

He reached over, and pulled open the table drawer. Connie sat at the table in the sunshine of the doorway.

'Flossie!' he said to the dog, who was lying on a little mat at the stair foot. 'Go an' hark, hark!'

He lifted his finger, and his 'hark!' was very vivid. The dog trotted out to reconnoitre.

'Are you sad today?' she asked him.

He turned his blue eyes quickly, and gazed direct on her.

'Sad! no, bored! I had to go getting summonses for two poachers I caught, and oh well, I don't like people.'

He spoke cold, good English, and there was anger in his voice.

'Do you hate being a gamekeeper?' she asked.

'Being a gamekeeper, no! So long as I'm left alone. But when I have to go messing around at the police-station, and various other places, and waiting for a lot of fools to attend to me . . . oh well, I get mad . . . ' and he smiled, with a certain faint humour.

'Couldn't you be really independent?' she asked.

'Me? I suppose I could, if you mean manage to exist on my pension. I could! But I've got to work, or I should die. That is, I've got to have something that keeps me occupied. And I'm not in a good enough temper to work for myself. It's got to be a sort of job for somebody else, or I should throw it up in a month, out of bad temper. So altogether I'm very well off here, especially lately . . . '

He laughed at her again, with mocking humour.

'But why are you in a bad temper?' she asked. 'Do you mean you are *always* in a bad temper?'

'Pretty well,' he said, laughing. 'I don't quite digest my bile.'

'But what bile?' she said.

'Bile!' he said. 'Don't you know what that is?' She was silent, and disappointed. He was taking no notice of her.

'I'm going away for a while next month,' she said.

'You are! Where to?'

'Venice.'

'Venice! With Sir Clifford? For how long?'

'For a month or so,' she replied. 'Clifford won't go.'

'He'll stay here?' he asked.

'Yes! He hates to travel as he is.'

'Ay, poor devil!' he said, with sympathy.

There was a pause.

'You won't forget me when I'm gone, will you?' she asked. Again he lifted his eyes and looked full at her.

'Forget?' he said. 'You know nobody forgets. It's not a question of memory.'

She wanted to say: 'What then?' but she didn't. Instead, she said in a mute kind of voice: 'I told Clifford I might have a child.'

Now he really looked at her, intense and searching.

'You did?' he said at last. 'And what did he say?'

'Oh, he wouldn't mind. He'd be glad, really, so long as it seemed to be his.' She dared not look up at him.

He was silent a long time, then he gazed again on her face.

'No mention of *me*, of course?' he said.

'No. No mention of you,' she said.

'No, he'd hardly swallow me as a substitute breeder. Then where are you supposed to be getting the child?'

'I might have a love affair in Venice,' she said.

'You might,' he replied slowly. 'So that's why you're going?'

'Not to have the love affair,' she said, looking up at him, pleading.

'Just the appearance of one,' he said.

There was silence. He sat staring out the window, with a faint grin, half mockery, half bitterness, on his face. She hated his grin.

'You've not taken any precautions against having a child then?' he asked her suddenly. 'Because I haven't.'

'No,' she said faintly. 'I should hate that.'

He looked at her, then again with the peculiar subtle grin out of the window. There was a tense silence.

At last he turned to her and said satirically, 'That was why you wanted me then, to get a child?'

She hung her head.

'No. Not really,' she said.

'What then, *really*?' he asked rather bitingly.

She looked up at him reproachfully, saying: 'I don't know.'

He broke into a laugh.

'Then I'm damned if I do,' he said.

There was a long pause of silence, a cold silence.

'Well,' he said at last. 'It's as your Ladyship likes. If you get the baby, Sir Clifford's welcome to it. I shan't have lost anything. On the contrary, I've had a very nice experience, very nice indeed!' – and he stretched in a half suppressed sort of yawn. 'If you've made use of me,' he said, 'it's not the first time I've been made use of; and I don't suppose it's ever been as pleasant as this time, though of course one can't feel tremendously dignified about it.' He stretched again, curiously, his muscles quivering, and his jaw oddly set.

'But I didn't make use of you,' she said, pleading.

'At your Ladyship's service,' he replied.

'No,' she said. 'I liked your body.'

'Did you?' he replied, and he laughed. 'Well then, we're quits, because I liked yours.'

He looked at her with queer darkened eyes.

'Would you like to go upstairs now?' he asked her, in a strangled sort of voice.

'No, not here. Not now!' she said heavily, though if he had used any power over her, she would have gone, for she had no strength against him.

He turned his face away again, and seemed to forget her.

'I want to touch you like you touch me,' she said. 'I've never really touched your body.'

He looked at her, and smiled again. 'Now?' he said.

'No! No! Not here! At the hut. Would you mind?'

'How do I touch you?' he asked.

'When you feel me.'

He looked at her, and met her heavy, anxious eyes.

'And do you like it when I feel you?' he asked, laughing at her still.

'Yes, do you?' she said.

'Oh, me!' Then he changed his tone. 'Yes,' he said. 'You know without asking.' Which was true.

She rose and picked up her hat. 'I must go,' she said.

'Will you go?' he replied politely.

She wanted him to touch her, to say something to her, but he said nothing, only waited politely.

'Thank you for the tea,' she said.

'I haven't thanked your Ladyship for doing me the honours of my teapot,' he said.

She went down the path, and he stood in the doorway, faintly grinning. Flossie came running with her tail lifted. And Connie had to plod dumbly across into the wood, knowing he was standing there watching her, with that incomprehensible grin on his face.

She walked home very much downcast and annoyed. She didn't at all like his saying he had been made use of; because, in a sense, it was true. But he oughtn't to have said it. Therefore, again, she was divided between two feelings: resentment against him, and a desire to make it up with him.

She passed a very uneasy and irritated tea-time, and at once went up to her room. But when she was there it was no good; she could neither sit nor stand. She would have to do something about it. She would have to go back to the hut; if he was not there, well and good.

She slipped out of the side door, and took her way direct and a little sullen. When she came to the clearing she was terribly uneasy. But there he was again, in his shirt-sleeves, stooping, letting the hens out of the coops, among the chicks that were now growing a little gawky, but were much more trim than hen-chickens.

She went straight across to him.

'You see I've come!' she said.

'Ay, I see it!' he said, straightening his back, and looking at her with a faint amusement.

'Do you let the hens out now?' she asked.

'Yes, they've sat themselves to skin and bone,' he said. 'An' now they're not all that anxious to come out an' feed. There's no self in a sitting hen; she's all in the eggs or the chicks.'

The poor mother-hens; such blind devotion! even to eggs not their own! Connie looked at them in compassion. A helpless silence fell between the man and the woman.

'Shall us go i' th' 'ut?' he asked.

'Do you want me?' she asked, in a sort of mistrust.

'Ay, if you want to come.'

She was silent.

'Come then!' he said.

And she went with him to the hut. It was quite dark when he had shut the door, so he made a small light in the lantern, as before.

'Have you left your underthings off?' he asked her.

'Yes!'

'Ay, well, then I'll take my things off too.'

He spread the blankets, putting one at the side for a coverlet. She took off her hat, and shook her hair. He sat down, taking off his shoes and gaiters, and undoing his cord breeches.

'Lie down then!' he said, when he stood in his shirt. She obeyed in silence, and he lay beside her, and pulled the blanket over them both.

'There!' he said.

And he lifted her dress right back, till he came even to her breasts. He kissed them softly, taking the nipples in his lips in tiny caresses.

'Eh, but tha'rt nice, tha'rt nice!' he said, suddenly rubbing his face with a snuggling movement against her warm belly.

And she put her arms round him under his shirt, but she was afraid, afraid of his thin, smooth, naked body, that seemed so powerful, afraid of the violent muscles. She shrank, afraid.

And when he said, with a sort of little sigh: 'Eh, tha'rt nice!' something in her quivered, and something in her spirit stiffened in resistance: stiffened from the terribly physical intimacy, and from the peculiar haste of his possession. And this time the sharp ecstasy of her own passion did not overcome her; she lay with her hands inert on his striving body, and do what she might, her spirit seemed to look on from the top of her head, and the butting of his haunches seemed ridiculous to her, and the sort of anxiety of his penis to come to its little evacuating crisis seemed farcical. Yes, this was love, this ridiculous bouncing of the buttocks, and the wilting of the poor insignificant, moist little penis. This was the divine love! After all, the moderns were right when they felt contempt for the performance; for it was a performance. It was quite true, as some poets said, that the God who created man must have had a sinister sense of humour, creating him a reasonable being, yet forcing him to take this ridiculous posture, and driving him with blind craving for this ridiculous performance. Even a Maupassant found it a humiliating anticlimax. Men despised the intercourse act, and yet did it.

Cold and derisive her queer female mind stood apart, and though she lay perfectly still, her impulse was to heave her loins, and throw the man out, escape his ugly grip, and the butting overriding of his absurd haunches. His body was a foolish, impudent, imperfect thing, a little disgusting in its unfinished clumsiness. For surely a complete evolution would eliminate this performance, this 'function'.

And yet when he had finished, soon over, and lay very very still, receding into silence, and a strange, motionless distance, far, farther than the horizon of her awareness, her heart began to weep. She could feel him ebbing away, ebbing away, leaving her there like a stone on a shore. He was withdrawing, his spirit was leaving her. He knew.

And in real grief, tormented by her own double consciousness and reaction, she began to weep. He took no notice, or did not even know. The storm of weeping swelled and shook her, and shook him.

'Ay!' he said. 'It was no good that time. You wasn't there.' So he knew! Her sobs became violent.

'But what's amiss?' he said. 'It's once in a while that way.'

'I . . . I can't love you,' she sobbed, suddenly feeling her heart breaking.

'Canna ter? Well, dunna fret! There's no law says as tha's got to. Ta'e it for what it is.'

He still lay with his hand on her breast. But she had drawn both her hands from him.

His words were small comfort. She sobbed aloud.

'Nay, nay!' he said. 'Ta'e the thick wi' th' thin. This wor' a bit o' thin for once.'

She wept bitterly, sobbing. 'But I want to love you, and I can't. It only seems horrid.'

He laughed a little, half bitter, half amused.

'It isna horrid,' he said, 'even if tha thinks it is. An' tha canna ma'e it horrid. Dunna fret thysen about lovin' me. Tha'lt niver force thysen to 't. There's sure to be a bad nut in a basketful. Tha mun ta'e th' rough wi' th' smooth.'

He took his hand away from her breast, not touching her. And now she was untouched she took an almost perverse satisfaction in it. She hated the dialect: the *thee* and the *tha* and the *thysen*. He could get up if he liked, and stand there above her buttoning down those absurd corduroy breeches, straight in front of her. After all, Michaelis had had the decency to turn away. This man was so assured in himself, he didn't know what a clown other people found him, a half-bred fellow.

Yet, as he was drawing away, to rise silently and leave her, she clung to him in terror.

'Don't! Don't go! Don't leave me! Don't be cross with me! Hold me! Hold me fast!' she whispered in blind frenzy, not even knowing what she said, and clinging to him with uncanny force. It was from herself she wanted to be saved, from her own inward anger and resistance. Yet how powerful was that inward resistance that possessed her!

He took her in his arms again and drew her to him, and suddenly she became small in his arms, small and nestling. It was gone, the resistance was gone, and she began to melt in a marvellous peace. And as she melted small and wonderful in his arms, she became infinitely desirable to him, all his blood-vessels seemed to scald with intense yet tender desire, for her, for her softness, for the penetrating beauty of her in his arms, passing into his blood. And softly, with that marvellous swoon-like caress of his hand in pure soft desire, softly he stroked the silky slope of her loins, down, down between her soft warm buttocks, coming nearer and nearer to the very quick of her. And she felt him like a flame of desire, yet tender, and she felt herself melting in the flame. She let herself go. She felt his penis risen against her with silent amazing force and assertion, and she let herself go to him. She yielded with a quiver that was like death, she went all open to him. And oh, if he were not tender to her now, how cruel, for she was all open to him and helpless!

She quivered again at the potent inexorable entry inside her, so strange and terrible. It might come with the thrust of a sword in her softly-opened body, and that would be death. She clung in a sudden anguish of terror. But it came with a strange slow thrust of peace, the dark thrust of peace and a ponderous, primordial tenderness, such as made the world in the beginning. And her terror subsided in her breast, her breast dared to be gone in peace, she held nothing. She dared to let go everything, all herself, and be gone in the flood.

And it seemed she was like the sea, nothing but dark waves rising and heaving, heaving with a great swell, so that slowly her whole darkness was in motion, and she was ocean rolling its dark, dumb mass. Oh, and far down inside her the deeps parted and rolled asunder, in long, far-travelling billows, and ever, at the quick of her, the depths parted and rolled asunder, from the centre of soft plunging, as the plunger went deeper and deeper, touching lower, and she was deeper and deeper and deeper disclosed, the heavier the billows of her rolled away to some shore, uncovering her, and closer and closer plunged the palpable unknown, and further and further rolled the waves of herself away from herself, leaving her, till suddenly, in a soft, shuddering convulsion, the quick of all her plasm was touched, she knew herself touched, the consummation was upon her, and she was gone. She was gone, she was not, and she was born: a woman.

Ah, too lovely, too lovely! In the ebbing she realised all the loveliness. Now all her body clung with tender love to the unknown man, and blindly to the wilting penis, as it so tenderly, frailly, unknowingly withdrew, after the fierce thrust of its potency. As it drew out and left her body, the secret, sensitive thing, she gave an unconscious cry of pure loss, and she tried to put it back. It had been so perfect! And she loved it so!

And only now she became aware of the small, bud-like reticence and tenderness of the penis, and a little cry of wonder and poignancy escaped her again, her woman's heart crying out over the tender frailty of that which had been the power.

'It was so lovely!' she moaned. 'It was so lovely!' But he said nothing, only softly kissed her, lying still above her. And she moaned with a sort of bliss, as a sacrifice, and a new-born thing.

And now in her heart the queer wonder of him was awakened. A man! the strange potency of manhood upon her! Her hands strayed over him, still a little afraid. Afraid of that strange, hostile, slightly repulsive thing that he had been to her, a man. And now she touched him, and it was the sons of god with the daughters of men.[80] How beautiful he felt, how pure in tissue! How lovely, how lovely, strong, and yet pure and delicate, such stillness of the sensitive body! Such utter stillness of potency and delicate flesh. How beautiful! How beautiful! Her hands came timorously down his back, to the soft, smallish globes of the buttocks. Beauty! What beauty! a sudden little flame of new awareness went through her. How was it possible, this beauty here, where she had previously only been repelled? The unspeakable beauty to the touch, of the warm, living buttocks! The life within life, the sheer warm, potent loveliness. And the strange weight of the balls between his legs! What a mystery! What a strange heavy weight of mystery, that could lie soft and heavy in one's hand! The roots, root of all that is lovely, the primeval root of all full beauty.

She clung to him, with a hiss of wonder that was almost awe, terror. He held her close, but he said nothing. He would never say anything. She crept nearer to him, nearer, only to be near to the sensual wonder of him. And out of his utter, incomprehensible stillness, she felt again the slow, momentous, surging rise of the phallus again, the other power. And her heart melted out with a kind of awe.

And this time his being within her was all soft and iridescent, purely soft and iridescent, such as no consciousness could seize. Her whole self quivered unconscious and alive, like plasm. She could not know what it was. She could not remember what it had been. Only that it had been more lovely than anything ever could be. Only that. And afterwards she was utterly still, utterly unknowing, she was not aware for how long. And he was still with her, in an unfathomable silence along with her. And of this, they would never speak.

When awareness of the outside began to come back, she clung to his breast, murmuring: 'My love! my love!' And he held her silently. And she curled on his breast, perfect.

But his silence was fathomless. His hands held her like flowers, so still and strange. 'Where are you?' she whispered to him. 'Where are you? Speak to me! Say something to me!'

He kissed her softly, murmuring: 'Ay, my lass!'

But she did not know what he meant, she did not know where he was. In his silence he seemed lost to her.

'You love me, don't you?' she murmured.

'Ay, tha knows!' he said.

'But tell me!' she pleaded.

'Ay! Ay! 'asn't ter felt it?' he said dimly, but softly and surely. And she clung close to him, closer. He was so much more peaceful in love than she was, and she wanted him to reassure her.

'You do love me!' she whispered, assertive. And his hands stroked her softly, as if she were a flower, without the quiver of desire, but with delicate nearness. And still there haunted her a restless necessity to get a grip on love.

'Say you'll always love me!' she pleaded.

'Ay!' he said, abstractedly. And she felt her questions driving him away from her.

'Mustn't we get up?' he said at last.

'No!' she said.

But she could feel his consciousness straying, listening to the noises outside.

'It'll be nearly dark,' he said. And she heard the pressure of circumstance in his voice. She kissed him, with a woman's grief at yielding up her hour.

He rose, and turned up the lantern, then began to pull on his clothes, quickly disappearing inside them. Then he stood there, above her, fastening his breeches and looking down at her with dark, wide eyes, his face a little flushed and his hair ruffled, curiously warm and still and beautiful in the dim light of the lantern, so beautiful, she would never tell him how beautiful. It made her want to cling fast to him, to hold him, for there was a warm, half-sleepy remoteness in his beauty that made her want to cry out and clutch him, to have him. She would never have him. So she lay on the blanket with curved, soft naked haunches, and he had no idea what she was thinking, but to him too she was beautiful, the soft, marvellous thing he could go into, beyond everything.

'I love thee that I can go into thee,' he said.

'Do you like me?' she said, her heart beating.

'It heals it all up, that I can go into thee. I love thee that tha opened to me. I love thee that I came into thee like that.'

He bent down and kissed her soft flank, rubbed his cheek against it, then covered it up.

'And will you never leave me?' she said.

'Dunna ask them things,' he said.

'But you do believe I love you?' she said.

'Tha loved me just now, wider than iver tha thout tha would. But who knows what'll 'appen, once tha starts thinkin' about it!'

'No, don't say those things! And you don't really think that I wanted to make use of you, do you?'

'How?'

'To have a child – ?'

'Now anybody can 'ave any childt i' th' world,' he said, as he sat down fastening on his leggings.

'Ah no!' she cried. 'You don't mean it?'

'Eh well!' he said, looking at her under his brows. 'This wor t' best.'

She lay still. He softly opened the door. The sky was dark blue, with crystalline, turquoise rim. He went out, to shut up the hens, speaking softly to his dog. And she lay and wondered at the wonder of life, and of being.

When he came back she was still lying there, glowing like a gypsy. He sat on the stool by her.

'Tha mun come one naight ter th' cottage, afore tha goos; sholl ter?' he asked, lifting his eyebrows as he looked at her, his hands dangling between his knees.

'Sholl ter?' she echoed, teasing.

He smiled.

'Ay, sholl ter?' he repeated.

'Ay!' she said, imitating the dialect sound.

'Yi!' he said.

'Yi!' she repeated.

'An' slaip wi' me,' he said. 'It needs that. When sholt come?'

'When sholl I?' she said.

'Nay,' he said, 'tha canna do't. When sholt come then?'

''Appen Sunday,' she said.

''Appen a' Sunday! Ay!'

He laughed at her quickly.

'Nay, tha canna,' he protested.

'Why canna I?' she said.

He laughed. Her attempts at the dialect were so ludicrous, somehow.

'Coom then, tha mun goo!' he said.

'Mun I?' she said.

'Maun Ah!' he corrected.

'Why should I say *maun* when you said *mun*,' she protested. 'You're not playing fair.'

'Arena Ah!' he said, leaning forward and softly stroking her face.

'Th'art good cunt, though, aren't ter? Best bit o' cunt left on earth. When ter likes! When tha'rt willin'!'

'What is cunt?' she said.

'An' doesn't ter know? Cunt! It's thee down theer; an' what I get when I'm i'side thee, and what tha gets when I'm i'side thee; it's a' as it is, all on't.'

'All on't,' she teased. 'Cunt! It's like fuck then.'

'Nay nay! Fuck's only what you do. Animals fuck. But cunt's a lot more than that. It's thee, dost see: an' tha'rt a lot besides an animal, aren't ter? – even ter fuck? Cunt! Eh, that's the beauty o' thee, lass!'

She got up and kissed him between the eyes, that looked at her so dark and soft and unspeakably warm, so unbearably beautiful.

'Is it?' she said. 'And do you care for me?'

He kissed her without answering.

'Tha mun goo, let me dust thee,' he said.

His hand passed over the curves of her body, firmly, without desire, but with soft, intimate knowledge.

As she ran home in the twilight the world seemed a dream; the trees in the park seemed bulging and surging at anchor on a tide, and the heave of the slope to the house was alive.

Chapter 13

ON SUNDAY Clifford wanted to go into the wood. It was a lovely morning, the pear blossom and plum had suddenly appeared in the world, in a wonder of white here and there.

It was cruel for Clifford, while the world bloomed, to have to be helped from chair to bath-chair. But he had forgotten, and even seemed to have a certain conceit of himself in his lameness. Connie still suffered, having to lift his inert legs into place. Mrs Bolton did it now, or Field.

She waited for him at the top of the drive, at the edge of the screen of beeches. His chair came puffing along with a sort of valetudinarian slow importance. As he joined his wife he said, 'Sir Clifford on his foaming steed!'

'Snorting, at least!' she laughed.

He stopped and looked round at the façade of the long, low old brown house.

'Wragby doesn't wink an eyelid!' he said. 'But then why should it! I ride upon the achievements of the mind of man, and that beats a horse.'

'I suppose it does. And the souls in Plato[81] riding up to heaven in a two-horse chariot would go in a Ford car now,' she said.

'Or a Rolls-Royce: Plato was an aristocrat!'

'Quite! No more black horse to thrash and maltreat. Plato never thought we'd go one better than his black steed and his white steed, and have no steeds at all, only an engine!'

'Only an engine and gas!' said Clifford.

'I hope I can have some repairs done to the old place next year. I think I shall have about a thousand to spare for that: but work costs so much!' he added.

'Oh good!' said Connie. 'If only there aren't more strikes!'

'What would be the use of their striking again! Merely ruin the industry, what's left of it: and surely the owls are beginning to see it!'

'Perhaps they don't mind ruining the industry,' said Connie.

'Ah, don't talk like a woman! The industry fills their bellies, even if it can't keep their pockets quite so flush,' he said, using turns of speech that oddly had a twang of Mrs Bolton.

'But didn't you say the other day that you were a conservative-anarchist?' she asked innocently.

'And did you understand what I meant?' he retorted. 'All I meant is, people can be what they like and feel what they like and do what they like, strictly privately, so long as they keep the *form* of life intact, and the apparatus.'

Connie walked on in silence a few paces. Then she said, obstinately, 'It sounds like saying an egg may go as addled as it likes, so long as it keeps its shell on whole. But addled eggs do break of themselves.'

'I don't think people are eggs,' he said. 'Not even angels' eggs, my dear little evangelist.'

He was in rather high feather this bright morning. The larks were trilling away over the park, the distant pit in the hollow was fuming silent steam. It was almost like old days, before the war. Connie didn't really want to argue. But then she did not really want to go to the wood with Clifford either. So she walked beside his chair in a certain obstinacy of spirit.

'No,' he said. 'There will be no more strikes, if the thing is properly managed.'

'Why not?'

'Because strikes will be made as good as impossible.'

'But will the men let you?' she asked.

'We shan't ask them. We shall do it while they aren't looking: for their own good, to save the industry.'

'For your own good too,' she said.

'Naturally! For the good of everybody. But for their good even more than mine. I can live without the pits. They can't. They'll starve if there are no pits. I've got other provision.'

They looked up the shallow valley at the mine, and beyond it, at the black-lidded houses of Teac Teveshall crawling like some serpent up the hill. From the old brown church the bells were ringing: Sunday, Sunday, Sunday!

'But will the men let you dictate terms?' she said.

'My dear, they will have to: if one does it gently.'

'But mightn't there be a mutual understanding?'

'Absolutely: when they realise that the industry comes before the individual.'

'But must you own the industry?' she said.

'I don't. But to the extent I do own it, yes, most decidedly. The ownership of property has now become a religious question: as it has been since Jesus and St Francis. The point is *not*: take all thou hast and give to the poor, but use all thou hast to encourage the industry and give work to the poor. It's the only way to feed all the mouths and clothe all the bodies. Giving away all we have to the poor spells starvation for the poor just as much as for us. And universal starvation is no high aim. Even general poverty is no lovely thing. Poverty is ugly.'

'But the disparity?'

'That is fate. Why is the star Jupiter bigger than the star Neptune? You can't start altering the make-up of things!'

'But when this envy and jealousy and discontent has once started –' she began.

'Do your best to stop it. Somebody's *got* to be boss of the show.'

'But who is boss of the show?' she asked.

'The men who own and run the industries.'

There was a long silence.

'It seems to me they're a bad boss,' she said.

'Then you suggest what they should do.'

'They don't take their boss-ship seriously enough,' she said.

'They take it far more seriously than you take your ladyship,' he said.

'That's thrust upon me. I don't really want it,' she blurted out. He stopped the chair and looked at her.

'Who's shirking their responsibility now!' he said. 'Who is trying to get away *now* from the responsibility of their own boss-ship, as you call it?'

'But I don't want any boss-ship,' she protested.

'Ah! But that is funk. You've got it: fated to it. And you should live up to it. Who has given the colliers all they have that's worth having: all their political liberty, and their education, such as it is, their sanitation, their health-conditions, their books, their music, everything. Who has given it them? Have colliers given it to colliers? No! All the Wragbys and Shipleys in England have given their part, and must go on giving. There's your responsibility.'

Connie listened, and flushed very red.

'I'd like to give something,' she said. 'But I'm not allowed. Everything is to be sold and paid for now; and all the things you mention now, Wragby and Shipley *sells* them to the people, at a good profit. Everything is sold. You don't give one heartbeat of real sympathy. And besides, who has taken away from the people their natural life and manhood, and given them this industrial horror? Who has done that?'

'And what must I do?' he asked, green. 'Ask them to come and pillage me?'

'Why is Tevershall so ugly, so hideous? Why are their lives so hopeless?'

'They built their own Tevershall, that's part of their display of freedom. They built themselves their pretty Tevershall, and they live their own pretty lives. I can't live their lives for them. Every beetle must live its own life.'

'But you make them work for you. They live the life of your coalmine.'

'Not at all. Every beetle finds its own food. Not one man is forced to work for me.'

'Their lives are industrialised and hopeless, and so are ours,' she cried.

'I don't think they are. That's just a romantic figure of speech, a relic of the swooning and die-away romanticism. You don't look at all a hopeless figure standing there, Connie my dear.'

Which was true. For her dark-blue eyes were flashing, her colour was hot in her cheeks, she looked full of a rebellious passion far from the dejection of hopelessness. She noticed, in the tussocky places of the grass, cottony young cowslips standing up still bleared in their down. And she wondered with rage, why it was she felt Clifford was so *wrong*, yet she couldn't say it to him, she could not say exactly *where* he was wrong.

'No wonder the men hate you,' she said.

'They don't!' he replied. 'And don't fall into errors: in your sense of the word, they are *not* men. They are animals you don't understand, and never could. Don't thrust your illusions on other people. The masses were always the same, and will always be the same. Nero's slaves were extremely little different from our colliers or the Ford motor car workmen. I mean Nero's mine slaves and his field slaves. It is the masses: they are the unchangeable. An individual may emerge from the masses. But the emergence doesn't alter the mass. The masses are unalterable. It is one of the most momentous facts of social science. *Panem et circenses!*[82] Only today education is one of the bad substitutes for a circus. What is wrong today, is that we've made a profound hash of the circuses part of the programme, and poisoned our masses with a little education.'

When Clifford became really roused in his feelings about the common people, Connie was frightened. There was something devastatingly true in what he said. But it was a truth that killed.

Seeing her pale and silent, Clifford started the chair again, and no more was said till he halted again at the wood gate, which she opened.

'And what we need to take up now,' he said, 'is whips, not swords. The masses have been ruled since time began, and till time ends, ruled they will have to be. It is sheer hypocrisy and farce to say they can rule themselves.'

'But can you rule them?' she asked.

'I? Oh yes! Neither my mind nor my will is crippled, and I don't rule with my legs. I can do my share of ruling: absolutely, my share; and give me a son, and he will be able to rule his portion after me.'

'But he wouldn't be your own son, of your own ruling class; or perhaps not,' she stammered.

'I don't care who his father may be, so long as he is a healthy man not below normal intelligence. Give me the child of any healthy, normally intelligent man, and I will make a perfectly competent Chatterley of him. It is not who begets us, that matters, but where fate places us. Place any child among the ruling classes, and he will grow up, to his own extent, a ruler. Put kings' and dukes' children among the masses, and they'll be little plebeians, mass products. It is the overwhelming pressure of environment.'

'Then the common people aren't a race, and the aristocrats aren't blood,' she said.

'No, my child! All that is romantic illusion. Aristocracy is a function, a part of fate. And the masses are a functioning of another part of fate. The individual hardly matters. It is a question of which function you are brought up to and adapted to. It is not the individuals that make an aristocracy: it is the functioning of the aristocratic whole. And it is the functioning of the whole mass that makes the common man what he is.'

'Then there is no common humanity between us all!'

'Just as you like. We all need to fill our bellies. But when it comes to expressive or executive functioning, I believe there is a gulf and an absolute one, between the ruling and the serving classes. The two functions are opposed. And the function determines the individual.'

Connie looked at him with dazed eyes.

'Won't you come on?' she said.

And he started his chair. He had said his say. Now he lapsed into his peculiar and rather vacant apathy, that Connie found so trying. In the wood, anyhow, she was determined not to argue.

In front of them ran the open cleft of the riding, between the hazel walls and the gay grey trees. The chair puffed slowly on, slowly surging into the forget-me-nots that rose up in the drive like milk froth, beyond the hazel shadows. Clifford steered the middle course, where feet passing had kept a channel through the flowers. But Connie, walking behind, had watched the wheels jolt over the wood-ruff and the bugle, and squash the little yellow cups of the creeping-jenny. Now they made a wake through the forget-me-nots.

All the flowers were there, the first bluebells in blue pools, like standing water.

'You are quite right about its being beautiful,' said Clifford. 'It is so amazingly. What is *quite* so lovely as an English spring!'

Connie thought it sounded as if even the spring bloomed by act of Parliament. An English spring! Why not an Irish one? or Jewish? The chair moved slowly ahead, past tufts of sturdy bluebells that stood up like wheat, and over grey burdock leaves. When they came to the open place where the trees had been felled, the light flooded in rather stark. And the bluebells made sheets of bright blue colour, here and there, sheering off into lilac and purple. And between, the bracken was lifting its brown curled heads, like legions of young snakes with a new secret to whisper to Eve.

Clifford kept the chair going till he came to the brow of the hill; Connie followed slowly behind. The oak-buds were opening soft and brown. Everything came tenderly out of the old hardness. Even the snaggy craggy oak trees put out the softest young leaves, spreading thin, brown little wings like young bat-wings in the light. Why had men never any newness in them, any freshness to come forth with! Stale men!

Clifford stopped the chair at the top of the rise and looked down. The bluebells washed blue like flood-water over the broad riding, and lit up the downhill with a warm blueness.

'It's a very fine colour in itself,' said Clifford, 'but useless for making a painting.'

'Quite!' said Connie, completely uninterested.

'Shall I venture as far as the spring?' said Clifford.

'Will the chair get up again?' she said.

'We'll try; nothing venture, nothing win!'

And the chair began to advance slowly, joltingly down the beautiful broad riding washed over with blue encroaching hyacinths. Oh last of all ships, through the hyacinthian shallows! Oh pinnace on the last wild waters, sailing in the last voyage of our civilisation! Whither, O weird wheeled ship, your slow course steering.[83] Quiet and complacent, Clifford sat at the wheel of adventure: in his old black hat and tweed jacket, motionless and cautious. Oh Captain, my Captain,[84] our splendid trip is done! Not yet though! Downhill, in the wake, came Constance in her grey dress, watching the chair jolt downwards.

They passed the narrow track to the hut. Thank heaven it was not wide enough for the chair: hardly wide enough for one person. The chair reached the bottom of the slope, and swerved round, to disappear. And Connie heard a low whistle behind her. She glanced sharply round: the keeper was striding downhill towards her, his dog keeping behind him.

'Is Sir Clifford going to the cottage?' he asked, looking into her eyes.

'No, only to the well.'

'Ah! Good! Then I can keep out of sight. But I shall see you tonight. I shall wait for you at the park gate about ten.'

He looked again direct into her eyes.

'Yes,' she faltered.

They heard the Papp! Papp! of Clifford's horn, tooting for Connie. She 'Coo-eed!' in reply. The keeper's face flickered with a little grimace, and with his hand he softly brushed her breast upwards, from underneath. She looked at him, frightened, and started running down the hill, calling Coo-ee! again to Clifford. The man above watched her, then turned, grinning faintly, back into his path.

She found Clifford slowly mounting to the spring, which was halfway up the slope of the dark larchwood. He was there by the time she caught him up.

'She did that all right,' he said, referring to the chair.

Connie looked at the great grey leaves of burdock that grew out ghostly from the edge of the larchwood. The people call it Robin Hood's Rhubarb. How silent and gloomy it seemed by the well! Yet the water bubbled so bright, wonderful! And there were bits of eyebright and strong blue bugle . . . and there, under the bank, the yellow earth was moving. A mole! It emerged, rowing its pink hands, and waving its blind gimlet of a face, with the tiny pink nose-tip uplifted.

'It seems to see with the end of its nose,' said Connie.

'Better than with its eyes!' he said. 'Will you drink?'

'Will you?'

She took an enamel mug from a twig on a tree, and stooped to fill it for him. He drank in sips. Then she stooped again, and drank a little herself.

'So icy!' she said gasping.

'Good, isn't it! Did you wish?'

'Did you?'

'Yes, I wished. But I won't tell.'

She was aware of the rapping of a woodpecker, then of the wind, soft and eerie through the larches. She looked up. White clouds were crossing the blue.

'Clouds!' she said.

'White lambs only,' he replied.

A shadow crossed the little clearing. The mole had swum out on to the soft yellow earth.

'Unpleasant little beast, we ought to kill him,' said Clifford.

'Look! he's like a parson in a pulpit,' said she.

She gathered some sprigs of woodruff and brought them to him.

'New-mown hay!' he said. 'Doesn't it smell like the romantic ladies of the last century, who had their heads screwed on the right way after all!'

She was looking at the white clouds.

'I wonder if it will rain,' she said.

'Rain! Why! Do you want it to?'

They started on the return journey, Clifford jolting cautiously downhill. They came to the dark bottom of the hollow, turned to the right, and after a hundred yards swerved up the foot of the long slope, where bluebells stood in the light.

'Now, old girl!' said Clifford, putting the chair to it.

It was a steep and jolty climb. The chair pugged slowly, in a struggling unwilling fashion. Still, she nosed her way up unevenly, till she came to where the hyacinths were all around her, then she balked, struggled, jerked a little way out of the flowers, then stopped.

'We'd better sound the horn and see if the keeper will come,' said Connie. 'He could push her a bit. For that matter, I will push. It helps.'

'We'll let her breathe,' said Clifford. 'Do you mind putting a scotch under the wheel?'

Connie found a stone, and they waited. After a while Clifford started his motor again, then set the chair in motion. It struggled and faltered like a sick thing, with curious noises.

'Let me push!' said Connie, coming up behind.

'No! Don't push!' he said angrily. 'What's the good of the damned thing, if it has to be pushed! Put the stone under!'

There was another pause, then another start; but more ineffectual than before.

'You *must* let me push,' said she. 'Or sound the horn for the keeper.'

'Wait!'

She waited; and he had another try, doing more harm than good.

'Sound the horn then, if you won't let me push,' she said.

'Hell! Be quiet a moment!'

She was quiet a moment: he made shattering efforts with the little motor.

'You'll only break the thing down altogether, Clifford,' she remonstrated; 'besides wasting your nervous energy.'

'If I could only get out and look at the damned thing!' he said, exasperated. And he sounded the horn stridently. 'Perhaps Mellors can see what's wrong.'

They waited, among the mashed flowers under a sky softly curdling with cloud. In the silence a wood-pigeon began to coo, roo-hoo hoo! roo-hoo hoo! Clifford shut her up with a blast on the horn.

The keeper appeared directly, striding inquiringly round the corner. He saluted.

'Do you know anything about motors?' asked Clifford sharply.

'I am afraid I don't. Has she gone wrong?'

'Apparently!' snapped Clifford.

The man crouched solicitously by the wheel, and peered at the little engine.

'I'm afraid I know nothing at all about these mechanical things, Sir Clifford,' he said calmly. 'If she has enough petrol and oil – '

'Just look carefully and see if you can see anything broken,' snapped Clifford.

The man laid his gun against a tree, took off his coat and threw it beside it. The brown dog sat guard. Then he sat down on his heels and peered under the chair, poking with his finger at the greasy little engine, and resenting the grease-marks on his clean Sunday shirt.

'Doesn't seem anything broken,' he said. And he stood up, pushing back his hat from his forehead, rubbing his brow and apparently studying.

'Have you looked at the rods underneath?' asked Clifford. 'See if they are all right!'

The man lay flat on his stomach on the floor, his neck pressed back, wriggling under the engine and poking with his finger. Connie thought what a pathetic sort of thing a man was, feeble and small-looking, when he was lying on his belly on the big earth.

'Seems all right as far as I can see,' came his muffled voice.

'I don't suppose you can do anything,' said Clifford.

'Seems as if I can't!' And he scrambled up and sat on his heels, collier fashion. 'There's certainly nothing obviously broken.'

Clifford started his engine, then put her in gear. She would not move.

'Run her a bit hard, like,' suggested the keeper.

Clifford resented the interference: but he made his engine buzz like a bluebottle. Then she coughed and snarled and seemed to go better.

'Sounds as if she'd come clear,' said Mellors.

But Clifford had already jerked her into gear. She gave a sick lurch and ebbed weakly forwards.

'If I give her a push, she'll do it,' said the keeper, going behind.

'Keep off!' snapped Clifford. 'She'll do it by herself.'

'But Clifford!' put in Connie from the bank, 'You know it's too much for her. Why are you so obstinate!'

Clifford was pale with anger. He jabbed at his levers. The chair gave a sort of scurry, reeled on a few more yards, and came to her end amid a particularly promising patch of bluebells.

'She's done!' said the keeper. 'Not power enough.'

'She's been up here before,' said Clifford coldly.

'She won't do it this time,' said the keeper.

Clifford did not reply. He began doing things with his engine, running her fast and slow as if to get some sort of tune out of her. The wood re-echoed with weird noises. Then he put her in gear with a jerk, having jerked off his brake.

'You'll rip her inside out,' murmured the keeper.

The chair charged in a sick lurch sideways at the ditch.

'Clifford!' cried Connie, rushing forward.

But the keeper had got the chair by the rail. Clifford, however, putting on all his pressure, managed to steer into the riding, and with a strange noise the chair was fighting the hill. Mellors pushed steadily behind, and up she went, as if to retrieve herself.

'You see, she's doing it!' said Clifford, victorious, glancing over his shoulder. There he saw the keeper's face.

'Are you pushing her?'

'She won't do it without.'

'Leave her alone. I asked you not.'

'She won't do it.'

'*Let her try!*' snarled Clifford, with all his emphasis.

The keeper stood back: then turned to fetch his coat and gun. The chair seemed to strangle immediately. She stood inert. Clifford, seated a prisoner, was white with vexation. He jerked at the levers with his hand, his feet were no good. He got queer noises out of her. In savage impatience he moved little handles and got more noises out of her. But she would not budge. No, she would not budge. He stopped the engine and sat rigid with anger.

Constance sat on the bank and looked at the wretched and trampled bluebells. 'Nothing quite so lovely as an English spring.' 'I can do my share of ruling.' 'What we need to take up now is whips, not swords.' 'The ruling classes!'

The keeper strode up with his coat and gun, Flossie cautiously at his heels. Clifford asked the man to do something or other to the engine. Connie, who understood nothing at all of the technicalities of motors, and who had had experience of breakdowns, sat patiently on the bank as if she were a cipher. The keeper lay on his stomach again. The ruling classes and the serving classes!

He got to his feet and said patiently, 'Try her again, then.'

He spoke in a quiet voice, almost as if to a child.

Clifford tried her, and Mellors stepped quickly behind and began to push. She was going, the engine doing about half the work, the man the rest.

Clifford glanced round, yellow with anger.

'Will you get off there!'

The keeper dropped his hold at once, and Clifford added: 'How shall I know what she is doing!'

The man put his gun down and began to pull on his coat. He'd done. The chair began slowly to run backwards.

'Clifford, your brake!' cried Connie.

She, Mellors, and Clifford moved at once, Connie and the keeper jostling lightly. The chair stood. There was a moment of dead silence.

'It's obvious I'm at everybody's mercy!' said Clifford. He was yellow with anger.

No one answered. Mellors was slinging his gun over his shoulder, his face queer and expressionless, save for an abstracted look of patience. The dog Flossie, standing on guard almost between her master's legs, moved uneasily, eyeing the chair with great suspicion and dislike, and very much perplexed between the three human beings. The *tableau vivant*[85] remained set among the squashed blue-bells, nobody proffering a word.

'I expect she'll have to be pushed,' said Clifford at last, with an affectation of *sang froid*.

No answer. Mellors' abstracted face looked as if he had heard nothing. Connie glanced anxiously at him. Clifford too glanced round.

'Do you mind pushing her home, Mellors!' he said in a cool, superior tone. 'I hope I have said nothing to offend you,' he added, in a tone of dislike.

'Nothing at all, Sir Clifford! Do you want me to push that chair?'

'If you please.'

The man stepped up to it: but this time it was without effect. The brake was jammed. They poked and pulled, and the keeper took off his gun and his coat once more. And now Clifford said never a word. At last the keeper heaved the back of the chair off the ground and, with an instantaneous push of his foot, tried to loosen the wheels. He failed, the chair sank. Clifford was clutching the sides. The man gasped with the weight.

'Don't do it!' cried Connie to him.

'If you'll pull the wheel that way, so!' he said to her, showing her how.

'No! You mustn't lift it! You'll strain yourself,' she said, flushed now with anger.

But he looked into her eyes and nodded. And she had to go and take hold of the wheel, ready. He heaved and she tugged, and the chair reeled.

'For God's sake!' cried Clifford in terror.

But it was all right, and the brake was off. The keeper put a stone under the wheel, and went to sit on the bank, his heart beating and his face white with the effort, semi-conscious. Connie looked at him, and almost cried with anger. There was a pause and a dead silence. She saw his hands trembling on his thighs.

'Have you hurt yourself?' she asked, going to him.

'No. No!' He turned away almost angrily.

There was dead silence. The back of Clifford's fair head did not move. Even the dog stood motionless. The sky had clouded over.

At last he sighed, and blew his nose on his red handkerchief.

'That pneumonia took a lot out of me,' he said.

No one answered. Connie calculated the amount of strength it must have taken to heave up that chair and the bulky Clifford: too much, far too much! If it hadn't killed him!

He rose, and again picked up his coat, slinging it through the handle of the chair.

'Are you ready, then, Sir Clifford?'

'When you are!'

He stooped and took out the scotch, then put his weight against the chair. He was paler than Connie had ever seen him: and more absent. Clifford was a heavy man: and the hill was steep. Connie stepped to the keeper's side.

'I'm going to push too!' she said.

And she began to shove with a woman's turbulent energy of anger. The chair went faster. Clifford looked round.

'Is that necessary?' he said.

'Very! Do you want to kill the man! If you'd let the motor work while it would – '

But she did not finish. She was already panting. She slackened off a little, for it was surprisingly hard work.

'Ay! slower!' said the man at her side, with a faint smile of his eyes.

'Are you sure you've not hurt yourself?' she said fiercely.

He shook his head. She looked at his smallish, short, alive hand, browned by the weather. It was the hand that caressed her. She had never even looked at it before. It seemed so still, like him, with a curious inward stillness that made her want to clutch it, as if she could not reach it. All her soul suddenly swept towards him: he was so silent, and out of reach! And he felt his limbs revive. Shoving with his left hand, he laid his right on her round white wrist, softly enfolding her wrist, with a caress. And the flame of strength went down his back and his loins, reviving him. And she bent suddenly and kissed his hand. Meanwhile the back of Clifford's head was held sleek and motionless, just in front of them.

At the top of the hill they rested, and Connie was glad to let go. She had had fugitive dreams of friendship between these two men: one her husband, the other the father of her child. Now she saw the screaming absurdity of her dreams. The two males were as hostile as fire and water. They mutually exterminated one another. And she realised for the first time, what a queer subtle thing hate is. For the first time, she had consciously and definitely hated Clifford, with vivid hate: as if he ought to be obliterated from the face of the earth. And it was strange, how free and full of life it made her feel, to hate him and to admit it fully to herself. 'Now I've hated him, I shall never be able to go on living with him,' came the thought into her mind.

On the level the keeper could push the chair alone. Clifford made a little conversation with her, to show his complete composure: about Aunt Eva, who was at Dieppe, and about Sir Malcolm, who had written to ask would Connie drive with him in his small car, to Venice, or would she and Hilda go by train.

'I'd much rather go by train,' said Connie. 'I don't like long motor drives, especially when there's dust. But I shall see what Hilda wants.'

'She will want to drive her own car, and take you with her,' he said.

'Probably! I must help up here. You've no idea how heavy this chair is.'

She went to the back of the chair, and plodded side by side with the keeper, shoving up the pink path. She did not care who saw.

'Why not let me wait, and fetch Field. He is strong enough for the job,' said Clifford.

'It's so near,' she panted.

But both she and Mellors wiped the sweat from their faces when they came to the top. It was curious, but this bit of work together had brought them much closer than they had been before.

'Thanks so much, Mellors,' said Clifford, when they were at the house door. 'I must get a different sort of motor, that's all. Won't you go to the kitchen and have a meal? It must be about time.'

'Thank you, Sir Clifford. I was going to my mother for dinner today, Sunday.'

'As you like.'

Mellors slung into his coat, looked at Connie, saluted, and was gone. Connie, furious, went upstairs.

At lunch she could not contain her feeling.

'Why are you so abominably inconsiderate, Clifford?' she said to him.

'Of whom?'

'Of the keeper! If that is what you call ruling classes, I'm sorry for you.'

'Why?'

'A man who's been ill, and isn't strong! My word, if I were the serving classes, I'd let you wait for service. I'd let you whistle.'

'I quite believe it.'

'If he'd been sitting in a chair with paralysed legs, and behaved as you behaved, what would you have done for *him*?'

'My dear evangelist, this confusing of persons and personalities is in bad taste.'

'And your nasty, sterile want of common sympathy is in the worst taste imaginable. *Noblesse oblige!*[86] You and your ruling class!'

'And to what should it oblige me? To have a lot of unnecessary emotions about my gamekeeper? I refuse. I leave it all to my evangelist.'

'As if he weren't a man as much as you are, my word!'

'My gamekeeper to boot, and I pay him two pounds a week and give him a house.'

'Pay him! What do you think you pay for, with two pounds a week and a house?'

'His services.'

'Bah! I would tell you to keep your two pounds a week and your house.'

'Probably he would like to: but can't afford the luxury!'

'You, and *rule*!' she said. 'You don't rule, don't flatter yourself. You have only got more than your share of the money, and make people work for you for two pounds a week, or threaten them with starvation. Rule! What do you give forth of rule? Why, you're dried up! You only bully with your money, like any Jew or any Schieber!'[87]

'You are very elegant in your speech, Lady Chatterley!'

'I assure you, you were very elegant altogether out there in the wood. I was utterly ashamed of you. Why, my father is ten times the human being you are: you *gentleman*!'

He reached and rang the bell for Mrs Bolton. But he was yellow at the gills.

She went up to her room, furious, saying to herself, 'Him and buying people! Well, he doesn't buy me, and therefore there's no need for me to stay with him. Dead fish of a gentleman, with his celluloid soul! And how they take one in, with their manners and their mock wistfulness and gentleness. They've got about as much feeling as celluloid has.'

She made her plans for the night, and determined to get Clifford off her mind. She didn't want to hate him. She didn't want to be mixed up very intimately with him in any sort of feeling. She wanted him not to know anything at all about herself: and especially, not to know anything about her feeling for the keeper. This squabble of her attitude to the servants was an old one. He found her too familiar, she found him stupidly insentient, tough and india-rubbery where other people were concerned.

She went downstairs calmly, with her old demure bearing, at dinner-time. He was still yellow at the gills: in for one of his liver bouts, when he was really very queer. He was reading a French book.

'Have you ever read Proust?' he asked her.

'I've tried, but he bores me.'

'He's really very extraordinary.'

'Possibly! But he bores me: all that sophistication! He doesn't have feelings, he only has streams of words about feelings. I'm tired of self-important mentalities.'

'Would you prefer self-important animalities?'

'Perhaps! But one might possibly get something that wasn't self-important.'

'Well, I like Proust's subtlety and his well-bred anarchy.'

'It makes you very dead, really.'

'There speaks my evangelical little wife.'

They were at it again, at it again! But she couldn't help fighting him. He seemed to sit there like a skeleton, sending out a skeleton's cold grizzly *will* against her. Almost she could feel the skeleton clutching her and pressing her to its cage of ribs. He too was really up in arms: and she was a little afraid of him.

She went upstairs as soon as possible, and went to bed quite early. But at half-past nine she got up, and went outside to listen. There was no sound. She slipped on a dressing-gown and went downstairs. Clifford and Mrs Bolton were playing cards, gambling. They would probably go on until midnight.

Connie returned to her room, threw her pyjamas on the tossed bed, put on a thin nightdress and over that a woollen day-dress, put on rubber tennis-shoes, and then a light coat. And she was ready. If she met anybody, she was just going out for a few minutes. And in the morning, when she came in again, she would just have been for a little walk in the dew, as she fairly often did before breakfast. For the rest, the only danger was that someone should go into her room during the night. But that was most unlikely: not one chance in a hundred.

Betts had not yet locked up. He fastened up the house at ten o'clock, and unfastened it again at seven in the morning. She slipped out silently and unseen. There was a half-moon shining, enough to make a little light in the world, not enough to show her up in her dark-grey coat. She walked quickly across the park, not really in the thrill of the assignation, but with a certain anger and rebellion burning in her heart. It was not the right sort of heart to take to a love-meeting. But *à la guerre comme à la guerre!*[88]

Chapter 14

WHEN SHE GOT NEAR the park-gate, she heard the click of the latch. He was there, then, in the darkness of the wood, and had seen her!

'You are good and early,' he said out of the dark. 'Was everything all right?'

'Perfectly easy.'

He shut the gate quietly after her, and made a spot of light on the dark ground, showing the pallid flowers still standing there open in the night. They went on apart, in silence.

'Are you sure you didn't hurt yourself this morning with that chair?' she asked.

'No, no!'

'When you had that pneumonia, what did it do to you?'

'Oh nothing! it left my heart not so strong and the lungs not so elastic. But it always does that.'

'And you ought not to make violent physical efforts?'

'Not often.'

She plodded on in an angry silence.

'Did you hate Clifford?' she said at last.

'Hate him, no! I've met too many like him to upset myself hating him. I know beforehand I don't care for his sort, and I let it go at that.'

'What is his sort?'

'Nay, you know better than I do. The sort of youngish gentleman a bit like a lady, and no balls.'

'What balls?'

'Balls! A man's balls!'

She pondered this.

'But is it a question of that?' she said, a little annoyed.

'You say a man's got no brain, when he's a fool: and no heart, when he's mean; and no stomach when he's a funker. And when he's got none of that spunky wild bit of a man in him, you say he's got no balls. When he's sort of tame.'

She pondered this.

'And is Clifford tame?' she asked.

'Tame, and nasty with it: like most such fellows, when you come up against 'em.'

'And do you think you're not tame?'

'Maybe not quite!'

At length she saw in the distance a yellow light.

She stood still.

'There is a light!' she said.

'I always leave a light in the house,' he said.

She went on again at his side, but not touching him, wondering why she was going with him at all.

He unlocked, and they went in, he bolting the door behind them. As if it were a prison, she thought! The kettle was singing by the red fire, there were cups on the table.

She sat in the wooden armchair by the fire. It was warm after the chill outside.

'I'll take off my shoes, they are wet,' she said.

She sat with her stockinged feet on the bright steel fender. He went to the pantry, bringing food: bread and butter and pressed tongue. She was warm: she took off her coat. He hung it on the door.

'Shall you have cocoa or tea or coffee to drink?' he asked.

'I don't think I want anything,' she said, looking at the table. 'But you eat.'

'Nay, I don't care about it. I'll just feed the dog.'

He tramped with a quiet inevitability over the brick floor, putting food for the dog in a brown bowl. The spaniel looked up at him anxiously.

'Ay, this is thy supper, tha nedna look as if tha wouldna get it!' he said.

He set the bowl on the stairfoot mat, and sat himself on a chair by the wall, to take off his leggings and boots. The dog, instead of eating, came to him again, and sat looking up at him, troubled.

He slowly unbuckled his leggings. The dog edged a little nearer.

'What's amiss wi' thee then? Art upset because there's somebody else here? Tha'rt a female, tha art! Go an' eat thy supper.'

He put his hand on her head, and the bitch leaned her head sideways against him. He slowly, softly pulled the long silky ear.

'There!' he said. 'There! Go an' eat thy supper! Go!'

He tilted his chair towards the pot on the mat, and the dog meekly went, and fell to eating.

'Do you like dogs?' Connie asked him.

'No, not really. They're too tame and clinging.'

He had taken off his leggings and was unlacing his heavy boots. Connie had turned from the fire. How bare the little room was! Yet over his head on the wall hung a hideous enlarged photograph of a young married couple, apparently him and a bold-faced young woman, no doubt his wife.

'Is that you?' Connie asked him.

He twisted and looked at the enlargement above his head.

'Ay! Taken just afore we were married, when I was twenty-one.' He looked at it impassively.

'Do you like it?' Connie asked him.

'Like it? No! I never liked the thing. But she fixed it all up to have it done, like.'

He returned to pulling off his boots.

'If you don't like it, why do you keep it hanging there? Perhaps your wife would like to have it,' she said.

He looked up at her with a sudden grin.

'She carted off ivrything as was worth taking from th' 'ouse,' he said. 'But she left *that*!'

'Then why do you keep it? for sentimental reasons?'

'Nay, I niver look at it. I hardly knowed it wor theer. It's bin theer sin we come to this place.'

'Why don't you burn it?' she said.

He twisted round again and looked at the enlarged photograph. It was framed in a brown-and-gilt frame, hideous. It showed a clean-shaven, alert, very young-looking man in a rather high collar, and a somewhat plump, bold young woman with hair fluffed out and crimped, and wearing a dark satin blouse.

'It wouldn't be a bad idea, would it?' he said.

He had pulled off his boots, and put on a pair of slippers. He stood up on the chair, and lifted down the photograph. It left a pale place on the greenish wallpaper.

'No use dusting it now,' he said, setting the thing against the wall.

He went to the scullery, and returned with hammer and pincers. Sitting where he had sat before, he started to tear off the back-paper from the big frame, and to pull out the sprigs that held the back-board in position, working with the immediate quiet absorption that was characteristic of him.

He soon had the nails out: then he pulled out the backboards, then the enlargement itself, in its solid white mount. He looked at the photograph with amusement.

'Shows me for what I was, a young curate, and her for what she was, a bully,' he said. 'The prig and the bully!'

'Let me look!' said Connie.

He did look indeed very clean-shaven and very clean altogether, one of the clean young men of twenty years ago. But even in the photograph his eyes were alert and dauntless. And the woman was not altogether a bully, though her jowl was heavy. There was a touch of appeal in her.

'One never should keep these things,' said Connie.

'That one shouldn't! One should never have them made!'

He broke the cardboard photograph and mount over his knee, and when it was small enough, put it on the fire.

'It'll spoil the fire though,' he said.

The glass and the backboards he carefully took upstairs.

The frame he knocked asunder with a few blows of the hammer, making the stucco fly. Then he took the pieces into the scullery.

'We'll burn that tomorrow,' he said. 'There's too much plaster-moulding on it.'

Having cleared away, he sat down.

'Did you love your wife?' she asked him.

'Love?' he said. 'Did you love Sir Clifford?'

But she was not going to be put off.

'But you cared for her?' she insisted.

'Cared?' He grinned.

'Perhaps you care for her now,' she said.

'Me!' His eyes widened. 'Ah no, I can't think of her,' he said quietly.

'Why?'

But he shook his head.

'Then why don't you get a divorce? She'll come back to you one day,' said Connie.

He looked up at her sharply.

'She wouldn't come within a mile of me. She hates me a lot worse than I hate her.'

'You'll see she'll come back to you.'

'That she never shall. That's done! It would make me sick to see her.'

'You will see her. And you're not even legally separated, are you?'

'No.'

'Ah well, then she'll come back, and you'll have to take her in.'

He gazed at Connie fixedly. Then he gave the queer toss of his head.

'You may be right. I was a fool ever to come back here. But I felt stranded, and had to go somewhere. A man's a poor bit of a wastrel, blown about. But you're right. I'll get a divorce and get clear. I hate those things like death, officials and courts and judges. But I've got to get through with it. I'll get a divorce.'

And she saw his jaw set. Inwardly she exulted.

'I think I will have a cup of tea now,' she said.

He rose to make it. But his face was set.

As they sat at table she asked him, 'Why did you marry her? She was commoner than yourself. Mrs Bolton told me about her. She could never understand why you married her.'

He looked at her fixedly.

'I'll tell you,' he said. 'The first girl I had, I began with when I was sixteen. She was a schoolmaster's daughter over at Ollerton, pretty, beautiful really. I was supposed to be a clever sort of young fellow from Sheffield Grammar School, with a bit of French and German, very much up aloft. She was the romantic sort that hated common-ness. She egged me on to poetry and reading: in a way, she made a man of me. I read and I thought like a house on fire, for her. And I was a clerk in Butterley offices, thin, white-faced fellow fuming with all

the things I read. And about *everything* I talked to her: but everything.
We talked ourselves into Persepolis and Timbuctoo.[89] We were the
most literary-cultured couple in ten counties. I held forth with rapture
to her, positively with rapture. I simply went up in smoke. And she
adored me. The serpent in the grass was sex. She somehow didn't
have any; at least, not where it's supposed to be. I got thinner and
crazier. Then I said we'd got to be lovers. I talked her into it, as usual.
So she let me. I was excited, and she never wanted it. She just didn't
want it. She adored me, she loved me to talk to her and kiss her: in
that way she had a passion for me. But the other, she just didn't want.
And there are lots of women like her. And it was just the other that I
did want. So there we split. I was cruel, and left her. Then I took on
with another girl, a teacher, who had made a scandal by carrying on
with a married man and driving him nearly out of his mind. She was a
soft, white-skinned, soft sort of a woman, older than me, and played
the fiddle. And she was a demon. She loved everything about love,
except the sex. Clinging, caressing, creeping into you in every way:
but if you forced her to the sex itself, she just ground her teeth and
sent out hate. I forced her to it, and she could simply numb me with
hate because of it. So I was balked again. I loathed all that. I wanted a
woman who wanted me, and wanted *it*.

'Then came Bertha Coutts. They'd lived next door to us when I
was a little lad, so I knew 'em all right. And they were common.
Well, Bertha went away to some place or other in Birmingham; she
said, as a lady's companion; everybody else said, as a waitress or
something in a hotel. Anyhow just when I was more than fed up with
that other girl, when I was twenty-one, back comes Bertha, with airs
and graces and smart clothes and a sort of bloom on her: a sort of
sensual bloom that you'd see sometimes on a woman, or on a trolly.[90]
Well I was in a state of murder. I chucked up my job at Butterley
because I thought I was a weed, clerking there: and I got on as
overhead blacksmith at Tencvershall: shoeing horses mostly. It had
been my dad's job, and I'd always been with him. It was a job I liked:
handling horses: and it came natural to me. So I stopped talking
"fine", as they call it, talking proper English, and went back to
talking broad. I still read books, at home: but I blacksmithed and had
a pony-trap of my own, and was My Lord Duckfoot.[91] My dad left me
three hundred pounds when he died. So I took on with Bertha, and I
was glad she was common. I wanted her to be common. I wanted to
be common myself. Well, I married her, and she wasn't bad. Those
other "pure" women had nearly taken all the balls out of me, but she
was all right that way. She wanted me, and made no bones about it.

And I was as pleased as punch. That was what I wanted: a woman who *wanted* me to fuck her. So I fucked her like a good un. And I think she despised me a bit, for being so pleased about it, and bringin' her her breakfast in bed sometimes. She sort of let things go, didn't get me a proper dinner when I came home from work, and if I said anything, flew out at me. And I flew back, hammer and tongues. She flung a cup at me and I took her by the scruff of the neck and squeezed the life out of her. That sort of thing! But she treated me with insolence. And she got so's she'd never have me when I wanted her: never. Always put me off, brutal as you like. And then when she'd put me right off, and I didn't want her, she'd come all lovey-dovey, and get me. And I always went. But when I had her, she'd never come off when I did. Never! She'd just wait. If I kept back for half an hour, she'd keep back longer. And when I'd come and really finished, then she'd start on her own account, and I had to stop inside her till she brought herself off, wriggling and shouting, she'd clutch clutch with herself down there, an' then she'd come off, fair in ecstasy. And then she'd say: That was lovely! Gradually I got sick of it: and she got worse. She sort of got harder and harder to bring off, and she'd sort of tear at me down there, as if it was a beak tearing at me. By God, you think a woman's soft down there, like a fig. But I tell you the old rampers have beaks between their legs, and they tear at you with it till you're sick. Self! Self! Self! all self! tearing and shouting! They talk about men's selfishness, but I doubt if it can ever touch a woman's blind beakishness, once she's gone that way. Like an old trull![92] And she couldn't help it. I told her about it, I told her how I hated it. And she'd even try. She'd try to lie still and let *me* work the business. She'd try. But it was no good. She got no feeling off it, from my working. She had to work the thing herself, grind her own coffee. And it came back on her like a raving necessity, she had to let herself go, and tear, tear, tear, as if she had no sensation in her except in the top of her beak, the very outside top tip, that rubbed and tore. That's how old whores used to be, so men used to say. It was a low kind of self-will in her, a raving sort of self-will: like in a woman who drinks. Well in the end I couldn't stand it. We slept apart. She herself had started it, in her bouts when she wanted to be clear of me, when she said I bossed her. She had started having a room for herself. But the time came when I wouldn't have her coming to my room. I wouldn't.

'I hated it. And she hated me. My God, how she hated me before that child was born! I often think she conceived it out of hate. Anyhow, after the child was born I left her alone. And then came the war, and I joined up. And I didn't come back till I knew she was with that fellow at Stacks Gate.'

He broke off, pale in the face.

'And what is the man at Stacks Gate like?' asked Connie.

'A big baby sort of fellow, very low-mouthed. She bullies him, and they both drink.'

'My word, if she came back!'

'My God, yes! I should just go, disappear again.'

There was a silence. The pasteboard in the fire had turned to grey ash.

'So when you did get a woman who wanted you,' said Connie, 'you got a bit too much of a good thing.'

'Ay! Seems so! Yet even then I'd rather have her than the never-never ones: the white love of my youth, and that other poison-smelling lily, and the rest.'

'What about the rest?' said Connie.

'The rest? There is no rest. Only to my experience the mass of women are like this: most of them want a man, but don't want the sex, but they put up with it, as part of the bargain. The more old-fashioned sort just lie there like nothing and let you go ahead. They don't mind afterwards: then they like you. But the actual thing itself is nothing to them, a bit distasteful. And most men like it that way. I hate it. But the sly sort of women who are like that pretend they're not. They pretend they're passionate and have thrills. But it's all cockaloopy. They make it up. Then there's the ones that love everything, every kind of feeling and cuddling and going off, every kind except the natural one. They always make you go off when you're *not* in the only place you should be, when you go off. Then there's the hard sort, that are the devil to bring off at all, and bring themselves off, like my wife. They want to be the active party. Then there's the sort that's just dead inside: but dead: and they know it. Then there's the sort that puts you out before you really "come", and go on writhing their loins till they bring themselves off against your thighs. But they're mostly the Lesbian sort. It's astonishing how Lesbian women are, consciously or unconsciously. Seems to me they're nearly all Lesbian.'

'And do you mind?' asked Connie.

'I could kill them. When I'm with a woman who's really Lesbian, I fairly howl in my soul, wanting to kill her.'

'And what do you do?'

'Just get away as fast as I can.'

'But do you think Lesbian women any worse than homosexual men?'

'*I* do! Because I've suffered more from them. In the abstract, I've no idea. When I get with a Lesbian woman, whether she knows she's one or not, I see red. No, no! But I wanted to have nothing to do with any woman any more. I wanted to keep to myself: keep my privacy and my decency.'

He looked pale, and his brows were sombre.

'And were you sorry when I came along?' she asked.

'I was sorry and I was glad.'

'And what are you now?'

'I'm sorry, from the outside: all the complications and the ugliness and recrimination that's bound to come, sooner or later. That's when my blood sinks, and I'm low. But when my blood comes up, I'm glad. I'm even triumphant. I was really getting bitter. I thought there was no real sex left: never a woman who'd really "come" naturally with a man: except black women, and somehow, well, we're white men: and they're a bit like mud.'

'And now, are you glad of me?' she asked.

'Yes! When I can forget the rest. When I can't forget the rest, I want to get under the table and die.'

'Why under the table?'

'Why?' he laughed. 'Hide, I suppose. Baby!'

'You do seem to have had awful experiences of women,' she said.

'You see, I couldn't fool myself. That's where most men manage. They take an attitude, and accept a lie. I could never fool myself. I knew what I wanted with a woman, and I could never say I'd got it when I hadn't.'

'But have you got it now?'

'Looks as if I might have.'

'Then why are you so pale and gloomy?'

'Bellyful of remembering: and perhaps afraid of myself.'

She sat in silence. It was growing late.

'And you do think it's important, a man and a woman?' she asked him.

'For me it is. For me it's the core to my life: if I have a right relation with a woman.'

'And if you didn't get it?'

'Then I'd have to do without.'

Again she pondered, before she asked, 'And do you think you've always been right with women?'

'God, no! I let my wife get to what she was: my fault a good deal. I spoilt her. And I'm very mistrustful. You'll have to expect it. It takes a lot to make me trust anybody, inwardly. So perhaps I'm a fraud too. I mistrust. And tenderness is not to be mistaken.'

She looked at him.

'You don't mistrust with your body, when your blood comes up,' she said. 'You don't mistrust then, do you?'

'No, alas! That's how I've got into all the trouble. And that's why my mind mistrusts so thoroughly.'

'Let your mind mistrust. What does it matter!'

The dog sighed with discomfort on the mat. The ash-clogged fire sank.

'We *are* a couple of battered warriors,' said Connie.

'Are you battered too?' he laughed. 'And here we are returning to the fray!'

'Yes! I feel really frightened.'

'Ay!'

He got up, and put her shoes to dry, and wiped his own and set them near the fire. In the morning he would grease them. He poked the ash of pasteboard as much as possible out of the fire. 'Even burnt, it's filthy,' he said. Then he brought sticks and put them on the hob for the morning. Then he went out awhile with the dog.

When he came back, Connie said, 'I want to go out too, for a minute.'

She went alone into the darkness. There were stars overhead. She could smell flowers on the night air. And she could feel her wet shoes getting wetter again. But she felt like going away, right away from him and everybody.

It was chilly. She shuddered, and returned to the house. He was sitting in front of the low fire.

'Ugh! Cold!' she shuddered.

He put the sticks on the fire, and fetched more, till they had a good crackling chimneyful of blaze. The rippling running yellow flame made them both happy, warmed their faces and their souls.

'Never mind!' she said, taking his hand as he sat silent and remote. 'One does one's best.'

'Ay!' He sighed, with a twist of a smile.

She slipped over to him, and into his arms, as he sat there before the fire.

'Forget then!' she whispered. 'Forget!'

He held her close, in the running warmth of the fire. The flame itself was like a forgetting. And her soft, warm, ripe weight! Slowly his blood turned, and began to ebb back into strength and reckless vigour again.

'And perhaps the women *really* wanted to be there and love you properly, only perhaps they couldn't. Perhaps it wasn't all their fault,' she said.

'I know it. Do you think I don't know what a broken-backed snake that's been trodden on I was myself!'

She clung to him suddenly. She had not wanted to start all this again. Yet some perversity had made her.

'But you're not now,' she said. 'You're not that now: a broken-backed snake that's been trodden on.'

'I don't know what I am. There's black days ahead.'

'No!' she protested, clinging to him. 'Why? Why?'

'There's black days coming for us all and for everybody,' he repeated with a prophetic gloom.

'No! You're not to say it!'

He was silent. But she could feel the black void of despair inside him. That was the death of all desire, the death of all love: this despair that was like the dark cave inside the men, in which their spirit was lost.

'And you talk so coldly about sex,' she said. 'You talk as if you had only wanted your own pleasure and satisfaction.'

She was protesting nervously against him.

'Nay!' he said. 'I wanted to have my pleasure and satisfaction of a woman, and I never got it: because I could never get my pleasure and satisfaction of *her* unless she got hers of me at the same time. And it never happened. It takes two.'

'But you never believed in your women. You don't even believe really in me,' she said.

'I don't know what believing in a woman means.'

'That's it, you see!'

She still was curled on his lap. But his spirit was grey and absent, he was not there for her. And everything she said drove him further.

'But what *do* you believe in?' she insisted.

'I don't know.'

'Nothing, like all the men I've ever known,' she said.

They were both silent. Then he roused himself and said, 'Yes, I do believe in something. I believe in being warm-hearted. I believe especially in being warm-hearted in love, in fucking with a warm heart. I believe if men could fuck with warm hearts, and the women take it warm-heartedly, everything would come all right. It's all this cold-hearted fucking that is death and idiocy.'

'But you don't fuck me cold-heartedly,' she protested.

'I don't want to fuck you at all. My heart's as cold as cold potatoes just now.'

'Oh!' she said, kissing him mockingly. 'Let's have them *sautées*.' He laughed, and sat erect.

'It's a fact!' he said. 'Anything for a bit of warm-heartedness. But the women don't like it. Even you don't really like it. You like good, sharp, piercing cold-hearted fucking, and then pretending it's all sugar. Where's your tenderness for me? You're as suspicious of me as a cat is of a dog. I tell you it takes two even to be tender and warm-hearted. You love fucking all right: but you want it to be called something grand and mysterious, just to flatter your own self-importance. Your own self-importance is more to you, fifty times more, than any man, or being together with a man.'

'But that's what I'd say of you. Your own self-importance is everything to you.'

'Ay! Very well then!' he said, moving as if he wanted to rise. 'Let's keep apart then. I'd rather die than do any more cold-hearted fucking.'

She slid away from him, and he stood up.

'And do you think *I* want it?' she said.

'I hope you don't,' he replied. 'But anyhow, you go to bed an' I'll sleep down here.'

She looked at him. He was pale, his brows were sullen, he was as distant in recoil as the cold pole. Men were all alike.

'I can't go home till morning,' she said.

'No! Go to bed. It's a quarter to one.'

'I certainly won't,' she said.

He went across and picked up his boots.

'Then I'll go out!' he said.

He began to put on his boots. She stared at him.

'Wait!' she faltered. 'Wait! What's come between us?'

He was bent over, lacing his boot, and did not reply. The moments passed. A dimness came over her, like a swoon. All her consciousness died, and she stood there wide-eyed, looking at him from the unknown, knowing nothing any more.

He looked up, because of the silence, and saw her wide-eyed and lost. And as if a wind tossed him he got up and hobbled over to her, one shoe off and one shoe on, and took her in his arms, pressing her against his body, which somehow felt hurt right through. And there he held her, and there she remained.

Till his hands reached blindly down and felt for her, and felt under the clothing to where she was smooth and warm.

'Ma lass!' he murmured. 'Ma little lass! Dunna let's fight! Dunna let's niver fight! I love thee an' th' touch on thee. Dunna argue wi' me! Dunna! Dunna! Dunna! Let's be together.'

She lifted her face and looked at him.

'Don't be upset,' she said steadily. 'It's no good being upset. Do you really want to be together with me?'

She looked with wide, steady eyes into his face. He stopped, and went suddenly still, turning his face aside. All his body went perfectly still, but did not withdraw.

Then he lifted his head and looked into her eyes, with his odd, faintly mocking grin, saying: 'Ay-ay! Let's be together on oath.'

'But really?' she said, her eyes filling with tears.

'Ay really! Heart an' belly an' cock.'

He still smiled faintly down at her, with the flicker of irony in his eyes, and a touch of bitterness.

She was silently weeping, and he lay with her and went into her there on the hearthrug, and so they gained a measure of equanimity. And then they went quickly to bed, for it was growing chill, and they had tired each other out. And she nestled up to him, feeling small and enfolded, and they both went to sleep at once, fast in one sleep. And so they lay and never moved, till the sun rose over the wood and day was beginning.

Then he woke up and looked at the light. The curtains were drawn. He listened to the loud wild calling of blackbirds and thrushes in the wood. It would be a brilliant morning, about half-past five, his hour for rising. He had slept so fast! It was such a new day! The woman was still curled asleep and tender. His hand moved on her, and she opened her blue, wondering eyes, smiling unconsciously into his face.

'Are you awake?' she said to him.

He was looking into her eyes. He smiled, and kissed her. And suddenly she roused and sat up.

'Fancy that I am here!' she said.

She looked round the whitewashed little bedroom with its sloping ceiling and gable window where the white curtains were closed. The room was bare save for a little yellow-painted chest of drawers, and a chair: and the smallish white bed in which she lay with him.

'Fancy that we are here!' she said, looking down at him. He was lying watching her, stroking her breasts with his fingers, under the thin nightdress. When he was warm and smoothed out, he looked young and handsome. His eyes could look so warm. And she was fresh and young like a flower.

'I want to take this off!' he said, gathering the thin batiste night-dress and pulling it over her head. She sat there with bare shoulders and longish breasts faintly golden. He loved to make her breasts swing softly, like bells.

'You must take off your pyjamas too,' she said.

'Eh, nay!'

'Yes! Yes!' she commanded.

And he took off his old cotton pyjama-jacket, and pushed down the trousers. Save for his hands and wrists and face and neck he was white as milk, with fine slender muscular flesh. To Connie he was suddenly piercingly beautiful again, as when she had seen him that afternoon washing himself.

Gold of sunshine touched the closed white curtains. She felt it wanted to come in.

'Oh, do let's draw the curtains! The birds are singing so! Do let the sun in,' she said.

He slipped out of bed with his back to her, naked and white and thin, and went to the window, stooping a little, drawing the curtains and looking out for a moment. The back was white and fine, the small buttocks beautiful with an exquisite, delicate manliness, the back of the neck ruddy and delicate and yet strong.

There was an inward, not an outward strength in the delicate fine body.

'But you are beautiful!' she said. 'So pure and fine! Come!' She held her arms out.

He was ashamed to turn to her, because of his aroused nakedness.

He caught his shirt off the floor, and held it to him, coming to her.

'No!' she said, still holding out her beautiful slim arms from her drooping breasts. 'Let me see you!'

He dropped the shirt and stood still, looking towards her. The sun through the low window sent in a beam that lit up his thighs and slim belly, and the erect phallos rising darkish and hot-looking from the little cloud of vivid gold-red hair. She was startled and afraid.

'How strange!' she said slowly. 'How strange he stands there! So big! and so dark and cocksure! Is he like that?'

The man looked down the front of his slender white body, and laughed. Between the slim breasts the hair was dark, almost black. But at the root of the belly, where the phallos rose thick and arching, it was gold-red, vivid in a little cloud.

'So proud!' she murmured, uneasy. 'And so lordly! Now I know why men are so overbearing! But he's lovely, *really*. Like another being! A bit terrifying! But lovely really! And he comes to *me*! – ' She caught her lower lip between her teeth, in fear and excitement.

The man looked down in silence at the tense phallos, that did not change. 'Ay!' he said at last, in a little voice. 'Ay ma lad! tha'rt theer right enough. Yi, tha mun rear thy head! Theer on thy own, eh? an' ta'es no count o' nob'dy! Tha ma'es nowt o' me, John Thomas.[93] Art boss? of me? Eh well, tha'rt more cocky than me, an' tha says less. John Thomas! Dost want *her*? Dost want my lady Jane? Tha's dipped me in again, tha hast. Ay, an' tha comes up smilin.' Ax 'er then! Ax lady Jane! Say: Lift up your heads o' ye gates, that the king of glory may come in.[94] Ay, th' cheek on thee! Cunt, that's what tha'rt after. Tell lady Jane tha wants cunt. John Thomas, an' th' cunt o' lady Jane! – '

'Oh, don't tease him,' said Connie, crawling on her knees on the bed towards him and putting her arms round his white slender loins, and drawing him to her so that her hanging, swinging breasts touched the tip of the stirring, erect phallos, and caught the drop of moisture. She held the man fast.

'Lie down!' he said. 'Lie down! Let me come!'

He was in a hurry now.

And afterwards, when they had been quite still, the woman had to uncover the man again, to look at the mystery of the phallos.

'And now he's tiny, and soft like a little bud of life!' she said, taking the soft small penis in her hand. 'Isn't he somehow lovely! so on his own, so strange! And so innocent! And he comes so far into me! You must *never* insult him, you know. He's mine too. He's not only yours. He's mine! And so lovely and innocent!' And she held the penis soft in her hand.

He laughed.

'Blest be the tie that binds our hearts in kindred love,'[95] he said.

'Of course!' she said. 'Even when he's soft and little I feel my heart simply tied to him. And how lovely your hair is here! quite quite different!'

'That's John Thomas's hair, not mine!' he said.

'John Thomas! John Thomas!' and she quickly kissed the soft penis, that was beginning to stir again.

'Ay!' said the man, stretching his body almost painfully. 'He's got his root in my soul, has that gentleman! An' sometimes I don' know what ter do wi' him. Ay, he's got a will of his own, an' it's hard to suit him. Yet I wouldn't have him killed.'

'No wonder men have always been afraid of him!' she said. 'He's rather terrible.'

The quiver was going through the man's body, as the stream of consciousness again changed its direction, turning downwards. And he was helpless, as the penis in slow soft undulations filled and surged and rose up, and grew hard, standing there hard and overweening, in its curious towering fashion. The woman too trembled a little as she watched.

'There! Take him then! He's thine,' said the man.

And she quivered, and her own mind melted out. Sharp soft waves of unspeakable pleasure washed over her as he entered her, and started the curious molten thrilling that spread and spread till she was carried away with the last, blind flush of extremity.

He heard the distant hooters of Stacks Gate, for seven o'clock. It was Monday morning. He shivered a little, and with his face between her breasts pressed her soft breasts up over his ears, to deafen him.

She had not even heard the hooters. She lay perfectly still, her soul washed transparent.

'You must get up, mustn't you?' he muttered.

'What time?' came her colourless voice.

'Seven-o'clock blowers a bit sin'.'

'I suppose I must.'

She was resenting, as she always did, the compulsion from outside.

He sat up and looked blankly out of the window.

'You do love me, don't you?' she asked calmly.

He looked down at her.

'Tha knows what tha knows. What dost ax for!' he said, a little fretfully.

'I want you to keep me, not to let me go,' she said.

His eyes seemed full of a warm, soft darkness that could not think.

'When? Now?'

'Now in your heart. Then I want to come and live with you always, soon.'

He sat naked on the bed, with his head dropped, unable to think.

'Don't you want it?' she asked.

'Ay!' he said.

Then with the same eyes darkened with another flame of consciousness, almost like sleep, he looked at her.

'Dunna ax me nowt now,' he said. 'Let me be. I like thee. I luv thee when tha lies theer. A woman's a lovely thing when 'er's deep ter fuck, and cunt's good. Ah luv thee, thy legs, an' th' shape on thee, an' th' womanness on thee. Ah luv th' womanness on thee. Ah luv thee wi' my ba's an' wi' my heart. But dunna ax me nowt. Dunna ma'e me say nowt. Let me stop as I am while I can. Tha can ax me ivrything after. Now let me be, let me be!'

And softly, he laid his hand over her mound of Venus, on the soft brown maiden-hair, and himself sat still and naked on the bed, his face motionless in physical abstraction, almost like the face of Buddha. Motionless, and in the invisible flame of another consciousness, he sat with his hand on her, and waited for the turn.

After a while, he reached for his shirt and put it on, dressed himself swiftly in silence, looked at her once as she still lay naked and faintly golden like a Gloire de Dijon rose on the bed, and was gone. She heard him downstairs opening the door.

And still she lay musing, musing. It was very hard to go: to go out of his arms. He called from the foot of the stairs: 'Half-past seven!' She sighed, and got out of bed. The bare little room! Nothing in it at all but the small chest of drawers and the smallish bed. But the board floor was scrubbed clean. And in the corner by the window gable was a shelf with some books, and some from a circulating library. She looked. There were books about Bolshevist Russia, books of travel, a volume about the atom and the electron, another about the composition of the earth's core, and the causes of earthquakes: then a few novels: then three books on India. So! He was a reader after all.

The sun fell on her naked limbs through the gable window. Outside she saw the dog Flossie roaming round. The hazel-brake was misted with green, and dark-green dogs-mercury under. It was a clear clean morning, with birds flying and triumphantly singing. If only she could stay! If only there weren't the other ghastly world of smoke and iron! If only *he* would make her a world.

She came downstairs, down the steep, narrow wooden stairs. Still she would be content with this little house, if only it were in a world of its own.

He was washed and fresh, and the fire was burning.

'Will you eat anything?' he said.

'No! Only lend me a comb.'

She followed him into the scullery, and combed her hair before the handbreadth of mirror by the back door. Then she was ready to go.

She stood in the little front garden, looking at the dewy flowers, the grey bed of pinks in bud already.

'I would like to have all the rest of the world disappear,' she said, 'and live with you here.'

'It won't disappear,' he said.

They went almost in silence through the lovely dewy wood. But they were together in a world of their own.

It was bitter to her to go on to Wragby.

'I want soon to come and live with you altogether,' she said as she left him.

He smiled, unanswering.

She got home quietly and unremarked, and went up to her room.

Chapter 15

THERE WAS A LETTER from Hilda on the breakfast-tray. 'Father is going to London this week, and I shall call for you on Thursday week, June 17th. You must be ready so that we can go at once. I don't want to waste time at Wragby, it's an awful place. I shall probably stay the night at Retford with the Colemans, so I should be with you for lunch Thursday. Then we could start at tea-time, and sleep perhaps in Grantham. It is no use our spending an evening with Clifford. If he hates your going, it would be no pleasure to him.'

So! She was being pushed round on the chessboard again.

Clifford hated her going, but it was only because he didn't feel *safe* in her absence. Her presence, for some reason, made him feel safe, and free to do the things he was occupied with. He was a great deal at the pits, and wrestling in spirit with the almost hopeless problems of getting out his coal in the most economical fashion and then selling it when he'd got it out. He knew he ought to find some way of *using* it, or converting it, so that he needn't sell it, or needn't have the chagrin of failing to sell it. But if he made electric power, could he sell that or use it? And to convert into oil was as yet too costly and too elaborate. To keep industry alive there must be more industry, like a madness.

It was a madness, and it required a madman to succeed in it. Well, he was a little mad. Connie thought so. His very intensity and acumen in the affairs of the pits seemed like a manifestation of madness to her, his very inspirations were the inspirations of insanity.

He talked to her of all his serious schemes, and she listened in a kind of wonder, and let him talk. Then the flow ceased, and he turned on the loudspeaker, and became a blank, while apparently his schemes coiled on inside him like a kind of dream.

And every night now he played pontoon,[96] that game of the Tommies, with Mrs Bolton, gambling with sixpences. And again, in the gambling he was gone in a kind of unconsciousness, or blank intoxication, or intoxication of blankness, whatever it was. Connie could not bear to see him. But when she had gone to bed, he and Mrs Bolton would gamble on till two and three in the morning, safely, and with strange lust. Mrs Bolton was caught in the lust as much as Clifford: the more so, as she nearly always lost.

She told Connie one day: 'I lost twenty-three shillings to Sir Clifford last night.'

'And did he take the money from you?' asked Connie, aghast.

'Why of course, my Lady! Debt of honour!'

Connie expostulated roundly, and was angry with both of them. The upshot was, Sir Clifford raised Mrs Bolton's wages a hundred a year, and she could gamble on that. Meanwhile, it seemed to Connie, Clifford was really going deader.

She told him at length she was leaving on the seventeenth.

'Seventeenth!' he said. 'And when will you be back?'

'By the twentieth of July at the latest.'

'Yes! the twentieth of July.'

Strangely and blankly he looked at her, with the vagueness of a child, but with the queer blank cunning of an old man.

'You won't let me down, now, will you?' he said.

'How?'

'While you're away. I mean, you're sure to come back?'

'I'm as sure as I can be of anything, that I shall come back.'

'Yes! Well! Twentieth of July!'

He looked at her so strangely.

Yet he really wanted her to go. That was so curious. He wanted her to go, positively, to have her little adventures and perhaps come home pregnant, and all that. At the same time, he was afraid of her going.

She was quivering, watching her real opportunity for leaving him altogether, waiting till the time, herself, himself, should be ripe.

She sat and talked to the keeper of her going abroad.

'And then when I come back,' she said, 'I can tell Clifford I must leave him. And you and I can go away. They never need even know it is you. We can go to another country, shall we? To Africa or Australia. Shall we?'

She was quite thrilled by her plan.

'You've never been to the Colonies, have you?' he asked her.

'No! Have you?'

'I've been in India, and South Africa, and Egypt.'

'Why shouldn't we go to South Africa?'

'We might!' he said slowly.

'Or don't you want to?' she asked.

'I don't care. I don't much care what I do.'

'Doesn't it make you happy? Why not? We shan't be poor. I have about six hundred a year, I wrote and asked. It's not much, but it's enough, isn't it?'

'It's riches to me.'

'Oh, how lovely it will be!'

'But I ought to get divorced, and so ought you, unless we're going to have complications.'

There was plenty to think about.

Another day she asked him about himself. They were in the hut, and there was a thunderstorm.

'And weren't you happy when you were a lieutenant and an officer and a gentleman?'

'Happy? All right. I liked my Colonel.'

'Did you love him?'

'Yes! I loved him.'

'And did he love you?'

'Yes! In a way, he loved me.'

'Tell me about him.'

'What is there to tell? He had risen from the ranks. He loved the army. And he had never married. He was twenty years older than me. He was a very intelligent man: and alone in the army, as such a man is: a passionate man in his way: and a very clever officer. I lived under his spell while I was with him. I sort of let him run my life. And I never regret it.'

'And did you mind very much when he died?'

'I was as near death myself. But when I came to, I knew another part of me was finished. But then I had always known it would finish in death. All things do, as far as that goes.'

She sat and ruminated. The thunder crashed outside. It was like being in a little ark in the Flood.

'You seem to have such a lot *behind* you,' she said.

'Do I? It seems to me I've died once or twice already. Yet here I am, pegging on, and in for more trouble.'

She was thinking hard, yet listening to the storm.

'And weren't you happy as an officer and a gentleman, when your Colonel was dead?'

'No! They were a mingy lot.' He laughed suddenly. 'The Colonel used to say: Lad, the English middle classes have to chew every mouthful thirty times because their guts are so narrow, a bit as big as a pea would give them a stoppage. They're the mingiest set of ladylike snipe[97] ever invented: full of conceit of themselves, frightened even if their boot-laces aren't correct, rotten as high game, and always in the right. That's what finishes me up. Kow-tow, kow-tow, arse-licking till their tongues are tough: yet they're always in the right. Prigs on top of everything. Prigs! A generation of ladylike prigs with half a ball each – '

Connie laughed. The rain was rushing down.

'He hated them!'

'No,' said he. 'He didn't bother. He just disliked them. There's a difference. Because, as he said, the Tommies are getting just as priggish and half-balled and narrow-gutted. It's the fate of mankind, to go that way.'

'The common people too, the working people?'

'All the lot. Their spunk is gone dead. Motor cars and cinemas and aeroplanes suck the last bit out of them. I tell you, every generation breeds a more rabbity generation, with india-rubber tubing for guts and tin legs and tin faces. Tin people! It's all a steady sort of Bolshevism just killing off the human thing, and worshipping the mechanical thing. Money, money, money! All the modern lot get their real kick out of killing the old human feeling out of man, making mincemeat of the old Adam and the old Eve. They're all alike. The world is all alike: kill off the human reality, a quid for every foreskin, two quid for each pair of balls. What is cunt but machine-fucking! It's all alike. Pay 'em money to cut off the world's cock. Pay money, money, money to them that will take spunk out of mankind, and leave 'em all little twiddling machines.'

He sat there in the hut, his face pulled to mocking irony. Yet even then, he had one ear set backwards, listening to the storm over the wood. It made him feel so alone.

'But won't it ever come to an end?' she said.

'Ay, it will. It'll achieve its own salvation. When the last real man is killed, and they're *all* tame: white, black, yellow, all colours of tame ones: then they'll *all* be insane. Because the root of sanity is in the balls. Then they'll all be *insane*, and they'll make their grand *auto da fe*. You know *auto da fe* means *act of faith*? Ay well, they'll make their own grand little act of faith. They'll offer one another up.'

'You mean kill one another?'

'I do, duckie! If we go on at our present rate then in a hundred years' time there won't be ten thousand people in this island: there may not be ten. They'll have lovingly wiped each other out.' The thunder was rolling further away.

'How nice!' she said.

'Quite nice! To contemplate the extermination of the human species and the long pause that follows before some other species crops up, it calms you more than anything else. And if we go on in this way, with everybody, intellectuals, artists, government, indust-rialists and workers all frantically killing off the last human feeling, the last bit of their intuition, the last healthy instinct; if it goes on in algebraical progression, as it is going on: then ta-tah! to the human species! Goodbye! darling! the serpent swallows itself and leaves a void, considerably messed up, but not hopeless. Very nice! When savage wild dogs bark in Wragby, and savage wild pit-ponies stamp on Tevershall pit-bank! *te deum laudamus!* [98]

Connie laughed, but not very happily.

'Then you ought to be pleased that they are all Bolshevists,' she said. 'You ought to be pleased that they hurry on towards the end.'

'So I am. I don't stop 'em. Because I couldn't if I would.'

'Then why are you so bitter?'

'I'm not! If my cock gives its last crow, I don't mind.'

'But if you have a child?' she said.

He dropped his head.

'Why,' he said at last. 'It seems to me a wrong and bitter thing to do, to bring a child into this world.'

'No! Don't say it! Don't say it!' she pleaded. 'I think I'm going to have one. Say you'll be pleased.' She laid her hand on his.

'I'm pleased for you to be pleased,' he said. 'But for me it seems a ghastly treachery to the unborn creature.'

'Ah no!' she said, shocked. 'Then you *can't* ever really want me! You *can't* want me, if you feel that!'

Again he was silent, his face sullen. Outside there was only the threshing of the rain.

'It's not quite true!' she whispered. 'It's not quite true! There's another truth.' She felt he was bitter now partly because she was leaving him, deliberately going away to Venice. And this half pleased her.

She pulled open his clothing and uncovered his belly, and kissed his navel. Then she laid her cheek on his belly, and pressed her arm round his warm, silent loins. They were alone in the flood.

'Tell me you want a child, in hope!' she murmured, pressing her face against his belly. 'Tell me you do!'

'Why!' he said at last: and she felt the curious quiver of changing consciousness and relaxation going through his body. 'Why I've thought sometimes if one but tried, here among th' colliers even! They're workin' bad now, an' not earnin' much. If a man could say to 'em: Dunna think o' nowt but th' money. When it comes ter *wants*, we want but little. Let's not live for money – '

She softly rubbed her cheek on his belly, and gathered his balls in her hand. The penis stirred softly, with strange life, but did not rise up. The rain beat bruisingly outside.

'Let's live for summat else. Let's not live ter make money, neither for us-selves nor for anybody else. Now we're forced to. We're forced to make a bit for us-selves, an' a fair lot for th' bosses. Let's stop it! Bit by bit, let's stop it. We needn't rant an' rave. Bit by bit, let's drop the whole industrial life, an' go back. The least little bit o' money'll do. For everybody, me an' you, bosses an' masters, even th' king. The least little bit o' money'll really do. Just make up your mind to it, an' you've got out o' th' mess.' He paused, then went on, 'An I'd tell 'em: Look! Look at Joe! He moves lovely! Look how he moves, alive and aware. He's beautiful! An' look at Jonah! He's clumsy, he's ugly, because he's niver willin' to rouse himself. I'd tell 'em: Look! look at yourselves! one shoulder higher than t'other, legs twisted, feet all lumps! What have yer done ter yerselves, wi' the blasted work? Spoilt yerselves. No need to work that much. Take yer clothes off an' look at yourselves. Yer ought ter be alive an' beautiful, an' yer ugly an' half dead. So I'd tell 'em. An' I'd get my men to wear different clothes: 'appen close red trousers, bright red, an' little short white jackets. Why, if men had red, fine legs, that alone would change them in a month. They'd begin to be men again, to be men! An' the women could dress as they liked. Because if once the men walked with legs close bright scarlet, and buttocks nice and showing scarlet under a little white jacket: then the women 'ud begin to be women. It's because th' men *aren't* men, that th' women have to be. An' in time pull down Tevershall and build a few beautiful buildings, that would hold us all. An' clean the country up again. An' not have many children, because the world is overcrowded.

'But I wouldn't preach to the men: only strip 'em an' say: Look at yourselves! That's workin' for money! Hark at yourselves! That's working for money. You've been working for money! Look at Tevershall! It's horrible. That's because it was built while you were working for money. Look at your girls! They don't care about you, you don't care about them. It's because you've spent your time working an' caring for money. You can't talk nor move nor live, you can't properly be with a woman. You're not alive. Look at yourselves!'

There fell a complete silence. Connie was half listening, and threading in the hair at the root of his belly a few forget-me-nots that she had gathered on the way to the hut. Outside, the world had gone still, and a little icy.

'You've got four kinds of hair,' she said to him. 'On your chest it's nearly black, and your hair isn't dark on your head: but your moustache is hard and dark red, and your hair here, your love-hair, is like a little bush of bright red-gold mistletoe. It's the loveliest of all!'

He looked down and saw the milky bits of forget-me-nots in the hair on his groin.

'Ay! That's where to put forget-me-nots, in the man-hair, or the maiden-hair. But don't you care about the future?'

She looked up at him.

'Oh, I do, terribly!' she said.

'Because when I feel the human world is doomed, has doomed itself by its own mingy beastliness, then I feel the Colonies aren't far enough. The moon wouldn't be far enough, because even there you could look back and see the earth, dirty, beastly, unsavoury among all the stars: made foul by men. Then I feel I've swallowed gall, and it's eating my inside out, and nowhere's far enough away to get away. But when I get a turn, I forget it all again. Though it's a shame, what's been done to people these last hundred years: men turned into nothing but labour-insects, and all their manhood taken away, and all their real life. I'd wipe the machines off the face of the earth again, and end the industrial epoch absolutely, like a black mistake. But since I can't, an' nobody can, I'd better hold my peace, an' try an' live my own life: if I've got one to live, which I rather doubt.'

The thunder had ceased outside, but the rain which had abated, suddenly came striking down, with a last blench of lightning and mutter of departing storm. Connie was uneasy. He had talked so long now, and he was really talking to himself, not to her. Despair seemed to come down on him completely, and she was feeling happy, she hated despair. She knew her leaving him, which he had only just realised inside himself, had plunged him back into this mood. And she triumphed a little.

She opened the door and looked at the straight heavy rain, like a steel curtain, and had a sudden desire to rush out into it, to rush away. She got up, and began swiftly pulling off her stockings, then her dress and underclothing, and he held his breath. Her pointed keen animal breasts tipped and stirred as she moved. She was ivory-coloured in the greenish light. She slipped on her rubber shoes again and ran out with a wild little laugh, holding up her breasts to the heavy rain and spreading her arms, and running blurred in the rain with the eurhythmic dance-movements[99] she had learned so long ago in Dresden. It was a strange pallid figure lifting and falling, bending so the rain beat and glistened on the full haunches, swaying up again and coming belly-forward through the rain, then stooping again so that only the full loins and buttocks were offered in a kind of homage towards him, repeating a wild obeisance.

He laughed wryly, and threw off his clothes. It was too much. He jumped out, naked and white, with a little shiver, into the hard slanting rain. Flossie sprang before him with a frantic little bark.

Connie, her hair all wet and sticking to her head, turned her hot face and saw him. Her blue eyes blazed with excitement as she turned and ran fast, with a strange charging movement, out of the clearing and down the path, the wet boughs whipping her. She ran, and he saw nothing but the round wet head, the wet back leaning forward in flight, the rounded buttocks twinkling: a wonderful cowering female nakedness in flight.

She was nearly at the wide riding when he came up and flung his naked arm round her soft, naked-wet middle. She gave a shriek and straightened herself, and the heap of her soft, chill flesh came up against his body. He pressed it all up against him, madly, the heap of soft, chilled female flesh that became quickly warm as flame, in contact. The rain streamed on them till they smoked. He gathered her lovely, heavy posteriors one in each hand and pressed them in towards him in a frenzy, quivering motionless in the rain. Then suddenly he tipped her up and fell with her on the path, in the roaring silence of the rain, and short and sharp, he took her, short and sharp and finished, like an animal.

He got up in an instant, wiping the rain from his eyes.

'Come in,' he said, and they started running back to the hut. He ran straight and swift: he didn't like the rain. But she came slower, gathering forget-me-nots and campion and bluebells, running a few steps and watching him fleeing away from her.

When she came with her flowers, panting to the hut, he had already started a fire, and the twigs were crackling. Her sharp breasts rose and fell, her hair was plastered down with rain, her face was flushed ruddy and her body glistened and trickled. Wide-eyed and breathless, with a small wet head and full, trickling, naïve haunches, she looked another creature.

He took the old sheet and rubbed her down, she standing like a child. Then he rubbed himself, having shut the door of the hut. The fire was blazing up. She ducked her head in the other end of the sheet, and rubbed her wet hair.

'We're drying ourselves together on the same towel, we shall quarrel!' he said.

She looked up for a moment, her hair all odds and ends.

'No!' she said, her eyes wide. 'It's not a towel, it's a sheet.'

And she went on busily rubbing her head, while he busily rubbed his.

Still panting with their exertions, each wrapped in an army blanket, but the front of the body open to the fire, they sat on a log side by side before the blaze, to get quiet. Connie hated the feel of the blanket against her skin. But now the sheet was all wet.

She dropped her blanket and kneeled on the clay hearth, holding her head to the fire, and shaking her hair to dry it. He watched the beautiful curving drop of her haunches. That fascinated him today. How it sloped with a rich down-slope to the heavy roundness of her buttocks! And in between, folded in the secret warmth, the secret entrances!

He stroked her tail with his hand, long and subtly taking in the curves and the globe-fullness.

'Tha's got such a nice tail on thee,' he said, in the throaty caressive dialect. 'Tha's got the nicest arse of anybody. It's the nicest, nicest woman's arse as is! An' ivry bit of it is woman, woman sure as nuts. Tha'rt not one o' them button-arsed lasses as should be lads, are ter! Tha's got a real soft sloping bottom on thee, as a man loves in 'is guts. It's a bottom as could hold the world up, it is!'

All the while he spoke he exquisitely stroked the rounded tail, till it seemed as if a slippery sort of fire came from it into his hands. And his fingertips touched the two secret openings to her body, time after time, with a soft little brush of fire.

'An' if tha shits an' if tha pisses, I'm glad. I don't want a woman as couldna shit nor piss.'

Connie could not help a sudden snort of astonished laughter, but he went on unmoved.

'Tha'rt real, tha art! Tha'rt real, even a bit of a bitch. Here tha shits an' here tha pisses: an' I lay my hand on 'em both an' like thee for it. I like thee for it. Tha's got a proper, woman's arse, proud of itself. It's none ashamed of itself, this isna.'

He laid his hand close and firm over her secret places, in a kind of close greeting.

'I like it,' he said. 'I like it! An' if I only lived ten minutes, an' stroked thy arse an' got to know it, I should reckon I'd lived *one* life, see ter! Industrial system or not! Here's one o' my lifetimes.'

She turned round and climbed into his lap, clinging to him. 'Kiss me!' she whispered.

And she knew the thought of their separation was latent in both their minds, and at last she was sad.

She sat on his thighs, her head against his breast, and her ivory-gleaming legs loosely apart, the fire glowing unequally upon them. Sitting with his head dropped, he looked at the folds of her body in the fire-glow, and at the fleece of soft brown hair that hung down to a point between her open thighs. He reached to the table behind, and took up her bunch of flowers, still so wet that drops of rain fell on to her.

'Flowers stops out of doors all weathers,' he said. 'They have no houses.'

'Not even a hut!' she murmured.

With quiet fingers he threaded a few forget-me-not flowers in the fine brown fleece of the mound of Venus.

'There!' he said. 'There's forget-me-nots in the right place!'

She looked down at the milky odd little flowers among the brown maiden-hair at the lower tip of her body.

'Doesn't it look pretty!' she said.

'Pretty as life,' he replied.

And he stuck a pink campion-bud among the hair.

'There! That's me where you won't forget me! That's Moses in the bulrushes.'

'You don't mind, do you, that I'm going away?' she asked wistfully, looking up into his face.

But his face was inscrutable, under the heavy brows. He kept it quite blank.

'You do as you wish,' he said.

And he spoke in good English.

'But I won't go if you don't wish it,' she said, clinging to him.

There was silence. He leaned and put another piece of wood on the fire. The flame glowed on his silent, abstracted face. She waited, but he said nothing.

'Only I thought it would be a good way to begin a break with Clifford. I do want a child. And it would give me a chance to, to – ' she resumed.

'To let them think a few lies,' he said.

'Yes, that among other things. Do you want them to think the truth?'

'I don't care what they think.'

'I do! I don't want them handling me with their unpleasant cold minds, not while I'm still at Wragby. They can think what they like when I'm finally gone.'

He was silent.

'But Sir Clifford expects you to come back to him?'

'Oh, I must come back,' she said: and there was silence.

'And would you have a child in Wragby?' he asked.

She closed her arm round his neck.

'If you wouldn't take me away, I should have to,' she said.

'Take you where to?'

'Anywhere! away! But right away from Wragby.'

'When?'

'Why, when I come back.'

'But what's the good of coming back, doing the thing twice, if you're once gone?' he said.

'Oh, I must come back. I've promised! I've promised so faithfully. Besides, I come back to you, really.'

'To your husband's gamekeeper?'

'I don't see that that matters,' she said.

'No?' He mused a while. 'And when would you think of going away again, then; finally? When exactly?'

'Oh, I don't know. I'd come back from Venice. And then we'd prepare everything.'

'How prepare?'

'Oh, I'd tell Clifford. I'd have to tell him.'

'Would you!'

He remained silent. She put her arms fast round his neck.

'Don't make it difficult for me,' she pleaded.

'Make what difficult?'

'For me to go to Venice and arrange things.'

A little smile, half a grin, flickered on his face.

'I don't make it difficult,' he said. 'I only want to find out just what you are after. But you don't really know yourself. You want to take time: get away and look at it. I don't blame you. I think you're wise. You may prefer to stay mistress of Wragby. I don't blame you. I've no Wragbys to offer. In fact, you know what you'll get out of me. No, no, I think you're right! I really do! And I'm not keen on coming to live on you, being kept by you. There's that too.'

She felt somehow as if he were giving her tit for tat.

'But you want me, don't you?' she asked.

'Do you want me?'

'You know I do. *That's* evident.'

'Quite! And *when* do you want me?'

'You know we can arrange it all when I come back. Now I'm out of breath with you. I must get calm and clear.'

'Quite! Get calm and clear!'

She was a little offended.

'But you trust me, don't you?' she said.

'Oh, absolutely!'

She heard the mockery in his tone.

'Tell me then,' she said flatly; 'do you think it would be better if I *don't* go to Venice?'

'I'm sure it's better if you *do* go to Venice,' he replied in the cool, slightly mocking voice.

'You know it's next Thursday?' she said.

'Yes!'

She now began to muse. At last she said, 'And we *shall* know better where we are when I come back, shan't we?'

'Oh surely!'

The curious gulf of silence between them!

'I've been to the lawyer about my divorce,' he said, a little constrainedly.

She gave a slight shudder.

'Have you!' she said. 'And what did he say?'

'He said I ought to have done it before; that may be a difficulty. But since I was in the army, he thinks it will go through all right. If only it doesn't bring *her* down on my head!'

'Will she have to know?'

'Yes! she is served with a notice: so is the man she lives with, the co-respondent.'

'Isn't it hateful, all the performances! I suppose I'd have to go through it with Clifford.'

There was a silence.

'And of course,' he said, 'I have to live an exemplary life for the next six or eight months.[100] So if you go to Venice, there's temptation removed for a week or two, at least.'

'Am I temptation!' she said, stroking his face. 'I'm so glad I'm temptation to you! Don't let's think about it! You frighten me when you start thinking: you roll me out flat. Don't let's think about it. We can think so much when we are apart. That's the whole point! I've been thinking, I *must* come to you for another night before I go. I must come once more to the cottage. Shall I come on Thursday night?'

'Isn't that when your sister will be there?'

'Yes! But she said we would start at tea-time. So we could start at tea-time. But she could sleep somewhere else and I could sleep with you.'

'But then she'd have to know.'

'Oh, I shall tell her. I've more or less told her already. I must talk it all over with Hilda. She's a great help, so sensible.'

He was thinking of her plan.

'So you'd start off from Wragby at tea-time, as if you were going to London? Which way were you going?'

'By Nottingham and Grantham.'

'And then your sister would drop you somewhere and you'd walk or drive back here? Sounds very risky, to me.'

'Does it? well, then, Hilda could bring me back. She could sleep at

Mansfield, and bring me back here in the evening, and fetch me again in the morning. It's quite easy.'

'And the people who see you?'

'I'll wear goggles and a veil.'

He pondered for some time.

'Well,' he said. 'You please yourself as usual.'

'But wouldn't it please you?'

'Oh yes! It'd please me all right,' he said a little grimly. 'I might as well smite while the iron's hot.'

'Do you know what I thought?' she said suddenly. 'It suddenly came to me. You are the "Knight of the Burning Pestle"!'[101]

'Ay! And you? Are you the Lady of the Red-Hot Mortar?'

'Yes!' she said. 'Yes! You're Sir Pestle and I'm Lady Mortar.'

'All right, then I'm knighted. John Thomas is Sir John, to your Lady Jane.'

'Yes! John Thomas is knighted! I'm my-lady-maiden-hair, and you must have flowers too. Yes!'

She threaded two pink campions in the bush of red-gold hair above his penis.

'There!' she said. 'Charming! Charming! Sir John!'

And she pushed a bit of forget-me-not in the dark hair of his breast.

'And you won't forget me *there*, will you?' She kissed him on the breast, and made two bits of forget-me-not lodge one over each nipple, kissing him again.

'Make a calendar of me!'[102] he said. He laughed, and the flowers shook from his breast.

'Wait a bit!' he said.

He rose, and opened the door of the hut. Flossie, lying in the porch, got up and looked at him.

'Ay, it's me!' he said.

The rain had ceased. There was a wet, heavy, perfumed stillness. Evening was approaching.

He went out and down the little path in the opposite direction from the riding. Connie watched his thin, white figure, and it looked to her like a ghost, an apparition moving away from her.

When she could see it no more, her heart sank. She stood in the door of the hut, with a blanket round her, looking into the drenched, motionless silence.

But he was coming back, trotting strangely, and carrying flowers. She was a little afraid of him, as if he were not quite human. And when he came near, his eyes looked into hers, but she could not understand the meaning.

He had brought columbines and campions, and new-mown hay, and oak-tufts and honeysuckle in small bud. He fastened fluffy young oak-sprays round her breasts, sticking in tufts of bluebells and campion: and in her navel he poised a pink campion flower, and in her maiden-hair were forget-me-nots and wood-ruff.

'That's you in all your glory!' he said. 'Lady Jane, at her wedding with John Thomas.'

And he stuck flowers in the hair of his own body, and wound a bit of creeping-jenny round his penis, and stuck a single bell of a hyacinth in his navel. She watched him with amusement, his odd intentness. And she pushed a campion flower in his moustache, where it stuck, dangling under his nose.

'This is John Thomas marryin' Lady Jane,' he said. 'An' we mun let Constance an' Oliver go their ways. Maybe – '

He spread out his hand with a gesture, and then he sneezed, sneezing away the flowers from his nose and his navel. He sneezed again.

'Maybe what?' she said, waiting for him to go on.

He looked at her a little bewildered.

'Eh?' he said.

'Maybe what? Go on with what you were going to say,' she insisted.

'Ay, what *was* I going to say?'

He had forgotten. And it was one of the disappointments of her life, that he never finished.

A yellow ray of sun shone over the trees.

'Sun!' he said. 'And time you went. Time, my Lady, time! What's that as flies without wings, your Ladyship? Time! Time!'

He reached for his shirt.

'Say good-night! to John Thomas,' he said, looking down at his penis. 'He's safe in the arms of creeping-jenny! Not much burning pestle about him just now.'

And he put his flannel shirt over his head.

'A man's most dangerous moment,' he said, when his head had emerged, 'is when he's getting into his shirt. Then he puts his head in a bag. That's why I prefer those American shirts, that you put on like a jacket.' She still stood watching him. He stepped into his short drawers, and buttoned them round the waist.

'Look at Jane!' he said. 'In all her blossoms! Who'll put blossoms on you next year, Jinny? Me, or somebody else? "Goodbye, my bluebell, farewell to you!"[103] I hate that song, it's early war days.' He then sat down, and was pulling on his stockings. She still stood unmoving. He laid his hand on the slope of her buttocks. 'Pretty little Lady Jane!' he said. 'Perhaps in Venice you'll find a man who'll put jasmine in your maiden-hair, and a pomegranate flower in your navel. Poor little lady Jane!'

'Don't say those things!' she said. 'You only say them to hurt me.'

He dropped his head. Then he said, in dialect, 'Ay, maybe I do, maybe I do! Well then, I'll say nowt, an' ha' done wi't. But tha mun dress thysen, all' go back to thy stately homes of England,[104] how beautiful they stand. Time's up! Time's up for Sir John, an' for little Lady Jane! Put thy shimmy[105] on, Lady Chatterley! Tha might be anybody, standin' there be-out even a shimmy, an' a few rags o' flowers. There then, there then, I'll undress thee, tha bob-tailed young throstle.' And he took the leaves from her hair, kissing her damp hair, and the flowers from her breasts, and kissed her breasts, and kissed her navel, and kissed her maiden-hair, where he left the flowers threaded. 'They mun stop while they will,' he said. 'So! There tha'rt bare again, nowt but a bare-arsed lass an' a bit of a Lady Jane! Now put thy shimmy on, for tha mun go, or else Lady Chatterley's goin' to be late for dinner, an' where 'ave yer been to my pretty maid!'[106]

She never knew how to answer him when he was in this condition of the vernacular. So she dressed herself and prepared to go a little ignominiously home to Wragby. Or so she felt it: a little ignominiously home.

He would accompany her to the broad riding. His young pheasants were all right under the shelter.

When he and she came out on to the riding, there was Mrs Bolton faltering palely towards them.

'Oh, my Lady, we wondered if anything had happened!'

'No! Nothing has happened.'

Mrs Bolton looked into the man's face, that was smooth and new-looking with love. She met his half-laughing, half-mocking eyes. He always laughed at mischance. But he looked at her kindly.

'Evening, Mrs Bolton! Your Ladyship will be all right now, so I can leave you. Good-night to your Ladyship! Good-night, Mrs Bolton!'

He saluted and turned away.

Chapter 16

CONNIE ARRIVED HOME to an ordeal of cross-questioning. Clifford had been out at tea-time, had come in just before the storm, and where was her Ladyship? Nobody knew, only Mrs Bolton suggested she had gone for a walk into the wood. Into the wood, in such a storm! – Clifford for once let himself get into a state of nervous frenzy. He started at every flash of lightning, and blenched at every roll of thunder. He looked at the icy thunder-rain as if it were the end of the world. He got more and more worked up.

Mrs Bolton tried to soothe him.

'She'll be sheltering in the hut, till it's over. Don't worry, her Ladyship is all right.'

'I don't like her being in the wood in a storm like this! I don't like her being in the wood at all! She's been gone now more than two hours. When did she go out?'

'A little while before you came in.'

'I didn't see her in the park. God knows where she is and what has happened to her.'

'Oh, nothing's happened to her. You'll see, she'll be home directly after the rain stops. It's just the rain that's keeping her.'

But her Ladyship did not come home directly the rain stopped. In fact time went by, the sun came out for his last yellow glimpse, and there still was no sign of her. The sun was set, it was growing dark, and the first dinner-gong had rung.

'It's no good!' said Clifford in a frenzy. 'I'm going to send out Field and Betts to find her.'

'Oh don't do that!' cried Mrs Bolton. 'They'll think there's a suicide or something. Oh, don't start a lot of talk going. Let me slip over to the hut and see if she's not there. I'll find her all right.'

So, after some persuasion, Clifford allowed her to go.

And so Connie had come upon her in the drive, alone and palely loitering.[107]

'You mustn't mind me coming to look for you, my Lady! But Sir Clifford worked himself up into such a state. He made sure you were struck by lightning, or killed by a falling tree. And he was determined to send Field and Betts to the wood to find the body. So I thought I'd better come, rather than set all the servants agog.'

She spoke nervously. She could still see on Connie's face the smoothness and the half-dream of passion, and she could feel the irritation against herself.

'Quite!' said Connie. And she could say no more.

The two women plodded on through the wet world, in silence, while great drops splashed like explosions in the wood. When they came to the park, Connie strode ahead, and Mrs Bolton panted a little. She was getting plumper.

'How foolish of Clifford to make a fuss!' said Connie at length, angrily, really speaking to herself.

'Oh, you know what men are! They like working themselves up. But he'll be all right as soon as he sees your Ladyship.'

Connie was very angry that Mrs Bolton knew her secret: for certainly she knew it.

Suddenly Constance stood still on the path.

'It's monstrous that I should have to be followed!' she said, her eyes flashing.

'Oh! your Ladyship, don't say that! He'd certainly have sent the two men, and they'd have come straight to the hut. I didn't know where it was, really.'

Connie flushed darker with rage, at the suggestion. Yet, while her passion was on her, she could not lie. She could not even pretend there was nothing between herself and the keeper. She looked at the other woman, who stood so sly, with her head dropped: yet somehow, in her femaleness, an ally.

'Oh well!' she said. 'If it is so it is so. I don't mind!'

'Why you're all right, my Lady! You've only been sheltering in the hut. It's absolutely nothing.'

They went on to the house. Connie marched in to Clifford's room, furious with him, furious with his pale, overwrought face and prominent eyes.

'I must say, I don't think you need send the servants after me!' she burst out.

'My God!' he exploded. 'Where have you been, woman? You've been gone hours, hours, and in a storm like this! What the hell do you go to that bloody wood for? What have you been up to? It's hours even since the rain stopped, hours! Do you know what time it is? You're enough to drive anybody mad. Where have you been? What in the name of hell have you been doing?'

'And what if I don't choose to tell you?' She pulled her hat from her head and shook her hair.

He looked at her with his eyes bulging, and yellow coming into the whites. It was very bad for him to get into these rages: Mrs Bolton had a weary time with him, for days after. Connie felt a sudden qualm.

'But really!' she said, milder. 'Anyone would think I'd been I don't know where! I just sat in the hut during all the storm, and made myself a little fire, and was happy.'

She spoke now easily. After all, why work him up any more! He looked at her suspiciously.

'And look at your hair!' he said; 'look at yourself!'

'Yes!' she replied calmly. 'I ran out in the rain with no clothes on.'

He stared at her speechless.

'You must be mad!' he said.

'Why? To like a shower-bath from the rain?'

'And how did you dry yourself?'

'On an old towel and at the fire.'

He still stared at her in a dumbfounded way.

'And supposing anybody came,' he said.

'Who would come?'

'Who? Why, anybody! And Mellors. Does he come? He must come in the evenings.'

'Yes, he came later, when it had cleared up, to feed the pheasants with corn.'

She spoke with amazing nonchalance. Mrs Bolton, who was listening in the next room, heard in sheer admiration. To think a woman could carry it off so naturally!

'And suppose he'd come while you were running about in the rain with nothing on, like a maniac?'

'I suppose he'd have had the fright of his life, and cleared out as fast as he could.'

Clifford still stared at her transfixed. What he thought in his under-consciousness he would never know. And he was too much taken aback to form one clear thought in his upper consciousness. He just simply accepted what she said, in a sort of blank. And he admired her. He could not help admiring her. She looked so flushed and handsome and smooth: love smooth.

'At least,' he said, subsiding, 'you'll be lucky if you've got off without a severe cold.'

'Oh, I haven't got a cold,' she replied. She was thinking to herself of the other man's words: Tha's got the nicest woman's arse of anybody! She wished, she dearly wished she could tell Clifford that this had been said to her, during the famous thunderstorm. However! She bore herself rather like an offended queen, and went upstairs to change.

That evening, Clifford wanted to be nice to her. He was reading one of the latest scientific-religious books: he had a streak of a spurious sort of religion in him, and was egocentrically concerned with the future of his own ego. It was like his habit to make conversation to Connie about some book, since the conversation between them had to be made, almost chemically. They had almost chemically to concoct it in their heads.

'What do you think of this, by the way?' he said, reaching for his book. 'You'd have no need to cool your ardent body by running out in the rain, if only we had a few more aeons of evolution behind us. Ah, here it is! – "The universe shows us two aspects: on one side it is physically wasting, on the other it is spiritually ascending." '[108]

Connie listened, expecting more. But Clifford was waiting. She looked at him in surprise.

'And if it spiritually ascends,' she said, 'what does it leave down below, in the place where its tail used to be?'

'Ah!' he said. 'Take the man for what he means. *Ascending* is the opposite of his *wasting*, I presume.'

'Spiritually blown out, so to speak!'

'No, but seriously, without joking: do you think there is anything in it?'

She looked at him again.

'Physically wasting?' she said. 'I see you getting fatter, and I'm not wasting myself. Do you think the sun is smaller than he used to be? He's not to me. And I suppose the apple Adam offered Eve wasn't really much bigger, if any, than one of our orange pippins. Do you think it was?'

'Well, hear how he goes on: "It is thus slowly passing, with a slowness inconceivable in our measures of time, to new creative conditions, amid which the physical world, as we at present know it, will be represented by a ripple barely to be distinguished from nonentity." '

She listened with a glisten of amusement. All sorts of improper things suggested themselves. But she only said, 'What silly hocus-pocus! As if his little conceited consciousness could know what was happening as slowly as all that! It only means *he*'s a physical failure on the earth, so he wants to make the whole universe a physical failure. Priggish little impertinence!'

'Oh, but listen! Don't interrupt the great man's solemn words! – "The present type of order in the world has risen from an un-imaginable past, and will find its grave in an unimaginable future. There remains the inexhaustive realm of abstract forms, and creativity with its shifting character ever determined afresh by its own creatures, and God, upon whose wisdom all forms of order depend." – There, that's how he winds up!'

Connie sat listening contemptuously.

'He's spiritually blown out,' she said. 'What a lot of stuff! Un-imaginables, and types of order in graves, and realms of abstract forms, and creativity with a shifty character, and God mixed up with forms of order! Why, it's idiotic!'

'I must say, it is a little vaguely conglomerate, a mixture of gases, so to speak,' said Clifford. 'Still, I think there is something in the idea that the universe is physically wasting and spiritually ascending.'

'Do you? Then let it ascend, so long as it leaves me safely and solidly physically here below.'

'Do you like your physique?' he asked.

'I love it!' And through her mind went the words: It's the nicest, nicest woman's arse as is!

'But that is really rather extraordinary, because there's no denying it's an encumbrance. But then I suppose a woman doesn't take a supreme pleasure in the life of the mind.'

'Supreme pleasure?' she said, looking up at him. 'Is that sort of idiocy the supreme pleasure of the life of the mind? No thank you! Give me the body. I believe the life of the body is a greater reality than the life of the mind: when the body is really wakened to life. But so many people, like your famous wind-machine, have only got minds tacked on to their physical corpses.'

He looked at her in wonder.

'The life of the body,' he said, 'is just the life of the animals.'

'And that's better than the life of professional corpses. But it's not true! The human body is only just coming to real life. With the Greeks it gave a lovely flicker, then Plato and Aristotle killed it, and Jesus finished it off. But now the body is coming really to life, it is really rising from the tomb. And it will be a lovely, lovely life in the lovely universe, the life of the human body.'

'My dear, you speak as if you were ushering it all in! True, you are going away on a holiday: but don't please be quite so indecently elated about it. Believe me, whatever God there is is slowly eliminating the guts and alimentary system from the human being, to evolve a higher, more spiritual being.'

'Why should I believe you, Clifford, when I feel that whatever God there is has at last wakened up in my guts, as you call them, and is rippling so happily there, like dawn. Why should I believe you, when I feel so very much the contrary?'

'Oh, exactly! And what has caused this extraordinary change in you? running out stark naked in the rain, and playing Bacchante? desire for sensation, or the anticipation of going to Venice?'

'Both! Do you think it is horrid of me to be so thrilled at going off?' she said.

'Rather horrid to show it so plainly.'

'Then I'll hide it.'

'Oh, don't trouble! You almost communicate a thrill to me. I almost feel that it is *I* who am going off.'

'Well, why don't you come?'

'We've gone over all that. And as a matter of fact, I suppose your greatest thrill comes from being able to say a temporary farewell to all this. Nothing so thrilling, for the moment, as Goodbye-to-it-all! – But every parting means a meeting elsewhere. And every meeting is a new bondage.'

'I'm not going to enter any new bondages.'

'Don't boast, while the gods are listening,' he said.

She pulled up short.

'No! I won't boast!' she said.

But she was thrilled, none the less, to be going off: to feel bonds snap. She couldn't help it.

Clifford, who couldn't sleep, gambled all night with Mrs Bolton, till she was too sleepy almost to live.

And the day came round for Hilda to arrive. Connie had arranged with Mellors that if everything promised well for their night together, she would hang a green shawl out of the window. If there were frustration, a red one.

Mrs Bolton helped Connie to pack.

'It will be so good for your Ladyship to have a change.'

'I think it will. You don't mind having Sir Clifford on your hands alone for a time, do you?'

'Oh no! I can manage him quite all right. I mean, I can do all he needs me to do. Don't you think he's better than he used to be?'

'Oh much! You do wonders with him.'

'Do I though! But men are all alike: just babies, and you have to flatter them and wheedle them and let them think they're having their own way. Don't you find it so, my Lady?'

'I'm afraid I haven't much experience.'

Connie paused in her occupation.

'Even your husband, did you have to manage him, and wheedle him like a baby?' she asked, looking at the other woman.

Mrs Bolton paused too.

'Well!' she said. 'I had to do a good bit of coaxing, with him too. But he always knew what I was after, I must say that. But he generally gave in to me.'

'He was never the lord and master thing?'

'No! At least there'd be a look in his eyes sometimes, and then I knew *I'd* got to give in. But usually he gave in to me. No, he was never lord and master. But neither was I. I knew when I could go no further with him, and then I gave in: though it cost me a good bit, sometimes.'

'And what if you had held out against him?'

'Oh, I don't know. I never did. Even when he was in the wrong, if he was fixed, I gave in. You see I never wanted to break what was between us. And if you really set your will against a man, that finishes it. If you care for a man, you have to give in to him once he's really determined; whether you're in the right or not, you have to give in. Else you break something. But I must say, Ted 'ud give in to me sometimes, when I was set on a thing, and in the wrong. So I suppose it cuts both ways.'

'And that's how you are with all your patients?' asked Connie.

'Oh, that's different. I don't care at all, in the same way. I know what's good for them, or I try to, and then I just contrive to manage them for their own good. It's not like anybody as you're really fond of. It's quite different. Once you've been really fond of a man, you can be affectionate to almost any man, if he needs you at all. But it's not the same thing. You don't really *care*. I doubt, once you've *really* cared, if you can ever really care again.'

These words frightened Connie.

'Do you think one can only care once?' she asked.

'Or never. Most women never care, never begin to. They don't know what it means. Nor men either. But when I see a woman as cares, my heart stands still for her.'

'And do you think men easily take offence?'

'Yes! If you wound them on their pride. But aren't women the same? Only our two prides are a bit different.'

Connie pondered this. She began again to have some misgiving about her going away. After all, was she not giving her man the go-by, if only for a short time? And he knew it. That's why he was so queer and sarcastic.

Still! the human existence is a good deal controlled by the machine of external circumstance. She was in the power of this machine. She couldn't extricate herself all in five minutes. She didn't even want to.

Hilda arrived in good time on Thursday morning, in a nimble two-seater car, with her suitcase strapped firmly behind. She looked as demure and maidenly as ever, but she had the same will of her own. She had the very hell of a will of her own, as her husband had found out. But the husband was now divorcing her. Yes, she even made it easy for him to do that, though she had no lover. For the time being, she was 'off' men. She was very well content to be quite her own mistress: and mistress of her two children, whom she was going to bring up 'properly', whatever that may mean.

Connie was only allowed a suitcase, also. But she had sent on a trunk to her father, who was going by train. No use taking a car to

Venice. And Italy much too hot to motor in, in July. He was going comfortably by train. He had just come down from Scotland.

So, like a demure arcadian field-marshal, Hilda arranged the material part of the journey. She and Connie sat in the upstairs room, chatting.

'But Hilda!' said Connie, a little frightened. 'I want to stay near here tonight. Not here: near here!'

Hilda fixed her sister with grey, inscrutable eyes. She seemed so calm: and she was so often furious.

'Where, near here?' she asked softly.

'Well, you know I love somebody, don't you?'

'I gathered there was something.'

'Well he lives near here, and I want to spend this last night with him. I must! I've promised.'

Connie became insistent.

Hilda bent her Minerva-like head in silence. Then she looked up.

'Do you want to tell me who he is?' she said.

'He's our gamekeeper,' faltered Connie, and she flushed vividly, like a shamed child.

'Connie!' said Hilda, lifting her nose slightly with disgust: a motion she had from her mother.

'I know: but he's lovely really. He really understands tenderness,' said Connie, trying to apologise for him.

Hilda, like a ruddy, rich-coloured Athena,[109] bowed her head and pondered. She was really violently angry. But she dared not show it, because Connie, taking after her father, would straightway become obstreperous and unmanageable.

It was true, Hilda did not like Clifford: his cool assurance that he was somebody! She thought he made use of Connie shamefully and impudently. She had hoped her sister *would* leave him. But, being solid Scotch middle-class, she loathed any 'lowering' of oneself, or the family. She looked up at last.

'You'll regret it,' she said.

'I shan't,' cried Connie, flushed red. 'He's quite the exception. I *really* love him. He's lovely as a lover.'

Hilda still pondered.

'You'll get over him quite soon,' she said, 'and live to be ashamed of yourself because of him.'

'I shan't! I hope I'm going to have a child of his.'

'*Connie!*' said Hilda, hard as a hammer-stroke, and pale with anger.

'I shall if I possibly can. I should be fearfully proud if I had a child by him.'

It was no use talking to her. Hilda pondered.

'And doesn't Clifford suspect?' she said.

'Oh no! Why should he?'

'I've no doubt you've given him plenty of occasion for suspicion,' said Hilda.

'Not at all.'

'And tonight's business seems quite gratuitous folly. Where does the man live?'

'In the cottage at the other end of the wood.'

'Is he a bachelor?'

'No! His wife left him.'

'How old?'

'I don't know. Older than me.'

Hilda became more angry at every reply, angry as her mother used to be, in a kind of paroxysm. But still she hid it.

'I would give up tonight's escapade if I were you,' she advised calmly.

'I can't! I *must* stay with him tonight, or I can't go to Venice at all. I just can't.'

Hilda heard her father over again, and she gave way, out of mere diplomacy. And she consented to drive to Mansfield, both of them, to dinner, to bring Connie back to the lane-end after dark, and to fetch her from the lane-end the next morning, herself sleeping in Mansfield, only half an hour away, good going. But she was furious. She stored it up against her sister, this baulk in her plans.

Connie flung an emerald-green shawl over her window-sill.

On the strength of her anger, Hilda warmed towards Clifford. After all, he had a mind. And if he had no sex, functionally, all the better: so much the less to quarrel about! Hilda wanted no more of that sex business, where men became nasty, selfish little horrors. Connie really had less to put up with than many women, if she did but know it.

And Clifford decided that Hilda, after all, was a decidedly intelligent woman, and would make a man a first-rate helpmeet, if he were going in for politics for example. Yes, she had none of Connie's silliness, Connie was more a child: you had to make excuses for her, because she was not altogether dependable.

There was an early cup of tea in the hall, where doors were open to let in the sun. Everybody seemed to be panting a little.

'Goodbye, Connie girl! Come back to me safely.'

'Goodbye, Clifford! Yes, I shan't be long.' Connie was almost tender.

'Goodbye, Hilda! You will keep an eye on her, won't you?'

'I'll even keep two!' said Hilda. 'She shan't go very far astray.'

'It's a promise!'

'Goodbye, Mrs Bolton! I know you'll look after Sir Clifford nobly.'

'I'll do what I can, your Ladyship.'

'And write to me if there is any news, and tell me about Sir Clifford, how he is.'

'Very good, your Ladyship, I will. And have a good time, and come back and cheer us up.'

Everybody waved. The car went off. Connie looked back and saw Clifford sitting at the top of the steps in his house-chair. After all, he was her husband: Wragby was her home: circumstance had done it.

Mrs Chambers held the gate and wished her Ladyship a happy holiday. The car slipped out of the dark spinney that masked the park, on to the high-road where the colliers were trailing home. Hilda turned to the Crosshill Road, that was not a main road, but ran to Mansfield. Connie put on goggles. They ran beside the railway, which was in a cutting below them. Then they crossed the cutting on a bridge.

'That's the lane to the cottage!' said Connie.

Hilda glanced at it impatiently.

'It's a frightful pity we can't go straight off!' she said. 'We could have been in Pall Mall by nine o'clock.'

'I'm sorry for your sake,' said Connie, from behind her goggles.

They were soon at Mansfield, that once-romantic, now utterly disheartening colliery town. Hilda stopped at the hotel named in the motor car book, and took a room. The whole thing was utterly uninteresting, and she was almost too angry to talk. However, Connie *had* to tell her something of the man's history.

'*He! He!* What name do you call him by? You only say *he*,' said Hilda.

'I've never called him by any name: nor he me: which is curious, when you come to think of it. Unless we say Lady Jane and John Thomas. But his name is Oliver Mellors.'

'And how would you like to be Mrs Oliver Mellors, instead of Lady Chatterley?'

'I'd love it.'

There was nothing to be done with Connie. And anyhow, if the man had been a lieutenant in the army in India for four or five years, he must be more or less presentable. Apparently he had character. Hilda began to relent a little.

'But you'll be through with him in a while,' she said, 'and then you'll be ashamed of having been connected with him. One *can't* mix up with the working people.'

'But you are such a socialist! you're always on the side of the working classes.'

'I may be on their side in a political crisis, but being on their side makes me know how impossible it is to mix one's life with theirs. Not out of snobbery, but just because the whole rhythm is different.'

Hilda had lived among the real political intellectuals, so she was disastrously unanswerable.

The nondescript evening in the hotel dragged out, and at last they had a nondescript dinner. Then Connie slipped a few things into a little silk bag, and combed her hair once more.

'After all, Hilda,' she said, 'love can be wonderful; when you feel you *live*, and are in the very middle of creation.' It was almost like bragging on her part.

'I suppose every mosquito feels the same,' said Hilda.

'Do you think it does? How nice for it!'

The evening was wonderfully clear and long-lingering, even in the small town. It would be half-light all night. With a face like a mask, from resentment, Hilda started her car again, and the two sped back on their traces, taking the other road, through Bolsover.

Connie wore her goggles and disguising cap, and she sat in silence. Because of Hilda's opposition, she was fiercely on the side of the man, she would stand by him through thick and thin.

They had their headlights on, by the time they passed Crosshill, and the small lit-up train that chuffed past in the cutting made it seem like real night. Hilda had calculated the turn into the lane at the bridge-end. She slowed up rather suddenly and swerved off the road, the lights glaring white into the grassy, overgrown lane. Connie looked out. She saw a shadowy figure, and she opened the door.

'Here we are!' she said softly.

But Hilda had switched off the lights, and was absorbed backing, making the turn.

'Nothing on the bridge?' she asked shortly.

'You're all right,' said the man's voice.

She backed on to the bridge, reversed, let the car run forwards a few yards along the road, then backed into the lane, under a wych-elm tree, crushing the grass and bracken. Then all the lights went out. Connie stepped down. The man stood under the trees.

'Did you wait long?' Connie asked.

'Not so very,' he replied.

They both waited for Hilda to get out. But Hilda shut the door of the car and sat tight.

'This is my sister Hilda. Won't you come and speak to her? Hilda! This is Mr Mellors.'

The keeper lifted his hat, but went no nearer.

'Do walk down to the cottage with us, Hilda,' Connie pleaded. 'It's not far.'

'What about the car?'

'People do leave them on the lanes. You have the key.'

Hilda was silent, deliberating. Then she looked backwards down the lane.

'Can I back round the bush?' she said.

'Oh yes!' said the keeper.

She backed slowly round the curve, out of sight of the road, locked the car, and got down. It was night, but luminous dark. The hedges rose high and wild, by the unused lane, and very dark seeming. There was a fresh sweet scent on the air. The keeper went ahead, then came Connie, then Hilda, and in silence. He lit up the difficult places with a flashlight torch, and they went on again, while an owl softly hooted over the oaks, and Flossie padded silently around. Nobody could speak. There was nothing to say.

At length Connie saw the yellow light of the house, and her heart beat fast. She was a little frightened. They trailed on, still in Indian file.

He unlocked the door and preceded them into the warm but bare little room. The fire burned low and red in the grate. The table was set with two plates and two glasses, on a proper white tablecloth for once. Hilda shook her hair and looked round the bare, cheerless room. Then she summoned her courage and looked at the man.

He was moderately tall, and thin, and she thought him good-looking. He kept a quiet distance of his own, and seemed absolutely unwilling to speak.

'Do sit down, Hilda,' said Connie.

'Do!' he said. 'Can I make you tea or anything, or will you drink a glass of beer? It's moderately cool.'

'Beer!' said Connie.

'Beer for me, please!' said Hilda, with a mock sort of shyness. He looked at her and blinked.

He took a blue jug and tramped to the scullery. When he came back with the beer, his face had changed again.

Connie sat down by the door, and Hilda sat in his seat, with the back to the wall, against the window corner.

'That is his chair,' said Connie softly. And Hilda rose as if it had burnt her.

'Sit yer still, sit yer still! Ta'e ony cheer as yo'n a mind to, none of us is th' big bear,' he said, with complete equanimity.

And he brought Hilda a glass, and poured her beer first from the blue jug.

'As for cigarettes,' he said, 'I've got none, but 'appen you've got your own. I dunna smoke, mysen. Shall y' eat summat?' He turned direct to Connie. 'Shall t'eat a smite o' summat, if I bring it thee? Tha can usually do wi' a bite.' He spoke the vernacular with a curious calm assurance, as if he were the landlord of the inn.

'What is there?' asked Connie, flushing.

'Boiled ham, cheese, pickled wa'nuts, if yer like. Nowt much.'

'Yes,' said Connie. 'Won't you, Hilda?'

Hilda looked up at him.

'Why do you speak Yorkshire?' she said softly.

'That! That's non Yorkshire, that's Derby.'

He looked back at her with that faint, distant grin.

'Derby, then! Why do you speak Derby? You spoke natural English at first.'

'Did Ah though? An' canna Ah change if Ah'n a mind to 't? Nay, nay, let me talk Derby if it suits me. If yo'n nowt against it.'

'It sounds a little affected,' said Hilda.

'Ay, 'appen so! An' up i' Tevershall yo'd sound affected.' He looked again at her, with a queer calculating distance, along his cheek-bones: as if to say: Yi, an' who are you?

He tramped away to the pantry for the food.

The sisters sat in silence. He brought another plate, and knife and fork. Then he said, 'An' if it's the same to you, I s'll ta'e my coat off, like I allers do.'

And he took off his coat, and hung it on the peg, then sat down to table in his shirt-sleeves: a shirt of thin, cream-coloured flannel.

' 'Elp yerselves!' he said. ' 'Elp yerselves! Dunna wait fr axin'!'

He cut the bread, then sat motionless. Hilda felt, as Connie once used to, his power of silence and distance. She saw his smallish, sensitive, loose hand on the table. He was no simple working man, not he: he was acting! acting!

'Still!' she said, as she took a little cheese. 'It would be more natural if you spoke to us in normal English, not in vernacular.'

He looked at her, feeling her devil of a will.

'Would it?' he said in the normal English. 'Would it? Would anything that was said between you and me be quite natural, unless you said you wished me to hell before your sister ever saw me again: and unless I said something almost as unpleasant back again? Would anything else be natural?'

'Oh yes!' said Hilda. 'Just good manners would be quite natural.'

'Second nature, so to speak!' he said: then he began to laugh. 'Nay,' he said. 'I'm weary o' manners. Let me be!'

Hilda was frankly baffled and furiously annoyed. After all, he might show that he realised he was being honoured. Instead of which, with his play-acting and lordly airs, he seemed to think it was he who was conferring the honour. Just impudence! Poor misguided Connie, in the man's clutches!

The three ate in silence. Hilda looked to see what his table-manners were like. She could not help realising that he was instinctively much more delicate and well-bred than herself. She had a certain Scottish clumsiness. And moreover, he had all the quiet self-contained assurance of the English, no loose edges. It would be very difficult to get the better of him.

But neither would he get the better of her.

'And do you really think,' she said, a little more humanly, 'it's worth the risk?'

'Is what worth what risk?'

'This escapade with my sister.'

He flickered his irritating grin.

'Yo' maun ax 'er!'

Then he looked at Connie.

'Tha comes o' thine own accord, lass, doesn't ter? It's non me as forces thee?'

Connie looked at Hilda.

'I wish you wouldn't cavil, Hilda.'

'Naturally I don't want to. But someone has to think about things. You've got to have some sort of continuity in your life. You can't just go making a mess.'

There was a moment's pause.

'Eh, continuity!' he said. 'An' what by that? What continuity 'ave yer got i' *your* life? I thought you was gettin' divorced. What continuity's that? Continuity o' yer own stubbornness. I can see that much. An' what good's it goin' to do yer? You'll be sick o' yer continuity afore yer a fat sight older. A stubborn woman an' 'er own self-will: ay, they make a fast continuity, they do. Thank heaven, it isn't me as 'as got th' andlin' of yer!'

'What right have you to speak like that to me?' said Hilda.

'Right! What right ha' yo' ter start harnessin' other folks i' your continuity? Leave folks to their own continuities.'

'My dear man, do you think I am concerned with you?' said Hilda softly.

'Ay,' he said. 'Yo' are. For it's a force-put. Yo' more or less my sister-in-law.'

'Still far from it, I assure you.'

'Not a' that far, I assure *you*. I've got my own sort o' continuity, back your life! Good as yours, any day. An' if your sister there comes ter me for a bit o' cunt an' tenderness, she knows what she's after. She's been in my bed afore: which you 'aven't, thank the Lord, with your continuity.' There was a dead pause, before he added: ' – Eh, I don't wear me breeches arse-forrards. An' if I get a windfall, I thank my stars. A man gets a lot of enjoyment out o' that lass theer, which is more than anybody gets out o' th' likes o' you. Which is a pity, for you might 'appen a' bin a good apple, 'stead of a handsome crab. Women like you needs proper graftin'.'

He was looking at her with an odd, flickering smile, faintly sensual and appreciative.

'And men like you,' she said, 'ought to be segregated: justifying their own vulgarity and selfish lust.'

'Ay, ma'am! It's a mercy there's a few men left like me. But you deserve what you get: to be left severely alone.'

Hilda had risen and gone to the door. He rose and took his coat from the peg.

'I can find my way quite well alone,' she said.

'I doubt you can't,' he replied easily.

They tramped in ridiculous file down the lane again, in silence. An owl still hooted. He knew he ought to shoot it.

The car stood untouched, a little dewy. Hilda got in and started the engine. The other two waited.

'All I mean,' she said from her entrenchment, 'is that I doubt if you'll find it's been worth it, either of you!'

'One man's meat is another man's poison,' he said, out of the darkness. 'But it's meat an' drink to me.'

The lights flared out.

'Don't make me wait in the morning, Connie.'

'No, I won't. Good-night!'

The car rose slowly on to the high-road, then slid swiftly away, leaving the night silent.

Connie timidly took his arm, and they went down the lane. He did not speak. At length she drew him to a standstill.

'Kiss me!' she murmured.

'Nay, wait a bit! Let me simmer down,' he said.

That amused her. She still kept hold of his arm, and they went quickly down the lane, in silence. She was so glad to be with him, just now. She shivered, knowing that Hilda might have snatched her away. He was inscrutably silent.

When they were in the cottage again, she almost jumped with pleasure, that she should be free of her sister.

'But you were horrid to Hilda,' she said to him.

'She should ha' been slapped in time.'

'But why? and she's *so* nice.'

He didn't answer, went round doing the evening chores, with a quiet, inevitable sort of motion. He was outwardly angry, but not with her. So Connie felt. And his anger gave him a peculiar handsomeness, an inwardness and glisten that thrilled her and made her limbs go molten.

Still, he took no notice of her.

Till he sat down and began to unlace his boots. Then he looked up at her from under his brows, on which the anger still sat firm.

'Shan't you go up?' he said. 'There's a candle!'

He jerked his head swiftly to indicate the candle burning on the table. She took it obediently, and he watched the full curve of her hips as she went up the first stairs.

It was a night of sensual passion, in which she was a little startled and almost unwilling: yet pierced again with piercing thrills of sensuality, different, sharper, more terrible than the thrills of tenderness, but, at the moment, more desirable. Though a little frightened, she let him have his way, and the reckless, shameless sensuality shook her to her foundations, stripped her to the very last, and made a different woman of her. It was not really love. It was not voluptuousness. It was sensuality sharp and searing as fire, burning the soul to tinder.

Burning out the shames, the deepest, oldest shames, in the most secret places. It cost her an effort to let him have his way and his will of her. She had to be a passive, consenting thing, like a slave, a physical slave. Yet the passion licked round her, consuming, and when the sensual flame of it pressed through her bowels and breast, she really though she was dying: yet a poignant, marvellous death.

She had often wondered what Abélard meant, when he said that in their year of love he and Heloïse[110] had passed through all the stages and refinements of passion. The same thing, a thousand years ago: ten thousand years ago! The same on the Greek vases, everywhere! The refinements of passion, the extravagances of sensuality! And necessary, forever necessary, to burn out false shames and smelt out the heaviest ore of the body into purity. With the fire of sheer sensuality.

In the short summer night she learnt so much. She would have thought a woman would have died of shame. Instead of which, the shame died. Shame, which is fear: the deep organic shame, the old, old physical fear which crouches in the bodily roots of us, and can only be chased away by the sensual fire, at last it was roused up and routed by the phallic hunt of the man, and she came to the very heart of the jungle of herself. She felt, now, she had come to the real bedrock of her nature, and was essentially shameless. She was her sensual self, naked and unashamed. She felt a triumph, almost a vainglory. So! That was how it was! That was life! That was how oneself really was! There was nothing left to disguise or be ashamed of. She shared her ultimate nakedness with a man, another being.

And what a reckless devil the man was! really like a devil! One had to be strong to bear him. But it took some getting at, the core of the physical jungle, the last and deepest recess of organic shame. The phallos alone could explore it. And how he had pressed in on her!

And how, in fear, she had hated it. But how she had really wanted it! She knew now. At the bottom of her soul, fundamentally, she had needed this phallic hunting out, she had secretly wanted it, and she had believed that she would never get it. Now suddenly there it was, and a man was sharing her last and final nakedness, she was shameless.

What liars poets and everybody were! They made one think one wanted sentiment. When what one supremely wanted was this piercing, consuming, rather awful sensuality. To find a man who dared do it, without shame or sin or final misgiving! If he had been ashamed afterwards, and made one feel ashamed, how awful! What a pity most men are so doggy, a bit shameful, like Clifford! Like Michaelis even! Both sensually a bit doggy and humiliating. The supreme pleasure of the mind! And what is that to a woman? What is it, really, to the man either! He becomes merely messy and doggy, even in his mind. It needs sheer sensuality even to purify and quicken the mind. Sheer fiery sensuality, not messiness.

Ah, God, how rare a thing a man is! They are all dogs that trot and sniff and copulate. To have found a man who was not afraid and not ashamed! She looked at him now, sleeping so like a wild animal asleep, gone, gone in the remoteness of it. She nestled down, not to be away from him.

Till his rousing waked her completely. He was sitting up in bed, looking down at her. She saw her own nakedness in his eyes, immediate knowledge of her. And the fluid, male knowledge of herself seemed to flow to her from his eyes and wrap her voluptuously. Oh, how voluptuous and lovely it was to have limbs and body half-asleep, heavy and suffused with passion!

'Is it time to wake up?' she said.

'Half-past six.'

She had to be at the lane-end at eight. Always, always, always this compulsion on one!

'I might make the breakfast and bring it up here; should I?' he said.

'Oh yes!'

Flossie whimpered gently below. He got up and threw off his pyjamas, and rubbed himself with a towel. When the human being is full of courage and full of life, how beautiful it is! So she thought, as she watched him in silence.

'Draw the curtain, will you?'

The sun was shining already on the tender green leaves of morning, and the wood stood bluey-fresh, in the nearness. She sat up in bed, looking dreamily out through the dormer window, her naked arms pushing her naked breasts together. He was dressing himself. She was half-dreaming of life, a life together with him: just a life.

He was going, fleeing from her dangerous, crouching nakedness.

'Have I lost my nightie altogether?' she said.

He pushed his hand down in the bed, and pulled out the bit of flimsy silk.

'I knowed I felt silk at my ankles,' he said.

But the nightdress was slit almost in two.

'Never mind!' she said. 'It belongs here, really. I'll leave it.'

'Ay, leave it, I can put it between my legs at night, for company. There's no name nor mark on it, is there?'

She slipped on the torn thing, and sat dreamily looking out of the window. The window was open, the air of morning drifted in, and the sound of birds. Birds flew continuously past. Then she saw Flossie roaming out. It was morning.

Downstairs she heard him making the fire, pumping water, going out at the back door. By and by came the smell of bacon, and at length he came upstairs with a huge black tray that would only just go through the door. He set the tray on the bed, and poured out the tea. Connie squatted in her torn nightdress, and fell on her food hungrily. He sat on the one chair, with his plate on his knees.

'How good it is!' she said. 'How nice to have breakfast together.'

He ate in silence, his mind on the time that was quickly passing. That made her remember.

'Oh, how I wish I could stay here with you, and Wragby were a million miles away! It's Wragby I'm going away from really. You know that, don't you?'

'Ay!'

'And you promise we will live together and have a life together, you and me! You promise me, don't you?'

'Ay! When we can.'

'Yes! And we *will*! we *will*, won't we?' She leaned over, making the tea spill, catching his wrist.

'Ay!' he said, tidying up the tea.

'We can't possibly *not* live together now, can we?' she said appealingly.

He looked up at her with his flickering grin.

'No!' he said. 'Only you've got to start in twenty-five minutes.'

'Have I?' she cried. Suddenly he held up a warning finger, and rose to his feet.

Flossie had given a short bark, then three loud sharp yaps of warning.

Silent, he put his plate on the tray and went downstairs. Constance heard him go down the garden path. A bicycle bell tinkled outside there.

'Morning, Mr Mellors! Registered letter!'

'Oh ay! Got a pencil?'

'Here y'are!'

There was a pause.

'Canada!' said the stranger's voice.

'Ay! That's a mate o' mine out there in British Columbia. Dunno what he's got to register.'

' 'Appen sent y'a fortune, like.'

'More like wants summat.'

Pause.

'Well! Lovely day again!'

'Ay!'

'Morning!'

'Morning!'

After a time he came upstairs again, looking a little angry.

'Postman,' he said.

'Very early!' she replied.

'Rural round; he's mostly here by seven, when he does come.'

'Did your mate send you a fortune?'

'No! Only some photographs and papers about a place out there in British Columbia.'

'Would you go there?'

'I thought perhaps we might.'

'Oh yes! I believe it's lovely!'

But he was put out by the postman's coming.

'Them damned bikes, they're on you afore you know where you are. I hope he twigged nothing.'

'After all, what could he twig!'

'You must get up now, and get ready. I'm just goin' ter look round outside.'

She saw him go reconnoitring into the lane, with dog and gun. She went downstairs and washed, and was ready by the time he came back, with the few things in the little silk bag.

He locked up, and they set off, but through the wood, not down the lane. He was being wary.

'Don't you think one lives for times like last night?' she said to him.

'Ay! But there's the rest o' times to think on,' he replied, rather short.

They plodded on down the overgrown path, he in front, in silence.

'And we *will* live together and make a life together, won't we?' she pleaded.

'Ay!' he replied, striding on without looking round. 'When t' time comes! Just now you're off to Venice or somewhere.'

She followed him dumbly, with sinking heart. Oh, now she *was* to go!

At last he stopped.

'I'll just strike across here,' he said, pointing to the right.

But she flung her arms round his neck, and clung to him.

'But you'll keep the tenderness for me, won't you?' she whispered. 'I loved last night. But you'll keep the tenderness for me, won't you?'

He kissed her and held her close for a moment. Then he sighed, and kissed her again.

'I must go an' look if th' car's there.'

He strode over the low brambles and bracken, leaving a trail through the fern. For a minute or two he was gone. Then he came striding back.

'Car's not there yet,' he said. 'But there's the baker's cart on t' road.'

He seemed anxious and troubled.

'Hark!'

They heard a car softly hoot as it came nearer. It slowed up on the bridge.

She plunged with utter mournfulness in his track through the fern, and came to a huge holly hedge. He was just behind her.

'Here! Go through there!' he said, pointing to a gap. 'I shan't come out.'

She looked at him in despair. But he kissed her and made her go. She crept in sheer misery through the holly and through the wooden fence, stumbled down the little ditch and up into the lane, where Hilda was just getting out of the car in vexation.

'Why you're there!' said Hilda. 'Where's *he?*'

'He's not coming.'

Connie's face was running with tears as she got into the car with her little bag. Hilda snatched up the motoring helmet with the disfiguring goggles.

'Put it on!' she said. And Connie pulled on the disguise, then the long motoring coat, and she sat down, a goggling, inhuman, unrecognisable creature. Hilda started the car with a businesslike motion. They heaved out of the lane, and were away down the road. Connie had looked round, but there was no sight of him. Away! Away! She sat in bitter tears. The parting had come so suddenly, so unexpectedly. It was like death.

'Thank goodness you'll be away from him for some time!' said Hilda, turning to avoid Crosshill village.

Chapter 17

'YOU SEE, HILDA,' said Connie after lunch, when they were nearing London, 'you have never known either real tenderness or real sensuality: and if you do know them, with the same person, it makes a great difference.'

'For mercy's sake don't brag about your experiences!' said Hilda. 'I've never met the man yet who was capable of intimacy with a woman, giving himself up to her. That was what I wanted. I'm not keen on their self-satisfied tenderness, and their sensuality. I'm not content to be any man's little petsy-wetsy, nor his *chair à plaisir*[111] either. I wanted a complete intimacy, and I didn't get it. That's enough for me.'

Connie pondered this. Complete intimacy! She supposed that meant revealing everything concerning yourself to the other person, and his revealing everything concerning himself. But that was a bore. And all that weary self-consciousness between a man and a woman! a disease!

'I think you're too conscious of yourself all the time, with everybody,' she said to her sister.

'I hope at least I haven't a slave nature,' said Hilda.

'But perhaps you have! Perhaps you are a slave to your own idea of yourself.'

Hilda drove in silence for some time after this piece of unheard-of insolence from that chit Connie.

'At least I'm not a slave to somebody else's idea of me: and the somebody else a servant of my husband's,' she retorted at last, in crude anger.

'You see, it's not so,' said Connie calmly.

She had always let herself be dominated by her elder sister. Now, though somewhere inside herself she was weeping, she was free of the dominion of *other women*. Ah! that in itself was a relief, like being given another life: to be free of the strange dominion and obsession of *other women*. How awful they were, women!

She was glad to be with her father, whose favourite she had always been. She and Hilda stayed in a little hotel off Pall Mall, and Sir Malcolm was in his club. But he took his daughters out in the evening, and they liked going with him.

He was still handsome and robust, though just a little afraid of the new world that had sprung up around him. He had got a second wife in Scotland, younger than himself, and richer. But he had as many holidays away from her as possible: just as with his first wife.

Connie sat next to him at the opera. He was moderately stout, and had stout thighs, but they were still strong and well-knit, the thighs of a healthy man who had taken his pleasure in life. His good-humoured selfishness, his dogged sort of independence, his unrepenting sensuality, it seemed to Connie she could see them all in his well-knit straight thighs. Just a man! And now becoming an old man, which is sad. Because in his strong, thick male legs there was none of the alert sensitiveness and power of tenderness which is the very essence of youth, that which never dies, once it is there.

Connie woke up to the existence of legs. They became more important to her than faces, which are no longer very real. How few people had live, alert legs! She looked at the men in the stalls. Great puddingy thighs in black pudding-cloth, or lean wooden sticks in black funeral stuff, or well-shaped young legs without any meaning whatever, either sensuality or tenderness or sensitiveness, just mere leggy ordinariness that pranced around. Not even any sensuality like her father's. They were all daunted, daunted out of existence.

But the women were not daunted. The awful mill-posts of most females! really shocking, really enough to justify murder! Or the poor thin pegs! or the trim neat things in silk stockings, without the slightest look of life! Awful, the millions of meaningless legs prancing meaninglessly around!

But she was not happy in London. The people seemed so spectral and blank. They had no alive happiness, no matter how brisk and good-looking they were. It was all barren. And Connie had a woman's blind craving for happiness, to be assured of happiness.

In Paris at any rate she felt a bit of sensuality still. But what a weary, tired, worn-out sensuality. Worn-out for lack of tenderness. Oh! Paris was sad. One of the saddest towns: weary of its now-mechanical sensuality, weary of the tension of money, money, money, weary even of resentment and conceit, just weary to death, and still not sufficiently Americanised or Londonised to hide the weariness under a mechanical jig-jig-jig! Ah, these manly he-men, these *flâneurs*,[112] the oglers, these eaters of good dinners! How weary they were! weary, worn-out for lack of a little tenderness, given and taken. The efficient, sometimes charming women knew a thing or two about the sensual realities: they had that pull over their jigging English sisters. But they knew even less of tenderness. Dry, with the endless dry tension of will, they too were wearing out. The human world was just getting worn out. Perhaps it would turn fiercely destructive. A sort of anarchy! Clifford and his conservative anarchy! Perhaps it wouldn't be conservative much longer. Perhaps it would develop into a very radical anarchy.

Connie found herself shrinking and afraid of the world. Sometimes she was happy for a little while in the Boulevards or in the Bois or the Luxembourg Gardens. But already Paris was full of Americans and English, strange Americans in the oddest uniforms, and the usual dreary English that are so hopeless abroad.

She was glad to drive on. It was suddenly hot weather, so Hilda was going through Switzerland and over the Brenner, then through the Dolomites down to Venice. Hilda loved all the managing and the driving and being mistress of the show. Connie was quite content to keep quiet.

And the trip was really quite nice. Only Connie kept saying to herself: Why don't I really care? Why am I never really thrilled? How awful, that I don't really care about the landscape any more! But I don't. It's rather awful. I'm like Saint Bernard,[113] who could sail down the lake of Lucerne without ever noticing that there were even mountain and green water. I just don't care for landscape any more. Why should one stare at it? Why should one? I refuse to.

No, she found nothing vital in France or Switzerland or the Tyrol or Italy. She just was carted through it all. And it was all less real than Wragby. Less real than the awful Wragby! She felt she didn't care if she never saw France or Switzerland or Italy again. They'd keep. Wragby was more real.

As for people! people were all alike, with very little difference. They all wanted to get money out of you: or, if they were travellers, they wanted to get enjoyment, perforce, like squeezing blood out of a stone. Poor mountains! poor landscape! it all had to be squeezed and squeezed and squeezed again, to provide a thrill, to provide enjoyment. What did people mean, with their simply *determined* enjoying of themselves?

No! said Connie to herself. I'd rather be at Wragby, where I can go about and be still, and not stare at anything or do any performing of any sort. This tourist performance of enjoying oneself is too hopelessly humiliating: it's such a failure.

She wanted to go back to Wragby, even to Clifford, even to poor crippled Clifford. He wasn't such a fool as this swarming holidaying lot, anyhow.

But in her inner consciousness she was keeping touch with the other man. She mustn't let her connection with him go: oh, she mustn't let it go, or she was lost, lost utterly in this world of riff-raffy expensive people and joy-hogs. Oh, the joy-hogs! Oh 'enjoying oneself!' Another modern form of sickness.

They left the car in Mestre, in a garage, and took the regular steamer over to Venice. It was a lovely summer afternoon, the shallow lagoon rippled, the full sunshine made Venice, turning its back to them across the water, look dim.

At the station quay they changed to a gondola, giving the man the address. He was a regular gondolier in a white-and-blue blouse, not very good-looking, not at all impressive.

'Yes! The Villa Esmeralda! Yes! I know it! I have been the gondolier for a gentleman there. But a fair distance out!'

He seemed a rather childish, impetuous fellow. He rowed with a certain exaggerated impetuosity, through the dark side-canals with the horrible, slimy green walls, the canals that go through the poorer quarters, where the washing hangs high up on ropes, and there is a slight, or strong odour of sewage.

But at last he came to one of the open canals with pavement on either side, and looping bridges, that run straight, at right-angles to the Grand Canal. The two women sat under the little awning, the man was perched above, behind them.

'Are the signorine staying long at the Villa Esmeralda?' he asked, rowing easy, and wiping his perspiring face with a white-and-blue handkerchief.

'Some twenty days: we are both married ladies,' said Hilda, in her curious hushed voice, that made her Italian sound so foreign.

'Ah! Twenty days!' said the man. There was a pause. After which he asked: 'Do the signore want a gondolier for the twenty days or so that they will stay at the Villa Esmeralda? Or by the day, or by the week?'

Connie and Hilda considered. In Venice, it is always preferable to have one's own gondola, as it is preferable to have one's own car on land.

'What is there at the Villa? what boats?'

'There is a motor-launch, also a gondola. But – ' The *but* meant: they won't be your property.

'How much do you charge?'

It was about thirty shillings a day, or ten pounds a week.

'Is that the regular price?' asked Hilda.

'Less, Signora, less. The regular price – '

The sisters considered.

'Well,' said Hilda, 'come tomorrow morning, and we will arrange it. What is your name?'

His name was Giovanni, and he wanted to know at what time he should come, and then, for whom should he say he was waiting. Hilda had no card. Connie gave him one of hers. He glanced at it swiftly, with his hot, southern blue eyes, then glanced again.

'Ah!' he said, lighting up. 'Milady! Milady, isn't it?'

'Milady Costanza!' said Connie.

He nodded, repeating: 'Milady Costanza!' and putting the card carefully away in his blouse.

The Villa Esmeralda was quite a long way out, on the edge of the lagoon looking towards Chioggia. It was not a very old house, and pleasant, with the terraces looking seawards, and below, quite a big garden with dark trees, walled in from the lagoon.

Their host was a heavy, rather coarse Scotchman who had made a good fortune in Italy before the war, and had been knighted for his ultra-patriotism during the war. His wife was a thin, pale, sharp kind of person with no fortune of her own, and the misfortune of having to regulate her husband's rather sordid amorous exploits. He was terribly tiresome with the servants. But having had a slight stroke during the winter, he was now more manageable.

The house was pretty full. Besides Sir Malcolm and his two daughters, there were seven more people, a Scotch couple, again with two daughters; a young Italian Contessa, a widow; a young Georgian prince, and a youngish English clergyman who had had pneumonia and was being chaplain to Sir Alexander for his health's sake. The prince was penniless, good-looking, would make an excellent chauffeur, with the necessary impudence, and basta![114] The Contessa was a quiet little puss with a game on somewhere. The clergyman was a raw simple fellow from a Bucks vicarage: luckily he had left his wife and two children at home. And the Guthries, the family of four, were good solid Edinburgh middle class, enjoying everything in a solid fashion, and daring everything while risking nothing.

Connie and Hilda ruled out the prince at once. The Guthries were more or less their own sort, substantial, but boring: and the girls wanted husbands. The chaplain was not a bad fellow, but too deferential. Sir Alexander, after his slight stroke, had a terrible heaviness in his joviality, but he was still thrilled at the presence of so many handsome young women. Lady Cooper was a quiet, catty person who had a thin time of it, poor thing, and who watched every other woman with a cold watchfulness that had become her second nature, and who said cold, nasty little things which showed what an utterly low opinion she had of all human nature. She was also quite venomously overbearing with the servants, Connie found: but in a quiet way. And she skilfully behaved so that Sir Alexander should think that *he* was lord and monarch of the whole caboosh, with his stout, would-be-genial paunch, and his utterly boring jokes, his humourosity, as Hilda called it.

Sir Malcolm was painting. Yes, he still would do a Venetian lagoonscape, now and then, in contrast to his Scottish landscapes. So in the morning he was rowed off with a huge canvas, to his 'site'. A little later, Lady Cooper would be rowed off into the heart of the city, with sketching-block and colours. She was an inveterate water-colour painter, and the house was full of rose-coloured palaces, dark canals, swaying bridges, medieval façades, and so on. A little later the Guthries, the prince, the countess, Sir Alexander, and sometimes Mr Lind, the chaplain, would go off to the Lido, where they would bathe; coming home to a late lunch at half-past one.

The house-party, as a house-party, was distinctly boring. But this did not trouble the sisters. They were out all the time. Their father took them to the exhibition, miles and miles of weary paintings. He took them to all the cronies of his in the Villa Lucchese, he sat with them on warm evenings in the piazza, having got a table at Florian's: he took them to the theatre, to the Goldoni[115] plays. There were illuminated water-fêtes, there were dances. This was a holiday-place of all holiday-places. The Lido, with its acres of sun-pinked or pyjamaed bodies, was like a strand with an endless heap of seals come up for mating. Too many people in the piazza, too many limbs and trunks of humanity on the Lido, too many gondolas, too many motor-launches, too many steamers, too many pigeons, too many ices, too many cocktails, too many menservants wanting tips, too many languages rattling, too much, too much sun, too much smell of Venice, too many cargoes of strawberries, too many silk shawls, too many huge, raw-beef slices of watermelon on stalls: too much enjoyment, altogether far too much enjoyment!

Connie and Hilda went around in their sunny frocks. There were dozens of people they knew, dozens of people knew them. Michaelis turned up like a bad penny. 'Hullo! Where you staying? Come and have an ice-cream or something! Come with me somewhere in my gondola.' Even Michaelis *almost* sunburned: though sun-cooked is more appropriate to the look of the mass of human flesh.

It was pleasant in a way. It was *almost* enjoyment. But anyhow, with all the cocktails, all the lying in warmish water and sunbathing on hot sand in hot sun, jazzing with your stomach up against some fellow in the warm nights, cooling off with ices, it was a complete narcotic. And that was what they all wanted, a drug: the slow water, a drug; the sun, a drug; jazz, a drug; cigarettes, cocktails, ices, vermouth. To be drugged! Enjoyment! Enjoyment!

Hilda half liked being drugged. She liked looking at all the women, speculating about them. The women were absorbingly interested in the women. How does she look! what man has she captured? what fun is she getting out of it? – The men were like great dogs in white flannel trousers, waiting to be patted, waiting to wallow, waiting to plaster some woman's stomach against their own, in jazz.

Hilda liked jazz, because she could plaster her stomach against the stomach of some so-called man, and let him control her movements from the visceral centre, here and there across the floor, and then she could break loose and ignore 'the creature'. He had been merely made use of. Poor Connie was rather unhappy. She wouldn't jazz, because she simply couldn't plaster her stomach against some 'creature's' stomach. She hated the conglomerate mass of nearly nude flesh on the Lido: there was hardly enough water to wet them all. She disliked Sir Alexander and Lady Cooper. She did not want Michaelis or anybody else trailing her.

The happiest times were when she got Hilda to go with her away across the lagoon, far across to some lonely shingle-bank, where they could bathe quite alone, the gondola remaining on the inner side of the reef.

Then Giovanni got another gondolier to help him, because it was a long way and he sweated terrifically in the sun. Giovanni was very nice: affectionate, as the Italians are, and quite passionless. The Italians are not passionate: passion has deep reserves. They are easily moved, and often affectionate, but they rarely have any abiding passion of any sort.

So Giovanni was already devoted to his ladies, as he had been devoted to cargoes of ladies in the past. He was perfectly ready to prostitute himself to them, if they wanted him: he secretly hoped they would want him. They would give him a handsome present, and it would come in very handy, as he was just going to be married. He told them about his marriage, and they were suitably interested.

He thought this trip to some lonely bank across the lagoon probably meant business: business being *l'amore*, love. So he got a mate to help him, for it *was* a long way: and after all, they were two ladies. Two ladies, two mackerels! Good arithmetic! Beautiful ladies, too! He was justly proud of them. And though it was the Signora who paid him and gave him orders, he rather hoped it would be the young milady who would select him for *l'amore*. She would give more money too.

The mate he brought was called Daniele. He was not a regular gondolier, so he had none of the cadger and prostitute about him. He was a sandola man, a sandola being a big boat that brings in fruit and produce from the islands.

Daniele was beautiful, tall and well-shapen, with a light round head of little, close-pale-blond curls, and a good-looking man's face, a little like a lion, and long-distance blue eyes. He was not effusive, loquacious, and bibulous like Giovanni. He was silent and he rowed with a strength and ease as if he were alone on the water. The ladies were ladies, remote from him. He did not even look at them. He looked ahead.

He was a real man, a little angry when Giovanni drank too much wine and rowed awkwardly, with effusive shoves of the great oar. He was a man as Mellors was a man, unprostituted. Connie pitied the wife of the easily-overflowing Giovanni. But Daniele's wife would be one of those sweet Venetian women of the people whom one still sees, modest and flower-like in the back of that labyrinth of a town.

Ah, how sad that man first prostitutes woman, then woman prostitutes man. Giovanni was pining to prostitute himself, dribbling like a dog, wanting to give himself to a woman. And for money!

Connie looked at Venice far off, low and rose-coloured upon the water. Built of money, blossomed of money, and dead with money.

The money-deadness! Money, money, money, prostitution and deadness.

Yet Daniele was still a man capable of a man's free allegiance. He did not wear the gondolier's blouse: only the knitted blue jersey. He was a little wild, uncouth and proud. So he was hireling to the rather doggy Giovanni, who was hireling again of two women. So it is! When Jesus refused the devil's money,[116] he left the devil like a Jewish banker, master of the whole situation.

Connie would come home from the blazing light of the lagoon in a kind of stupor, to find letters from home. Clifford wrote regularly. He wrote very good letters: they might all have been printed in a book. And for this reason Connie found them not very interesting.

She lived in the stupor of the light of the lagoon, the lapping saltiness of the water, the space, the emptiness, the nothingness: but health, health, complete stupor of health. It was gratifying, and she was lulled away in it, not caring for anything. Besides, she was pregnant. She knew now. So the stupor of sunlight and lagoon salt and sea-bathing and lying on shingle and finding shells and drifting away, away in a gondola was completed by the pregnancy inside her, another fullness of health, satisfying and stupefying.

She had been at Venice a fortnight, and she was to stay another ten days or a fortnight. The sunshine blazed over any count of time, and the fullness of physical health made forgetfulness complete. She was in a sort of stupor of well-being.

From which a letter from Clifford roused her.

We too have had our mild local excitement. It appears the truant wife of Mellors, the keeper, turned up at the cottage, and found herself unwelcome. He packed her off and locked the door. Report has it, however, that when he returned from the wood he found the no longer fair lady firmly established in his bed, in *puris naturalibus*;[117] or one should say, in *impuris naturalibus*. She had broken a window and got in that way. Unable to evict the somewhat man-handled Venus from his couch, he beat a retreat and retired, it is said, to his mother's house in Tevershall. Meanwhile the Venus of Stacks Gate is established in the cottage, which she claims is her home, and Apollo, apparently, is domiciled in Tevershall.

I repeat this from hearsay, as Mellors has not come to me personally. I had this particular bit of local garbage from our garbage bird, our ibis, our scavenging turkey-buzzard, Mrs Bolton. I would not have repeated it had she not exclaimed: her Ladyship will go no more to the wood if *that* woman's going to be about!

I like your picture of Sir Malcolm striding into the sea with white hair blowing and pink flesh glowing. I envy you that sun. Here it rains. But I don't envy Sir Malcolm his inveterate mortal carnality. However, it suits his age. Apparently one grows more carnal and more mortal as one grows older. Only youth has a taste of immortality –

This news affected Connie in her state of semi-stupefied well-being with vexation amounting to exasperation. Now she had got to be bothered by that beast of a woman! Now she must start and fret! She had no letter from Mellors. They had agreed not to write at all, but now she wanted to hear from him personally. After all, he was the father of the child that was coming. Let him write!

But how hateful! Now everything was messed up. How foul those low people were! How nice it was here, in the sunshine and the indolence, compared to that dismal mess of that English Midlands! After all, a clear sky was almost the most important thing in life.

She did not mention the fact of her pregnancy, even to Hilda. She wrote to Mrs Bolton for exact information.

Duncan Forbes, an artist friend of theirs, had arrived at the Villa Esmeralda, coming north from Rome. Now he made a third in the gondola, and he bathed with them across the lagoon, and was their escort: a quiet, almost taciturn young man, very advanced in his art.

She had a letter from Mrs Bolton:

You will be pleased, I am sure, my Lady, when you see Sir Clifford. He's looking quite blooming and working very hard, and very hopeful. Of course he is looking forward to seeing you among us again. It is a dull house without my Lady, and we shall all welcome her presence among us once more.

About Mr Mellors, I don't know how much Sir Clifford told you. It seems his wife came back all of a sudden one afternoon, and he found her sitting on the doorstep when he came in from the wood. She said she was come back to him and wanted to live with him again, as she was his legal wife, and he wasn't going to divorce her. Because it seems Mr Mellors was trying for a divorce. But he wouldn't have anything to do with her, and wouldn't let her in the house, and did not go in himself, he went back into the wood without ever opening the door.

But when he came back after dark, he found the house broken into, so he went upstairs to see what she'd done, and he found her in bed without a rag on her. He offered her money, but she said she was his wife and he must take her back. I don't know what sort

of a scene they had. His mother told me about it, she's terribly
upset. Well he told her he'd die rather than ever live with her
again, so he took his things and went straight to his mother's on
Tevershall hill. He stopped the night and went to the wood next
day through the park, never going near the cottage. It seems he
never saw his wife that day. But the day after she was at her
brother Dan's at Beggarlee, swearing and carrying on, saying she
was his legal wife, and that he'd been having women at the
cottage, because she'd found a scent-bottle in his drawer, and
gold-tipped cigarette-ends on the ash-heap, and I don't know
what all. Then it seems the postman Fred Kirk says he heard
somebody talking in Mr Mellors' bedroom early one morning,
and a motor car had been in the lane.

Mr Mellors stayed on with his mother, and went to the wood
through the park, and it seems she stayed on at the cottage. Well,
there was no end of talk. So at last Mr Mellors and Tom Phillips
went to the cottage and fetched away most of the furniture and
bedding, and unscrewed the handle of the pump, so she was
forced to go. But instead of going back to Stacks Gate she went
and lodged with that Mrs Swain at Beggarlee, because her brother
Dan's wife wouldn't have her. And she kept going to old Mrs
Mellors' house, to catch him, and she began swearing he'd got in
bed with her in the cottage, and she went to a lawyer to make him
pay her an allowance. She's grown heavy, and more common than
ever, and as strong as a bull. And she goes about saying the most
awful things about him, how he has women at the cottage, and
how he behaved to her when they were married, the low, beastly
things he did to her, and I don't know what all. I'm sure it's awful,
the mischief a woman can do, once she starts talking. And no
matter how low she may be, there'll be some as will believe her,
and some of the dirt will stick. I'm sure the way she makes out
that Mr Mellors was one of those low, beastly men with women, is
simply shocking. And people are only too ready to believe things
against anybody, especially things like that. She declares she'll
never leave him alone while he lives. Though what I say is, if he
was so beastly to her, why is she so anxious to go back to him? But
of course she's coming near her change of life, for she's years
older than he is. And these common, violent women always go
partly insane when the change of life comes upon them –

This was a nasty blow to Connie. Here she was, sure as life,
coming in for her share of the lowness and dirt. She felt angry with

him for not having got clear of Bertha Coutts: nay, for ever having married her. Perhaps he had a certain hankering after lowness. Connie remembered the last night she had spent with him, and shivered. He had known all that sensuality, even with Bertha Coutts! It was really rather disgusting. It would be well to be rid of him, clear of him altogether. He was perhaps really common, really low.

She had a revulsion against the whole affair, and almost envied the Guthrie girls their gawky inexperience and crude maidenliness. And she now dreaded the thought that anybody would know about herself and the keeper. How unspeakably humiliating! She was weary, afraid, and felt a craving for utter respectability, even for the vulgar and deadening respectability of the Guthrie girls. If Clifford knew about her affair, how unspeakably humiliating! She was afraid, terrified of society and its unclean bite. She almost wished she could get rid of the child again, and be quite clear. In short, she fell into a state of funk.

As for the scent-bottle, that was her own folly. She had not been able to refrain from perfuming his one or two handkerchiefs and his shirts in the drawer, just out of childishness, and she had left a little bottle of Coty's Wood-violet perfume, half empty, among his things. She wanted him to remember her in the perfume. As for the cigarette-ends, they were Hilda's.

She could not help confiding a little in Duncan Forbes. She didn't say she had been the keeper's lover, she only said she liked him, and told Forbes the history of the man.

'Oh,' said Forbes, 'you'll see, they'll never rest till they've pulled the man down and done him in. If he has refused to creep up into the middle classes, when he had a chance; and if he's a man who stands up for his own sex, then they'll do him in. It's the one thing they won't let you be, straight and open in your sex. You can be as dirty as you like. In fact the more dirt you do on sex, the better they like it. But if you believe in your own sex, and won't have it done dirt to: they'll down you. It's the one insane taboo left: sex as a natural and vital thing. They won't have it, and they'll kill you before they'll let you have it. You'll see, they'll hound that man down. And what's he done, after all? If he's made love to his wife all ends on, hasn't he a right to? She ought to be proud of it. But you see, even a low bitch like that turns on him, and uses the hyena instinct of the mob against sex, to pull him down. You have a snivel and feel sinful or awful about your sex, before you're allowed to have any. Oh, they'll hound the poor devil down.'

Connie had a revulsion in the opposite direction now. What had he done, after all? what had he done to herself, Connie, but give her an exquisite pleasure and a sense of freedom and life? He had released her warm, natural sexual flow. And for that they would hound him down.

No no, it should not be. She saw the image of him, naked white with tanned face and hands, looking down and addressing his erect penis as if it were another being, the odd grin flickering on his face. And she heard his voice again: Tha's got the nicest woman's arse of anybody! And she felt his hand warmly and softly closing over her tail again, over her secret places, like a benediction. And the warmth ran through her womb, and the little flames flickered in her knees, and she said: Oh no! I mustn't go back on it! I must not go back on him. I must stick to him and to what I had of him, through everything. I had no warm, flamy life till he gave it me. And I won't go back on it.

She did a rash thing. She sent a letter to Ivy Bolton, enclosing a note to the keeper, and asking Mrs Bolton to give it him. And she wrote to him:

> I am very much distressed to hear of all the trouble your wife is making for you, but don't mind it, it is only a sort of hysteria. It will all blow over as suddenly as it came. But I'm awfully sorry about it, and I do hope you are not minding very much. After all, it isn't worth it. She is only a hysterical woman who wants to hurt you. I shall be home in ten days' time, and I do hope everything will be all right.

A few days later came a letter from Clifford. He was evidently upset.

> I am delighted to hear you are prepared to leave Venice on the sixteenth. But if you are enjoying it, don't hurry home. We miss you, Wragby misses you. But it is essential that you should get your full amount of sunshine, sunshine and pyjamas, as the advertisements of the Lido say. So please do stay on a little longer, if it is cheering you up and preparing you for our sufficiently awful winter. Even today, it rains.
>
> I am assiduously, admirably looked after by Mrs Bolton. She is a queer specimen. The more I live, the more I realise what strange creatures human beings are. Some of them might just as well have a hundred legs, like a centipede, or six, like a lobster. The human consistency and dignity one has been led to expect from one's fellow-men seem actually non-existent. One doubts if they exist to any startling degree even in oneself.
>
> The scandal of the keeper continues and gets bigger like a

snowball. Mrs Bolton keeps me informed. She reminds me of a fish which, though dumb, seems to be breathing silent gossip through its gills, while ever it lives. All goes through the sieve of her gills, and nothing surprises her. It is as if the events of other people's lives were the necessary oxygen of her own.

She is preoccupied with the Mellors scandal, and if I will let her begin, she takes me down to the depths. Her great indignation, which even then is like the indignation of an actress playing a role, is against the wife of Mellors, whom she persists in calling Bertha Coutts. I have been to the depths of the muddy lives of the Bertha Couttses of this world, and when, released from the current of gossip, I slowly rise to the surface again, I look at the daylight in wonder that it ever should be.

It seems to me absolutely true, that our world, which appears to us the surface of all things, is really the *bottom* of a deep ocean: all our trees are submarine growths, and we are weird, scaly-clad submarine fauna, feeding ourselves on offal like shrimps. Only occasionally the soul rises gasping through the fathomless fathoms under which we live, far up to the surface of the ether, where there is true air. I am convinced that the air we normally breathe is a kind of water, and men and women are a species of fish.

But sometimes the soul does come up, shoots like a kittiwake into the light, with ecstasy, after having preyed on the submarine depths. It is our mortal destiny, I suppose, to prey upon the ghastly subaqueous life of our fellow-men, in the submarine jungle of mankind. But our immortal destiny is to escape, once we have swallowed our swimmy catch, up again into the bright ether, bursting out from the surface of Old Ocean into real light. Then one realises one's eternal nature.

When I hear Mrs Bolton talk, I feel myself plunging down, down, to the depths where the fish of human secrets wriggle and swim. Carnal appetite makes one seize a beakful of prey: then up, up again, out of the dense into the ethereal, from the wet into the dry. To you I can tell the whole process. But with Mrs Bolton I only feel the downward plunge, down, horribly, among the sea-weeds and the pallid monsters of the very bottom.

I am afraid we are going to lose our gamekeeper. The scandal of the truant wife, instead of dying down, has reverberated to greater and greater dimensions. He is accused of all unspeakable things, and curiously enough, the woman has managed to get the bulk of the colliers' wives behind her, gruesome fish, and the village is putrescent with talk.

I hear this Bertha Coutts besieges Mellors in his mother's house, having ransacked the cottage and the hut. She seized one day upon her own daughter, as that chip of the female block was returning from school; but the little one, instead of kissing the loving mother's hand, bit it firmly, and so received from the other hand a smack in the face which sent her reeling into the gutter: whence she was rescued by an indignant and harassed grandmother.

The woman has blown off an amazing quantity of poison-gas. She has aired in detail all those incidents of her conjugal life which are usually buried down in the deepest grave of matrimonial silence, between married couples. Having chosen to exhume them, after ten years of burial, she has a weird array. I hear these details from Linley and the doctor: the latter being amused. Of course there is really nothing in it. Humanity has always had a strange avidity for unusual sexual postures, and if a man likes to use his wife, as Benvenuto Cellini says, 'in the Italian way',[118] well that is a matter of taste. But I had hardly expected our gamekeeper to be up to so many tricks. No doubt Bertha Coutts herself first put him up to them. In any case, it is a matter of their own personal squalor, and nothing to do with anybody else.

However, everybody listens: as I do myself. A dozen years ago, common decency would have hushed the thing. But common decency no longer exists, and the colliers' wives are all up in arms and unabashed in voice. One would think every child in Tevershall, for the last fifty years, had been an immaculate conception, and every one of our nonconformist females was a shining Joan of Arc. That our estimable gamekeeper should have about him a touch of Rabelais[119] seems to make him more monstrous and shocking than a murderer like Crippen.[120] Yet these people in Tevershall are a loose lot, if one is to believe all accounts.

The trouble is, however, the execrable Bertha Coutts has not confined herself to her own experiences and sufferings. She has discovered, at the top of her voice, that her husband has been 'keeping' women down at the cottage, and has made a few random shots at naming the women. This has brought a few decent names trailing through the mud, and the thing has gone quite considerably too far. An injunction has been taken out against the woman.

I have had to interview Mellors about the business, as it was impossible to keep the woman away from the wood. He goes about as usual, with his Miller-of-the-Dee air,[121] I cares for nobody, no not I, if nobody cares for me! Nevertheless, I shrewdly suspect he feels like a dog with a tin can tied to its tail: though he makes a very good show of pretending the tin can isn't there. But I hear that in the village the women call away their children if he is passing, as if he were the Marquis de Sade[122] in person. He goes on with a certain impudence, but I am afraid the tin can is firmly tied to his tail, and that inwardly he repeats, like Don Rodrigo[123] in the Spanish ballad: 'Ah, now it bites me where I most have sinned!'

I asked him if he thought he would be able to attend to his duty in the wood, and he said he did not think he had neglected it. I told him it was a nuisance to have the woman trespassing: to which he replied that he had no power to arrest her. Then I hinted at the scandal and its unpleasant course. 'Ay,' he said. 'Folks should do their own fuckin', then they wouldn't want to listen to a lot of clatfart[124] about another man's.'

He said it with some bitterness, and no doubt it contains the real germ of truth. The mode of putting it, however, is neither delicate nor respectful. I hinted as much, and then I heard the tin can rattle again. 'It's not for a man i' the shape you're in, Sir Clifford, to twit me for havin' a cod atween my legs.'

These things, said indiscriminately to all and sundry, of course do not help him at all, and the rector, and Linley, and Burroughs all think it would be as well if the man left the place.

I asked him if it was true that he entertained ladies down at the cottage, and all he said was: 'Why, what's that to you, Sir Clifford?' I told him I intended to have decency observed on my estate, to which he replied: 'Then you mun button the mouths o' a' th' women.' – When I pressed him about his manner of life at the cottage, he said: 'Surely you might ma'e a scandal out o' me an' my bitch Flossie. You've missed summat there.' As a matter of fact, for an example of impertinence he'd be hard to beat.

I asked him if it would be easy for him to find another job. He said: 'If you're hintin' that you'd like to shunt me out of this job, it'd be easy as wink.' So he made no trouble at all about leaving at the end of next week, and apparently is willing to initiate a young fellow, Joe Chambers, into as many mysteries of the craft as possible. I told him I would give him a month's wages extra, when he left. He said he'd rather I kept my money, as I'd no occasion to ease my conscience. I asked him what he meant, and he said: 'You don't owe me nothing extra, Sir Clifford, so don't pay me nothing extra. If you think you see my shirt hanging out, just tell me.'

Well, there is the end of it for the time being. The woman has gone away: we don't know where to: but she is liable to arrest if she shows her face in Tevershall. And I hear she is mortally afraid of gaol, because she merits it so well. Mellors will depart on Saturday week, and the place will soon become normal again.

Meanwhile, my dear Connie, if you would enjoy to stay in Venice or in Switzerland till the beginning of August, I should be glad to think you were out of all this buzz of nastiness, which will have died quite away by the end of the month.

So you see, we are deep-sea monsters, and when the lobster walks on mud, he stirs it up for everybody. We must perforce take it philosophically.

The irritation, and the lack of any sympathy in any direction, of Clifford's letter, had a bad effect on Connie. But she understood it better when she received the following from Mellors:

The cat is out of the bag, along with various other pussies. You have heard that my wife Bertha came back to my unloving arms, and took up her abode in the cottage: where, to speak disrespectfully, she smelled a rat, in the shape of a little bottle of Coty. Other evidence she did not find, at least for some days, when she began to howl about the burnt photograph. She noticed the glass and the backboard in the square bedroom. Unfortunately, on the backboard somebody had scribbled little sketches, and the initials, several times repeated: C.S.R. This, however, afforded no clue until she broke into the hut, and found one of your books, an autobiography of the actress Judith,[125] with your name, Constance Stewart Reid, on the front page. After this, for some days she went round loudly saying that my paramour was no less a person than Lady Chatterley herself. The news came at last to the rector, Mr Burroughs, and to Sir Clifford. They then proceeded to take legal steps against my liege lady, who for her part disappeared, having always had a mortal fear of the police.

Sir Clifford asked to see me, so I went to him. He talked around things and seemed annoyed with me. Then he asked if I knew that even her Ladyship's name had been mentioned. I said I never listened to scandal, and was surprised to hear this bit from Sir Clifford himself. He said, of course it was a great insult, and I told him there was Queen Mary[126] on a calendar in the scullery, no doubt because Her Majesty formed part of my harem. But he didn't appreciate the sarcasm. He as good as told me I was a disreputable character who walked about with my breeches' buttons undone, and I as good as told him he'd nothing to unbutton anyhow, so he gave me the sack, and I leave on Saturday week, and the place thereof shall know me no more.[127]

I shall go to London, and my old landlady, Mrs Inger, 17 Coburg Square, will either give me a room or will find one for me.

Be sure your sins will find you out, especially if you're married and her name's Bertha –

There was not a word about herself, or to her. Connie resented this. He might have said some few words of consolation or reassurance. But she knew he was leaving her free, free to go back to Wragby and to Clifford. She resented that too. He need not be so falsely chivalrous. She wished he had said to Clifford: 'Yes, she is my lover and my mistress and I am proud of it!' But his courage wouldn't carry him so far.

So her name was coupled with his in Tevershall! It was a mess. But that would soon die down.

She was angry, with the complicated and confused anger that made her inert. She did not know what to do nor what to say, so she said and did nothing. She went on at Venice just the same, rowing out in the gondola with Duncan Forbes, bathing, letting the days slip by. Duncan, who had been rather depressingly in love with her ten years ago, was in love with her again. But she said to him: 'I only want one thing of men, and that is, that they should leave me alone.'

So Duncan left her alone: really quite pleased to be able to. All the same, he offered her a soft stream of a queer, inverted sort of love. He wanted to be *with* her.

'Have you ever thought,' he said to her one day, 'how very little people are connected with one another. Look at Daniele! He is handsome as a son of the sun. But see how alone he looks in his handsomeness. Yet I bet he has a wife and family, and couldn't possibly go away from them.'

'Ask him,' said Connie.

Duncan did so. Daniele said he was married, and had two children, both male, aged seven and nine. But he betrayed no emotion over the fact.

'Perhaps only people who are capable of real togetherness have that look of being alone in the universe,' said Connie. 'The others have a certain stickiness, they stick to the mass, like Giovanni.' 'And,' she thought to herself, 'like you, Duncan.'

Chapter 18

SHE HAD TO MAKE UP HER MIND what to do. She would leave Venice on the Saturday that he was leaving Wragby: in six days' time. This would bring her to London on the Monday following, and she would then see him. She wrote to him to the London address, asking him to send her a letter to Hartland's hotel, and to call for her on the Monday evening at seven.

Inside herself, she was curiously and complicatedly angry, and all her responses were numb. She refused to confide even in Hilda, and Hilda, offended by her steady silence, had become rather intimate with a Dutch woman. Connie hated these rather stifling intimacies between women, intimacy into which Hilda always entered ponderously.

Sir Malcolm decided to travel with Connie, and Duncan could come on with Hilda. The old artist always did himself well: he took berths on the Orient Express, in spite of Connie's dislike of *trains de luxe*, the atmosphere of vulgar depravity there is aboard them nowadays. However, it would make the journey to Paris shorter.

Sir Malcolm was always uneasy going back to his wife. It was habit carried over from the first wife. But there would be a house-party for the grouse, and he wanted to be well ahead. Connie, sunburnt and handsome, sat in silence, forgetting all about the landscape.

'A little dull for you, going back to Wragby,' said her father, noticing her glumness.

'I'm not sure I shall go back to Wragby,' she said, with startling abruptness, looking into his eyes with her big blue eyes. His big blue eyes took on the frightened look of a man whose social conscience is not quite clear.

'You mean you'll stay on in Paris a while?'

'No! I mean never go back to Wragby.'

He was bothered by his own little problems, and sincerely hoped he was getting none of hers to shoulder.

'How's that, all at once?' he asked.

'I'm going to have a child.'

It was the first time she had uttered the words to any living soul, and it seemed to mark a cleavage in her life.

'How do you know?' said her father.

She smiled.

'How *should* I know?'

'But not Clifford's child, of course?'

'No! Another man's.'

She rather enjoyed tormenting him.

'Do I know the man?' asked Sir Malcolm.

'No! You've never seen him.'

There was a long pause.

'And what are your plans?'

'I don't know. That's the point.'

'No patching it up with Clifford?'

'I suppose Clifford would take it,' said Connie. 'He told me, after last time you talked to him, he wouldn't mind if I had a child: so long as I went about it discreetly.'

'Only sensible thing he could say, under the circumstances. Then I suppose it'll be all right.'

'In what way?' said Connie, looking into her father's eyes. They were big blue eyes rather like her own, but with a certain uneasiness in them, a look sometimes of an uneasy little boy, sometimes a look of sullen selfishness, usually good-humoured and wary.

'You can present Clifford with an heir to all the Chatterleys, and put another baronet in Wragby.'

Sir Malcolm's face smiled with a half-sensual smile.

'But I don't think I want to,' she said.

'Why not? Feeling entangled with the other man? Well! If you want the truth from me, my child, it's this. The world goes on. Wragby stands and will go on standing. The world is more or less a fixed thing, and externally, we have to adapt ourselves to it. Privately, in my private opinion, we can please ourselves. Emotions change. You may like one man this year and another next. But Wragby still stands. Stick by Wragby as far as Wragby sticks by you. Then please yourself. But you'll get very little out of making a break. You can make a break if you wish. You have an independent income, the only thing that never lets you down. But you won't get much out of it. Put a little baronet in Wragby. It's an amusing thing to do.'

And Sir Malcolm sat back and smiled again. Connie did not answer.

'I hope you had a real man at last,' he said to her after a while, sensually alert.

'I did. That's the trouble. There aren't many of them about,' she said.

'No, by God!' he mused. 'There aren't! Well, my dear, to look at you, he was a lucky man. Surely he wouldn't make trouble for you?'

'Oh no! He leaves me my own mistress entirely.'

'Quite! Quite! A genuine man would.'

Sir Malcolm was pleased. Connie was his favourite daughter, he had always liked the female in her. Not so much of her mother in her as in Hilda. And he had always disliked Clifford. So he was pleased, and very tender with his daughter, as if the unborn child were his child.

He drove with her to Hartland's hotel, and saw her installed: then went round to his club. She had refused his company for the evening.

She found a letter from Mellors: 'I won't come round to your hotel, but I'll wait for you outside the Golden Cock in Adam Street at seven.'

There he stood, tall and slender, and so different, in a formal suit of thin dark cloth. He had a natural distinction, but he had not the cut-to-pattern look of her class. Yet, she saw at once, he could go anywhere. He had a native breeding which was really much nicer than the cut-to-pattern class thing.

'Ah, there you are! How well you look!'

'Yes! But not you.'

She looked in his face anxiously. It was thin, and the cheek-bones showed. But his eyes smiled at her, and she felt at home with him. There it was: suddenly, the tension of keeping up her appearances fell from her. Something flowed out of him physically, that made her feel inwardly at ease and happy, at home. With a woman's now alert instinct for happiness, she registered it at once. 'I'm happy when he's there!' Not all the sunshine of Venice had given her this inward expansion and warmth.

'Was it horrid for you?' she asked as she sat opposite him at table. He was too thin; she saw it now. His hand lay as she knew it, with that curious loose forgottenness of a sleeping animal. She wanted so much to take it and kiss it. But she did not quite dare.

'People are always horrid,' he said.

'And did you mind very much?'

'I minded, as I always shall mind. And I knew I was a fool to mind.'

'Did you feel like a dog with a tin can tied to its tail? Clifford said you felt like that.'

He looked at her. It was cruel of her at that moment: for his pride had suffered bitterly.

'I suppose I did,' he said.

She never knew the fierce bitterness with which he resented insult.

There was a long pause.

'And did you miss me?' she asked.

'I was glad you were out of it.'

Again there was a pause.

'But did people *believe* about you and me?' she asked.

'No! I don't think so for a moment.'

'Did Clifford?'

'I should say not. He put it off without thinking about it. But naturally it made him want to see the last of me.'

'I'm going to have a child.'

The expression died utterly out of his face, out of his whole body. He looked at her with darkened eyes, whose look she could not understand at all: like some dark-flamed spirit looking at her.

'Say you're glad!' she pleaded, groping for his hand. And she saw a certain exultance spring up in him. But it was netted down by things she could not understand.

'It's the future,' he said.

'But aren't you glad?' she persisted.

'I have such a terrible mistrust of the future.'

'But you needn't be troubled by any responsibility. Clifford would have it as his own, he'd be glad.'

She saw him go pale, and recoil under this. He did not answer.

'Shall I go back to Clifford, and put a little baronet into Wragby?' she asked.

He looked at her, pale and very remote. The ugly little grin flickered on his face.

'You wouldn't have to tell him who the father was?'

'Oh!' she said; 'he'd take it even then, if I wanted him to.'

He thought for a time.

'Ay!' he said at last, to himself. 'I suppose he would.'

There was silence. A big gulf was between them.

'But you don't want me to go back to Clifford, do you?' she asked him.

'What do you want yourself?' he replied.

'I want to live with you,' she said simply.

In spite of himself, little flames ran over his belly as he heard her say it, and he dropped his head. Then he looked up at her again, with those haunted eyes.

'If it's worth it to you,' he said. 'I've got nothing.'

'You've got more than most men. Come, you know it,' she said.

'In one way, I know it.' He was silent for a time, thinking. Then he resumed: 'They used to say I had too much of the woman in me. But it's not that. I'm not a woman because I don't want to shoot birds, neither because I don't want to make money, or get on. I could have got on in the army, easily, but I didn't like the army. Though I could manage the men all right: they liked me and they had a bit of a holy fear of me when I got mad. No, it was stupid, dead-handed higher authority that made the army dead: absolutely fool-dead. I like men, and men like me. But I can't stand the twaddling bossy impudence of the people who run this world. That's why I can't get on. I hate the impudence of money, and I hate the impudence of class. So in the world as it is, what have I to offer a woman?'

'But why offer anything? It's not a bargain. It's just that we love one another,' she said.

'Nay, nay! It's more than that. Living is moving and moving on. My life won't go down the proper gutters, it just won't. So I'm a bit of a waste ticket by myself. And I've no business to take a woman into my life, unless my life does something and gets somewhere, inwardly at least, to keep us both fresh. A man must offer a woman *some* meaning in his life, if it's going to be an isolated life, and if she's a genuine woman. I can't be just your male concubine.'

'Why not?' she said.

'Why, because I can't. And you would soon hate it.'

'As if you couldn't trust me,' she said.

The grin flickered on his face.

'The money is yours, the position is yours, the decisions will lie with you. I'm not just my Lady's fucker, after all.'

'What else are you?'

'You may well ask. It no doubt is invisible. Yet I'm something to myself at least. I can see the point of my own existence, though I can quite understand nobody else's seeing it.'

'And will your existence have less point, if you live with me?'

He paused a long time before replying: 'It might.'

She too stayed to think about it.

'And what is the point of your existence?'

'I tell you, it's invisible. I don't believe in the world, not in money, nor in advancement, nor in the future of our civilisation. If there's got to be a future for humanity, there'll have to be a very big change from what now is.'

'And what will the real future have to be like?'

'God knows! I can feel something inside me, all mixed up with a lot of rage. But what it really amounts to, I don't know.'

'Shall I tell you?' she said, looking into his face. 'Shall I tell you what you have that other men don't have, and that will make the future? Shall I tell you?'

'Tell me then,' he replied.

'It's the courage of your own tenderness, that's what it is like when you put your hand on my tail and say I've got a pretty tail.'

The grin came flickering on his face.

'That!' he said.

Then he sat thinking.

'Ay!' he said. 'You're right. It's that really. It's that all the way through. I knew it with the men. I had to be in touch with them, physically, and not go back on it. I had to be bodily aware of them and a bit tender to them, even if I put 'em through hell. It's a question of awareness, as Buddha said. But even he fought shy of the bodily awareness, and that natural physical tenderness, which is the best, even between men; in a proper manly way. Makes 'em really manly, not so monkeyish. Ay! it's tenderness, really; it's cunt-awareness. Sex is really only touch, the closest of all touch. And it's touch we're afraid of. We're only half-conscious, and half alive. We've got to come alive and aware. Especially the English have got to get into touch with one another, a bit delicate and a bit tender. It's our crying need.'

She looked at him.

'Then why are you afraid of me?' she said.

He looked at her a long time before he answered.

'It's the money, really, and the position. It's the world in you.'

'But isn't there tenderness in me?' she said wistfully.

He looked down at her, with darkened, abstract eyes.

'Ay! It comes an' goes, like in me.'

'But can't you trust it between you and me?' she asked, gazing anxiously at him.

She saw his face all softening down, losing its armour.

'Maybe!' he said.

They were both silent.

'I want you to hold me in your arms,' she said. 'I want you to tell me you are glad we are having a child.'

She looked so lovely and warm and wistful, his bowels stirred towards her.

'I suppose we can go to my room,' he said. 'Though it's scandalous again.'

But she saw the forgetfulness of the world coming over him again, his face taking the soft, pure look of tender passion.

They walked by the remoter streets to Coburg Square, where he had a room at the top of the house, an attic room where he cooked for himself on a gas ring. It was small, but decent and tidy.

She took off her things, and made him do the same. She was lovely in the soft first flush of her pregnancy.

'I ought to leave you alone,' he said.

'No!' she said. 'Love me! Love me, and say you'll keep me. Say you'll keep me! Say you'll never let me go, to the world nor to anybody.'

She crept close against him, clinging fast to his thin, strong naked body, the only home she had ever known.

'Then I'll keep thee,' he said. 'If tha wants it, then I'll keep thee.' He held her round and fast.

'And say you're glad about the child,' she repeated. 'Kiss it! Kiss my womb and say you're glad it's there.'

But that was more difficult for him.

'I've a dread of puttin' children i' th' world,' he said. 'I've such a dread o' th' future for 'em.'

'But you've put it into me. Be tender to it, and that will be its future already. Kiss it!'

He quivered, because it was true. 'Be tender to it, and that will be its future.' – At that moment he felt a sheer love for the woman. He kissed her belly and her mound of Venus, to kiss close to the womb and the foetus within the womb.

'Oh, you love me! You love me!' she said, in a little cry like one of her blind, inarticulate love cries. And he went in to her softly, feeling the stream of tenderness flowing in release from his bowels to hers, the bowels of compassion kindled between them.

And he realised as he went into her that this was the thing he had to do, to come into tender touch, without losing his pride or his dignity or his integrity as a man. After all, if she had money and means, and he had none, he should be too proud and honourable to hold back his tenderness from her on that account. 'I stand for the touch of bodily awareness between human beings,' he said to himself, 'and the touch of tenderness. And she is my mate. And it is a battle against the money, and the machine, and the insentient ideal monkeyishness of the world. And she will stand behind me there. Thank God I've got a woman! Thank God I've got a woman who is with me, and tender and aware of me. Thank God she's not a bully, nor a fool. Thank God she's a tender, aware woman.' And as his seed sprang in her, his soul sprang towards her too, in the creative act that is far more than procreative.

She was quite determined now that there should be no parting between him and her. But the ways and means were still to settle.

'Did you hate Bertha Coutts?' she asked him.

'Don't talk to me about her.'

'Yes! You must let me. Because once you liked her. And once you were as intimate with her as you are with me. So you have to tell me. Isn't it rather terrible, when you've been intimate with her, to hate her so? Why is it?'

'I don't know. She sort of kept her will ready against me, always, always: her ghastly female will: her freedom! A woman's ghastly freedom that ends in the most beastly bullying! Oh, she always kept her freedom against me, like vitriol in my face.'

'But she's not free of you even now. Does she still love you?'

'No no! If she's not free of me, it's because she's got that mad rage, she must try to bully me.'

'But she must have loved you.'

'No! Well, in specks she did. She was drawn to me. And I think even that she hated. She loved me in moments. But she always took it back, and started bullying. Her deepest desire was to bully me, and there was no altering her. Her *will* was wrong, from the first.'

'But perhaps she felt you didn't really love her, and she wanted to make you.'

'My God, it was bloody making.'

'But you didn't really love her, did you? You did her that wrong.'

'How could I? I began to. I began to love her. But somehow, she always ripped me up. No, don't let's talk of it. It was a doom, that was. And she was a doomed woman. This last time, I'd have shot her like I shoot a stoat, if I'd but been allowed: a raving, doomed thing in the shape of a woman! If only I could have shot her, and ended the whole misery! It ought to be allowed. When a woman gets absolutely possessed by her own will, her own will set against everything, then it's fearful, and she should be shot at last.'

'And shouldn't men be shot at last, if they get possessed by their own will?'

'Ay! – the same! But I must get free of her, or she'll be at me again. I wanted to tell you. I must get a divorce if I possibly can. So we must be careful. We mustn't really be seen together, you and I. I never, *never* could stand it if she came down on me and you.'

Connie pondered this.

'Then we can't be together?' she said.

'Not for six months or so. But I think my divorce will go through in September; then till March.'

'But the baby will probably be born at the end of February,' she said.

He was silent.

'I could wish the Cliffords and Berthas all dead,' he said.

'It's not being very tender to them,' she said.

'Tender to them? Yea, even then the tenderest thing you could do for them, perhaps, would be to give them death. They can't live! They only frustrate life. Their souls are awful inside them. Death ought to be sweet to them. And I ought to be allowed to shoot them.'

'But you wouldn't do it,' she said.

'I would though! and with less qualms than I shoot a weasel. It anyhow has a prettiness and a loneliness. But they are legion. Oh, I'd shoot them.'

'Then perhaps it is just as well you daren't.'

'Well.'

Connie had now plenty to think of. It was evident he wanted absolutely to be free of Bertha Coutts. And she felt he was right. The last attack had been too grim. – This meant her living alone, till spring. Perhaps she could get divorced from Clifford. But how? If Mellors were named, then there was an end to *his* divorce. How loathsome! Couldn't one go right away, to the far ends of the earth, and be free from it all?

One could not. The far ends of the world are not five minutes from Charing Cross, nowadays. While the wireless is active, there are no far ends of the earth. Kings of Dahomey and Lamas of Tibet listen in to London and New York.

Patience! Patience! The world is a vast and ghastly intricacy of mechanism, and one has to be very wary, not to get mangled by it.

Connie confided in her father.

'You see, Father, he was Clifford's gamekeeper: but he was an officer in the army in India. Only he is like Colonel C. E. Florence,[128] who preferred to become a private soldier again.'

Sir Malcolm, however, had no sympathy with the unsatisfactory mysticism of the famous C. E. Florence. He saw too much advertisement behind all the humility. It looked just like the sort of conceit the knight most loathed, the conceit of self-abasement.

'Where did your gamekeeper spring from?' asked Sir Malcolm irritably.

'He was a collier's son in Tevershall. But he's absolutely presentable.'

The knighted artist became more angry.

'Looks to me like a gold-digger,' he said. 'And you're a pretty easy gold-mine, apparently.'

'No, Father, it's not like that. You'd know if you saw him. He's a man. Clifford always detested him for not being humble.'

'Apparently he had a good instinct, for once.'

What Sir Malcolm could not bear was the scandal of his daughter's having an intrigue with a gamekeeper. He did not mind the intrigue: he minded the scandal.

'I care nothing about the fellow. He's evidently been able to get round you all right. But by God, think of all the talk. Think of your stepmother, how she'll take it!'

'I know,' said Connie. 'Talk is beastly: especially if you live in society. And he wants so much to get his own divorce. I thought we might perhaps say it was another man's child, and not mention Mellors' name at all.'

'Another man's! What other man's?'

'Perhaps Duncan Forbes. He has been our friend all his life. And he's a fairly well-known artist. And he's fond of me.'

'Well I'm damned! Poor Duncan! And what's he going to get out of it?'

'I don't know. But he might rather like it, even.'

'He might, might he? Well, he's a funny man if he does. Why, you've never even had an affair with him, have you?'

'No! But he doesn't really want it. He only loves me to be near him, but not to touch him.'

'My God, what a generation!'

'He would like me most of all to be a model for him to paint from. Only I never wanted to.'

'God help him! But he looks downtrodden enough for anything.'

'Still, you wouldn't mind so much the talk about him?'

'My God, Connie, all the bloody contriving!'

'I know! It's sickening! But what can I do?'

'Contriving, conniving; conniving, contriving! Makes a man think he's lived too long.'

'Come, Father, if you haven't done a good deal of contriving and conniving in your time, you may talk.'

'But it was different, I assure you.'

'It's *always* different.'

Hilda arrived, also furious when she heard of the new developments. And she also simply could not stand the thought of a public scandal about her sister and a gamekeeper. Too, too humiliating!

'Why should we not just disappear, separately, to British Columbia, and have no scandal?' said Connie.

But that was no good. The scandal would come out just the same. And if Connie was going with the man, she'd better be able to marry him. This was Hilda's opinion. Sir Malcolm wasn't sure. The affair might still blow over.

'But will you see him, Father?'

Poor Sir Malcolm! he was by no means keen on it. And poor Mellors, he was still less keen. Yet the meeting took place: a lunch in a private room at the club, the two men alone, looking one another up and down.

Sir Malcolm drank a fair amount of whisky, Mellors also drank. And they talked all the while about India, on which the young man was well informed.

This lasted during the meal. Only when coffee was served, and the waiter had gone, Sir Malcolm lit a cigar and said, heartily, 'Well, young man, and what about my daughter?'

The grin flickered on Mellors' face.

'Well, Sir, and what about her?'

'You've got a baby in her all right.'

'I have that honour!' grinned Mellors.

'Honour, by God!' Sir Malcolm gave a little squirting laugh, and became Scotch and lewd. 'Honour! How was the going, eh!? Good, my boy, what?'

'Good!'

'I'll bet it was! Ha-ha! My daughter, chip of the old block, what! I never went back on a good bit of fucking, myself. Though her mother, oh, holy saints!' He rolled his eyes to heaven. 'But you warmed her up, oh, you warmed her up, I can see that. Ha-ha! My blood in her! You set fire to her haystack all right. Ha-ha-ha! I was jolly glad of it, I can tell you. She needed it. Oh, she's a nice girl, she's a nice girl, and I knew she'd be good going, if only some damned man would set her stack on fire! Ha-ha-ha! A gamekeeper, eh, my boy! Bloody good poacher, if you ask me. Ha-ha! But now, look here, speaking seriously, what are we going to do about it? Speaking seriously, you know!'

Speaking seriously, they didn't get very far. Mellors, though a little tipsy, was much the soberer of the two. He kept the conversation as intelligent as possible: which isn't saying much.

'So you're a gamekeeper! Oh, you're quite right! That sort of game is worth a man's while, eh, what? The test of a woman is when you pinch her bottom. You can tell just by the feel of her bottom if she's going to come up all right. Ha-ha! I envy you, my boy. How old are you?'

'Thirty-nine.'

The knight lifted his eyebrows.

'As much as that! Well, you've another good twenty years, by the look of you. Oh, gamekeeper or not, you're a good cock. I can see that with one eye shut. Not like that blasted Clifford! A lily-livered hound with never a fuck in him, never had. I like you, my boy, I'll bet you've a good cod on you; oh, you're a bantam, I can see that. You're a fighter. Gamekeeper! Ha-ha, by crikey, I wouldn't trust my game to you! But look here, seriously, what are we going to do about it? The world's full of blasted old women.'

Seriously, they didn't do anything about it, except establish the old freemasonry of male sensuality between them.

'And look here, my boy, if ever I can do anything for you, you can rely on me. Gamekeeper! Christ, but it's rich! I like it! Oh, I like it! Shows the girl's got spunk. What? After all, you know, she has her own income, moderate, moderate, but above starvation. And I'll leave her what I've got. By God, I will. She deserves it for showing spunk, in a world of old women. I've been struggling to get myself clear of the skirts of old women for seventy years, and haven't managed it yet. But you're the man, I can see that.'

'I'm glad you think so. They usually tell me, in a sideways fashion, that I'm the monkey.'

'Oh, they would! My dear fellow, what could you be but a monkey, to all the old women?'

They parted most genially, and Mellors laughed inwardly all the time for the rest of the day.

The following day he had lunch with Connie and Hilda, at some discreet place.

'It's a very great pity it's such an ugly situation all round,' said Hilda.

'I had a lot o' fun out of it,' said he.

'I think you might have avoided putting children into the world until you were both free to marry and have children.'

'The Lord blew a bit too soon on the spark,' said he.

'I think the Lord had nothing to do with it. Of course Connie has enough money to keep you both, but the situation is unbearable.'

'But then you don't have to bear more than a small corner of it, do you?' said he.

'If you'd been in her own class.'

'Or if I'd been in a cage at the Zoo.'

There was silence.

'I think,' said Hilda, 'it will be best if she names quite another man as co-respondent, and you stay out of it altogether.'

'But I thought I'd put my foot right in.'

'I mean, in the divorce proceeding.'

He gazed at her in wonder. Connie had not dared mention the Duncan scheme to him.

'I don't follow,' he said.

'We have a friend who would probably agree to be named as co-respondent, so that your name need not appear,' said Hilda.

'You mean a man?'

'Of course!'

'But she's got no other?'

He looked in wonder at Connie.

'No, no!' she said hastily. 'Only that old friendship, quite simple, no love.'

'Then why should the fellow take the blame? If he's had nothing out of you?'

'Some men are chivalrous and don't only count what they get out of a woman,' said Hilda.

'One for me, eh? But who's the johnny?'

'A friend whom we've known since we were children in Scotland, an artist.'

'Duncan Forbes!' he said at once, for Connie had talked of him. 'And how would you shift the blame on to him?'

'They could stay together in some hotel, or she could even stay in his apartment.'

'Seems to me like a lot of fuss for nothing,' he said.

'What else do you suggest?' said Hilda. 'If your name appears, you will get no divorce from your wife, who is apparently quite an impossible person to be mixed up with.'

'All that!' he said grimly.

There was a long silence.

'We could go right away,' he said.

'There is no right away for Connie,' said Hilda. 'Clifford is too well known.'

Again the silence of pure frustration.

'The world is what it is. If you want to live together without being persecuted, you will have to marry. To marry, you both have to be divorced. So how are you both going about it?'

He was silent for a long time.

'How are *you* going about it for us?' he said.

'We will see if Duncan will consent to figure as co-respondent: then we must get Clifford to divorce Connie: and you must go on with your divorce, and you must both keep apart till you are free.'

'Sounds like a lunatic asylum.'

'Possibly! And the world would look on you as lunatics: or worse.'

'What is worse?'

'Criminals, I suppose.'

'Hope I can plunge in the dagger a few more times yet,' he said, grinning. Then he was silent, and angry.

'Well!' he said at last. 'I agree to anything. The world is a raving idiot, and no man can kill it: though I'll do my best. But you're right. We must rescue ourselves as best we can.'

He looked in humiliation, anger, weariness and misery at Connie.

'Ma lass!' he said. 'The world's goin' to put salt on thy tail.'

'Not if we don't let it,' she said.

She minded this conniving against the world less than he did.

Duncan, when approached, also insisted on seeing the delinquent gamekeeper, so there was a dinner, this time in his flat: the four of them. Duncan was a rather short, broad, dark-skinned, taciturn Hamlet of a fellow with straight black hair and a weird Celtic conceit of himself. His art was all tubes and valves and spirals and strange colours, ultra-modern, yet with a certain power, even a certain purity of form and tone: only Mellors thought it cruel and repellent. He did not venture to say so, for Duncan was almost insane on the point of his art, it was a personal cult, a personal religion with him.

They were looking at the pictures in the studio, and Duncan kept his smallish brown eyes on the other man. He wanted to hear what the gamekeeper would say. He knew already Connie's and Hilda's opinions.

'It is like a pure bit of murder,' said Mellors at last; a speech Duncan by no means expected from a gamekeeper.

'And who is murdered?' asked Hilda, rather coldly and sneeringly.

'Me! It murders all the bowels of compassion in a man.'

A wave of pure hate came out of the artist. He heard the note of dislike in the other man's voice, and the note of contempt. And he himself loathed the mention of bowels of compassion. Sickly sentiment!

Mellors stood rather tall and thin, worn-looking, gazing with flickering detachment, that was something like the dancing of a moth on the wing, at the pictures.

'Perhaps stupidity is murdered; sentimental stupidity,' sneered the artist.

'Do you think so? I think all these tubes and corrugated vibrations are stupid enough for anything, and pretty sentimental. They show a lot of self-pity and an awful lot of nervous self-opinion, seems to me.'

In another wave of hate, the artist's face looked yellow. But with a sort of silent hauteur he turned the pictures to the wall.

'I think we may go to the dining-room,' he said.

And they trailed off, dismally.

After coffee, Duncan said, 'I don't at all mind posing as the father of Connie's child. But only on the condition that she'll come and pose as a model for me. I've wanted her for years, and she's always refused.' He uttered it with the dark finality of an inquisitor announcing an *auto da fé*.

'Ah!' said Mellors. 'You only do it on condition, then?'

'Quite! I only do it on that condition.' The artist tried to put the utmost contempt of the other person into his speech. He put a little too much.

'Better have me as a model at the same time,' said Mellors. 'Better do us in a group, Vulcan and Venus under the net of art.[129] I used to be a blacksmith, before I was a gamekeeper.'

'Thank you,' said the artist. 'I don't think Vulcan has a figure that interests me.'

'Not even if it was tubified and titivated up?'

There was no answer. The artist was too haughty for further words.

It was a dismal party, in which the artist henceforth steadily ignored the presence of the other man, and talked only briefly, as if the words were wrung out of the depths of his gloomy portentousness, to the women.

'You didn't like him, but he's better than that, really. He's really kind,' Connie explained as they left.

'He's a little black pup with a corrugated distemper,' said Mellors.

'No, he wasn't nice today.'

'And will you go and be a model to him?'

'Oh, I don't really mind any more. He won't touch me. And I don't mind anything, if it paves the way to a life together for you and me.'

'But he'll only shit on you on canvas.'

'I don't care. He'll only be painting his own feelings for me, and I don't mind if he does that. I wouldn't have him touch me, not for anything. But if he thinks he can do anything with his owlish arty staring, let him stare. He can make as many empty tubes and corrugations out of me as he likes. It's his funeral. He hated you for what you said: that his tubified art is sentimental and self-important. But of course it's true.'

Chapter 19

DEAR CLIFFORD – I am afraid what you foresaw has happened. I am really in love with another man, and I do hope you will divorce me. I am staying at present with Duncan in his flat. I told you he was at Venice with us. I'm awfully unhappy for your sake: but do try to take it quietly. You don't really need me any more, and I can't bear to come back to Wragby. I'm most awfully sorry. But do try to forgive me, and divorce me and find someone better. I'm not really the right person for you, I am too impatient and selfish, I suppose. But I can't ever come back to live with you again. And I feel so frightfully sorry about it all, for your sake. But if you don't let yourself get worked up, you'll see you won't mind so frightfully. You didn't really care about me personally. So do forgive me and get rid of me.

Clifford was not *inwardly* surprised to get this letter. Inwardly, he had known for a long time she was leaving him. But he had absolutely refused any outward admission of it. Therefore, outwardly, it came as the most terrible blow and shock to him. He had kept the surface of his confidence in her quite serene.

And that is how we are. By strength of will we cut off our inner intuitive knowledge from admitted consciousness. This causes a state of dread, or apprehension, which makes the blow ten times worse when it does fall.

Clifford was like a hysterical child. He gave Mrs Bolton a terrible shock, sitting up in bed ghastly and blank.

'Why, Sir Clifford, whatever's the matter?'

No answer! She was terrified lest he had had a stroke. She hurried and felt his face, took his pulse.

'Is there a pain? Do try and tell me where it hurts you. Do tell me!' No answer!

'Oh dear, oh dear! Then I'll telephone to Sheffield for Dr Carrington, and Dr Lecky may as well run round straight away.'

She was moving to the door, when he said in a hollow tone: 'No!'

She stopped and gazed at him. His face was yellow, blank, and like the face of an idiot.

'Do you mean you'd rather I didn't fetch the doctor?'

'Yes! I don't want him,' came the sepulchral voice.

'Oh, but Sir Clifford, you're ill, and I daren't take the responsibility. I *must* send for the doctor, or *I* shall be blamed.'

A pause: then the hollow voice said, 'I'm not ill. My wife isn't coming back.' – It was as if an image spoke.

'Not coming back? you mean her Ladyship?' Mrs Bolton moved a little nearer to the bed. 'Oh, don't you believe it. You can trust her Ladyship to come back.'

The image in the bed did not change, but it pushed a letter over the counterpane.

'Read it!' said the sepulchral voice.

'Why, if it's a letter from her Ladyship, I'm sure her Ladyship wouldn't want me to read her letter to you, Sir Clifford. You can tell me what she says, if you wish.'

But the face with the fixed blue eyes sticking out did not change.

'Read it!' repeated the voice.

'Why, if I must, I do it to obey you, Sir Clifford,' she said.

And she read the letter.

The face in the bed seemed to deepen its expression of wild, but motionless distraction. Mrs Bolton looked at it and was worried.

She knew what she was up against: male hysteria. She had not nursed soldiers without learning something about that very unpleasant disease.

She was a little impatient of Sir Clifford. Any man in his senses must have *known* his wife was in love with somebody else, and was going to leave him. Even, she was sure, Sir Clifford was inwardly absolutely aware of it, only he wouldn't admit it to himself. If he would have admitted it, and prepared himself for it; or if he would have admitted it, and actively struggled with his wife against it, that would have been acting like a man. But no! he knew it, and all the time tried to kid himself it wasn't so. He felt the devil twisting his tail, and pretended it was the angels smiling on him. This state of falsity had now brought on that crisis of falsity and dislocation, hysteria, which is a form of insanity. 'It comes,' she thought to herself, hating him a little, 'because he always thinks of himself. He's so wrapped up in his own immortal self, that when he does get a shock he's like a mummy tangled in its own bandages. Look at him!'

But hysteria is dangerous: and she was a nurse, it was her duty to pull him out. Any attempt to rouse his manhood and his pride would only make him worse: for his manhood was dead, temporarily if not finally. He would only squirm softer and softer, like a worm, and become more dislocated.

The only thing was to release his self-pity. Like the lady in Tennyson,[130] he must weep or he must die.

So Mrs Bolton began to weep first. She covered her face with her hand and burst into little wild sobs. 'I would never have believed it of her Ladyship, I wouldn't!' she wept, suddenly summoning up all her old grief and sense of woe, and weeping the tears of her own bitter chagrin. Once she started, her weeping was genuine enough, for she had had something to weep for.

Clifford thought of the way he had been betrayed by the woman Connie, and in a contagion of grief, tears filled his eyes and began to run down his cheeks. He was weeping for himself. Mrs Bolton, as soon as she saw the tears running over his blank face, hastily wiped her own wet cheeks on her little handkerchief, and leaned towards him.

'Now don't you fret, Sir Clifford!' she said, in a luxury of emotion. 'Now don't you fret, don't, you'll only do yourself an injury!'

His body shivered suddenly in an indrawn breath of silent sobbing, and the tears ran quicker down his face. She laid her hand on his arm, and her own tears fell again. Again the shiver went through him, like a convulsion, and she laid her arm round his shoulder. 'There, there! There, there! Don't you fret, then, don't you! Don't you fret!' she moaned to him, while her own tears fell. And she drew him to her, and held her arms round his great shoulders, while he laid his face on her bosom and sobbed, shaking and hulking his huge shoulders, whilst she softly stroked his dusky-blond hair and said: 'There! There! There! There then! There then! Never you mind! Never you mind, then!'

And he put his arms round her and clung to her like a child, wetting the bib of her starched white apron, and the bosom of her pale-blue cotton dress, with his tears. He had let himself go altogether, at last.

So at length she kissed him, and rocked him on her bosom, and in her heart she said to herself: 'Oh, Sir Clifford! Oh high and mighty Chatterleys! Is this what you've come down to!' And finally he even went to sleep, like a child. And she felt worn out, and went to her own room, where she laughed and cried at once, with a hysteria of her own. It was so ridiculous! It was so awful! Such a come-down! So shameful! And it *was* so upsetting as well.

After this, Clifford became like a child with Mrs Bolton. He would hold her hand, and rest his head on her breast, and when she once lightly kissed him, he said: 'Yes! Do kiss me! Do kiss me!' And when she sponged his great blond body, he would say the same: 'Do kiss me!' and she would lightly kiss his body, anywhere, half in mockery.

And he lay with a queer, blank face like a child, with a bit of the wonderment of a child. And he would gaze on her with wide, childish eyes, in a relaxation of madonna-worship. It was sheer relaxation on his part, letting go all his manhood, and sinking back to a childish position that was really perverse. And then he would put his hand into her bosom and feel her breasts, and kiss them in exaltation, the exaltation of perversity, of being a child when he was a man.

Mrs Bolton was both thrilled and ashamed, she both loved and hated it. Yet she never rebuffed nor rebuked him. And they drew into a closer physical intimacy, an intimacy of perversity, when he was a child stricken with an apparent candour and an apparent wonderment, that looked almost like a religious exaltation: the perverse and literal rendering of: 'except ye become again as a little child'.[131] – While she was the Magna Mater,[132] full of power and potency, having the great blond child-man under her will and her stroke entirely.

The curious thing was that when this child-man, which Clifford was now and which he had been becoming for years, emerged into the world, it was much sharper and keener than the real man he used to be. This perverted child-man was now a *real* businessman; when it was a question of affairs, he was an absolute he-man, sharp as a needle, and impervious as a bit of steel. When he was out among men, seeking his own ends, and 'making good' his colliery workings, he had an almost uncanny shrewdness, hardness, and a straight sharp punch. It was as if his very passivity and prostitution to the Magna Mater gave him insight into material business affairs, and lent him a certain remarkable inhuman force. The wallowing in private emotion, the utter abasement of his manly self, seemed to lend him a second nature, cold, almost visionary, business-clever. In business he was quite inhuman.

And in this Mrs Bolton triumphed. 'How he's getting on!' she would say to herself in pride. 'And that's my doing! My word, he'd never have got on like this with Lady Chatterley. She was not the one to put a man forward. She wanted too much for herself.'

At the same time, in some corner of her weird female soul, how she despised him and hated him! He was to her the fallen beast, the squirming monster. And while she aided and abetted him all she could, away in the remotest corner of her ancient healthy womanhood she despised him with a savage contempt that knew no bounds. The merest tramp was better than he.

His behaviour with regard to Connie was curious. He insisted on seeing her again. He insisted, moreover, on her coming to Wragby. On this point he was finally and absolutely fixed. Connie had promised to come back to Wragby, faithfully.

'But is it any use?' said Mrs Bolton. 'Can't you let her go, and be rid of her?'

'No! She said she was coming back, and she's got to come.'

Mrs Bolton opposed him no more. She knew what she was dealing with.

I needn't tell you what effect your letter has had on me [he wrote to Connie in London]. Perhaps you can imagine it if you try, though no doubt you won't trouble to use your imagination on my behalf.

I can only say one thing in answer: I must see you personally, here at Wragby, before I can do anything. You promised faithfully to come back to Wragby, and I hold you to the promise. I don't believe anything nor understand anything until I see you personally, here under normal circumstances. I needn't tell you that nobody here suspects anything, so your return would be quite normal. Then if you feel, after we have talked things over, that you still remain in the same mind, no doubt we can come to terms.

Connie showed this letter to Mellors.

'He wants to begin his revenge on you,' said he, handing the letter back.

Connie was silent. She was somewhat surprised to find that she was afraid of Clifford. She was afraid to go near him. She was afraid of him as if he were evil and dangerous.

'What shall I do?' she said.

'Nothing, if you don't want to do anything.'

She replied, trying to put Clifford off. He answered: 'If you don't come back to Wragby now, I shall consider that you are coming back one day, and act accordingly. I shall just go on the same, and wait for you here, if I wait for fifty years.'

She was frightened. This was bullying of an insidious sort. She had no doubt he meant what he said. He would not divorce her, and the child would be his, unless she could find some means of establishing its illegitimacy.

After a time of worry and harassment, she decided to go to Wragby. Hilda would go with her. She wrote this to Clifford. He replied: 'I shall not welcome your sister, but I shall not deny her the door. I have no doubt she has connived at your desertion of your duties and responsibilities, so do not expect me to show pleasure in seeing her.'

They went to Wragby. Clifford was away when they arrived. Mrs Bolton received them.

'Oh, your Ladyship, it isn't the happy home-coming we hoped for, is it!' she said.

'Isn't it?' said Connie.

So this woman knew! How much did the rest of the servants know or suspect?

She entered the house which now she hated with every fibre in her body. The great, rambling mass of a place seemed evil to her, just a menace over her. She was no longer its mistress, she was its victim.

'I can't stay long here,' she whispered to Hilda, terrified.

And she suffered going into her own bedroom, re-entering into possession as if nothing had happened. She hated every minute inside the Wragby walls.

They did not meet Clifford till they went down to dinner. He was dressed, and with a black tie: rather reserved, and very much the superior gentleman. He behaved perfectly politely during the meal, and kept a polite sort of conversation going: but it seemed all touched with insanity.

'How much do the servants know?' asked Connie, when the woman was out of the room.

'Of your intentions? Nothing whatsoever.'

'Mrs Bolton knows.'

He changed colour.

'Mrs Bolton is not exactly one of the servants,' he said.

'Oh, I don't mind.'

There was tension till after coffee, when Hilda said she would go up to her room.

Clifford and Connie sat in silence when she had gone. Neither would begin to speak. Connie was so glad that he wasn't taking the pathetic line, she kept him up to as much haughtiness as possible. She just sat silent and looked down at her hands.

'I suppose you don't at all mind having gone back on your word?' he said at last.

'I can't help it,' she murmured.

'But if you can't, who can?'

'I suppose nobody.'

He looked at her with curious cold rage. He was used to her. She was as it were embedded in his will. How dared she now go back on him, and destroy the fabric of his daily existence? How dared she try to cause this derangement of his personality!

'And for *what* do you want to go back on everything?' he insisted.

'Love!' she said. It was best to be hackneyed.

'Love of Duncan Forbes? But you didn't think that worth having, when you met me. Do you mean to say you now love him better than anything else in life?'

'One changes,' she said.

'Possibly! Possibly you may have whims. But you still have to convince me of the importance of the change. I merely don't believe in your love of Duncan Forbes.'

'But why *should* you believe in it? You have only to divorce me, not to believe in my feelings.'

'And why should I divorce you?'

'Because I don't want to live here any more. And you really don't want me.'

'Pardon me! I don't change. For my part, since you are my wife, I should prefer that you should stay under my roof in dignity and quiet. Leaving aside personal feelings, and I assure you, on my part it is leaving aside a great deal, it is bitter as death to me to have this order of life broken up, here in Wragby, and the decent round of daily life smashed, just for some whim of yours.'

After a time of silence she said: 'I can't help it. I've got to go. I expect I shall have a child.'

He too was silent for a time.

'And is it for the child's sake you must go?' he asked at length.

She nodded.

'And why? Is Duncan Forbes so keen on his spawn?'

'Surely keener than you would be,' she said.

'But really? I want my wife, and I see no reason for letting her go. If she likes to bear a child under my roof, she is welcome, and the child is welcome: provided that the decency and order of life is preserved. Do you mean to tell me that Duncan Forbes has a greater hold over you? I don't believe it.'

There was a pause.

'But don't you see,' said Connie. 'I *must* go away from you, and I must live with the man I love.'

'No, I don't see it! I don't give tuppence for your love, nor for the man you love. I don't believe in that sort of cant.'

'But you see, I do.'

'Do you? My dear Madam, you are too intelligent, I assure you, to believe in your own love for Duncan Forbes. Believe me, even now you really care more for me. So why should I give in to such nonsense!'

She felt he was right there. And she felt she could keep silent no longer.

'Because it isn't Duncan that I *do* love,' she said, looking up at him. 'We only said it was Duncan, to spare your feelings.'

'To spare my feelings?'

'Yes! Because who I really love, and it'll make you hate me, is Mr Mellors, who was our gamekeeper here.'

If he could have sprung out of his chair, he would have done so. His face went yellow, and his eyes bulged with disaster as he glared at her.

Then he dropped back in the chair, gasping and looking up at the ceiling.

At length he sat up.

'Do you mean to say you're telling me the truth?' he asked, looking gruesome.

'Yes! You know I am.'

'And when did you begin with him?'

'In the spring.'

He was silent like some beast in a trap.

'And it *was* you, then, in the bedroom at the cottage?'

So he had really inwardly known all the time.

'Yes!'

He still leaned forward in his chair, gazing at her like a cornered beast.

'My God, you ought to be wiped off the face of the earth!'

'Why?' she ejaculated faintly.

But he seemed not to hear her.

'That scum! That bumptious lout! That miserable cad! And carrying on with him all the time, while you were here and he was one of my servants! My God, my God, is there any end to the beastly lowness of women!'

He was beside himself with rage, as she knew he would be.

'And you mean to say you want to have a child to a cad like that?'

'Yes! I'm going to.'

'You're going to! You mean you're sure! How long have you been sure?'

'Since June.'

He was speechless, and the queer blank look of a child came over him again.

'You'd wonder,' he said at last, 'that such beings were ever allowed to be born.'

'What beings?' she asked.

He looked at her weirdly, without an answer. It was obvious he couldn't even accept the fact of the existence of Mellors, in any connection with his own life. It was sheer, unspeakable, impotent hate.

'And do you mean to say you'd marry him? – and bear his foul name?' he asked at length.

'Yes, that's what I want.'

He was again as if dumbfounded.

'Yes!' he said at last. 'That proves that what I've always thought about you is correct: you're not normal, you're not in your right senses. You're one of those half-insane, perverted women who must run after depravity, the *nostalgie de la boue*.'[133]

Suddenly he had become almost wistfully moral, seeing himself the incarnation of good, and people like Mellors and Connie the incarnation of mud, of evil. He seemed to be growing vague, inside a nimbus.

'So don't you think you'd better divorce me and have done with it?' she said.

'No! You can go where you like, but I shan't divorce you,' he said idiotically.

'Why not?'

He was silent, in the silence of imbecile obstinacy.

'Would you even let the child be legally yours, and your heir?' she said.

'I care nothing about the child.'

'But if it's a boy it will be legally your son, and it will inherit your title, and have Wragby.'

'I care nothing about that,' he said.

'But you *must*! I shall prevent the child from being legally yours, if I can. I'd so much rather it were illegitimate, and mine: if it can't be Mellors'.'

'Do as you like about that.'

He was immovable.

'And won't you divorce me?' she said. 'You can use Duncan as a pretext! There'd be no need to bring in the real name. Duncan doesn't mind.'

'*I* shall never divorce you,' he said, as if a nail had been driven in.

'But why? Because I want you to?'

'Because I follow my own inclination, and I'm not inclined to.'

It was useless. She went upstairs and told Hilda the upshot.

'Better get away tomorrow,' said Hilda, 'and let him come to his senses.'

So Connie spent half the night packing her really private and personal effects. In the morning she had her trunks sent to the station, without telling Clifford. She decided to see him only to say goodbye, before lunch.

But she spoke to Mrs Bolton.

'I must say goodbye to you, Mrs Bolton, you know why. But I can trust you not to talk.'

'Oh, you can trust me, your Ladyship, though it's a sad blow for us here, indeed. But I hope you'll be happy with the other gentleman.'

'The other gentleman! It's Mr Mellors, and I care for him. Sir Clifford knows. But don't say anything to anybody. And if one day you think Sir Clifford may be willing to divorce me, let me know, will you? I should like to be properly married to the man I care for.'

'I'm sure you would, my Lady! Oh, you can trust me. I'll be faithful to Sir Clifford, and I'll be faithful to you, for I can see you're both right in your own ways.'

'Thank you! And look! I want to give you this – may I?

So Connie left Wragby once more, and went on with Hilda to Scotland. Mellors went into the country and got work on a farm. The idea was, he should get his divorce, if possible, whether Connie got hers or not. And for six months he should work at farming, so that eventually he and Connie could have some small farm of their own, into which he could put his energy. For he would have to have some work, even hard work, to do, and he would have to make his own living, even if her capital started him.

So they would have to wait till spring was in, till the baby was born, till the early summer came round again.

The Grange Farm, Old Heanor, 29 September
I got on here with a bit of contriving, because I knew Richards, the company engineer, in the army. It is a farm belonging to Butler and Smitham Colliery Company, they use it for raising hay and oats for the pit-ponies; not a private concern. But they've got cows and pigs and all the rest of it, and I get thirty shillings a week as labourer. Rowley, the farmer, puts me on to as many jobs as he can, so that I can learn as much as possible between now and next Easter. I've not heard a thing about Bertha. I've no idea why she didn't show up at the divorce, nor where she is nor what she's up to. But if I keep quiet till March I suppose I shall be free. And don't you bother about Sir Clifford. He'll want to get rid of you one of these days. If he leaves you alone, it's a lot.

I've got lodgings in a bit of an old cottage in Engine Row, very decent. The man is engine-driver at High Park, tall, with a beard, and very chapel. The woman is a birdy bit of a thing who loves anything superior, King's English and allow-me! all the time. But they lost their only son in the war, and it's sort of knocked a hole in them. There's a long gawky lass of a daughter training for a schoolteacher, and I help her with her lessons sometimes, so we're quite the family. But they're very decent people, and only too kind to me. I expect I'm more coddled than you are.

I like farming all right. It's not inspiring, but then I don't ask to be inspired. I'm used to horses, and cows, though they are very female, have a soothing effect on me. When I sit with my head in her side, milking, I feel very solaced. They have six rather fine Herefords. Oat-harvest is just over and I enjoyed it, in spite of sore hands and a lot of rain. I don't take much notice of people, but get on with them all right. Most things one just ignores.

The pits are working badly; this is a colliery district like Tevershall, only prettier. I sometimes sit in the Wellington and talk to the men. They grumble a lot, but they're not going to alter anything. As everybody says, the Notts–Derby miners have got their hearts in the right place. But the rest of their anatomy must be in the wrong place, in a world that has no use for them. I like them, but they don't cheer me much: not enough of the old fighting-cock in them. They talk a lot about nationalisation, nationalisation of royalties, nationalisation of the whole industry. But you can't nationalise coal and leave all the other industries as they are. They talk about putting coal to new uses, like Sir Clifford is trying to do. It may work here and there, but not as a general thing, I doubt. Whatever you make you've got to sell it. The men are very apathetic. They feel the whole damned thing is doomed, and I believe it is. And they are doomed along with it. Some of the young ones spout about a Soviet, but there's not much conviction in them. There's no sort of conviction about anything, except that it's all a muddle and a hole. Even under a Soviet you've still got to sell coal: and that's the difficulty.

We've got this great industrial population, and they've got to be fed, so the damn show has to be kept going somehow. The women talk a lot more than the men, nowadays, and they are a sight more cocksure. The men are limp, they feel a doom somewhere, and they go about as if there was nothing to be done. Anyhow nobody knows what should be done, in spite of all the talk. The young ones get mad because they've no money to spend. Their whole life depends on spending money, and now they've got none to spend. That's our civilisation and our education: bring up the masses to depend entirely on spending money, and then the money gives out. The pits are working two days, two and a half days a week, and there's no sign of betterment even for the winter. It means a man bringing up a family on twenty-five and thirty shillings. The women are the maddest of all. But then they're the maddest for spending, nowadays.

If you could only tell them that living and spending isn't the same thing! But it's no good. If only they were educated to *live* instead of earn and spend, they could manage very happily on twenty-five shillings. If the men wore scarlet trousers as I said, they wouldn't think so much of money: if they could dance and hop and skip, and sing and swagger and be handsome, they could do with very little cash. And amuse the women themselves, and be amused by the women. They ought to learn to be naked and handsome, and to sing in a mass and dance the old group dances, and carve the stools they sit on, and embroider their own emblems. Then they wouldn't need money. And that's the only way to solve the industrial problem: train the people to be able to live and live in handsomeness, without needing to spend. But you can't do it. They're all one-track minds nowadays. Whereas the mass of people oughtn't even to try to think, because they *can't*. They should be alive and frisky, and acknowledge the great god Pan. He's the only god for the masses, forever. The few can go in for higher cults if they like. But let the mass be forever pagan.

But the colliers aren't pagan, far from it. They're a sad lot, a deadened lot of men: dead to their women, dead to life. The young ones scoot about on motorbikes with girls, and jazz when they get a chance. But they're very dead. And it needs money. Money poisons you when you've got it, and starves you when you haven't.

I'm sure you're sick of all this. But I don't want to harp on myself, and I've nothing happening to me. I don't like to think too much about you, in my head, that only makes a mess of us both. But of course what I live for now is for you and me to live together. I'm frightened, really. I feel the devil in the air, and he'll try to get us. Or not the devil, Mammon: which I think, after all, is only the mass-will of people, wanting money and hating life. Anyhow I feel great grasping white hands in the air, wanting to get hold of the throat of anybody who tries to live, to live beyond money, and squeeze the life out. There's a bad time coming. There's a bad time coming, boys, there's a bad time coming![134] If things go on as they are, there's nothing lies in the future but death and destruction, for these industrial masses. I feel my inside turn to water sometimes, and there you are, going to have a child by me. But never mind. All the bad times that ever have been, haven't been able to blow the crocus out: not even the love of women. So they won't be able to blow out my wanting you, nor the little glow there is between you and me. We'll be together next year. And though I'm frightened, I believe in your being with me. A man has to fend and fettle for the best, and then trust in something beyond himself. You can't insure against the future, except by really believing in the best bit of you, and in the power beyond it. So I believe in the little flame between us. For me now, it's the only thing in the world. I've got no friends, not inward friends. Only you. And now the little flame is all I care about in my life. There's the baby, but that is a side issue. It's my Pentecost, the forked flame[135] between me and you. The old Pentecost isn't quite right. Me and God is a bit uppish, somehow. But the little forked flame between me and you: there you are! That's what I abide by, and will abide by, Cliffords and Berthas, colliery companies and governments and the money-mass of people all notwithstanding.

That's why I don't like to start thinking about you actually. It only tortures me, and does you no good. I don't want you to be away from me. But if I start fretting it wastes something. Patience, always patience. This is my fortieth winter. And I can't help all the winters that have been. But this winter I'll stick to my little Pentecost flame, and have some peace. And I won't let the breath of people blow it out. I believe in a higher mystery, that doesn't let even the crocus be blown out. And if you're in Scotland and I'm in the Midlands, and I can't put my arms round you, and wrap my legs round you, yet I've got something of you. My soul softly flaps in the little Pentecost flame with you, like the peace of fucking. We fucked a flame into being. Even the flowers are fucked into being between the sun and the earth. But it's a delicate thing, and takes patience and the long pause.

So I love chastity now, because it is the peace that comes of fucking. I love being chaste now. I love it as snowdrops love the snow. I love this chastity, which is the pause of peace of our fucking, between us now like a snowdrop of forked white fire. And when the real spring comes, when the drawing together comes, then we can fuck the little flame brilliant and yellow, brilliant. But not now, not yet! Now is the time to be chaste, it is so good to be chaste, like a river of cool water in my soul. I love the chastity now that it flows between us. It is like fresh water and rain. How can men want wearisomely to philander. What a misery to be like Don Juan, and impotent ever to fuck oneself into peace, and the little flame alight, impotent and unable to be chaste in the cool between-whiles, as by a river.

Well, so many words, because I can't touch you. If I could sleep with my arms round you, the ink could stay in the bottle. We could be chaste together just as we can fuck together. But we have to be separate for a while, and I suppose it is really the wiser way. If only one were sure.

Never mind, never mind, we won't get worked up. We really trust in the little flame, and in the unnamed god that shields it from being blown out. There's so much of you here with me, really, that it's a pity you aren't all here.

Never mind about Sir Clifford. If you don't hear anything from him, never mind. He can't really do anything to you. Wait, he will want to get rid of you at last, to cast you out. And if he doesn't, we'll manage to keep clear of him. But he will. In the end he will want to spew you out as the abominable thing.

Now I can't even leave off writing to you.

But a great deal of us is together, and we can but abide by it, and steer our courses to meet soon. John Thomas says good-night to Lady Jane, a little droopingly, but with a hopeful heart.

NOTES

1 (p. 2) *the once well-known R.A.*   a reference to the Royal Academy of Arts, founded in 1768. Membership is limited to eighty artists, only about half of whom are painters.

2 (p. 2) *cultivated Fabians*   The Fabian Society was founded in 1883 to promulgate socialist ideas.

3 (p. 2) *Wandervogel songs*   literally the songs of migratory birds but in fact those sung by members of the German Wandervogel youth movement while hiking or rambling.

4 (p. 4) *L'amour avait passé par là*   Love had passed that way (French)

5 (p. 6) *the red-faced Kitchener*   having played a prominent role in the Boer War, Kitchener became Secretary of State for War in 1914.

6 (p. 6) *the Tommies*   popular expression for ordinary soldiers

7 (p. 7) *Lloyd George*   the Liberal politician who replaced Asquith as prime minister in 1916

8 (p. 7) *Horatio Bottomley*   A rabid journalist and owner of the fiercely patriotic journal *John Bull*, Bottomley was imprisoned for fraud after the war.

9 (p. 9) *pit bank*   probably a reference to the mound of coal left over after those parts suitable for sale had been hived off by the *screens* mentioned two lines above

10 (p. 11) *ne plus ultra*   the ultimate in perfection; literally: no more beyond (Latin)

11 (p. 13) *corpus delicti*   Latin phrase commonly used to describe the body of a murder victim but referring rather to the sum of the facts which constitute an offence in law

12 (p. 13) *demi-monde*   French expression for a social circle outside the confines of bourgeois respectability. A *demi-mondaine* was likely to be a rich man's mistress.

13 (p. 23) *Une immense espérence a traversé la terre*   A great hope has passed over the earth – from a poem by Alfred de Musset (1810–57)

14 (p. 27) *English Man of Letters*   reference to a series of popular monographs on famous writers *English Men of Letters*, which appeared between 1878 and 1919 and were edited by John Morley.

15 (p. 27) *hors de combat*   out of action (French)

16 (p. 28) *arriviste*   someone on the make and determined to succeed (French)

17 (p. 29) *Blest be the tie that binds . . . other*   from a hymn by the Reverend John Fawcett (1740–1817). The second line should read: 'Our hearts in Christian love'.

18 (p. 29) *Alcibiades*   like *Protagoras* a member of Socrates' circle but, unlike him, a soldier rather than a philosopher

19 (p. 30) *ex cathedra*   literally 'from the chair' but meaning: of an authority which does not permit itself to be questioned (Latin)

20 (p. 30) *as if the ass had spoken*   The reference is to the Old Testament story of Balaam's talking ass (see Numbers 22), a particular favourite of Lawrence's.

21 (p. 32) *If they be not nice to me . . . they be?*   modification of lines in 'A Lover's Resolution' by George Withers (1588–1667): 'If she be not so to me / What care I how fair she be?'

22 (p. 33) *Hildebrand*   name of the monk who became Pope Gregory VII (1021–85), a strong supporter of priestly celibacy

23 (p. 33) *riding*   a track through a wood primarily intended for those on horseback

24 (p. 36) *Where are the snows of yesteryear?*   English version of a famous line from the *Grand Testament* of François Villon (1431–63): 'Où sont les neiges d'antan?'

25 (p. 44) *my-eye-Betty-Martin*   'all my eye and Betty Martin' is a popular phrase of uncertain origin which characterises whatever the speaker feels is complete nonsense.

26 (p. 48) *Charlestoned*   The charleston, danced to the rhythms of ragtime jazz, had first become popular in the mid 1920s.

27 (p. 48) *Methuselah*   According to the Bible, Methuselah lived for almost a thousand years.

28 (p. 50) *blackleading*   Blacklead was a graphite product used for making an iron stove or fire-grate shine.

29 (p. 52) étape *after* étape   stage after stage (French)

30 (p. 52) *after Henry James*   It was not Henry James who talked of the bitch goddess of success but his brother William (1842–1910), in a letter to H. G. Wells.

31 (p. 52) *cock-a-hoopy*   arrogant, boastful

32 (p. 54) *Go ye into the streets . . . a man*   modification of *Jeremiah*, 5:1 ('Run ye to and fro through the streets of Jerusalem, and see now, and know, and seek in the broad places thereof, if ye can find a man, if there be *any* that executeth judgement, that seeketh the truth . . . ')

33 (p. 54) *C'est une autre chose*   That's something else (French)

34 (p. 64) *cri de coeur*   a cry from the heart (French)

35 (p. 68) *butty*   a miner who leased a part of the coal-face from the mine's owners and then worked it with a small team of colleagues whom he himself paid. Lawrence's father was a butty for most of his working life.

36 (p. 70) *Touch not the nettle . . . to loose*   popular song from the 1840s with words attributed to Sir Walter Scott

37 (p. 71) *Seasons return but not to me . . . or Morn*   See John Milton, *Paradise Lost*, iii, 41–2.

38 (p. 71) *Pale beyond porch and portal*   from 'The Garden of Proserpine' by Algernon Charles Swinburne (1837–1909)

39 (p. 72) *Ye must be born again! I believe in the resurrection of the body*   The first phrase is from John 3:7; the second from what is known as 'the Apostles Creed', an affirmation of faith for baptismal candidates developed in the early days of the Christian church.

40 (p. 72) *Except a grain of wheat . . . by no means bring forth*   a version of John 12:24. (The apparent quotation which follows is unidentified.)

41 (p. 72) *The world has grown pale with thy breath*   from Swinburne's 'Hymn to Proserpine'. *Persephone*, in the following line, is the Latin version of Proserpine, queen of the underworld but also goddess of spring.

42 (p. 72) *Absalom*   third son of King David, killed after he had led a rebellion against his father. Fleeing on horseback, his hair caught in a tree.

43 (p. 77) *Sweeter than the lids of Juno's eyes*   See William Shakespeare, *The Winter's Tale* 4, 4

44 (p. 79) *Thou still unravished bride of quietness*   from 'Ode on a Grecian Urn' by John Keats (1795–1821)

45 (p. 84) *piquet or bezique*   fashionable card games of French origin

46 (p. 84) *j'adoube*   saying this allows chess players to touch one of their pieces without then being obliged to move it (French)

47 (p. 85) *Miss Mitford*   Like George Eliot and Mrs Gaskell, Mary Russell Mitford was a nineteenth-century author who wrote memorable accounts of English provincial life.

48 (p. 87) *Princess Mary*   This daughter of George V married Henry George Lascelles in February 1922.

49 (p. 87) *Swan & Edgar*   well known London department store of Lawrence's time

50 (p. 88) *Primitive Methodist*   Primitive Methodism was founded in 1808 when Hugh Bourne was expelled from the main Methodist movement. It was known for its crusading, evangelical fervour.

51 (p. 89) *Palais-de-Danse*   pretentious French term for a dance-hall, and hence, two lines lower, '*the Pally*'

52 (p. 90) *stocking frames*   mechanical knitting machines, invented in 1589

53 (p. 91) *coppy*   thicket of small trees (dialect)

54 (p. 93) *the new Achilles*   The point is that when the mother of Achilles tried to make her baby immortal by dipping him in the Styx she held him by the heel which then became the only part of his body where he was still vulnerable.

55 (p. 104) '*ca' canny' creed*   The Scottish phrase in inverted commas refers to the deliberate slowing down of working practices, the 'go-slow'.

56 (p. 105) *dibbed about*   pecked (dialect)

57 (p. 110) *King Edward's time*   Edward VII was king between 1901 and 1910.

58 (p. 111) *warren*   originally an enclosure for small game animals

59 (p. 113) *gin close*   enclosed area in which 'gins', i.e. traps for rabbits and other small animals, are set

60 (p. 114) *Balaam's ass*   See Note 20 above.

61 (p. 117) *Iacchos*   another name of Bacchus, god of wine and ecstasy whose female votaries were known as Bacchantes (see the line above)

62 (p. 120) '*For hands she hath none . . . of hair . . .*'   from Swinburne's 'The Pilgrims'

63 (p. 121) '*Who knoweth the mysteries of the will . . . the angels –* '   The epigraph to *Ligeia* by Edgar Allan Poe, a story about which Lawrence writes interestingly in his *Studies in Classic American Literature*.

65 (p. 127) *cinquecento furniture* furniture from the sixteenth century (Italian)

66 (p. 127) *Sir Edward Landseer(s) . . . William Henry Hunt* popular English painters of the nineteenth century (Landseer specialised in the painting of animals)

67 (p. 130) *bag wigs* type of wig from the eighteenth century, popular with doctors and lawyers (bag refers to the way the hair was tied up)

68 (p. 131) *Gare du Nord* station in Paris where the trains from England still arrive

69 (p. 135) *Chadwick Hall* an obvious reference to Hardwick Hall, near Chesterfield in Derbyshire

70 (p. 136) *Good Queen Anne and Tom Jones* Anne reigned from 1702 to 1714 but Henry Fielding's novel *Tom Jones* was not published until 1749.

71 (p. 137) *Sandringham* country estate in Norfolk bought by the future Edward VII in 1863

72 (p. 140) *Nurse Cavell* Edith Cavell (1865–1915) was a heroine of the First World War. Matron of a Brussels hospital when the Germans invaded Belgium, she was shot for helping allied soldiers avoid capture.

73 (p. 140) *Saint George of Cappadocia* The intended reference seems to be to England's patron saint.

74 (p. 140) *Roman de la rose* title of a famous French poem of the thirteenth century closely associated with the cult of courtly love

75 (p. 141) *au très petit sérieux* facetious opposite of *au grand sérieux* i.e. very seriously (French)

76 (p. 141) *The fault, dear Brutus . . . we are underlings* William Shakespeare, *Julius Caesar*, 1, 2

77 (p. 142) *wezzle-brained* thoughtless (dialect)

78 (p. 143) *dool-owls* ghosts, hobgoblins (dialect)

79 (p. 144) *dutch oven* receptacle for cooking on an open fire

80 (p. 153) *the sons of god with the daughters of men* a memory of the first two verses of Genesis 6

81 (p. 156) *the souls in Plato* reference to Plato's allegory of the soul as drawn in a chariot by two horses, the white one representing spirit and the black one the body with all its passions

82 (p. 160) *Panem et circenses!* bread and circuses, the cynical conservative's formula for keeping the populace quiet (Latin). The source is Juvenal's tenth satire.

83 (p. 162) *Whither, O weird wheeled ship . . . steering*   modification of lines from 'A Passer-by' by Robert Bridges (1844–1930)

84 (p. 162) *Oh, Captain, my Captain . . . is done*   modification of lines from *Drumtaps* by Walt Whitman (1819–92)

85 (p. 166) *tableau vivant*   a living picture (French)

86 (p. 169) *Noblesse oblige!*   rank carries with it responsibilities and obligations (French)

87 (p. 170) *any Schieber*   profiteer (German)

88 (p. 171) *à la guerre comme à la guerre*   The nearest English equivalent of this French saying is 'all's fair in love and war'.

89 (p. 176) *Persepolis and Timbuctoo*   the ancient capital of Persia and a fabled African city on the southern edge of the Sahara but both used here to indicate whatever is remote and exotic

90 (p. 176) *a trolly*   a trollop

91 (p. 176) *My Lord Duckfoot*   slang for someone who puts on airs

92 (p. 177) *trull*   prostitute

93 (p. 185) *John Thomas*   one of the colloquial ways of referring to the penis

94 (p. 185) *Lift up your heads o' ye gates . . . may come in*   Psalms 24:7

95 (p. 185) *Blest be the tie that binds . . . love*   See Note 17 above.

96 (p. 188) *pontoon*   simple card game known in France as *vingt-et-un* and in the United States as blackjack

97 (p. 190) *mingiest set of ladylike snipe*   mingiest is from mingy meaning mean and snipe (a game bird) is a traditional term of abuse.

98 (p. 192) *te deum laudamus*   We praise thee, O God (Latin)

99 (p. 194) *eurhythmic dance-movements*   series of co-ordinated movements to music, somewhere between modern dance and gymnastics, originally devised by Emile Jacques-Dalcroze (1865–1950) as an aid to musical development. There was a well-known Eurhythmic Institute near Dresden.

100 (p. 199) *an exemplary life for the next six or eight months*   In divorce proceedings of this time a 'decree nisi' was first granted and then made absolute six months later if, in the meantime, there was no new evidence relevant to the case.

101 (p. 200) *Knight of the Burning Pestle*   title of a comedy by Francis Beaumont (1584–1616)

102 (p. 200) *make a calendar of me*   because printed calendars often had floral decorations

103 (p. 201) *'Goodbye, my bluebell . . . to you!'* popular song from the early 1900s

104 (p. 202) *stately homes of England, how beautiful they stand* Mellors is quoting from 'The Homes of England' by Felecia Dorothea Hemans (1793–1835).

105 (p. 202) *shimmy* deformation of the French *chemise*, probably meaning here a petticoat

106 (p. 202) *where 'ave yer been to my pretty maid* line from a popular nursery rhyme

107 (p. 203) *alone and palely loitering* line from 'La belle dame sans merci' by Keats

108 (p. 206) *The universe shows us two aspects . . . ascending* This and the subsequent quotation are from *Religion in the Making* (1926) by Alfred North Whitehead.

109 (p. 210) *Athena* Greek goddess of war (Minerva was her Roman name)

110 (p. 218) *Abélard . . . Heloïse* famous French lovers from the twelfth century. He was a priest and she became a nun after her relations had castrated him.

111 (p. 223) *chair à plaisir* flesh always available, on tap (French)

112 (p. 225) *flâneurs* idle men about town (French)

113 (p. 225) *Saint Bernard* St Bernard of Clairvaux (1090–1153), whose trip on the lake was an exercise in mortification

114 (p. 228) *basta!* enough! (Italian)

115 *Goldoni* Carlo Goldoni (1707–93) was a successful eighteenth-century dramatist from Venice.

116 (p. 231) *When Jesus refused the devil's money* an episode from Jesus' forty days in the wilderness. See Matthew 4:8–11.

117 (p. 231) *in puris naturalibus* in a state of nature and thus stark naked (Latin)

118 (p. 237) *as Benvenuto Cellini says, 'in the Italian way'* In a translation of the memoirs of Cellini (1500–71), which Lawrence probably read, J. A. Symonds defines the Italian way as anal intercourse.

119 (p. 237) *Rabelais* French writer of the fifteenth century famous for his plain speaking and bawdy humour

120 (p. 237) *Crippen* a reference to Dr Hawley Henry Crippen, hanged in 1910 for poisoning his wife

121 (p. 237) *Miller-of-the-Dee air*   'The Miller of Dee' is a folk song from the eighteenth century with words as Clifford quotes them.

122 (p. 238) *Marquis de Sade*   French author (1740–1814) of *Justine* and other novels of sadistic male fantasy

123 (p. 238) *Don Rodrigo*   protagonist of the Spanish ballad 'The Penitence of Don Roderick' who is punished for sexual indiscretions by having to hold a serpent with two heads, one of which bites into his heart and the other into his genitals

124 (p. 238) *clatfart*   dialect word for useless, idle talk

125 (p. 239) *the actress Judith*   Judith was the stage name of the celebrated French actress Julie Bernat (1827–1912).

126 (p. 239) *Queen Mary*   wife of George V

127 (p. 239) *the place thereof shall know me no more*   slight modification of Psalms 103:16

128 (p. 249) *Colonel C. E. Florence*   reference to Colonel T. E. Lawrence (of Arabia) who gave up his fame and rank to serve as an aircraftsman under the name of Shaw

129 (p. 254) *Vulcan and Venus under the net of art*   It was the blacksmith Vulcan, Roman god of fire, who in fact trapped his wife Venus and her lover Mars under a net when they were sleeping together.

130 (p. 257) *like the lady in Tennyson*   a reference to Tennyson's 'The Princess' (1850)

131 (p. 258) *except ye become . . . child*   Lawrence has conflated Matthew 18:3 with Mark 10:15

132 (p. 258) *Magna Mater*   Great Mother (Latin)

133 (p. 263) *nostalgie de la boue*   French expression meaning 'longing for mud' (a regressive desire to return to one's low origins)

134 (p. 267) *there's a bad time coming*   ironic adaptation of a popular song of the mid-nineteenth century with the refrain: 'There's a good time coming, boys'

135 (p. 267) *Pentecost, the forked flame*   At Pentacost or Whitsun, fifty days after Easter, the Holy Spirit descended on the apostles 'in cloven tongues like as of fire'.